Overcoming

Overcoming

Marjorie S. Chilton

PALMETTO
PUBLISHING

Charleston, SC
www.PalmettoPublishing.com

Overcoming

Cover photo by Gary L. Chilton

First Edition

Hardcover ISBN: 979-8-8229-0465-1

Paperback ISBN: 979-8-8229-0466-8

eBook ISBN: 979-8-8229-0467-5

Acknowledgments

Warm thanks to Fries resident Raymond Davis, who told me about the bell that woke the town, and to Doug Long who shared how his grandfather helped build the dam on the New River for the Fries mill. Many heartfelt thanks to Sherry Turner for her patience and technical expertise. Love and thanks to Gary and John Allen who are always supportive and keep life interesting.

Overcoming is a work of fiction. All characters are fictitious as are the village The Falls, the Wide River, and the town of St. Claire, Virginia. But the inspiration for St. Claire is a real town named Fries (pronounced freeze), Virginia, located on the New River. At the beginning of the twentieth century, Colonel Francis Henry Fries bought land along the New River and with the labor of local men built a dam, hundreds of houses, and a cotton mill. The mill was in operation from 1903 until 1989. From the beginning mountain music has been an important part of the culture of Fries. There are music festivals in May and September, a Fiddlers' Convention in August, and a jam session every Thursday night at the Fries

Recreation Center. The mill was torn down, but the large bell that once stood on top of the mill and was rung to wake the residents was moved to the small business district where it sits today.

Chapter 1

Serena

THE BAPTIST MINISTER set out from home on a long walk to visit a member of his flock. Normally he would have driven his car, but the government was rationing gasoline, and this little inconvenience made him feel he was contributing to the war effort. Besides, it was a perfect day for a long walk, and he said a silent prayer of thanks for spring, the lovely respite between the cold of winter and the humid heat of the southern summer. It was a sunny day with just a hint of cool breeze that brought sweet smells to his senses. Everywhere, grass had greened, and azaleas of every color bloomed all over the town. Usually he would enjoy a walk on such a lovely day, but today he felt unprepared and inadequate for the encounter to come. As a pastor to his flock, it was part of his job to comfort the bereaved, to help them find the strength to go on living. But so far, he had been unable to breach the wall of sadness that had closed in around this young woman. On his last visit, he had practically pleaded with her to come back to church "where there are people who care about you, who want to comfort you." She had finally said she would think about it, but he felt certain she had only said that to get rid of him. Well, she couldn't get rid of him that easily. He would try again today, and with this determination, he picked up a little speed.

Serena had come here in 1931 because she had accepted a job teaching at the junior high school. Two things had happened rather quickly after her arrival: first, she'd established herself as a serious and superb teacher of seventh grade American history, and second, she had captured the heart of the once confirmed bachelor, George Lowell.

George taught world history and civics in the high school. The minister did not know exactly how they had met, but since the two buildings were joined, there were probably opportunities for this to happen. George was an attractive man, and over the decade he had been in town, many a single woman had set her cap for him only to give up. The attraction between George and Serena was not a mystery, for they were both attractive and obviously both teachers of social studies. Both also attended services at the minister's church. He had heard some time ago that it was the music rather than his sermons that kept them in his flock. (He had to admit that though he worked very hard to preach uplifting messages of God's love and forgiveness and guidance these sermons paled in comparison to the soaring music presented every Sunday by organist, pianist, and choir.) Whatever the attraction, they fell in love and had a lovely June wedding in her home church in St. Claire, a small mountain town with the distinction of being the home of a small college and a large textile mill whose machines ran on the power of the Wide River. The minister had had the honor and pleasure of sharing a place in the ceremony by leading the benedictory prayer.

A reception was held at the lovely old home of Serena's grandparents, who, to the astonishment of the minister, were in their nineties and still tottering about and being looked after by their younger daughter, Serena's aunt Amelia, who had never married. Serena's father was in his seventies and her mother in her sixties. They owned St. Claire's only general store and lived in an apartment above it. In time, he learned that her parents had given up on having children when they were surprised by a very late pregnancy. Serena was not only an only child but an only grandchild and only niece to her mother's sister. Serena had been reared and cherished by these five aging adults.

The minister and his wife had so enjoyed that day in St. Claire, such a picturesque little town nestled in a forest of pines and spruce, great oaks, maples, and tall poplars. And Serena's family were so warm and welcoming and were delighted with George and so happy for Serena.

They had hated to leave such a joyous gathering and relived much of the day as they drove down the mountain and home. He remembered how his wife had commented on how fortunate this family had been that they had all lived to see Serena grow up, settled in her profession, and married to a fine man.

Tragically, over the following six years, four of them would die: Serena's mother of cancer, her grandfather of pneumonia, her grandmother peacefully in her sleep, and her father after a fall from a ladder in his store.

They had been an unusually congenial group of people who truly enjoyed each other's company. They had gathered every Sunday after church for a meal and conversation around the Lawrence dining room table where they discussed the minister's sermon, talked about local and world events, and caught up with the happenings in each other's lives over the past week. There was always laughter.

Serena felt deeply the loss of each one of her family. It seemed impossible that they were gone, that they would not be there to welcome her home when she visited or celebrate her achievements with her as they always had in the past. Never again would they gather around the table to talk and laugh and celebrate a holiday or just celebrate their belonging to each other.

Fortunately, Serena had married a man who was like them, sharing their same values of honesty, integrity, and compassion. George had also borne great loss in his life, and now his understanding and compassion allowed Serena to grieve for her lost loved ones and grow to accept their absence. After her father's death, she returned to her classroom and, in time, to home improvement projects.

When George had first moved here, he had bought an old cottage on a pretty tree-lined street. He had made necessary repairs inside and out, built bookshelves on one wall in the living room and, over the years, filled them with his ever-increasing collection. He had also built himself a desk and a chair. For the kitchen, he had built a table and one chair and for the bedroom, a single bed. To store his clothes, he had bought a chifforobe at an estate sale. He had painted every room white.

When Serena had entered the picture, changes took place in this small cottage. The minister had dropped by one afternoon for a short visit and found George hard at work building a double bed. He had already added another chair to the kitchen table. After their marriage, many more welcome changes appeared: a comfortable sofa, chair, end table, a painting of the Wide River done by a local artist in St. Claire, family photographs, a houseplant, and an area rug in the living room, two more chairs in the kitchen, modern cabinets, and yellow paint on the walls. These were the only rooms the minister visited, but he suspected the rest of the house had benefited from Serena's efforts.

Serena had inherited her father's store and had promoted to manager the young man who had helped him run it. As the depression waned, the store was turning enough profit that Serena and George had been able to afford to rent a cottage at the coast for several weeks during the summer. They spent their days reading, walking on the beach, fishing, and making plans for the years to come. After seven years of marriage, many couples become bored with their lives and each other, but this was not so for George and Serena. They loved history, geography, and politics and never ran out of things to talk about. Their conversations stimulated discussions that carried over in their classrooms. As the world grew closer to war, they renewed their love and held each other close.

On December 7, 1941, news came of the Japanese attack on Pearl Harbor. George and Serena knew, without a doubt, that America would immediately enter the war. George was forty years old and uncertain whether he would be drafted but very certain that he would volunteer. Serena pleaded with him to wait, even as her own sense of duty to country left her feeling guilty for doing so. He hated the thought of leaving her, but he knew he would hate himself even more if he shirked his responsibility to join the fight against the Nazi tyranny that threatened the world.

In the days that followed, George informed his principal and his students of his intentions to join the navy in January. This would give the principal time to find a replacement and time for George to settle his affairs in his classroom to enable an orderly transition. He also needed time to say goodbye to his students, because he always became emotionally attached to his students and they to him. He wanted them to know how he hated to leave them, and to convey to them how important it was that they, too, become a part of the war effort. He told them that the government would be asking citizens to participate, and he hoped that each of them would be the good citizens he knew they were. On the last day of school before Christmas, he said, "This may be a long war, and if so, many of you will be called up. I do hope and pray that we all come back, but it is likely that won't happen. And there will be a lot of people left hurting. But for those who do return, there is something you can do: you can be kind to each other and especially kind to the ones who are hurting."

George and Serena spent a bittersweet Christmas in St. Claire with Aunt Amelia and her friend Carole who taught biology at the college and who had moved in years earlier to help Amelia care for her mother after her father's death. They attended a Christmas concert at the college before the students left for the holidays, and a children's nativity play at church. Amelia wanted to continue the family tradition of having an open house for neighbors and friends on the twenty-third, so the four of them spent all day on the twenty-first baking cookies and little cakes. The next day, George and Serena scoured the woods for a tree while Amelia baked a ham. After supper, they decorated the tree and admired their work while they drank hot cocoa. The next day, dozens and dozens of little biscuits came out of the oven and were filled with small pieces of ham.

While Amelia and Carole prepared these, Serena and George washed the punch bowl and cups borrowed from the college and then set about readying the dining room for the night's gathering. By seven thirty, the house was filled with friends happy to feel the warmth of each other's company and the lovely tree and table laden with food. It was a brief but welcome respite from the dark worries of things to come.

They spent Christmas Eve cleaning up, returning the borrowed items to the college, and cooking. They prepared enough food for their evening meal and for Christmas Day, and that night they listened to Prime Minister Churchill's Christmas Eve broadcast from the White House, where he and President Roosevelt were planning a strategy to defeat the Nazis. Churchill urged the country to put aside their worries for one night and allow the children to enjoy Christmas.

In the morning after breakfast, they exchanged gifts. George and Serena gave Amelia a polished oak walking stick and Carole a box of Whitman's chocolates. Amelia gave George a lovely set of cuff links that had been her father's. "These are for you when you return," she said. To Serena she gave her mother's string of pearls. Serena's gift to George was the latest edition of H. G. Wells's *Outline of History*. She knew he enjoyed reading a favorite book a second time. He was very pleased and anxious to see what had been updated from the 1930 version. He said that he would look forward all day during basic training to reading this book at night. George gave Serena a beautiful blue cashmere sweater that he clearly couldn't afford. She was delighted, said she'd never take it off.

After lunch, George and Serena bundled up and took a long walk. It had been a busy week with too much to do to dwell on George's plans to enlist in the navy. Now, though, his leaving loomed over them like an ominous dark cloud. They walked by the river holding thickly mittened hands but saying nothing. Finally, George broke the silence. "Serena, when this is all over, let's buy a little lot on the oceanfront. We could build a small house—we could do it ourselves and spend all summer there every summer. What do you think?"

"Oh, George, that's a wonderful idea."

The next day, they said goodbye to Amelia and Carole and returned home. They spent much of their time over the next week planning how they would save money to purchase the oceanfront lot and the materials for the house. They drew up a list of everything they would want in the house and then drew house plans. When they had settled on a plan, they filled time discussing how they would furnish the house, and Serena thought about how she would decorate it.

Having grown up in the Midwest, where most people had as much chance of seeing the ocean as they had of going to the moon, George was fascinated by these great bodies of water on either side of America. Before he met Serena, he had taken every opportunity to spend time on the coast and had found temporary summer jobs on fishing boats to finance his "vacations" by the sea. He was as thrilled as a child that he and Serena were able, for two straight summers, to spend real vacations there. So it was no real surprise that he would choose to join the navy over the army. Serena thought he would be less of a target on a ship than in a battle on land. Unfortunately, it is not the sailor but the ship that is the target. On August 9, 1942, the USS *Quincy* was headed for Guadalcanal when it was struck by a Japanese torpedo. Three hundred seventy men were killed, 167 wounded. The USS *Elliot* rescued 493 men from the shark-infested water and carried them back to Pearl Harbor for medical care.

When she received the telegram that George had been killed, the light went out in Serena's eyes. She walked to the bedroom and picked up the photograph she kept on the nightstand. It was her favorite picture of George, one she had taken on their last vacation at the beach. He was smiling and holding up a string of fish he had caught that morning. "Oh George, I hope you didn't suffer." She kissed his face as tears streamed down her own. She lay down on the bed and placed his picture over her heart and wept quietly. She thought of the last time she had seen him when he came home before shipping out. They had just a few days together. He had replaced a worn washer in the faucet in the kitchen sink to stop a drip and had tuned up the car. He said he didn't want her to have any trouble with that car and get stuck somewhere with him not here to fix it. They didn't have the gas to drive the seventy miles to the train station, so she had taken the bus with him, and they had sat as close as they could together, touching shoulders, holding hands. At the station, they had waited to approach the train until the "all aboard" announcement, then one last kiss, and George stepped onto the train and was gone. She would never touch him or kiss him or see him again.

The following days would be a blur. Early the next morning, Serena's neighbor Patsy stopped by to see if Serena would like to take a walk with her, something Patsy often did in good weather, and in summer sometimes Serena would go along. There was no answer at the door, and Patsy noticed that the newspaper was still lying on the porch where the boy had thrown it. She knocked again, and it opened to reveal Serena's tear-swollen face, her hair and clothes disheveled, her hand clutching a photograph. "What is wrong, Serena?" Patsy asked, but she already knew.

"George is gone, Patsy. He won't be coming back. They sent that awful telegram."

"Oh no, darling. I'm so sorry." She hugged her neighbor for a long time. Then she sat her down on the sofa and went to the kitchen to make coffee. Patsy sat with her and urged her to drink the coffee, and she learned that no one else knew about George. So Patsy called the minister, Amelia, and George's brother Edward in California. Edward would not be able to come to the memorial but would later call the minister. Patsy then talked Serena into taking a bath, ran it for her, and got out fresh clothes for her. People would be coming here. Out of the bath and dressed, Serena allowed Patsy to comb her hair. By the time the minister arrived, Serena was again sitting on the sofa. He had notified the deacons, who would tell their wives, who would prepare food for Serena. The minister had also called the principal of the junior high school, who would spread the word.

The next morning, the minister met the bus that brought Amelia. It had been many years since he had seen her, but he was surprised at how little she had aged—no, she actually seemed younger somehow than he had remembered. He gathered her things and drove her to Serena's house. Over the course of the day, they were joined by the high school principal, and plans were made for a memorial service. Serena sat on the sofa, Amelia by her side, often holding Serena's hand. Patsy had made a pot of coffee and gone home, so the minister kept the cups refreshed and served sandwiches brought earlier by a church member.

Throughout this, Serena sat quietly, only agreeing to this or that with a faint "yes" or "all right" but offering no suggestions. She sipped a bit of the coffee, ate nothing, and with a handkerchief dabbed the tears that ran down her cheeks. Finally she spoke up. “George had a fierce love for America. I’d like this service to reflect that.”

The memorial for George was held three days later on Sunday afternoon. The First Baptist Church comfortably held five hundred people. On this day, nearly seven hundred filled the sanctuary, sitting in overcrowded pews, in chairs brought from Sunday school rooms and the fellowship hall, or standing in the back or in the side aisles. As the church filled, the organist played the old and familiar hymns. Finally, a deacon led Serena and Amelia into the sanctuary from a side door to a seat on the front pew beside Patsy and her family, the school principals, and two of George’s fellow teachers. Row after row behind them were filled with other high school and junior high school teachers and students.

The minister stepped up to the pulpit and led the congregation in prayer. He then said, “We are gathered here today to honor the life of George Joseph Lowell and to honor his heartfelt love for this country. He died for this country, but before that, he spent his life making sure that the generation that followed him would understand what a precious gift they had been given to grow up with freedom: the freedom to worship as they choose, the freedom to choose their leaders, the freedom to pursue their dreams, even the freedom to complain about their government. In this hour of our sadness and grief, let us all remember and make room in our hearts for gratitude.

The combined choir and the high school chorus then sang a soaring rendition of "America the Beautiful" followed by a eulogy given by a former student who had been so inspired by her teacher that she went on to college, majored in history, and was now teaching in the adjoining county. She recalled Mr. Lowell's saying that American democracy was a great experiment, and while the British had thought it doomed to fail, Americans had proved them wrong, and the Brits now were ever so grateful to have been wrong. She was followed by a high school student who had been among George's last class. He described how Mr. Lowell would assign reading from the textbook for homework and the next day lead a discussion of that text. He would stop periodically and write on the board the major points to remember, and as he wrote, the students would copy his words in their notebooks. These notes became study guides of material certain to be covered on tests. "He didn't try to trip you up or surprise you on his tests. You always knew what to expect and what to study. He told us that if this war lasted for years, many of us would be called to serve, and he knew we would be scared, because he was scared, but he was more scared of living in a country ruled by a brute like Hitler than dying in a fight for freedom." As the boy sat down, the choir and chorus behind him rose to sing "The Battle Hymn of the Republic."

The minister returned to the pulpit and said, "George was reared on a farm in the Midwest. He told me once that it was a good life there with his parents and older brother. The work was hard, but they were a happy family. They became even happier when George was eight years old and a baby sister arrived. His brother Edward told me that George in particular was delighted with their baby sister. When his chores were done, he would look after her, talk to her, and tell her about his day at school and what he had learned. He would read to her and show her the pictures in his books. By the time she was four, he had taught her to count to ten, and she was beginning to read. When she entered first grade, the teacher had to scramble to find things for little Abbie to do, because she had already defeated every challenge of first grade. She was, of course, George Lowell's first student.

"In December 1918 the family welcomed home Edward, who had fought in France in the Great War. Their happiness was short lived. The flu epidemic of that year, spreading around the world, found its way into the Lowell farmhouse. Just before Christmas, both Mrs. Lowell and eight-year-old Abbie had sickened and died. George told me that he fully expected to also get sick, and that he hadn't cared if he did, he was so sad. But neither their father nor Edward or George were to even sicken. Their father, however, could not handle the loss of his wife and daughter. He gave in to his grief and gave up. Devastated as they were, a farm does not run itself, and Edward and George took over its operation. George returned to school to complete his final year. Before the summer was over, their father had died." (The minister knew this was not the time or place to explain that Mr. Lowell had taken up drinking and had stumbled one night into the path of a truck). "Edward and George buried their father in the cemetery next to their mother and went home and talked into the night. Before sunrise they had decided their course of action. They sold the farm, divided the money down the middle, and headed to the state capital, where they enrolled in college. They found a boarding-house and rented a room. They also found part-time jobs. Within three years, they had both graduated, Edward in engineering and George in history. On a June morning in 1922, George and Edward said goodbye as Edward boarded the train to California. On another train, George headed southeast. The two brothers would stay in touch through letters and once in a while a telephone call, but they would never see each other again.

"George knew that he wanted to live in a warm but temperate climate with all four seasons and no more than a day away from the ocean. While in college, he had studied the southern states and had taken every opportunity to talk with people from the mid-Atlantic area. He had settled on three small cities to visit. One of the three he eliminated because it just didn't feel right. The other two he liked very much, and he applied for a teaching position in both. In our town, he had rented a room in a boarding-house and submitted this address on both applications. Luckily for us he was hired. As his former students have attested, George was a great teacher, loved and respected by his students and his colleagues.

"For ten years he taught school, attended church, worked on the house he had bought, and slipped away to the coast to fish every chance he got. He seemed content. Then he met a lovely young lady, also a teacher, and they fell in love and married, and for the next ten years, George was happy."

As the organ softly played the Navy Hymn, a veteran of the Great War in dress uniform stepped down from the podium, approached Serena, and spoke these words. "On behalf of the president of the United States and the chief of naval operations, please accept this flag as a symbol of our appreciation for your husband's service to this country and a grateful navy." The choir and chorus then rose and sang the Navy Hymn.

The minister rose to give the benediction: "Heavenly Father, as we leave here today, our hearts are heavy for the loss of one we all loved. But our hearts are also grateful for his courage and his willingness to serve the country we all love. Help us, Lord, to summon our own courage as we grieve our loss and to find our place of service to you and to our country. In the name of Jesus Christ our Lord we pray, amen."

The new school year began the day after Labor Day, and Serena was there to welcome her new classes of seventh graders. If she had taken some time off, everyone would have understood, but she couldn't bear to be in the house where George no longer lived. It took all the strength she could muster to get through each day. She couldn't eat and lost weight, and one day she walked into the house and passed out. Patsy had seen her drive up, get out of the car, and stumble to the house. She ran over and found Serena passed out on the living room floor. Patsy wet a washcloth and placed it on her face. When Serena came to, Patsy helped her to the sofa and begged her to eat. Serena protested that she just could not swallow food. Patsy asked if she could drink. Serena said she could. Patsy went home and returned quickly with a glass of milk, orange juice, and a raw egg mixed together. Serena drank it and shortly was feeling better. Patsy's concoction became Serena's breakfast every morning. At lunch, she would drink tomato soup, and at night, she had chocolate milk with a beaten raw egg.

Serena and Patsy had been friendly neighbors all the time that Serena had lived next door, but now Patsy seriously took Serena under her wing. She would cook a bit extra of whatever she was having for supper and take a small portion to Serena. Gradually Serena began to recover her ability to swallow food. They would also talk about Serena's day and Patsy's day, or current events, or anything that had happened in the community. But Serena could not talk about George. She could not go back to church to hear the wonderful music she and George had loved so much. She could not go to the movies, because that too was something they had enjoyed together. She would listen to the news on the radio and to President Roosevelt's Fireside Chats because her students expected this, but she would not listen to *The Answer Man*, the program that broadcast questions from listeners and answers provided by a team of experts, or *The Major Bowes Amateur Hour*, because these were programs that she and George had enjoyed together.

Patsy suggested she listen to *Amos 'n' Andy* because it was funny, and Serena needed badly to laugh. Serena balked at this, but Patsy turned on the radio and insisted Serena sit down and listen. In spite of herself, Serena laughed for the first time since George's death. This program was broadcast nightly, and Serena tuned in several times, but comedy alone wasn't the same as comedy shared. It made her feel even lonelier.

One afternoon after school, as she sat at her desk in the empty classroom, a former student walked in leading a puppy of indeterminate heritage. "Mrs. Lowell, do you remember me? I'm Jimmie Lindsey."

"Of course I remember you. Everybody called you Jimmie Lin."

"They still do. And this little fellow, well, he don't have a name. We just call him 'Boy.' But see, Mr. Lowell told us lots of folks would be hurting because of this war, and we needed to help them if we could. So I brought him to you so, you know, you wouldn't be all by yourself."

Serena was just on the verge of telling Jimmie that she couldn't possibly keep this dog when it occurred to her that, in a way, the puppy was a gift from George as well as from this well-meaning boy.

"Jimmie, thank you so much for thinking of me. You are so kind." She reached down and petted the dog, and he wagged his tail.

"He likes you already, Mrs. Lowell. What are you going to name him?"

"Why, I'm going to name him 'Jimmie,' of course!"

Serena put her work away, put Jimmie in her car, and headed to the store, where she purchased a bag of dry dog food, a bowl for his food and one for his water, and a rug for him to sleep on. She didn't want him running loose—there was too much traffic—nor did she want to leave him inside alone all day while she was at work, so she turned to Patsy, who said she would be happy to take Jimmie for a walk on his leash every morning and back home with her for the rest of the day. Serena planned to eventually fence in her yard, but for now, Patsy had come to her rescue. And Jimmie, in spite of his expensive veterinary care, food, and trouble, proved to be a godsend. On days she felt she just couldn't leave her bed and face another day, she would force herself up to take Jimmie out to do his business and run around a bit in the yard. She began leaving school earlier in the afternoon, taking work home with her to do at night, with Jimmie lying on his rug next to her as she graded papers. Sometimes she would stop and reach down to pet him, and his tail would wag in appreciation. Sometimes she would sit down beside him and put her arms around him and draw him into her lap. When she was feeling particularly sad, Jimmie would come to her and lay his head in her lap, and as she stroked him, she would tell him about George and how terribly she missed him.

The minister had visited several times, bringing food his wife had prepared. They had invited her to have supper at their house twice, but Serena had made excuses. On one visit he had noticed a basket with unopened mail, which he assumed to be letters of sympathy. He had encouraged her to open these, had appealed to her conscience: if people were kind enough to send these, shouldn't she at least open them and say thank you when she next saw the sender?

One evening soon after his visit, she picked up the basket and looked through the letters, noting the return addresses with the senders' names. She stopped when she came to a letter from Miss Glenna McAllen. Serena knew only one person named Glenna, and she realized that she had never actually known Glenna's last name. They had first met in 1928 at Renney's Restaurant in the little community of The Falls, located about three miles from St. Claire. Renney's was a popular place known for really good country cooking at a good price. Renney did most of the cooking. Her husband raised most of the vegetables, which his mother canned in large quantities. He also raised chickens, and Monday through Saturday, fried chicken and gravy was on the menu. (Renney's was closed on Sundays.)

As a treat, Serena's family drove occasionally to Renney's for supper, and if they had been shopping or had other business in one of the larger towns down the mountain, they would stop here to eat or just have dessert before going home. On one particular evening, Serena and her mother had taken her grandmother down the mountain for a doctor appointment. Afterward, they had done a bit of shopping. Amelia was cooking for the menfolk at home, and the ladies had decided ahead of time to eat supper at Renney's. After the waitress took their order, Serena headed for the restroom. As she approached the last booth, she noticed a little girl, pencil in hand and head bent over a sheet of paper. On her way back she stopped. "Doing your homework?" The girl looked up, and Serena almost gasped. Sitting there in Renney's was truly the most beautiful child she had ever seen.

"Yes, ma'am. I'm doing arithmetic problems." No one had ever addressed Serena as "ma'am" before, and it made her feel rather grown up; on the other hand, it was a bit dishonest.

"You don't have to call me ma'am. I'm a student too. My name is Serena. What's your name?"

"Glenna, it's Irish. I was named for my grandfather in Ireland."

"That's a beautiful name, Glenna."

"Thank you, Serena is a beautiful name too."

"Thank you. My mother chose that name because it means calm. She hoped I would be a calm and quiet baby." Glenna did not smile. "Well, I'd better let you get back to work. It was very nice to meet you, Glenna."

Over the years, as most of Serena's visits to Renney's were in the late evenings, she would find Glenna there in the last booth immersed in her schoolwork but willing to leave it for a pleasant chat with Serena. She would learn that Glenna loved math and had plans to study bookkeeping and accounting.

George had teased her, pretended to be shocked that she wasn't going to study something really interesting like history. She was fourteen then and working as a waitress after school. A year later, she said she hoped to get a scholarship to college but still to study bookkeeping and accounting.

Serena had watched Glenna grow from a beautiful but sad little girl into a beautiful and confident, happy young lady. But then something had happened, and Glenna had quit school. As she opened the letter now, Serena remembered how disappointed she had been in Glenna. She opened the envelope and read the note:

August 14, 1942

Dear Serena,

Today there was a notice in the St. Claire paper that George was killed when the Japanese attacked his ship. Reading this, my heart just broke. Sometimes life hurts so bad you think you can't stand it, but you have to, and after a while it gets easier and you just go on and do the best you can. Anyway, I just wanted to say I'm so sorry. I'll pray for you every day.

Glenna

Tears came to Serena's eyes as she read the letter. She thought, "How right you are, Glenna, how right you are." Then she made a decision. She would go back to St. Claire for Christmas. No matter how painful it would be, she and Jimmie would go to St. Claire. Amelia would not want to come here without Carole, and Serena didn't have room for them both, so she would go there. She began making plans. If she got up earlier and walked to school, she could save her gas rations and by Christmas would have enough for a round trip to St. Claire. She would stop at Renney's and thank Glenna for the letter. Before she could change her mind, she sat down and wrote Amelia a letter to let her know her plans. When she finished, she called Jimmie, fastened his leash, and they walked the six blocks to the post office and sent the letter through the out-of-town mail.

On Saturday, the nineteenth of December, Serena and Jimmie headed up the mountain and, as planned, stopped at Renney's for lunch. After letting Jimmie out on his leash for a brief walk, Serena put him back in the car on his rug and went inside, where she was immediately greeted by Glenna. She took Glenna's hand and thanked her for her kind letter. Glenna asked how she was getting along, and Serena said, "It is just as you said in the letter: you don't want to keep going, but you have to, and you make yourself get up in the morning, and you go through the day, forcing yourself to meet your responsibilities. What about you? How are you doing?"

"Well, I'm okay. I can't complain." She started to say something else but stopped herself. "I'll get you some coffee," she said, then led Serena to a booth. They chatted briefly when she took Serena's order, and when she served it, and Serena felt that all was not okay with Glenna, but the restaurant had filled with customers, and there was no chance to really talk again. So Serena went on her way, wondering about Glenna, but soon was settled once again in the sad state of her own life and the gloomy prospects of Christmas with Amelia and Carole.

* * *

At last, the minister reached the house. He had grown warm in his dark suit and was relieved to see Serena's car in the driveway. She would be at home and perhaps offer him a glass of water. She answered the knock at the door, invited him in, and offered him a glass of ice water, which he readily accepted. "Have a seat in the living room while I get it," she said. When he walked into the room, he was surprised to find boxes full of books and half-empty shelves. He sat on the sofa and wondered what was happening.

When Serena returned with the water and a napkin, she took a seat herself and explained. "I am moving back to St. Claire when the school year is out. This house belongs to a life I had with George, and that life is over. I can't live here any longer. I've tried, but I just can't."

"But it hasn't been even a year yet. Should you make such an important decision so soon?"

"I know the common advice is, 'Don't make any big changes the first year after the death of your spouse,' but things have sort of fallen into place, and I feel strongly that it's the right thing to do. I haven't really spoken with you very much since before Christmas, when I went to St. Claire. I had hardly unpacked when Aunt Amelia and Carole told me they both planned to retire from the college. Carole, you know, taught biology there for many years, and Amelia taught piano. Carole's parents left her a bit of money, and Amelia inherited a considerable sum from my grandparents—most of it kept in a safe in the library, but that's another story. Anyway, they told me they didn't intend to live through another winter in St. Claire. They had bought a cottage in Key West, Florida, and they were going to move in May."

"What about the house in St. Claire?"

"Well, that was another surprise. I had always assumed that my grandparents had left the house and the money, if they had any, to Amelia and she would leave it to me, but in fact, they left the money to Amelia and the house to me, with Amelia having a lifetime right to live in it."

"That's a rather large house for one person and very expensive to keep up."

"Yes, it is. I know it is. Fortunately, it has always been kept in good repair, and as you know, it's already fenced in. My grandfather loved dogs, always kept two or three, so Jimmie will have more freedom to run and play."

"What will you do with this house?"

"I'm renting it to Patsy's daughter, Jane. Her husband is overseas, and she and her little girl have been living with Patsy and Arlen. Arlen works at night and sleeps during the day, and it's hard to keep the little one quiet all day. Besides, Jane's used to having her own place. They had a furnished apartment before the war, so now she'll have a furnished house. I'll just take these books and clothes and personal things. I've been saving my gasoline rations, and I'll have enough fuel to go up there next weekend and take as much as the car will hold. Then I'll have enough by June to make the final trip and take all the rest."

"Are you going to give up teaching?"

"No, that's another thing that has fallen into place. Over Christmas, Mr. Johnson came to the house to tell me that the seventh-grade teacher is retiring this year, and he offered me the position and asked me to think it over. I did, and I accepted his offer."

"Are you happy with your decision?"

"Happy?" she asked him with an incredulous tone. "Happiness isn't something I expect to feel again. Day in and day out, I am just trying to survive. During the day at school, I have to think about the children, about the lessons, all the things that have to be taken care of. And there's Jimmie here; we go for a walk every evening if the weather is good. When we get back, I feed him, and he takes a nap. I'll eat a little something, tidy up, and listen to the news, grade papers, plan for tomorrow. And then I'm clean out of distractions, and the only thing left is the long night. Awful as that is, weekends are worse. At least in St. Claire, everything around me won't be a reminder of George, and that big house needs a good cleaning and cleaning out. I'm also going to raise a garden this summer. There'll be plenty of distractions."

"Serena, tell me about the long nights."

"No, Pastor, I don't want to talk about it. I don't want to think about it. It's too painful."

"George was a good man; he deserves your grief. But grief is a burden, and a burden is meant to be shared with people who care about you. Share your grief and the burden is lightened. If you can't share with me, please find some other person to talk to. Don't try to go it alone, Serena. You are a good person, and a person who has much to give. Share your burden and share your gifts, and you may find your way back to happiness."

"Those are nice words, Pastor, but they're just words."

"They are words that mean something, Serena. You had a great loss, but there are many others all around us who are suffering. It's been my experience that the happiest people are the ones who busy themselves helping others."

"I'll pray for them, Pastor."

"I'm told that you write a quotation on the board each morning and lead your class in a discussion of its meaning. Here is one you might add to your list: 'The hands that help are holier than the lips that pray.'"

Serena made no comment, just sighed.

"I believe we are led to people who need our help, Serena."

Chapter 2

The Renegars

ON THE WAY to St. Claire and just before the road reaches the top of the mountain, any traveler who looked on the left would see a waterfall spilling into the pool before it made its way under a small bridge and continued down the mountain. The source of the waterfall was a branch of the Wide River. At a point miles away and long in the past, the waters of the Wide on the far right edge encountered a huge jumble of rocks, and some veered off to the right. There were some who speculated that this was a favorite place for the untold numbers of deer to stop and drink, and that they eventually wore down a deep path in the soil, allowing the water to leave the river and take a different course. Others who knew a bit more about science said it was no doubt all the ice that had once covered the mountain that caused this anomaly. One fellow who was one-eighth Cherokee swore that his ancestors had purposefully carved a trench to reroute the water to a favorite campground.

Whatever the cause of the divergence, the waterfall and pool attracted animals and Indians and eventually white settlers heading south to warmer climes and more promising opportunities. An apprentice surveyor told his cousins about the falls and the large area of level-to-hilly land on either side of the falls because he knew they wanted to build a tavern.

The boys' father, John Renegar, owned a large farm about thirty miles inland from this place, and on the side he raised hops and barley and brewed beer and ale for his family's use. His two youngest sons, Robert and Albert, who, like their siblings, had spent their lives laboring on the farm from sunup until sundown, had decided they wanted no part of farming, but they were inspired by the very fine beer and ale their father produced. Thus their dream of owning a tavern.

John Renegar was a generous man and loving father. He understood that he could not have achieved his success without the help of his wife and children. When his three daughters had married, he gave each a generous sum of money. He intended that upon his death, the farm would be divided between his two eldest sons. The house and two acres and enough money for her old age would be left to his wife. He decided he would do what he could to help Robert and Albert establish a tavern.

So he accompanied them to the falls, and he walked the land and observed the fine timber all over the property. He also discovered a spring with crystal-clear water. The boys could build the brewery around this spring. So he bought the land and helped his sons set up the brewery. He set aside more land on his farm to grow more hops and barley, which he would furnish until they could pay for it. Eventually he would sell enough timber off this land to recoup his investment.

Over two years, Robert and Albert, and during the winter their older brothers, cleared the land, built first a barn with living quarters for themselves, sowed grass, built a chicken house and a sheltered pen for hogs, and then built the tavern, with living quarters upstairs for themselves and rooms to let for travelers.

Even before the tavern opened, travelers who stopped at the falls to replenish their water supply and water their horses or oxen or the cow tied to the back of the wagon would wander over the trail to visit with the Renegars and share the news from the world beyond the mountain. The Renegars, in turn, shared their ale and venison stew. Often an evening of music ensued as both parties brought out fiddles, harmonicas, and whatever they had. Music, as much as beer and ale and good food, would always be a part of Renegar's Tavern and create a sense of comradery, even among strangers, and if only for a few hours from hard-lived lives.

Early on, Robert would marry Lucinda, his sweetheart from back home. They would have three children, but only Rob, the eldest, would remain to join his uncle Albert to run the tavern after his father's death. As more people settled in the area mostly over the mountain, the community around the tavern became known as The Falls, and in time a one-room schoolhouse was built. Albert spearheaded this project mainly because he had fallen in love with a beautiful woman named Rachael who had a son named Olan, whom Rachael was determined would be educated. Albert and Rachael would marry after her husband died. When they married, Lucinda moved to Richmond to live with her older son, who had become a Presbyterian minister, and her daughter, who kept house for her brother.

Rob would eventually marry Lydia, the schoolteacher Albert had hired, and their only child, Rebecca, would, at sixteen, marry Mitchell King. Mitch and Rebecca would eventually inherit and run the tavern. They had two children, Martin Renegar King, born in 1889, and Susan Irene King, born in 1891. She would always be called Renney.

Martin's parents and grandparents assumed that Martin would eventually become proprietor of Renegar's, but this was not meant to be. At a young age, he expressed his dislike for living over the tavern. He complained that it was like having company all the time. Martin liked people, enjoyed having conversations on any number of topics, but at the end of the day, when he finished his chores, he looked forward to quiet and privacy to read and think. The tavern was a noisy place at night, with fiddlers fiddling and singers singing and crowds imbibing the beer and ale his father provided. He wanted to live in a house and, very specifically, a house on the Wide River. It was a lovely, peaceful place to fish or just to walk and listen to the birds sing and the water ripple over the rocks. As a youngster, he would often walk the mile to the river carrying not a fishing pole but a book, find a place to sit, and lose himself in a story.

Renney, on the other hand, loved the tavern. She was a good student, but as soon as her homework was completed, she put all books aside and headed downstairs to the kitchen. At seven years old, she could be found standing on a wooden box, learning to make biscuits. By the time she was fifteen, she had mastered every item served at the tavern. Not only could she cook, she loved waiting on customers.

When Martin was thirteen years old, he contracted a bad case of mumps. He overheard the doctor tell his mother that he would never be able to father children. At the time, this news didn't mean much to him, but as he got older, he realized that all the girls he knew had one ambition: marry and have babies.

Martin liked girls, but he knew telling a girl he'd dated a time or two that he couldn't help her have babies would be embarrassing. To lead a girl on and let her fall in love with him, then tell her, would only mean heartbreak. To marry a girl and not tell her—well, his conscience wouldn't allow him to do that. So Martin avoided girls. He was a fine-looking young man, and many a girl sought his attention, but one by one they gave up and turned their attention elsewhere.

Martin was an affable young man, always courteous and friendly with family and customers, and he was dependable, never failing to keep the woodboxes filled for the stoves and the big fireplace in the dining room. This, and giving the dining room a thorough cleaning either late on Saturday night or at some point on Sunday, were his chores at the tavern.

When Martin completed the eighth grade in The Falls School, he insisted on continuing his education at the high school in St. Claire. He was the only one of his class to do this. (Two years later, Renney would do the same. Rebecca said this was due to the influence of her mother, Lydia, the former schoolteacher.) Martin and Renney would walk the three miles to St. Claire unless it was pouring down rain, sleet, or snow. In that case, their grandfather, Rob, would take them in his covered buggy and be there at three o'clock to bring them home.

When Mitch expressed concern about Martin's peculiarities, Rebecca would remind him of Martin's great-uncle, Paul, who was known as a "bookworm" and who had left home to live with his grandparents so he could go to school. They had sent him to college and seminary.

As for his apparent lack of interest in girls, Rebecca decided his bout with the mumps was likely the cause. She was right but for the wrong reason.

Long before Martin graduated from high school, he had gotten a part-time job at the textile mill in St. Claire. The day after graduation, the job became full time. The manager over workers recognized early on that Martin was very smart, so he apprenticed him to the mill's fixer, who knew everything about the machinery and, if something went wrong, could quickly determine and fix the problem. The present fixer was getting on in years and might, at any time, need to be replaced. His job paid more than any other of the workers' jobs because it required skills and knowledge and was essential to keep the machines running.

In spite of his feelings about living above the tavern, he would continue to live there and do his chores because he needed to save his money to buy land along the Wide River where some day he would build his house. He spent money only for shoes and clothing when he absolutely had to, and to attend concerts, plays, and the occasional lecture at the Jane Auditorium in St. Claire. The concerts featured local groups of fiddlers, singers, and cloggers much of the time but often the college choir and orchestra. Occasionally the college players would put on a play, which sometimes included local talent. Several times a year, there would be a lecturer of particular interest. Martin loved it and rarely missed Saturday night at the Jane.

By 1910, Martin had saved enough money to purchase three acres on The Falls side of the river, where the land was less expensive, and closer to the tavern, where he continued to live and do his chores. For three and a half years, he spent every free minute turning his dream into reality.

First, he cleared the site for a road from the main road to his property and the place he would build his house. He had the timber sawed into lumber and stored in the barn at the tavern. He had a well and septic tank dug because he knew that one day he would have indoor plumbing. He had been inspired by Olan Avery, a man who had grown up in The Falls and inherited land on the west side of the waterfall from his mother, Rachael, and his father, Greene Avery, whom some considered a tragic figure and others a comic one. Olan was well respected, and no one mentioned his father to him.

Olan had joined the army and spent his career with the Corps of Engineers. Early on, he had built a lovely cottage for his mother, who lived there after Albert died. After her death and his retirement, Olan and his wife had moved into the cottage and become friends with Rob and Lydia and eventually, in spite of their difference in age, with Martin.

Olan encouraged Martin to think of the future and the certainty that electricity would come to the mountain. Thus the septic tank and lines to the house. Olan also advised Martin to build the house on the highest place on the property and to build seven feet off the ground to mitigate damage from flooding.

With help from Mitch, when four hands were necessary, Martin built the house, as he had the money at the time, and on a cold night in November 1914, he spent the first night in his house by the river. He slept in a bed he had built himself on a mattress he had ordered from the Sears Roebuck catalog and on which he had spent his last dime. He wasn't worried. He slept soundly and woke at his usual early hour and made breakfast of bacon and eggs, pone bread and coffee. He ate his breakfast sitting in his rocking chair by the fire and looking out the window to the river beyond. Martin was home at last.

Chapter 3

St. Claire

BIG CHANGES HAD come to the mountain after the Civil War. The economy in the South was in ruins. People were desperate for work and US dollars. One man who was well aware of this and eager to take advantage was the owner of a textile mill in Massachusetts. John St. Claire was a wealthy man who dreamed of becoming even wealthier and he figured out how to do that.

The federal government, in an effort to create jobs in the southern states, offered tax benefits to companies that established locations below the Mason Dixon line. Besides the tax benefits, St. Claire knew that southern workers were willing to work for considerably lower wages than their counterparts in the north.

When a friend's son who had served as a scout for the Union Army mentioned the Wide River that ran through a large forested area, St. Claire said, "Tell me more." Shortly thereafter, the former scout took St. Claire to the mountain. They rented rooms at Renegar's Tavern and claimed to have come for the fishing. What they did was walk the land and study the river. St. Claire came away with no doubt that he had found the perfect place to build his new mill and the town of hundreds of houses around it.

He bought five hundred acres of land and hired a builder/engineer, William Lawrence and Sons, and in the spring of 1871, he sent word throughout the mountain of his intentions to build a mill and houses for the workers along the Wide River. There would be jobs for lumberjacks in the fall, construction jobs come spring, and later, jobs in the mill and houses at low rents for the workers and their families.

The word spread rapidly, and hundreds of men and boys showed up to work, and women came to cook for them. Tents were set up for those who had come from distances too far to allow them to travel back and forth every day.

While the dam was being built, other workers to the east were building houses on the hills above the river. They were basic four- and five-room, well-built houses from timber cut when the land had been cleared the previous fall. Other workers were building the mill once the river had been dammed. When that was completed, these workers turned their attention to the business district located downriver at some distance from and east of the mill. It lay west of the first houses.

The first building was the Wide River Hotel. When it was completed, St. Claire, his plant manager, and William Lawrence and his sons moved from the rough cabin they had occupied from the beginning and into the hotel. This hotel included a kitchen and dining room and lobby. A noted cook from Massachusetts was brought in to prepare meals for these men who had eaten most of their meals at Renegar's or cooked for themselves.

Close to the hotel, St. Claire had workers build a Catholic church. This ordinarily would have been a controversial thing to do in an area where anti-Catholic sentiments were the norm. But if a man was giving you a job you desperately needed, any prejudices you had against his religion could be conveniently overlooked. The workers did a fine job on Holy Angels Catholic Church. Later, after William Lawrence decided he wanted to retire here, he would build a nondenominational church for everybody else, but still later, mill workers would build a Baptist church, where most of them would attend.

Up the way on the left, a general store was built. It would be owned by the mill and overseen by one of St. Claire's managers, but in time, St. Claire tired of this and sold it to a young man named Jackson (Jack) Anderson. Jack would one day marry the granddaughter of William Lawrence, and they would become the parents of a daughter named Serena.

Room was left for other businesses that St. Claire and Lawrence were certain would come over time. Beyond the business district and where the river veered to the south, a school for grades one through six was built. A playground lay behind it. William Lawrence suggested the town should at least provide for a seventh and eighth grade, but St. Claire declared that mill workers had no use for more than a sixth-grade education. He said his managers would send their children off to private schools beyond sixth grade. (Later the state would require the town to build accommodations for the upper grades.)

One final project was built to ensure that workers showed up for work on time. Only the wealthy could afford timepieces, so workers built a tower and installed a huge bell, which would be rung every morning five times at five o'clock. Everyone in the town became accustomed to waking to the sound of this bell. It set babies to crying and dogs to barking, but the bell did its job, and the workers made it to the mill by six o'clock.

When all the workers' houses were finished and the mill was up and running, William Lawrence built a fine house for John St. Claire and his wife, who detested this little town her husband had created in the wilderness, as she called it. She would spend as little time here as she could. William also built houses for the mill managers. Those done, he built a fine house for himself and his wife, Jane, because he had fallen in love with this place, and he wanted to retire here and turn over the running of his business to his sons.

Jane Lawrence loved William and would have followed him anywhere. She was the sort of person who made the best of any situation in which she found herself. She was well educated and an accomplished pianist. She had grown up in a small college town in Pennsylvania, where her father owned a tool-making company.

Jane was well aware that everyone benefited from living in a college town. There were lectures on a variety of subjects by professors and guests. There were concerts and plays and political debates, all open to the public. There were night classes for those who could not afford to quit their jobs and attend school full time. Also, the college provided jobs for people in the community. Citizens of college towns tended to be better informed and better educated. Their lives were continuously enriched.

Jane decided St. Claire would be a wonderful place for a college, a liberal arts college with a particular focus on music. She had visited St. Claire during the building process and had sat on the porch of the hotel in the late evening listening to the music coming from the campsite. She wanted to join them, but she was afraid the men would consider that an intrusion. As she sat listening night after night, she came to the conclusion that these talented people needed a place to perform for a large audience. She really wanted to establish a college here, but an auditorium became her priority.

Over the months, as the building wound down, Jane decided what she wanted to do and how she would do it. She approached John St. Claire about building an auditorium so that the workers could perform their music for a large audience every Saturday night. She told him that music was one of the best ways for people to express their deepest feelings. Besides that, gathering together on a Saturday night for a musical performance was fun, and people needed to have fun. And some people needed to perform for an appreciative audience. It was like food for their souls. Finally, Jane said, "Your people will work harder when they have something to look forward to on the weekend."

St. Claire said he had built all he was going to build, but if she could raise the money, he would donate the land. Jane was certain he said this to get rid of her, but he did not know she was a wealthy woman in her own right, having inherited a large sum of money from her mother. Nor did he know that she had many wealthy friends back at home and musician friends who would be happy to give concerts to benefit the cause. She returned home almost immediately and set to work first with an architect, who designed the auditorium with a balcony and large stage with rooms for dressing, practicing, creating props, storage, and classes for the college she intended to start later on.

Six months later, when St. Claire had forgotten all about his promise, Jane visited him at the mill and informed him she had raised the money for the auditorium. He looked at her with confusion on his face. "What auditorium?"

Jane reminded him. He donated the land in the business district, and a sum of money. Jane decided to name the building after him, but when it was finished, and when the cover over the entrance was revealed on the day of its dedication, it read JANE LAWRENCE AUDITORIUM in large black letters. St. Claire announced to the crowd that he had gone behind her back and changed the name from his to hers because were it not for her, there would be no auditorium.

* * *

In very little time, the workers' houses in St. Claire filled up because workers' children grew up, got married, and were looking for places to live. Albert and Rob decided to build a few houses in The Falls and rent them to mill workers. They hired farmers who were also skilled at carpentry to build the houses after the harvesting season was over. They built five houses to start with and rented them as fast as they were finished. The next fall, they built five more. In time they decided being landlords for ten families was more than they could handle, so they approached their tenants with a proposition. Instead of paying rent, they could pay to own their own homes, and if they liked, they could build a small barn for a cow and graze it on the green in front of the houses where the tavern cows grazed. Not all wanted a cow, but all wanted to buy their houses. Albert had contracts drawn up by an attorney in Wytheville, and everyone signed the papers.

Within a year, Albert died and was buried beside his brother, Robert. Rachael received Albert's share of the monthly house payments until her death. What was left went to Rob by prior agreement. After Albert's death, Rachael moved into the house Olan had built for her, but she continued to cook at the tavern until Rob found a replacement, because Lydia had her hands full with Rebecca and all the cleaning.

Chapter 4

Charlie and Kathleen

IN APRIL 1917, the United States entered the Great War. Martin was twenty-eight years old; he registered for the draft and was given "eligible but deferred" status because there was no one else to do his job at the St. Claire mill. Charlie McAllen, age twenty-three, was not so lucky. He worked at the mill but as an unskilled laborer whose job was to lift heavy raw materials coming in and finished material going out; he could be replaced. He was given "eligible to serve" status and quickly drafted.

Charlie was the youngest of six children. His two older brothers were in their thirties, both married with children and deferred from serving. Charlie's remaining siblings were young women. Their father was a farmer who produced most of the food they ate and who worked in the timber industry and was a skilled carpenter.

Charlie's mother was a humorless, no-nonsense woman who believed that idle hands were the devil's workshop, and she had seen to it that her children were never idle and were in regular attendance at the Methodist church. They were absolutely forbidden to step foot in Renegar's Tavern.

Charlie's father was a mild-mannered man who loved to hear a good story, especially one that featured the comic circumstances caused by human foibles. He was kind and affectionate, and it was to him that his children came with a scraped knee or hurt feelings.

Charlie was like his father. He looked up to his papa and spent most of his time with him learning about farming and in his father's workshop about carpentry. As he grew up, he decided he would follow in his papa's footsteps. He would have a small farm, build his own house, and furnish it with things he made himself.

When Charlie completed the eighth grade, he got a job at the mill in St. Claire. Every week, he paid his mother a portion of his earnings because, though he did enough work on the farm to earn his keep, she washed and ironed his clothes and cooked all the meals and kept the house clean, and he appreciated this. He kept a bit of his earnings for himself, but most of his money went into a savings account in the bank in St. Claire. By the time he was drafted, he had saved enough to buy fifteen acres and a truck and enough to start building his house.

He had planned to start clearing his land, but that would have to wait.

Charlie faithfully wrote letters to "Dear Papa and Mother" all through the months of his training and on the voyage to France. He wrote about the soldiers he had met and about the awful conditions in the trenches. Then, in June, the letters stopped coming. Naturally, everyone in The Falls community feared the worst but kept praying all the harder for Charlie. Finally, in mid July a letter came. It was not in Charlie's handwriting, but written by a woman—a nurse?—whose name was Kathleen Quinn.

* * *

Charlie had been badly wounded and brought to a field hospital unconscious. Kathleen had talked to him each time she passed his bed, urging him to wake up. He was being given fluids intravenously through a tube connected to a glass of water protected from dirt and dust only by a layer of gauze. She knew this was risky but the only way to save his life as long as he was unconscious.

Finally, one day she said rather forcefully, "Charlie, you must wake up and drink some water!"

Barely above a whisper and without opening his eyes, Charlie said, "Let me go. Let me go."

"I can't let you go, Charlie. There are people in America who love you and are praying for you to come home. We can't disappoint them." Kathleen wet a cloth and gently washed his face. “I want you to tell me about those people back home, Charlie.” But Charlie had drifted off, and Kathleen had other patients to attend to, so she left him. But she would return as often as she could.

Three days later, when she approached his cot, intending to try to wake him as she did several times a day, she found him talking in his sleep. He seemed to be having a conversation with “Papa.” She didn’t know whether Papa was his father or grandfather, but she felt from what little she could understand that Papa was very important to him. After this, when she tried to wake him, she would say that Papa wanted him to wake up and drink water so he could get well and come home. One day when she said this, Charlie opened his eyes and asked, “Is Papa here?”

“No, Papa is at home praying for you to get well.”

Charlie said, “I wish he was here,” as tears rolled down his face.

“I wish he was here too, Charlie.” She wiped the tears from his face and asked him to drink some water so he could get better and go home and be with his papa. He drank water. Then he asked how she knew about Papa, and she told him he sometimes talked in his sleep.

Charlie’s pain lessened as he was healing, and he drank water and broth throughout the day. The IV was removed. When Kathleen checked on him, he began telling her about his papa and mama, his brothers and sisters, and their life on the farm, and the village called The Falls. He asked her to write a letter to his parents. He asked her about her family, and she told him about her parents and siblings, and life in Dublin on the Irish Sea.

When Charlie had first been brought to the field hospital, he had not been expected to survive. He was being kept there because the doctor feared moving him would cause injury to organs that were healing.

The first thing Kathleen had noticed about Charlie was how tall he was. His feet were at the very bottom of the cot. The second thing she had noticed was that he had such a sweet face, and as she got to know him, she realized he had a sweet, kind nature also.

When his pain subsided, the doctor ordered Charlie to be moved to a hospital behind the lines. Charlie squeezed Kathleen's hand as they said goodbye, and as she watched the ambulance move away with Charlie, tears sprang to her eyes. When the driver returned, he assured her that Charlie had made it just fine. She was so relieved to hear this that she began to cry again and quickly turned and walked away.

Kathleen knew that you were not supposed to allow yourself to fall in love with a patient, especially one who was American and Protestant. As a Catholic, Kathleen knew this would never work. She would have to forget about Charlie. Then she remembered the other thing she loved: nursing.

Kathleen was not a nurse, not officially. But she had known that she wanted to be a nurse since the age of eight when, one day, she accompanied her mother to the hospital in Dublin to visit her grandmother. It was there that she saw the ladies in their neatly pressed and starched blue dresses with white collars and cuffs and the little white hats with lace trim. She had watched these ladies as they made their way around the ward caring for and comforting their patients. Her mother told her these ladies were nurses. "They take care of their patients, Kathleen."

"Like I take care of Eileen," she thought. "Now I know the name for what I want to be."

Her sister Eileen was a Down syndrome baby, born when Kathleen was four years old. Kathleen had rocked Eileen's cradle to help her sleep, and in time she had learned to change her diapers and feed her with a spoon. When Eileen had finally learned to sit up, Kathleen would place her in the little wagon their father had made and pull her around the neighborhood. She would read her stories and encourage her to talk. When Kathleen was not in school, they were inseparable.

Their father was a fisherman. Early every morning, he went out on the cold Irish Sea to fish for cod. Some days he brought in quite a haul to sell in the market, but other days not so much. Their mother raised a garden and kept chickens behind the house they rented, so though they were poor, they always had something to eat.

Kathleen planned to get a job after she finished school and saved to pay for nurses training. But her father was out one day in a sea that turned rough. He fell and broke his arm and had to stop fishing. Kathleen's mother took a job in a bottle factory, and Kathleen delayed her plan in order to stay home and care for her father and Eileen. Her father's arm never regained enough strength for him to resume fishing, so he remained at home and took over the gardening and chickens. Three years after his accident, Eileen died in her sleep. She had not been expected to live long, but it was shocking and sad to lose her.

Kathleen began looking for work when she received a letter from her brother, who had gotten a job in London in a printing company. He and their cousin had a small flat there, and they were willing to make room for her because they were certain she could get a job as a cleaner in a large hospital. Her brother would send her the money for her passage on the ship to London. Kathleen bade her parents goodbye and sailed to London, where she was promptly hired by the hospital.

She was first assigned to scrub floors, but over the next two years, she would empty bedpans, wash sheets, and wash dishes, pots, and pans. Whatever she was told to do, she did well cheerfully. Because of her willingness to work hard without complaining and do it well, she was promoted to delivering meals to patients.

While she worked, she was also absorbing information from doctors and nurses. She had made friends early on with an older nurse, and whatever she overheard or observed and did not understand, this nurse would explain. At night, Kathleen would make notes of what she had learned during the day.

In 1914, a number of British soldiers were transferred from France to the hospital in London. Kathleen volunteered to remain after work hours to help them manage their meals, write letters, or just listen as they recounted the horrors they had endured. One day, a nurse who had observed the positive effects Kathleen's efforts had on these soldiers told her about the Voluntary Aid Detachment program, which offered civilian women the opportunity to provide services in field hospitals wherever British soldiers were serving. These were the kinds of services that Kathleen was providing to the soldiers here. The volunteers were called VADs, and there were opportunities for advanced training.

Kathleen was immediately interested because she wanted to help the soldiers, and this program would move her closer to achieving her goal of becoming a nurse. She was a few months shy of the minimum age requirement of twenty-three, but she applied anyway, with excellent recommendations from hospital staff.

Three months later, Kathleen found herself onboard a ship bound for France and life-changing events. She had received training in bathing and feeding patients, bedmaking, first aid, and cleaning. Many of these skills she had already acquired from her work in the hospital, but she welcomed the opportunity to learn and improve. In France in the following months, she was trained as a masseuse and in how to operate an X-ray machine. She took a class in cookery and driving an ambulance.

When Charlie was transferred out, Kathleen worked without stopping in an effort to rid her mind of him. When exhaustion demanded, she would stop and sleep, but Charlie returned in her dreams.

The ambulance driver nearly always returned with a report that Charlie was improving and that he missed her. Finally, he brought her a letter. Kathleen put the letter, unopened, into her pocket and carried it with her the rest of the day. After a late supper, she went to her tent, and by the light of a lantern she opened and read the letter.

September 22, 1918

Dear Kathleen,

Today I was allowed to leave the hospital and walk the short distance to church. It felt good to be out of here and to be wearing a uniform again and not bed clothes. The church was a Catholic church. I don't think there is any other kind in this town or maybe in France. I got there early and took a seat at the back. Soon the church filled up around me. I copied what they did—stood up when they did and sat down when they did. I didn't understand much of the songs they sang or the words the priest said, but somehow it still gave me comfort. I could feel the kindness and love for God.

They tell me I will be sent home before long. I would really love to see you before I leave. Do you think you could come for a visit? Well, Kathleen, the truth is that I have never missed anybody the way I miss you. Please come.

Yours,
Charlie

All the feelings Kathleen had tried so hard to repress came flooding back. She knew she would go to him and went immediately to her supervisor to ask for an assignment to drive the ambulance. "I need a day out of here," she said. Two days later, Kathleen drove a patient to the hospital. When he was unloaded, she parked the ambulance and made her way inside to find Charlie. She was told to wait on the porch. Fifteen minutes later, the door opened and Charlie appeared, tall and handsome in his uniform.

"Charlie!" She had never seen him standing up and dressed. He had gained weight and filled out the uniform nicely. "Charlie, you look so fine."

"And you look just beautiful, Kathleen, just beautiful," he said as he walked toward her. He took her hand to his lips and kissed it. "Let's go for a walk."

As they walked, he assured her he was feeling well. They went to a shop where a photographer took their picture and then to a café where they sat outside, ordered coffee, and talked. Charlie took her hand in his and said, "Kathleen, if we had more time, I would court you properly, but anytime now I'll be boarding a ship to go home. So I'm going to say what is in my heart. I love you. I want to spend the rest of my life with you. Will you marry me and come to America?"

"Oh Charlie, I love you. But you are Protestant and I am Catholic, and that's not going to change. It just won't work. Your family will never accept me, and my family won't accept you. Wherever we live, we'll be on a little island by ourselves, and we would begin to resent each other."

"No, you're wrong. I wrote my folks about you. I told them you saved my life."

"Charlie, the doctors and their medicine saved your life, not me."

"No, it was you, Kathleen. I was in terrible pain. I wanted to give up and go on, but you wouldn't let me go. Every time I saw your face, I wanted to live. My family will love you for saving me, and when they get to know you, they'll love you even more."

With the help of an interpreter, Charlie had already spoken with the priest and had promised to rear their children in the Catholic Church. The priest had agreed to marry them.

Kathleen wanted to believe that Charlie's family would accept her, because she could not bear to say goodbye to him knowing that they would never see each other again. So she agreed to marry him, and they bought rings and went to the church and were married that day.

Chapter 5

Bess

ON A COOL June day in 1917, a well-dressed woman appeared at Renegar's carrying a basket covered by a red-and-white-checked cloth. It was midafternoon, and only two customers were sitting at a table out front. The woman approached the lone waitress, introduced herself as Bess Hollars, and asked to speak with Mrs. King. The waitress said she would go and tell Mrs. King. When she returned, she led the woman to Rebecca's small office off the kitchen.

"Have a seat, Mrs. Hollars."

"Oh, Mrs. King, it's Miss Hollars. I'm not married. I am a baker, and I've brought samples of my baked goods for you to try because I would love to do your baking for you." She removed the cover from the basket and set it on Rebecca's desk.

Rebecca looked inside and said, "Let me get a plate and a cup of coffee. Would you care for a cup of coffee, Miss Hollars?"

"I would love a cup, if it's no trouble."

Rebecca soon returned carrying a tray with coffee, cream, and sugar, and a plate and utensils. When they were both settled with their coffee, she began tasting the samples, which had been wrapped in waxed paper. After trying a bite each of the chocolate cake, apple pie, and finally the doughnut, she would take a few sips of the coffee. "Where did you learn to bake like this, Miss Hollars?" she asked when she had finished. And Bess told Rebecca her story.

"I was adopted when I was a baby. The Hollarses had not been able to have children, and by the time they decided to adopt, they were in their forties, and they were told they were too old. Then their doctor told them about me. I had been released for adoption privately.

"My mother was so thrilled to have a baby, she gave me her undivided attention. Anytime I wasn't asleep, I was in her lap being rocked or later read to. When I started walking, I would follow her around as she did her housework, and she would tell me what she was doing and why it needed to be done. Of course, I don't remember all this, but she told me about it when I was older.

"What I do remember is when she began letting me make a cupcake. Whenever she made a cake, she would leave a half a cup of batter for me. I would spoon it into one space of a greased and floured muffin tin, and she would put it into the stove with her cake. And when they were baked and cooled, she would let me ice my cupcake. When I was old enough, she let me make a cake, with her supervision, of course. By the time I was ten years old, I could bake a cake all on my own.

"When I was in high school, I walked home from school and passed a bakery every day. One day, there was a beautifully decorated wedding cake in the window. I couldn't help but stop and stare at it. The owner noticed and came out to speak with me. I told him how much I enjoyed baking cakes and said I would love to learn to decorate a cake. It was his wife who did all the decorating. They ended up giving me a part-time job after school and on Saturdays, and she taught me how to decorate cakes. Of course, I also learned more about baking from them. I worked there full time when I finished school. I wanted to open my own shop someday, but when my father retired—he worked for the railroad—he wanted to come to St. Claire and spend his days fishing."

"You're not from here?" Rebecca asked.

"No, we lived in Richmond. Daddy and a group of men would come here every year to fish, and he always said he wanted to retire here. He bought property on the river and built a house. He sold our house in Richmond, of course. I could have stayed in Richmond and lived in a boardinghouse, but my mother was not well by then, and I felt she needed me, so I gave up my job and came with them.

"The bake shop in St. Claire's had no openings, so I got a job in the college cafeteria. Then Daddy had a heart attack and died. I quit my job to stay with Mother. She died three months ago."

"Oh, I'm so sorry, Miss Hollars. It can't be easy being alone."

"No, it isn't easy, but I stay busy. I have my church family, and I do get occasional orders for special cakes. But I need a steady income. I would really appreciate any orders you could give me."

"When my daughter comes in, we'll talk about it. Come back tomorrow, and I'll let you know."

Shortly after Bess left, Renney came in. She was pregnant with her third child and had been to the doctor in St. Claire. She stuck her head in her mother's office and asked, "Everything all right here?"

"Yes, pour yourself a glass of milk and get a plate and fork, and come in here."

When Renney returned, Rebecca placed the basket on her desk and explained the visit from Bess Hollars. Renney chose the chocolate cake first. One bite led to another. "I can't stop. It's so good!"

"Renney, drink some milk and eat some pie."

Renney declared the pie perfect. "The crust is so flaky." More milk and the doughnut followed. "Oh, Mama, I could eat every one of these."

"Don't do that. You'll make yourself sick. Let's save the rest for your daddy and Martin."

They talked it over and decided they would ask Bess to supply the pies, cakes, and doughnuts for the tavern. These items would surely bring in more customers more often. Rebecca and Renney would concentrate on the main courses.

Thereafter, Bess would arrive at five o'clock every morning with her baskets filled with pies, cakes, and doughnuts, and again at five o'clock in the afternoon with more of the same. Rebecca and Renney were correct in their prediction that these sweets would increase their business. Throughout the day, people would drop in to have a cup of coffee and a piece of pie or cake or a doughnut. Their business had always been good; now it was better.

Though Martin no longer lived at the tavern, he was always there every morning to fill the woodboxes and again in the afternoon. He would usually also eat breakfast and supper there, and his mother or Renney would pack his lunch. Bess also ate breakfast and supper at the tavern, as this saved her more time for baking. Because they both sat at the counter and were the only ones there most times at this early hour, they naturally became acquainted and, over time, developed a friendship. One morning Bess told him she had hardly slept the previous night for something running around in her attic. After work, he went to her house to take a look and discovered, as he had suspected, a squirrel had taken up residence in her attic. He set a trap to catch the offender, then cut down the tree limbs hanging over the house that had enabled the squirrel access to the roof. When the squirrel was caught, Martin removed the trap, and installed screens over the vent at each end of the house. Then he released the squirrel.

Bess, observing all Martin's efforts on her behalf, brought out her pocketbook and asked how much she owed him for all he had done. He said, "An apple pie this week and a cherry pie next week." So Martin became Bess's handyman who wanted his remuneration in pies, small cakes, or his absolute favorite, strawberry cobbler in June when the strawberries were in season.

Often, when Martin completed a chore, or at suppertime on Friday, their encounters involved long conversations. Martin had continued his education by attending the Thursday-night lectures given at the college by Dr. Thomas Lawrence, who would choose a part of the world, such as Latin America or the African continent. Dr. Lawrence was so knowledgeable and such a talented lecturer that Martin was eager to share with someone the fascinating things he learned every week, and Bess was a good listener. She would, in fact, have loved to attend these lectures, but she spent every evening and night baking for the next day's delivery. She was happy to learn secondhand what Dr. Lawrence had said.

There was no hint of romance between Martin and Bess. Theirs was a truly platonic relationship. Bess was only four years older than Martin, but she seemed older. She was overweight, and Martin was attracted to very slender females—not that he pursued any of them as far as anybody knew.

As for Bess, the only crush she ever had had been not on a boy but on a girl who had sat next to her in her freshman English class. The girl's name was Jeanette, and Bess thought it the perfect name for this lovely girl. Jeanette had dark, shiny, soft curly hair and blue eyes. Bess would have loved to just sit and gaze at Jeanette as you would at a beautiful portrait, but she forced herself not to do that. Only when their teacher said something amusing would Jeanette turn her lovely face to her, and they would smile as if they were enjoying something together.

Bess did not understand her feelings for Jeanette, but she thought they were certainly unnatural. She was afraid to mention this to anyone, especially her parents. She was not their natural child, only theirs by adoption. They might be so horrified that they would give her up as her real parents had done. So she kept her feelings to herself. She never had another class with Jeanette, and only rarely saw her in the hall, but soon after graduation, she found Jeanette's photograph with the announcement of her engagement in the paper. She cut out the picture and placed it in a book that she kept in a drawer in her bedside table. Often she would take it out and gaze at Jeanette as long as she liked.

Chapter 6

Ethel Ann

IN 1919, BESS was invited, as she had been the previous two years, to Christmas dinner with Mitch and Rebecca and their family. They always insisted she come, and Bess insisted on bringing a fruitcake and a chocolate cake.

The tavern always closed at 2:00 p.m. on Christmas Eve and opened up, as usual, at 5:30 a.m. the day after Christmas. But this year, Christmas Day was on Friday. The mill in St. Claire sometimes had work on Saturday, but this year it would be closed down until Monday. Mitch and Rebecca decided to do the same for the tavern. "Everybody needs a break," Rebecca had announced.

Everyone agreed except Bess, though she kept this to herself. She generally enjoyed her Sundays. The tavern was always closed on Sundays. She would have a leisurely breakfast, then get ready for church. After church, she would have lunch in the college cafeteria, often with other fellow congregants. Then she would head home and begin baking for the Monday morning delivery. But the thoughts of spending the rest of Christmas Day, then all day Saturday, alone and with nothing to do and no one to talk to, made her sad. Even the Jane Auditorium would be closed Saturday night.

Bess missed her parents every day, but at Christmas their absence was especially painful. Thinking back, she realized how much effort they had made to ensure that Christmas was a beautiful, magical time for her. Now they were gone, and they had taken the magic with them.

She would attend the Christmas Eve service at church. It would be a comfort to sit with the others in the church bathed in candlelight, hear the scripture describing the events at Bethlehem, and sing the carols. But when it was over, she would watch the families drive away together, while she would go home alone to an empty house, then have dinner with the Kings and Donneleys, a big happy family, which served only to demonstrate how alone she was in this world. Bess had no thoughts of others who were also alone and would enjoy some company and perhaps a cake or pie or bag of doughnuts. Bess had only thoughts of herself.

So it was with a heavy heart and a feeling of envy that Bess showed up for dinner at the tavern on Christmas Day. She brought the cakes, which Martin helped carry inside, and they were greeted with the praise and appreciation she expected. Bess was a well-mannered woman and answered appropriately, as she did throughout the meal.

One of the long tables had been covered with a large white cloth set for the family, including Renney and Jack and their three children and his mother, as well as Mitch, Rebecca, Martin, and Bess. Everyone here was associated with the tavern. Jack grew and his mother canned most of the vegetables served at the tavern, and his cows, chickens, and hogs produced most of the rest.

Martin kept the fires burning in the stove and fireplaces, and Rebecca, Renney, and Bess cooked the food that brought in the customers. Mitch caught the fish, hunted the deer for their venison, brewed the ale and beer, and kept order on Friday and Saturday nights when the music was loud and some of the customers had too much to drink.

When everyone was seated and Mitch had said grace, platters were passed, and there was not a moment of silence for half an hour or more until Mitch stood to speak. He said, "We have gathered here to celebrate the birth of our Lord, but it so happens that we are here also to celebrate one hundred years of Renegar's Tavern. We all know the history of this place, of Robert and Albert and Rob, then Rebecca, the Renegars who built this place and kept it going all these years. The community has grown up around it, and it has been a place not just to get a fine meal and a glass of good drink, but a place of music, joy, and fellowship. I want to thank each of you for the contributions you have made to the success of Renegar's." He then named each person and their contribution, ending with thanks to Rebecca for marrying him and giving him the best life a man could wish for.

"Now, you all know that on the sixteenth of January, Prohibition is coming to America. Our brewery will close down at midnight on December 31. We will continue to sell our beer and ale until the supply runs out or until January 16, whichever comes first. As of that day, Renegar's Tavern will be no more. That sign will come down, and a new sign will go up. That sign will say Renney's Restaurant."

Martin noticed that Bess was quieter than usual during the meal and afterward. He understood that this holiday had to be painful for her. Later in the afternoon, when the woodboxes were filled, he made up a basket of leftovers that he planned to share with Bess. They could have supper together and visit awhile, then he would go home, sit by the fire, and read.

The house Mr. Hollars had built was very simple and informal. It faced the river through thinly cleared woods. The front door opened into a large space that served as a sitting room, dining room, and kitchen. There was a bedroom off each end of this large space. A hall from the kitchen led to an icebox room on the left and a large washroom on the right, which included a hand pump connected to the well under the house below and a modern commode connected to a septic tank located some three hundred yards in the distance. These Mr. Hollars had installed at the insistence of his wife, who refused to move here without these conveniences. The hall straight ahead led to the back porch and the woods and an outhouse beyond.

When Martin knocked on the door, Bess opened it immediately. "I thought I heard a motor. Come in."

"I brought supper, thought we could eat and visit awhile, but if you have plans, I'll just leave yours here and take mine home."

"I have no plans, Martin. I have no baking to do, and I don't know what to do with myself."

He set the basket on the table and noticed a bottle of bourbon on the wooden counter where Bess created her baked goods. She had had this built after she got the job baking for the tavern. It was enclosed on the sitting/dining side and open on the kitchen side, revealing shelves for storing pans and supplies. Someday she planned to have doors installed to hide the shelves but did not want to spend the money now. A large flat piece of polished marble sat on top for rolling out dough and pie crusts. This had belonged to her mother.

Bess noticed that Martin saw the bourbon and she explained, "The whiskey belonged to my father. I decided to celebrate Christmas." She took a glass from the cupboard and poured a bit of bourbon in it, then filled it with ice water from a jug she had earlier brought in from the icebox. She handed the glass to Martin. "Have some."

Martin was not much of a drinker. Growing up in a tavern, he had seen some people drink and laugh and sing and dance, and others make fools of themselves, some others threaten violence; Mitch knew how to handle those. Being around it all had robbed alcohol of the forbidden nature that made it so enticing to his friends. He would not have chosen to be drinking this Christmas evening, but he had come here to cheer up a friend, so he took the glass offered him and took a sip.

He didn't know how much Bess had had to drink, but he figured she had not eaten since he had, so he took the food out of the basket and suggested they have supper. He sipped the watered-down bourbon as they ate.

They talked about the changes coming. Martin said his parents had known for a long time that he had no interest in running the tavern, and that Renney was the one to take over when they could not do it anymore. "That time isn't here yet, but they decided since it can no longer be a tavern, and the name has to change, and someday it will be Renney's, they would just go ahead and put her name on it. Besides that, everybody knows Renney, and everybody likes her."

Bess agreed, then said, "Tell me something. How did a Methodist church come to be located so close to Renegar's Tavern? As I understand it, the Renegars owned all the land around the tavern."

"You are right, they did. They donated the land for the school, and Albert and Grandpa Rob built those houses on the hill to rent but then sold them to the renters. Then one day this fellow appeared, driving a fine buggy, and introduced himself as Dr. Thomas, said he wanted to build a nice house on a large level lot. It so happened that Grandpa Rob needed money to hire a cook and a cleaner because Rachael, who had done some of both, had moved out of the tavern after Albert died, and she wanted to stop working, and my grandmother was busy with my mother, who was just a baby. So when this man said he really wanted the large lot not far from the tavern's barn, Rob sold it. He thought the man was a medical doctor, and that would be good for the community. It turns out the man was a doctor of theology, and the nice house was actually two houses—one for himself and one for God."

"Wasn't he suspicious? Weren't there already graves out there?

"Oh yes, Rob pointed that out, but the man said he didn't mind having quiet neighbors."

Bess laughed. "Was Rob upset when he realized he had been fooled?"

"He always said it taught him a lesson, but he figured the people around here needed a church. Of course, the Methodists hate alcohol and preach against it, but the church hasn't hurt our business. I am sure they are very happy about Prohibition, but I don't think people who drink will stop drinking. They will just buy it from bootleggers."

"What is it like to have grandparents?" Bess asked as she refreshed their drinks.

"You had no grandparents?"

"One was still living when I was adopted, but she died when I was very young. I have no memories of her."

"I am sorry you missed out, because it was wonderful having grandparents. We all lived together upstairs. It was like having four parents. Four people who love you unconditionally. My grandmother was the first teacher at the little school in The Falls. She read to us when we were little, and when we learned to read, we read to her. Grandpa took me fishing, and I just loved being at the river. I always knew I wanted to live by the river. Grandpa told me when I grew up, I could get a job, save my money, and buy land on the river, then build a house. He didn't try to talk me out of it. He told me how to do it."

"Are you as happy living on the river as you expected to be?"

"I love it, cannot imagine living anywhere else. What about you, Bess? You grew up in a city. Are you happy here?"

"I am happy when I have plenty of baking to do, and in the city I would probably have more to do than time to do it. When I'm not baking, I have time to think about how alone I am. I imagine I would be happier in the city."

As she stood and refreshed their drinks, Martin suggested that she could sell this house and return to the city, buy a store for a bakery, and live upstairs.

"Are you trying to get rid of me, Martin?"

"No, I just want everybody to be happy, that's all."

"Martin, you are such a nice man. How have you managed to remain single?"

"Well, I'll tell you, Bess." Probably because he had had two glasses of bourbon, Martin told Bess about his bout with mumps and the diagnosis of infertility and his decision to avoid romantic relationships.

Because of her more-than-three bourbons, Bess asked, "You have never slept with a woman?"

"I didn't say that, Bess. Sex isn't always about romance."

"Oh."

"Since we are getting rather personal here, why have you never married, Bess?"

"Husbands are too much trouble, Martin." He opened his mouth to object, but Bess interrupted, "Hear me out. If a woman has a husband, she has to clean his house, wash and iron his clothes, cook his meals, and wash his dishes and all the pots and pans it takes to cook those meals, and sleep with him, and unless he had a bad case of mumps (sorry) have his babies and take care of them. How on earth could I do that and do what I love, bake?

"Martin, baking for me isn't just about making something to eat. It's an art. You take the freshest ingredients and put them together just the right way in the correct amounts and bake them in just the right pans and at the right temperature for exactly the right time and remove them from their pans (if it's a cake) when the time is right. Then there's the frosting. But you get my point.

"Think about the chocolate cake I make for your mother. She places it in her clear glass-covered cake stand on the shelf behind the counter. It looks like a picture. Everyone who comes in the door sees that cake, and nine out of ten order a piece because it looks so good. And what's more, it reminds some of those customers of the cake their mothers made, and it may remind someone else who grew up really poor of how they stood outside a bakery window looking at a sweet thing they would love to eat, but they didn't have a penny to buy it, and how that hurt. But now, they do have some money, and they can have a piece of that cake, and that makes them happy. That is what art does; it stirs up feelings in people."

"I've never thought about it like that, but you're right. Cooking is an art."

"Life involves choices. I can't be happy without my baking, so I choose to bake."

"I, for one of many, I'm sure, am very glad you made that choice. Now will you excuse me? I need to go out for a minute."

While Martin was gone, Bess again refreshed their drinks and wound up the Victrola. When he returned, she visited the washroom, and Martin looked through her record collection and sipped his drink. When she returned, he said, "This makes me want to dance."

"The only dancing I've ever done was square dancing back in eighth grade. I don't know how to dance to that music."

"Well, it's time you learned," Martin held out his right hand. "Come on, Bess."

Bess took a few sips of her drink and walked into Martin's arms, and the dancing lesson began. She caught on quickly and was surprisingly light on her feet, which led Martin to ask, "Are you sure you haven't done this before?" She assured him she had not. They stopped only to wind up the Victrola and drink more bourbon, then resumed dancing. They had started out with the virtuous space between them, but as they drank and danced more, the space between them disappeared. Being held by another human being felt so good to Bess, who had not been hugged by anyone since her mother had gotten too sick and died. As they danced, her thoughts of Jeanette came to her, and she wondered if being made love to by a man would cure her of her unnatural desire. She could feel that something was happening to Martin. Without thinking, she asked Martin to make love to her.

When Martin woke up the next morning, the first thing he noticed was that he had a headache. The next thing he noticed was that he was not alone in bed. Then he remembered what happened. He had told her making love was not a good idea, because they were friends and this would change their relationship. She said she didn't want to die without ever making love, and he was the only man she trusted. His next thought was, "I will never touch another drop of alcohol again."

He got up and quietly felt around for his clothes, which he took into the sitting room, where he dressed in the dark. The stove in the kitchen was still warm because Bess had added wood the night before, prior to their dancing lesson. He lit a lantern and added more wood now. After a visit to the washroom, he made a pot of coffee and drank a cup. When his headache eased, he made a pan of biscuits. Bess got up and said good morning on her way to the washroom. She was wearing a gown and robe and bedroom slippers. Martin put the biscuits in the oven.

When Bess returned to the kitchen, she wanted only coffee. "I have a terrible headache. I guess this is what is called a hangover," she said as she took the cup of coffee Martin handed her. She then sat on the sofa and drank the coffee, resting her head on the back of the sofa between sips.

Martin stood behind the counter waiting to take out the biscuits and watched Bess. Finally he said, "I am sorry for what happened last night, Bess."

"You don't need to apologize, Martin. I got you drunk and lured you into my bed. It was lovely. I won't do it again, but it was lovely, and I do not regret it."

Later at home, Bess's words repeated in his mind. He hoped she meant it when she said it wouldn't happen again, but it didn't make sense that if you had a lovely experience, you would not want to repeat it. But he did not intend to waste time trying to figure this out. One thing was certain, he would not participate in any more "lovely" experiences with Bess.

Early on Monday, Bess arrived, as usual, as Martin was filling the woodboxes. She brought in two large baskets of pies and went back to her car for two more baskets with cakes and doughnuts. Renney looked over the items, made out the receipt, and paid Bess, then made the breakfast Bess always ordered: sausage, eggs, biscuits, and coffee. Bess was sitting at the counter when Martin brought his plate out and sat at the counter, one seat between them as usual.

They said good morning, and Martin asked what she had brought this morning, and she told him. They talked about the plan to eventually remove the long tables and build booths and smaller tables. They discussed the snow they expected to fall any time, and Martin said if it was bad, he would pick up her things and deliver them in the afternoon. When Renney brought out his lunch, Martin said goodbye and left for the mill.

Thus they seamlessly fell back into the relationship they had as though nothing unusual had happened between them. Then, on a cold clear day in February, Bess came in with three cakes, six pies, and enough doughnuts for the rest of the day and evening. She explained to Renney that she had some business to take care of and would not be back that evening, and probably not until the next afternoon. She asked for a sausage biscuit to go and left.

At seven fifteen that night, Martin was sitting in his chair by the fire reading when he heard a car drive up. He put the book down, slipped into his shoes, and went to the door to find Bess climbing the stairs to his porch.

"Bess," he called out, "come in out of the cold." Martin was not pleased to see her, but his good manners won out over his irritation. Once inside, she went to the fire to warm up. Martin drew up a chair for her to sit. "Is something wrong?" he asked.

"You had better sit down, Martin. We have a problem. I am pregnant."

Martin opened his mouth but was too stunned to speak. Finally, he said, "It cannot be. I heard the doctor say that I would never be able to father children."

"I told that to the doctor I saw today, and he said your doctor should have said you *might* not be able to father children." She told him the name of the doctor. "He was our family doctor in Richmond. He said abortion is illegal, but women have them all the time, and no one enforces the law. At first that's what I thought I would do, but then he said you have a right to know that you can father a child, and I thought this may be the only child you will ever have. So I told him I'd think it over and talk to you.

"On the train, on the way home, I thought about what a lonely life I live with no family. Even my parents were not really related to me. But this baby is my child, my real child. I felt better. But this isn't just about me. It is going to change both our lives."

As Martin sat listening to Bess and her shocking news, he experienced a myriad of emotions: despair at the thought of marrying this woman, anger at the doctor who had so casually announced to his mother that he would never be able to father children, excitement that he had, pity for Bess, who saw having a child as a relief from her aloneness, shame that he had been so foolish to get himself into this quandary, resignation that he would have to marry Bess and be a father to his child.

When Bess paused, Martin spoke. "Bess, surely you know that if you keep this baby, you will have to give up all your baking. A baby will take up all your time."

"Your mother didn't give up the tavern. Renney has kept working."

"My mother wasn't running the tavern when she had me and Renney, and when she worked there, her parents were there to take care of us. As for Renney, Jack's mother lives with them and looks after the little ones. You won't have that kind of help."

"I have some money, Martin. My father left a savings account, and I was able to save money too because I lived with them. I have been very careful not to use my savings except to pay the property taxes and a few other necessities. I'll hire someone to help me at first, and later I can keep the baby in the big room. Babies sleep most of the time. I can bake while she sleeps."

"You refer to the baby as a girl."

"I hope it will be a girl. If it's a boy, you will have to be more involved."

"Boy or girl, I'll have to be involved, Bess. I would never shirk my responsibility for my child."

"I know that, Martin. You are a good man. But I also know that this isn't what you want. I am not the woman you would choose to be the mother of your child, because you're not in love with me, and I am not in love with you. I have been in love. I know what that feels like, and this isn't it. But we are friends, and we do enjoy each other's company. If we keep the baby, we need to marry, but after a year or so, we can get a divorce. Now that you know you can have children, you'll be free to find someone and fall in love."

"Sounds like you have it all figured out, Bess."

"Well, I had that long train ride to think it through. Now I'm going home and will let you think it through. You let me know in a few days what you want to do. If you are unwilling to marry me, I will have an abortion, or I'll go somewhere else and tell people I adopted the baby. Either way, you will be free from the responsibility."

The next afternoon, Martin and Bess ate supper together as usual. He walked her to her car afterward and told her he would follow her home. Once there, they settled in the sitting room by the fire, and Martin asked if she had changed her mind about what she wanted to do. She said she wanted to keep the baby.

"Then we need to get married as soon as possible. We can go to the county seat tomorrow morning." Bess was a bit surprised but relieved. They discussed their living arrangements. Martin would continue to live in his house but would have telephones installed in both houses. He would be available if she needed him. He would pay the bills for both telephones. He would either borrow or buy a cradle and baby bed. After a few months, they could begin buying a few things the baby would need, and by the time she arrived, they would have what she needed. "Come April or May, we need to start looking for someone to help you with the baby during the day." They would share the cost. "I will spend the nights here, of course, after the baby comes, and when you start baking again, I'll deliver the things to Renney's and bring home supper for us in the evening."

The next morning, after Bess had made her delivery to Renney's and Martin filled the woodboxes, they each returned home and changed clothes, and, in Bess's car, Martin drove them to the county seat, where he purchased wedding rings, and afterward they were married in the courthouse. A number of shotgun weddings came to Martin's mind as he went through the proceedings, but in this case, there was no irate father and no shotgun that had driven him to this wedding. It was his conscience and the sense of responsibility instilled in him by his father and grandfather that had driven him to this place. Their example had taught him what it meant to be a man. And when the judge said, "You may kiss the bride," Martin smiled and kissed Bess on the lips.

Martin also took his bride out to lunch. Later, back in The Falls, Martin drove to Renney's in his truck. He gathered his family into the office and told them that he and Bess had gotten married because she was pregnant. He explained what happened and that neither of them was in love with the other but were doing the right thing. They did not want any celebration or have to pretend that it was something it wasn't, at least to his family. His family was completely surprised but agreed to their wishes. Rebecca said, "We will celebrate when the baby comes."

"Yes," he said.

Over the months that followed, people in the village became aware of the marriage and, later, that a baby was expected. A few tongues wagged, but many more than one had married for the same reason. Everybody liked Martin and loved Bess's cakes, pies, and doughnuts, even though they didn't really know her, so what gossip there was was mainly by females who had tried and failed to get Martin King to the altar.

The baby, Ethel Ann, named for Bess's mother, arrived on Saturday, October 2, 1920. Martin had hoped for a girl because it seemed so important to Bess. He moved a few of his things to Bess's house and into what had been her parents' bedroom. He had hired a Mrs. Cooke to stay with Bess during the day and do the laundry and cleaning.

Martin had little experience with babies. He had, on occasion, held Renney's babies, but never bathed one or changed a diaper. Now he was learning to do these things, and he would talk to Ethel Ann as he performed these necessary chores. When they were done, he enjoyed rocking her, often continuing to hold and rock her long after she had fallen asleep. Bess would go to bed early during these times so that she would be rested when the baby woke up demanding to be changed and nursed. For now, then, this forced little family settled into a comfortable routine.

Chapter 7

Glenna

KATHLEEN HAD REPORTED to her VAD supervisor that she had married Charlie on the day she returned to the field hospital. "Did you have sexual relations with him?" the supervisor asked.

"No," Kathleen answered.

"Then keep it to yourself. We need you here."

So Kathleen continued as before, caring for the wounded soldiers. She knew Charlie's home address since she had written letters for him, so at night she wrote to him. When he got home, there were a number of letters from Kathleen. She cautioned him to write to her as Kathleen Quinn.

When the war was over in November 1918, Kathleen applied for passage to America on a brides' ship. It would be many months before she would have a place on a ship, so she returned to Ireland for a long visit with her parents. They were upset that she had married a Protestant and tried to convince her to have the marriage annulled, remain in Ireland, and find a way to pursue her dream of becoming a nurse. She finally convinced them of her determination to be with Charlie and assured them that they would rear their children in the Catholic Church.

She got a job in the bottle factory where her mother worked and used the money to help her parents with food and rent and to buy wool material to make a warm winter coat, a winter dress, a pretty hat and leather gloves, and new shoes and stockings because she wanted to look nice for Charlie when she saw him again.

Due to the flu pandemic, it would be a year before she had a place on a brides' ship. In December 1919 she returned to France to brides' camp, where she learned about what to expect in America, and a week later, she boarded the ship for the six-week trip across the Atlantic.

When Charlie and Kathleen were reunited, it had been fourteen months since they had seen each other and the first time they had seen each other in street clothes. They had each worn their best to please the other, Charlie in a suit and tie and black overcoat and hat, and Kathleen in the warm winter coat and new dress she had made the year before. She was carrying a large canvas bag that contained everything she owned.

As the brides gathered to disembark from the ship, they were greeted by a sea of cheering men on the dock. Kathleen scanned the upturned faces and soon found

Charlie, taller than most of the others. He was looking for her, probably with a redhead in mind, but her hat covered her hair, so she noted where he was standing and walked through the crowd to him when she left the ship. His sweet face broke into a smile when he saw her, and she was quickly engulfed in his arms and off the ground.

Kathleen had expected they would spend a few days in New York and was disappointed when Charlie said he had to get back to work, so they would be leaving on the train that afternoon. On the way to the station, they stopped at a café for lunch, where she told him about the activities on the brides' ship. She had made friends with several women, but none who were bound for the Virginia mountains.

On the train heading south, she asked how his parents had reacted to the news that their daughter-in-law was a Catholic. Charlie said the whole family was anxious to meet her and were planning a big welcome dinner for her. "And they would like us to have a real wedding in the Methodist church."

"A real wedding? We had a real wedding, Charlie."

"I should have said another wedding, where all the family and friends can attend."

"Another wedding isn't necessary, Charlie. But we could have a reception and invite all the family and friends and have cake and punch."

"Or we could have another wedding and a reception, Kathleen."

"Charlie, why is a second wedding so important?"

Charlie looked away and did not answer.

"Charlie, why is a second wedding so important?"

"My mother says we are not really married."

"She thinks you are lying?"

"No, not that. She does not believe that God recognizes a Catholic wedding. She says we cannot live together until we have a real wedding."

"What?! Oh, oh, now I know why we couldn't stay in New York. Your mother would not allow it."

He did not deny this.

"You lied to me, Charlie. You said your family would accept me as I am. Obviously that is not the case."

"Kathleen, I did not lie. I thought they would be so grateful to you for saving my life that they would overlook that you are a Catholic. I guess they don't love me as much as I thought."

The train pulled into Boston, and Kathleen said, "Charlie, let's get off here. Boston is a big city. We can live here. You can be a Protestant and I can be a Catholic, and nobody will care."

"Oh, Kathleen, I can't live in a big city. I have land back home. I'm going to build us a house. I have a job."

"You also have a mother who runs your life. I will get off here and find a priest and have our marriage annulled, and I'll go back to Ireland where I belong."

She started to get up, but Charlie stopped her. "Please don't do that, Kathleen." He had turned toward her, and she saw there were tears in his eyes. "You are the only woman I have ever loved. If I have to choose between my mother and you, I choose you."

Kathleen could not bear to hurt Charlie. She remained in her seat.

The next morning the train pulled into St. Claire, where Charlie had left his truck. He carried Kathleen's bag and helped her into the truck, setting the bag at her feet. Deep snow lay on the ground everywhere except for the streets and pathways. As they drove through St. Claire, Charlie pointed out the Jane Auditorium and all the houses John St. Claire had built for the workers, then the Catholic church and the mill where he worked. Soon they were out in the country, with deep forests bordering the hills on the right and the far side of the river on the left. Now and then, Kathleen would see a house, and then they were crossing the long bridge over the river, and a mile down the road, they turned off the highway and into The Falls.

Renney's Restaurant sat on the left. There were no cars there. "It's closed on Sunday," he explained. A mountain of snow stood at the edge of the forest on the left side. The parking areas in front and on the side were cleared. Charlie pointed out the general store and a garage down the road straight ahead, but he turned left beside Renney's, and they passed outbuildings including a barn behind the restaurant, then a wooded area. Just beyond this sat a white clapboard house with a shoveled path to the mailbox and another to the church next door.

"This is the minister's house, and that's the Methodist church next door." The church matched the house, except it was much larger and had a steeple. Beyond the church lay the cemetery, then more woods, and beyond them the red brick schoolhouse. A field lay across the road, and Charlie identified it as a baseball field now covered in snow. One house sat just beyond and on the left. Then the road curved to the right and climbed the hill to a long row of small white houses that sat along the road that circled back down the hill and on to the garage and general store. Within the circle was a fenced cow pasture.

Charlie pulled the truck into the yard of the third house on the hill. Kathleen saw that an outbuilding lay straight ahead out back. Charlie explained that a past owner had built this for a cow, but they didn't have a cow. They walked to the house on the path Charlie had cleared, and Kathleen stood on the porch and looked out over the village, which was enclosed in thick forest. It felt a bit claustrophobic, but Charlie was calling her to come inside, so she shook off the feeling and followed him into the house. Charlie had intended to make their furniture in his father's workshop, but he had returned to work a few months after coming home, and he was so tired at the end of the day that he just could not summon the energy to do much of anything. So he had ordered the furniture from the Sears Roebuck catalog. "I hope you'll like it," he said as he showed her the bed and chifforobe.

"It is lovely, Charlie. I have never had anything so lovely. Thank you," she said as she hugged him. Then he showed her the table and chairs in the kitchen. She rubbed her hand on the smooth finish and sat in one of the chairs. "I will make cushions for the chairs and curtains for the windows."

"Well, I thought you might want to do that," he said and led her into the second bedroom, where a brand-new sewing machine sat with a padded stool.

"Oh, Charlie, this is wonderful!" she said as she lifted the cover and examined the machine. Then she hugged him again and cried for joy. "I never expected all this."

Charlie was touched and so happy he almost cried himself. He said he had bought only the most necessary things because he wanted her to choose the rest of the furnishings. He showed her the catalog and told her the general store here had material, but the general store in St. Claire had a better selection, according to his sister. He would give her money, and she could go shopping. "That would be a real treat," she said.

Kathleen unpacked her bag and hung up her few clothes. Then they freshened up and made their way to his parents' house, which was located on top of the mountain off a road where the forest had been cleared for farmland. Many of the people in the area had settled here and raised cattle, hogs, and chickens and grew wheat and all kinds of vegetables.

When they drove up to the house, Kathleen was surprised by the sight of a large farmhouse with a covered porch extending all along the front of the house. On both sides, trees, some evergreen and others leafless, stood in the snow. It was like a picture. Charlie parked beside the other cars, and before they got to the stone walkway to the house, Charlie's father and brothers came out the front door and stood smiling on the porch.

Mr. McAllen stepped forward. "Welcome, Kathleen. I'm Charlie's papa," he said as he took her hand in his. "And these are his brothers, Dave and Jim."

"It is a pleasure to meet you, Mr. McAllen."

"Not Mr. McAllen, Kathleen. Everybody calls me Papa. I hope you will too."

"Then thank you, Papa, Dave, Jim."

Once inside, the children gathered around and began introducing themselves. One named Benjamin said, "You talk funny." To which Kathleen responded with a smile and said, "No, you talk funny."

Everyone laughed.

They settled in comfortable chairs in the front room and asked her about her trip over on the brides' ship. As they were talking, Charlie's oldest sister came in, introduced herself, and gathered the children to settle them in the kitchen, where they would eat. Shortly thereafter, they were all called into the dining room, where an extra table had been added to the already long one to accommodate all the adults.

Mrs. McAllen came out of the kitchen, and Charlie introduced her to Kathleen. Mrs. McAllen was a stern-looking woman, her hair pulled tightly back from her face, not a wave nor a curl nor a smile to soften her appearance. Kathleen's first impression was that this woman was ready for battle. She said to Kathleen, "We appreciate all you did to help Charlie recover." It was said without warmth, as though it was necessary to be said and gotten out of the way.

"Thank you, Mrs. McAllen."

Mr. McAllen asked Charlie and Kathleen to sit at his right. Then everyone else took their places. Charlie's mother at the opposite end of the table, which Kathleen considered a blessing. Mr. McAllen said grace, and everyone began helping themselves to the dish in front of them and passing it to the left. Several platters of the same food had been placed strategically on the table, so there was no getting up to refill from the kitchen.

As they ate, Charlie's siblings shared stories with Kathleen about Charlie. Some were touching and others funny. Kathleen noticed though that his mother did not make any comments or laugh. One of Charlie's sisters asked how Kathleen had come to have her position in the field hospital in France. Kathleen told her that she had always wanted to be a nurse but didn't have the money, about going to London and working in the hospital, volunteering to help the soldiers, and learning about the VAD program.

Mrs. McAllen spoke up, saying, "Your parents let you take off like that on your own?"

"As I explained, my brother was in London, and I lived with him. I wouldn't have gone otherwise."

After the meal, Kathleen offered to help with the cleaning up, but Charlie's sisters would not hear of it. "You can help next time," one of them said. So Charlie took her on a tour of the farm, and then they joined the others in the front room. After a while Jim rose and said he had better be getting home, and the others followed. Mrs. McAllen said to Kathleen, "Charlie can bring in your things, and I'll show you to your room."

"Mrs. McAllen, I am not staying here. I'm going home with my husband."

"You will stay here until after the wedding," Mrs. McAllen insisted.

"There won't be another wedding, Mother," Charlie said. "We will be happy to have a reception for all the relatives and friends to meet Kathleen, but there won't be another wedding. The United States government recognizes our marriage as legal, and that should be good enough for you."

Mrs. McAllen stared at Charlie, turned around, and walked out of the room.

Kathleen would remain in The Falls for nearly twenty years, but never again was she to visit Charlie's parents' house.

* * *

Charlie and Kathleen wasted no time getting together to browse through the Sears Roebuck catalog. They chose a matching set of an overstuffed sofa and two chairs, end tables, and an area rug. Kathleen suggested they order an ottoman so Charlie could put his feet up after a hard day at the mill. They also ordered two lamps in anticipation of the electricity that they were certain would come soon. The lamps would just be for looks for ten long years. (Charlie would also later order a radio so they would be ready.)

Kathleen bought yellow-and-white-checked material and made curtains for the kitchen window and the back door. Of the same material she made cushions for the kitchen seats and backs. For the front room, she chose a wine-colored material to match the sofa and chairs. These she lined and made especially full so they could be closed to keep out the summer sun. She made green curtains for their bedroom but decided to wait about the curtains for the other bedroom because by then she suspected she was pregnant, and she wanted to know if the baby was a boy or girl.

If Kathleen had thought she would be shunned by the villagers who attended the Methodist church, she was in for a surprise. Though many had negative feelings about Catholicism, these people put those prejudices aside because Charlie let it be known that if it were not for her attention to him, he would not have lived to return home, and these people had prayed hard for his recovery. The way they saw it, God had used Kathleen to save Charlie, and who could argue with God?

In addition to that, while Kathleen might not have been a certified nurse, she knew more than anybody else in the village about medicine. She kept on hand Dakin's solution to prevent infection and gauze to cover wounds. Some women would come to her with their complaints, and if she knew something to help, she would tell them what to do. If not, her advice was to see the doctor in St. Claire. One overweight woman told Kathleen she was always hungry and very thirsty. Kathleen told her these were symptoms of diabetes and that now there was a treatment called insulin. She told the woman to go to the doctor without delay. Kathleen had been right, and this woman told everyone that Kathleen had saved her life. Most of those who sought her help needed first aid, and Kathleen was certified in this. She was called on so often that she organized a class in first aid, and later, another in the proper way to give a massage. (The women later reported that their husbands really appreciated this.)

Kathleen might also have thought that all of Charlie's family would have nothing to do with her, but she would have been wrong again. Charlie's father had visited them the next day after the "welcoming" dinner. He apologized for his wife's behavior. "She's a good woman, but she has strong and absolute views about religion, and she won't allow that anybody who disagrees with her has a right to believe something different. So don't expect her to come around to accepting you unless you give in and marry Charlie all over again in the Methodist church and, not only that, declare Catholicism evil and join the Methodist church. I don't expect you will do that, and frankly I wouldn't want you to do that. We are all Christians and love Jesus Christ, and we should love each other and not fight over the details. Charlie's brothers and sisters feel the same way I do, but they love their mother and don't want to get on her bad side, so you won't see much of them. Don't take that to mean that they don't accept you, because they do. What I am trying to say is that you do have a family here, and you can call on us if you need us. My wife accepts that she has no control over me, so I hope to visit you and Charlie regularly. I want to be a part of your family." Then he presented a gift of a few slices of ham he had cut for their breakfast the following morning. He would be a frequent visitor, always bringing something from his farm. Charlie's siblings also visited, but infrequently, and usually at night. They often brought something sweet like the fried apple pies Charlie especially liked or half of a pound cake. They wanted Charlie to know they loved him and accepted Kathleen as their sister-in-law.

* * *

On Monday, January 17, 1921, Kathleen gave birth to a baby girl. She was named Glenna Quinn McAllen after her grandfather Glenn. Had the baby been a boy, he would have been named after Charlie. Glenn's mother had insisted on naming her son after her little brother who had died, even though it meant a lifetime of teasing because his first and last names rhymed and inspired other children to add any number of silly verses to Glenn Quinn. Glenn learned to laugh along with his tormentors, but Kathleen knew the teasing must have hurt his feelings. She loved him dearly and wanted to honor him.

Papa McAllen had noticed that Kathleen had no rocking chair, and long before Glenna was born, he had gotten busy in his workshop and built one of oak lumber he had on hand. He had stained it a reddish brown and had someone he knew make padded cushions for the seat and back. Kathleen was thrilled with the chair. She said it was a work of art.

When Papa visited and saw his new granddaughter, he declared she was the most beautiful baby he had ever seen. He attended her christening at the Catholic church, standing with Charlie and Kathleen during the ceremony. For the rest of his life, he would be a real grandfather to Glenna, visiting often, taking her to the general store when she was a bit older to choose a Little Golden Book or to Renney's for hot chocolate. He always gave her a Christmas present, one of the most special being a wooden checkers set he had made and painted, including the little round playing pieces, half red and half black. Glenna and her papa spent many evenings playing checkers.

Charlie would sometimes take Kathleen and Glenna to the land he had bought before the war. He had intended to start building the house by now, but the furnishings for the rental house had eaten away at his savings. His sister had loaned him a cradle for Glenna, then a baby bed, but at over two years old, she needed a real bed, so he had once again turned to the catalog, and he and Kathleen ordered a bed, nightstand, dresser, and chifforobe.

When they visited the land, they would walk about and make plans where to build the house and the various outbuildings they would need. As time passed, Kathleen realized that they were just dreaming, that there would likely never be a house here. She saw that Charlie lacked the stamina for such an undertaking, most likely due to his serious injuries suffered in the war.

One Saturday in September 1924, Charlie went to Richmond with his brother Jim, who Charlie said had business to attend to and wanted Charlie to go with him. He had said not to wait up for him because they would be late coming back.

Though he was very late getting home, Charlie was up early the next morning. Kathleen was cooking breakfast when he said to leave that for a while. He took her hand and led her out the back door and around to the side of the house where he had parked a shiny new 1924 Model T Ford.

"Charlie, you bought this car?"

"Yes, it is ours."

He took her hand and led her to the car and helped her inside, then ran around and got in the driver's seat. She said, "I hardly know what to say. It's such a surprise."

Charlie said, "Kathleen, I am never going to be able to build the house for us. It's all I can do to work in the mill all day. I have kept hoping my strength would come back to the way I was before the war, but it hasn't, and it's not going to. I am not able to build a house or farm. It's been hard to give up that dream, but sometimes you just have to face facts, and the fact is I am as well as I am going to be.

"We have a nice little house here. You've made it so cozy and comfortable. We can go on living right here, but we don't have to stay here all the time. They're paving more and more of the roads now. We can take little trips to other places. There is a picture show in Wytheville. I would love for us to go there, and now we can. Riding in this car will be half the fun. Do you see, Kathleen?"

She took his hand in hers and said, "Yes, Charlie, I understand. This car is a lovely surprise. Thank you, darling." Kathleen did understand. She knew that Charlie was sincere in his desire to take Glenna and her places. But she also understood that the automobile had replaced the beloved horse now in the minds of men who loved the thrill of traveling fast in a vehicle under their control. If Charlie had been forced to give up his dream of building a house and a farm, she was happy that he had something that would bring him some joy.

Over the following years, they did enjoy the car, taking Sunday afternoon rides and, on many occasions, traveling to Wytheville to the picture show and eating supper in a little café there. They would ride in style to the Jane Auditorium on Saturday nights. Glenna would sit on Charlie's lap so she could see the performers. At home the car would be parked in what had been a barn but, with the owner's permission, had been turned into a garage. With help from Jim and Dave, Charlie had enlarged the entrance and built a swinging door. Besides Roy Capp's, it was the only garage in The Falls.

Chapter 8

BESS WAS DETERMINED to be with Ethel Ann all the time and also to resume baking as soon as possible. But nursing the baby every two or three hours proved to sap her strength, so it was over two months before she had the energy to bake anything. After that, as the baby began to sleep for longer between feedings and Bess slept more at night, she slowly resumed baking.

As soon as Ethel Ann woke up in the morning, Bess rolled her bed into the big room, and unless she was nursing, changing, or rocking her, this is where the baby remained all day, mostly sleeping. Bess could keep her eye on her and bake pies and cakes and doughnuts.

When the baby was awake, Bess could talk to her just as her mother had talked to Bess about whatever she was doing. While the baby slept, Bess worked quietly. If Ethel Ann woke up at an inconvenient time, Mrs. Cooke would change her diaper, and Bess would quickly finish what she needed to do, then nurse the baby. If Bess was nursing the baby and something needed to come out of the oven, Mrs. Cooke would take care of that.

This worked well for a while, but then Martin tired of the expense of keeping Mrs. Cooke full time. "I am a mill worker, Bess, not a wealthy man who can afford a full-time servant." Bess, who was bearing half the cost, also became concerned about expenses, as it took nearly all she was making to pay her half of Mrs. Cooke's wages. They decided that Mrs. Cooke could reduce her hours to two days per week to do the washing and cleaning. Mrs. Cooke was agreeable to this.

By now, Ethel Ann was over seven months old and had finally learned to sit up in a high chair. She was also sleeping less, so when she was awake, Bess sat her in the high chair very close to the counter so she could see her mother as she kneaded dough or rolled out crust or mixed cake batter. Ethel Ann had a rattle, and as Bess worked and talked or sang what she was doing, the baby would shake her rattle or, if she was teething, bite one of her teething rings. (Bess kept one in the icebox at all times.) For several months, this worked well except at times when Ethel Ann needed to be changed and fed and Bess was in the middle of something that had to be finished before she stopped. Ethel Ann would cry, and Bess would talk to her. By the time Bess was able to stop and take care of the baby, both were frustrated. In time, Bess began pacifying her daughter with a tiny bit of cake batter or the sweet syrup of pie filling on the tip of her finger.

Ethel Ann had been slow to turn over, sit up, crawl, and walk. Martin was no expert on child development, but he had watched Renney's children go through these developmental stages, and he knew that his daughter was not keeping up with normal expectations. Bess brushed off his concerns. "Children develop at their own pace," she said, parroting something she had once heard.

Martin ignored her and made it his business to interact with his daughter as much as he could. He continued to give her a bath each night, and once she was bathed, diapered, and dressed for bed, he would show her picture books and point out and name the things pictured. Later, he bought storybooks and read to her. She was not as interested as he would have liked, but what really concerned him was that her first word after dada and mama was "do-nut."

Ethel Ann was over eighteen months old when she began to walk. She did not want to sit in her highchair and would kick and cry when Bess forced her into the chair. But Bess could not have her walking all over the place, particularly near the hot stove, so she had bought a playpen and kept her in there while she did her baking. Ethel Ann, when not napping, wanted out to roam around. Thus a little piece of doughnut now and then to keep her quiet. In time, Ethel Ann learned to say and demand, "Do-nut!"

Martin told Bess that she must stop giving their daughter anything sweet. "It is not good for her. She is fat. She will be teased unmercifully when she goes to school. Make some applesauce out of sweet apples and let her eat that."

"Can you imagine what a mess that would be?" Bess asked him. He had said it didn't matter, that she could clean it up, but she ignored him and his concerns. He saw that she was not going to make applesauce, so he made a batch. Ethel Ann loved it. She made a mess but did learn to use the spoon. Martin cleaned up the mess.

It was at that point that Martin moved back to his house, and every night after he had delivered Bess's baked goods and brought home and eaten supper, he took Ethel Ann home with him. He couldn't do anything about what Bess did during the day, because he had to work, but he would limit Ethel Ann's time with her mother as much as possible. For all he knew, she might be giving the child doughnuts if she woke up in the middle of the night. He kept a fresh supply of homemade applesauce in his icebox, and whenever Ethel Ann called for a doughnut, he gave her applesauce. Often, she would throw a fit for a doughnut, but in time she learned it would do no good and settled for the applesauce.

On Saturday nights, he took Ethel Ann to the Jane Auditorium. Bess occasionally went with them, but most of the time, she preferred to stay home, wash and set her hair, and have a leisurely bath. On Sunday morning, she would pick up Ethel Ann and take her to church and to the college for lunch, then return her to Martin. Martin would do the thorough cleaning at the restaurant and eat lunch with his parents while Ethel Ann was with her mother.

Ethel Ann adjusted to her new life of living with parents at separate houses. At Martin's house, there were no doughnuts, only applesauce, but she had the run of the house and her own room. At Bess's house, there was little freedom, but there were doughnuts.

Martin did everything he could think of to stimulate Ethel Ann's interest in the world around her. When the days were warm and longer, he would take her fishing or on walks along the river. He put up a swing for her under an oak tree. He continued to read her stories and engage her in conversations. As she neared the time she would be going to school, he went through a trunk upstairs over the restaurant and found the blocks Rob had had made for him. His grandmother had painted a letter of the alphabet on one side of each of the twenty-six blocks and the numbers one through twenty-six on the opposite side. With these, he taught Ethel Ann the ABCs a few at a time. He taught her to count to ten, with the blocks turned so the letters were facedown and not confusing. He would stop when she became tired, because he didn't want her to dislike learning. He knew she was going to have a hard time in school and made up his mind to help her as much as he could. Then everything changed.

One Tuesday afternoon in June 1926, as Martin drove to Bess's house after work, he was thinking that he wished it was Friday with the weekend ahead, then chastised himself for wishing his life away. Just before reaching the house, he thought he smelled smoke. When he pulled up, he knew it was coming from the house. He jumped out of the truck, ran to the house, and flung open the door. He yelled out to Bess and Ethel Ann and ran to the stove, where something was burning. He grabbed the pitcher of water sitting by the stove, opened the oven door, and threw the water on what had been two pies. Then he ran to the bedroom, where he found Bess and Ethel Ann on the bed. Bess was staring at the ceiling. Ethel Ann was crying. "Bess, Bess," he said, but there was no answer. He touched her face. She was cold.

He picked up Ethel Ann, who kept saying, "I couldn't wake her up. I tried, Daddy, but I couldn't wake Mama up."

Martin said, "I'm sure you did, honey; I couldn't wake her up either." He carried her outside and sat her in his truck. "You stay right here, sugar, while I go back inside a minute."

Martin called the sheriff and told him what he had found when he arrived after work. He opened the windows to air out the house and walked back to Ethel Ann. She was still crying but had calmed down some. He wiped her face with his handkerchief. "It looks like your mama put two pies in the oven to bake. Can you tell me what happened after that?"

"Mama said she had a headache, and we went to bed. She told me to listen for the bell. I tried to wake her up, but she wouldn't. I tried to get the pies out so they wouldn't be burnded up, but I couldn't. It was too hot."

"So you went back and tried again to wake her up?"

Ethel Ann nodded and said she did.

The sheriff brought the doctor with him. They went inside and came back out in about ten minutes and spoke with Martin and Ethel Ann, who repeated what had happened.

The doctor took Martin aside and told him Bess had apparently had a massive stroke. The sheriff made arrangements for the body to be removed. Martin went back in and returned in just a minute with Ethel Ann's baby doll and a pair of her pajamas. Then he took her to Renney's where, after settling Ethel Ann with a glass of milk, told his parents and Renney what had happened. Then he returned to the house to wait for the ambulance that would take Bess away. While he waited, he packed all of his daughter's clothes that had remained at this house, then took the cakes and the bag of doughnuts outside. He threw the cakes into the woods, but the bag of doughnuts he stomped over and over and emptied in the woods. He went back into the house, and he stood at the bed and looked at his wife, whom he had once cared for as a friend but had come to dislike intensely. All she had cared about was baking, and she had stuffed their child with doughnuts to keep her quiet. He could not summon any pity, just relief that it was over. Then he went outside and waited for the ambulance.

When Martin returned to Renney's, Rebecca was holding Ethel Ann in her lap, telling her a story. When she saw him, she called out "Daddy," and held out her arms to him.

"She has had supper, Martin." He thanked his mother and took his daughter, and they walked upstairs together. He sat in the rocking chair in the sitting room and helped Ethel Ann into his lap. He reached into the bag he had left there earlier and pulled out "Dolly" and handed her to Ethel Ann.

"We are going to stay here tonight, honey."

"Where is Mama?"

"Well, you know you couldn't wake Mama up, and I couldn't wake her up. That's because she had a stroke. Sometimes when a person has a stroke, they pass away."

"They go away?"

"They go to heaven to be with Jesus. That's where your mama went."

"Will she be back tomorrow?"

"No, she won't ever come back, Ethel Ann. One day, many years from now, we will see her again when we pass away and go to heaven."

"I want my mama, Daddy. Make her come back."

"I can't, honey. She can't come back, but we will be okay. I'll take care of you. You will miss your mama, and you will feel sad, but in time you will feel better."

Martin rocked his child to sleep and laid her on his old bed that Rebecca had made up with fresh sheets. Then he went downstairs and called his supervisor and told him what had happened. He was told to take the rest of the week off, that if they had an emergency, they would call. Then he called Bess's pastor and made arrangements for the funeral for Thursday morning. Rebecca told him that Mary Davis, one of their waitresses and a part-time cook, would prepare lunch for the family and any of the mourners who wished to come. The restaurant would be closed after tonight until Friday morning.

Martin knew that Bess owned a grave plot at the cemetery in St. Claire. Her father had purchased three when they moved here. He was thankful for that. He called the funeral home and spoke with the owner, informing him of the plot bought by Mr. Hollars. He knew about this and would have the grave dug. They made an appointment for Martin to come to the funeral home in the morning to choose the coffin and take care of other matters.

Rebecca carried Martin his supper on a tray and set it on her desk. While he ate, they talked about finding someone to look after Ethel Ann while he was at work. She suggested Mrs. Cooke, who had helped Bess when Ethel Ann was a baby. He said he would visit her tomorrow. She said she would look after her tomorrow while he took care of the funeral arrangements. He was grateful and said so. Then he went upstairs to check on Ethel Ann. She had had a terrible day, and he was glad she could sleep.

Later, Rebecca and Mitch came up, and they talked into the night. Mitch had filled the woodboxes. Martin thanked him, said he had completely forgotten about them. Then he said good night and lay down beside his little girl and went to sleep.

The next morning, a wreath of white flowers was placed on the front door. A neatly printed sign said: "Due to the death of our daughter-in-law, Bess Hollars King, we will be closed until five thirty Friday morning."

Renney had taken care of this. She also prepared breakfast for everyone. Ethel Ann was very quiet during the meal. She had awakened in the night and had to go to the bathroom. She was confused and didn't know where she was. Martin took her to the outhouse. On the way back in, she asked him if they were going to live over the restaurant now. He told her no, that they would live in his house on the river. She said she was glad, because he had an indoor bathroom. Actually, his indoor bathroom required pumping many buckets of water in the pump house and carrying them inside and heating them on the stove for a bath. One bucket full of water was kept by the commode to flush it. When Ethel Ann was not there, he used the outhouse. Ethel Ann was not able to go back to sleep, so they talked about what Bess might be doing in heaven. Martin said she was probably visiting with her parents. He told her that he would be making funeral arrangements in the morning, and she would be spending the day with her grandparents. She had never been to a funeral, so he told her what to expect, and that she would wear her best dress and shoes and she would sit with him, and her grandparents, and Renney and Jack. She had finally gone back to sleep, but Martin remained awake and finally got up and made coffee.

When Martin started to leave, she cried to go with him, but he convinced her to stay by telling her that she would have to sit quietly all morning if she went. Mitch's suggestion for a ride in the buggy helped.

Martin first went back to the house to go through Bess's clothes to find something to bury her in. He found the dress she often wore to church and figured it was her favorite so laid it aside and found the underthings and stockings. It was too early to go to the funeral home, so he began to look through her things in case there were valuables or money he would not want to leave in the house for some thief. He found a pearl necklace and earrings that someday would be Ethel Ann's. Then he opened the drawer to the bedside table. There was a book of poetry. A bookmark protruded from the pages, and Martin opened the book to those pages. Cut from a newspaper was an announcement of the engagement of the lovely young woman in the photograph. The poem on the page was E. B. Browning's "How Do I Love Thee?"

"Oh my God," he thought, "Bess was a lesbian." He remembered that she had said she had been in love, knew how that felt. Later, when he had asked about it, she said it was impossible and would say no more. All that talk about not wanting to marry because husbands were too much trouble was a cover. Bess had had to hide what she was. He knew something about that. But she had freed him from his secret. And he would have kept hers if she had confided in him. His anger toward her waned.

Chapter 9

WHEN BESS DIED, Rebecca asked Kathleen if she would be interested in using Bess's recipe and making doughnuts for the restaurant. Kathleen agreed to give it a try and found that she enjoyed doing this and making a little money also, because Glenna seemed to outgrow her shoes and clothes every few months. So Rebecca gave Kathleen the recipe and the basket and cover Bess had used to transport the doughnuts, because she saw no reason for Kathleen to go to the expense of buying another basket and cover.

During the week, Charlie would deliver the doughnuts on his way to work, but on Saturday, if he was off and the weather was nice, Kathleen would walk to the restaurant to make the delivery.

Martin had to be at the restaurant early every morning to refill the woodboxes for the day. Since her mother's death, Ethel Ann had to come with him. Most of the time, she would go upstairs and get in his bed and go back to sleep, but since it was Saturday and he didn't have to go to work, they would be going back home. They were in the kitchen when Kathleen walked in carrying the basket of doughnuts.

When Ethel Ann spied Kathleen, she ran over and yelled, "That's my mama's doughnut basket!" She reached for the basket, but Kathleen held it up and Martin rushed over to try to shush her, but as he carried her up the steps, she continued to cry and call out for her mama and doughnuts.

Rebecca removed from the stove the pan of bacon she was frying and took the basket from Kathleen. She said she was sorry. "I don't know what we're going to do with that child. Bess stuffed her with doughnuts to keep her quiet, and Martin won't let her have any because she's too chubby. She has lost her mother and the doughnuts. Lord help us."

Kathleen said, "I will buy another basket and cloth. I can do that much."

"Thank you, Kathleen. I'll get your money."

Later Kathleen went to the general store and bought a dark basket and a yellow-and-white-checked cloth, but anytime in the future Ethel Ann saw Kathleen, she associated this red-haired woman with the loss of her mother and doughnuts, especially in the years that followed, when Kathleen began cooking in the restaurant and, following Martin's orders, would not give her a doughnut. In her child's mind, she decided that Kathleen was responsible for her mother's absence.

To make matters worse, the adults in her life had decided that to deal with the horror of lying beside her dead mother for hours, trying to wake her up and being unable to do that and keep the pies from burning, they should discourage her from mentioning her mother in the hopes that she would forget what had happened. Anytime Ethel Ann wanted to talk about Bess or ask questions, they would say, "She's in a better place now. Don't worry about her." Ethel Ann was left wondering why her mother had gone to a better place and left her behind. No one thought to allow the child to express her feelings. So her feelings festered and rankled, and Kathleen, and eventually Kathleen's child Glenna, became the objects of her resentment and eventually hatred.

Chapter 10

ONE SUMMER DAY in 1927, Charlie came home and announced that he needed glasses. He was having trouble reading the addresses on the shipment labels, and this was important because all the boxes going to the same place would be stored together and separately from those headed to another. The glasses helped for a while, but soon he needed a stronger prescription. Kathleen asked him if he had been exposed to the mustard gas used by the Germans during the war. He said he had. Her heart sank. Charlie was going blind.

By January, Charlie had completely lost his sight. Kathleen drove him down the mountain to a veterans' hospital, where he was examined but was given no hope for ever recovering his sight. He was given materials to help him learn Braille, a cane, and instructions on how to use the cane to navigate his way through his dark world. While there, Kathleen completed an application for veterans' benefits.

Charlie had understood that he was going blind even before he completely lost his sight, and he was determined not to become helpless and a burden on Kathleen. He began practicing doing chores and counting his steps and memorizing when to step up and down. He could help Kathleen by pumping water into a bucket and carrying it into the kitchen, and he could make the beds.

Years earlier, he had made a wagon for Glenna, and Kathleen used it to bring sacks of flour and sugar and other things from the store. Now Charlie would pull Glenna in the wagon to the store, counting his steps and memorizing the number, then return home with the groceries and Kathleen's baking supplies.

He knew he could no longer chop wood for the stove and fireplace, so he had the timber cut from his property, selling most of it and saving some, which his father stored in a barn. Charlie hired his nephew to chop the wood, load it into Charlie's truck, and park the truck in the garage beside the Model T. Charlie could fill a basket with wood from the truck and bring the wood in as needed.

Most of the money from the sale of the timber went into his savings account in the bank in St. Claire, but he kept out a large stack of ones and a smaller stack of fives. These he kept in a metal box in the chifforobe. While they waited for the veterans' benefits, they could use this money to pay rent, buy food, and any other necessity.

By now, Kathleen was baking cakes as well as doughnuts for Renney's, so she appreciated Charlie's bringing in the water and wood and groceries. He was also helpful keeping Glenna busy as she tagged along with him on these errands.

There was always plenty of work to do, but there was also time for fun. Saturday nights at the Jane had become a tradition for Charlie and Kathleen and now Glenna. Because Kathleen could drive, they could continue to attend the concerts and plays at the Jane, and on Sundays Kathleen and Glenna could attend early Mass. Charlie did not like being left alone, and soon he decided to join them. Two hours later, he and Glenna would walk to the Methodist church for the worship service. When they got home, Kathleen would have Sunday dinner ready, almost always fried chicken, Charlie's favorite.

Staying busy helped Charlie ward off the despair he felt, but at times the sadness won out. One day when he went out the back door and did not soon return, Kathleen went to look for him. She saw that the garage door was open, and she peeked inside. Charlie was sitting in the Ford, his arms around the steering wheel, his head resting on his arms. He was sobbing. She quietly backed away and went back into the house and began cooking lunch. She could not do anything to fix this awful thing that had happened to him, but she could give him the space and privacy to grieve his loss.

Late in the spring, the first VA check arrived. The first check included the benefits for the months since his application. It was promptly deposited into the savings account. The monthly benefit covered the rent and food and little else, but they were grateful to have it. Kathleen continued to do Renney's baking, and with her earnings, they could make it.

Glenna would start first grade in September, so Kathleen began making jumpers and blouses for her to wear. Each month, she would buy the material and notions, and in spare minutes throughout the day, she would cut and sew. When she finished these, she began knitting Glenna a new sweater.

Charlie asked Kathleen what else he could do to help her, and she suggested he could wash their clothes and sheets. She had gotten him started, but he learned quickly and soon took over this chore. Encouraged by his success, he suggested that he learn to braid Glenna's hair. Kathleen was skeptical, but she didn't want to discourage him, so she agreed to teach him. Glenna thought it was a wonderful idea, and she sat patiently on the ottoman, Charlie sitting behind her, and Kathleen standing beside the chair giving instructions. Learning to plait was easy, but achieving a result with both braids the same length and positioned the same on both sides proved to be a challenge. There were many do-overs and lots of laughter, but after a week Charlie had achieved a level of success approved by both Kathleen and Glenna.

Glenna was also eager to help her mother, and she became the official duster of all the furniture she could reach. She insisted on dusting every day so that Charlie said the poor dust mites didn't stand a chance of a long life in the McAllen household.

Little by little, Charlie accepted his condition, and with each new accomplishment, he became more confident that he could live a normal life. When September came, he walked Glenna to school and was there at two forty-five to walk her back home. Only if it was raining would he allow her to walk alone dressed in her rubber boots and a yellow rain slicker and carrying her umbrella, all ordered from the catalog. At these times, he and Kathleen would stand on the front porch, and as Kathleen described her progress down the street past the last house, around the curve, and down the hill, past the ballfield, and in the schoolhouse door, Charlie could watch their little scholar make her way to school.

After school, Glenna would proudly display the work she had done that day, describing it all to Charlie. As she learned to read, she would sit in his lap and read to him. If she encountered a word she didn't know, she would spell it, and he would help her sound it out. But those times were rare because Glenna was learning fast, and Charlie was filled with pride for her.

A few days before Christmas, the three of them walked carefully through the snow into the woods to find a tree, which Charlie managed to saw down as Kathleen directed. At home, Kathleen popped popcorn and threaded three needles, and they strung garlands. Every year since coming to America, she had bought two or three inexpensive red glass ball ornaments. She had also made angels by drawing and cutting out the forms from cereal boxes. She would cover the heads and make gowns with strands of white yarn, then knit wings that fit snugly over the cardboard. Kathleen kept these packed in two boxes and stored under the bed.

Before they could set up the tree, they had to move the radio from the corner. Normally Charlie took care of this, but this year his job was only to pick it up and set it on a small rug, and while Glenna held up the edge of the area rug, Kathleen dragged the smaller rug past the fireplace and into the bedroom. She said the radio would remain there until electricity came to the mountain.

That done, the tree was placed in the stand and stood in the corner. Kathleen guided Charlie to the tree and handed him the metal star they had bought their first Christmas. He felt the top of the tree and placed the star just right.

"Perfect!" Kathleen said. Then Glenna chose a red ball and hung it on one of the lower branches. Kathleen said she would hang an angel near the star. Charlie sat in his chair and imagined how the tree was decorated as Kathleen and Glenna discussed where they were hanging the ornaments and popcorn garland.

With help from his father, Charlie bought Kathleen a string of glass pearls, and he and Kathleen bought Glenna a storybook, a coloring book, a large box of crayons, and two new pairs of warm stockings. While she was at school, and after she was asleep at night, Kathleen knitted her a green pullover sweater. She was also knitting Charlie a soft scarf to keep his neck warm, and she had ordered for him a book of Wild West stories written in Braille, which he was learning.

Charlie's father took Glenna to St. Claire one Saturday to do a little shopping. In October, he had taken her to a photographer to have her picture taken. Now they were looking for a frame for the picture. Glenna chose the frame, and they had the saleslady put the picture in the frame and wrap it in brown paper secured with a red ribbon.

When Papa asked what she wanted to get for her father, she said without hesitation, "A whistle so he can scare away mean ol' snakes." Papa told her that was a good idea, and he suggested they buy a cowhide string to go with it so he could wear it around his neck and always have it handy. She said that was a good idea. Papa had it wrapped up in brown paper and secured with a red ribbon.

During the month of December, Charlie, Kathleen, and Glenna attended Dickens's *A Christmas Carol*, presented by the college players and some children in the community. They later returned to the Jane to attend a concert of secular and sacred Christmas music. They attended a play called *The First Christmas* at the Methodist church and Midnight Mass at the Catholic church on Christmas Eve.

Renney's was open for breakfast and lunch only on Christmas Eve and the day after Christmas with limited fare for both, only soup and sandwiches for lunch both days. Since Renney's was always closed on Sunday, and Christmas Day was on Tuesday, Kathleen did not have to bake for Renney's for four days. She was free to enjoy the holiday with Charlie and Glenna. She made a large batch of fudge, which she shared with Papa and neighbors. She made cinnamon rolls. They popped popcorn, this time to eat, and had hot chocolate, and Charlie and Kathleen told Glenna about their Christmases growing up.

On Christmas morning, Glenna slept a little longer, since they had been out late to Midnight Mass. Papa had given them a fresh ham, which Kathleen placed in the oven, then made coffee and pancakes. She and Charlie were eating when they heard squeals from the front room. They had laid her Santa Claus gifts out unwrapped. They left their breakfast to go to the front room and enjoy the excitement.

"Look what Santa brought me," she said, and immediately told her daddy about the storybook and the coloring book, and the biggest box of crayons she had ever seen. She wanted to get into her stocking and open the other presents, but Kathleen said to wait until after breakfast.

When they had all eaten, they returned to the front room, where Glenna presented her gifts first to Charlie and then to Kathleen. Charlie was touched that she wanted to protect him from snakes. He told her the whistle was a really good idea and put it around his neck. Kathleen loved the picture and the frame Glenna said she had picked out. She handed it to Charlie so he could feel the frame. Then Glenna cried because he could not see the picture. He took her into his arms and told her that her sweet face was permanently imprinted on his brain. Then he asked her how her hair was dressed in the picture, and she told him she had pigtails with navy blue ribbons. He asked what she was wearing, and she said a navy blue jumper and a white long-sleeved blouse. He asked if she was smiling, and she said she was. He told her he could see the picture.

Then he asked her to give his gift to Kathleen, and she did. Kathleen opened it and said, "Oh, Charlie, these are beautiful. I've never had anything so beautiful."

"They are glass, Kathleen. If I had the money, I would buy you real pearls."

"These are real to me, Charlie." She hugged and kissed him, then went to Glenna's room and fastened the pearls around her neck, and looked in the mirror above the dresser. She would take them off for now but later put on a nice dress and the pearls for Christmas dinner.

When she returned, she gave Charlie the scarf she had knitted for him, and then the book. He put the scarf around his neck and said it felt good. He was thrilled with the book, and he hugged and kissed her, and Glenna giggled. Then she opened her last present from Daddy and Mama. It was the green pullover sweater. She put it on over her pajamas, and she hugged her mother and then her daddy. Then she remembered her stocking, which was filled with two oranges, two Baby Ruth bars, and a dozen Bit-O-Honey bars. She was thrilled and wanted to eat an orange immediately. So Kathleen had her to sit at the table in the kitchen, and she sliced the orange and let Glenna do the peeling while she cleared the breakfast things away and washed the dishes. Charlie was immersed in his book.

Kathleen spent most of her day in the kitchen checking and basting the ham and preparing the vegetables, yeast rolls, and an Irish Christmas pudding. But at one point, she walked softly to the front room, where she saw that Charlie was reading his book, his feet resting on the ottoman, and Glenna was lying on her tummy, resting on her left arm and coloring in her coloring book, her crayons splayed out on the rug. It was a picture that she would remember the rest of her life.

Chapter 11

Eduardo (Edo)

SEVEN HUNDRED MILES to the north, another mother, Rosa Morelli, was watching her children enjoying their Christmas gifts, but she was watching one in particular, who was studying the map of the United States that she gave him. His teacher had told the class about the many places she saw and visited as her family moved from army post to army post as her father, an army major, was transferred over the years.

The teacher's descriptions had captured the imagination of Eduardo, her nine-year-old. He was busy finding the states of the places she talked about. These were places he wants to visit someday.

Rosa thought of her father, Eduardo, who grew up in Spain and wanted to visit all the countries around the Mediterranean Sea. Her grandfather had tried to talk him out of this. He had said, "Eduardo, if you touch one of the Moorish girls, they will cut off your head!" But her father was determined to go, and after nearly two years of traveling and working throughout North Africa, Palestine, and Lebanon, he was homesick and used the last of his money for fare on a merchant ship to Italy. He had planned to work his way overland back to Spain. Just off the ship, he showed up at a restaurant, broke and hungry, and appealed to the woman there to let him work for food. She was a widow with two small children who was trying her best to keep what had been her husband's restaurant.

She fed him, and he helped her. They fell in love and married and had a daughter they named Rosa. She thought that her son was like his grandfather, and she wondered if in some unlikely place, he would find love as her father did.

Chapter 12

TOWARD THE END of January 1929, Rebecca suffered an attack of appendicitis. While she was recuperating in the hospital in St. Claire, Renney asked Kathleen if she could come to the restaurant to work. Charlie assured her that he would be fine. He and Glenna would come to the restaurant for breakfast, and afterward she could go on to school, and he could walk home. There was snow on the ground, but he had rubber boots with threaded soles to prevent slipping, and he knew how many steps there were from Renney's to the back door of his house.

Kathleen suggested that he remain at the restaurant and visit with the customers, but he said no, that he wanted to go home. Kathleen, always torn between encouraging Charlie to be as independent as possible and cautioning him lest he become overconfident, stood outside the back door and watched as he made his way up the hill and to the back of the house. He had said when he got hungry, he would come back to the restaurant for lunch.

Charlie was pleased with himself for making the trip home in the snow with no problem. He took off his boots on the porch, went into the kitchen, removed his gloves and stuffed them into his coat pockets, then took off his hat, scarf, and coat and hung them on the peg by the door. He had one more story to read in the book Kathleen had given him, so he sat down with the book on his lap, his feet on the ottoman, and read the story. He had gotten quite good at reading Braille, and before an hour had passed, he had finished the story. He thought of taking a nap, but the three cups of coffee he drank for breakfast would not allow that. After Kathleen had left for Renney's, he had made the bed, filled the woodbox, and helped Glenna make her bed after she got up. When she was dressed, he had braided her hair, and then they had walked to Renney's. He had done the washing two days ago. He thought of all this and realized he had nothing to do but sit and hope his father would surprise him with a visit. He wished they had a telephone but then realized that the people he would enjoy talking with had no telephones, including his father. He decided he would have a telephone installed in this house and suggest Papa do the same.

Charlie thought about the radio he had bought, which sat silent in the bedroom because no electricity had come to the mountain. This would have been a perfect day to sit and listen to the news or music. He felt anger that other places had power but here there still was none, and there was nothing he could do about it. There was nothing he could do about much of anything, if you came right down to it, he thought. He felt frustrated and sad. Then he realized he needed to go to the toilet.

He put his book on the table beside his chair, pushed the ottoman away with his feet, got up, grabbed his cane, and walked to the kitchen, where he put on his coat, hat, and scarf, then went out to the porch, put on his boots, and walked to the toilet.

When he came out, he breathed in the cold, clean air of this snowy day, and he remembered how as a boy he had enjoyed being outside on such days when he and his brothers and sisters, once their chores were done, would divide themselves into two teams, with one of the oldest brothers on each team, and they would have snowball fights. Sometimes they would go sledding; sometimes they would just go exploring in the woods. Charlie smiled at the thoughts. He knew he couldn't do those things now, but then he remembered the path just a few feet away that ran behind all these houses and ended up at the road to St. Claire. It was a shortcut to the road. He had walked it when he had first rented the house. It was a well-worn path because kids and men headed to the river to fish would take this path, then walk up the road to another path that led to the river.

Charlie decided to use his cane to walk the path to the road and come back. So he took his gloves out of his coat pockets, put them on, and turned to the right, and with his cane, he found the opening from his yard to the path and turned left onto the path. He was on his way. He walked slowly, frequently waving his cane in front of him to ensure he had not veered off the path and close to walking into a tree. At one point, he realized he had forgotten to count his steps, but then realized that he could always turn left at the road and walk to Renney's if necessary.

When he got to the road, he knew it because he could feel the open space before him. This was one of the things he had learned since losing his sight. He considered turning left and following the road down to the turnoff to Renney's, but he had come this far on the path and felt confident he could make it back safely. So he turned around and started back.

After walking some distance, he began using his cane to locate the open space on the right that would lead to his house. When he found a clearing, he walked a few steps and straight into a tree. Panicked now, he stood still and fought down the fear he was feeling. Using his cane now, he turned around and found his way back to the path, but he was scared and wishing he had stayed at home in his chair. Suddenly he heard the sound of running behind him. He quickly turned around, lost his balance, and fell, hitting his head on a rock. The deer ran past him as he lay unconscious in the snow.

At Renney's the breakfast rush was over, and Kathleen began to worry about Charlie. She had never left him alone this long. She told Renney she needed to check on him and would be back shortly. She wrapped up a doughnut for him, bundled up, and walked home. When she walked into the house and called to him, there was no answer. She looked into each room, then went outside to see if he was in the toilet. Charlie was not in the toilet, but there were large footprints leading away from the toilet and toward the path. Following these, she saw him in the distance lying in the snow. She ran to him, knelt down, and determined that he was alive but unconscious. She ran through the woods to the house next door, banged on the door, and told her neighbor to go to Renney's or the school and call an ambulance, that Charlie had fallen in the snow. The neighbor gave her a blanket to cover Charlie. Kathleen ran back to Charlie and covered him with the blanket, then knelt back down and kissed his face and told him she knew he was cold but the ambulance was on the way. "We'll get you to the hospital and warm you up. Stay with me, Charlie. Please stay with me." Then she prayed.

Just as she had said, Charlie was taken to the hospital, where his wet clothes were removed and he was warmed with blankets. He was given fluids intravenously. The wound on his head was cleaned and treated, and his body temperature returned to normal, but he remained unconscious. The doctor told Kathleen, "We will just have to wait and see."

Charlie was moved to a room. His father arrived and sat in the room with Kathleen. Finally, she asked him to go to the school and bring Glenna to the hospital. Kathleen placed a chair by the bed, and Glenna stood on the chair, took her daddy's hand, and told him she was sorry he had fallen and hit his head, but she was sure he was going to be all right. Kathleen had told her that Charlie could hear her. So she told him what she had done at school that day, then took her little reader and read to him, describing the pictures as she went. Finally she said, "I love you, Daddy," as tears ran down her cheeks.

Kathleen told Glenna that the first time she saw Charlie, he was in bed and unconscious, and she had talked to him and told him to wake up and finally, one day when she told him to wake up, he had opened his eyes and smiled and told her she was a bossy woman.

Glenna laughed and felt better. But this time Charlie would not wake up. He was moved to the veterans' hospital down the mountain. Every Sunday for almost two years, Kathleen and Glenna would go to the hospital and sit by Charlie's bed, and Glenna would tell him about school, and she would read him a story. They would tell him everything that had happened in The Falls and St. Claire over the past week. They told him that electricity had come to the mountain, and described the programs they heard on the radio. They told him that Kathleen had gone to work full time at Renney's, and Glenna went to

Mrs. Oglesby's house after school and stayed there until Kathleen got off work.

They did not tell him about the Depression or that most of the money in his savings account had been lost. Before they left, they held his hands and kissed his cheeks and told him they loved him and missed him terribly and would see him next Sunday.

Just past five o'clock on a Tuesday morning in September 1931, someone knocked on the door. When Kathleen opened the door and saw the Methodist minister standing there, she began to cry. "He's gone. You've come to tell me he's gone."

She opened the screen door and backed away to let him inside. "I am so sorry, Kathleen." She had given the hospital the minister's number in case they needed to get in touch with her. He told her that a nurse making her rounds at three o'clock had found Charlie breathing funny, and she had stayed with him and held his hand until he slipped away.

"Oh, I must find out her name and thank her. I am so grateful he wasn't alone. He was so sweet and gentle."

"Yes, he was a fine man."

"Does Papa know?"

"No, I came to you first. Before I go tell him, is there anything I can do for you?"

"Yes, you could tell Renney and call Father O'Malley and let him know."

When the minister left, Kathleen went to their bedroom and picked up Charlie's pillow. Since the day of his accident, she had never laundered his pillowcase because it still had his scent. It was all she had left of him except the memories that came flooding back. He was a kind, gentle man, a genuinely good human being. It had been impossible not to fall in love with him.

"Mummy."

Kathleen turned around. Glenna was standing in the doorway. She put the pillow down and led Glenna to the front room, sat down, and took her child into her lap.

"Pastor Markley came earlier this morning with sad news for us, Glenna. Your daddy died this morning."

"He's not going to wake up?"

"No, his body won't wake up, but his soul is awake now, and he's gone to heaven, and Glenna, he's not blind anymore. He can see."

"I'm glad he can see, but I want him to come back. I want him here with us."

"So do I, darling, but he can't be with us anymore. We'll miss him terribly, but we'll be all right. You know when your daddy lost his sight he was very sad, but he was also brave. He learned to do all kinds of things to help our little family keep going. Now we have to be brave for each other." Kathleen held Glenna close and told her what would be happening in the days that followed.

Papa and Charlie's youngest sister, Margaret, came to the house midmorning. He hugged Kathleen and thanked her for making Charlie happy. Glenna ran to him, and he bent over and hugged her and told her how sorry he was that they had all lost Charlie. Then he asked her to show Margaret her pretty room. When they left the room, he wiped his eyes and told Kathleen that he had hoped with all his heart that Charlie would wake up, but in time he had come to believe that it was unlikely, so he had built a coffin for his son. He and Charlie's brothers had taken it to the church and set it inside. He wanted her to go to the church and see it. If she didn't like it, they would take it away, and he would help her buy another one.

Kathleen told Glenna she was going with Papa to the church and would be back shortly.

"Would you show Aunt Margaret where the coffee is and help her make a pot?" Glenna said she would.

Papa and Kathleen walked to the church. She was relieved that he had taken care of this and was certain the coffin would be more than acceptable because on that day ten years ago when she had been a guest in Papa's home, she had seen samples of the fine furniture he had made, as well as the rocking chair he had made for Charlie and her.

The coffin was made of walnut. The top had beveled sides, and the wood had been sanded to a fine finish. He had purchased padding for the interior. Kathleen could not imagine how painful it must have been for Charlie's father to build this. "It is a fine coffin, Papa. Thank you for doing this," she said through her tears. The next morning, Charlie's body was returned to The Falls. Kathleen had left his burial clothes at the church earlier that morning. The attendants who accompanied his body dressed him and placed him in the coffin. They draped an American flag over the bottom section of the coffin.

When she saw them drive away, Kathleen and Glenna walked down the hill and into the church. The minister was waiting for them, and he opened the coffin and stepped aside. Kathleen picked up Glenna so she could see her father. She looked at him and cried and said, "I wish you could wake up, Daddy. Can I kiss him, Mummy?"

"Yes, but he will feel cold."

Glenna bent over and kissed him, her tears dropping on his face. Kathleen set her down, and she touched his face and whispered, "I love you, Charlie." Then they walked out of the church and up the hill to the house.

The Methodist minister and Father O'Malley had conferred and decided that the Methodists would take food to the home of Charlie's parents, and the Catholics would take food to Kathleen's house. Renney's would take ham biscuits to both for breakfasts. Father O'Malley had visited Kathleen and Glenna as soon as he had gotten the word of Charlie's death, and he returned on Wednesday and brought food for lunch and again Wednesday night to accompany them to the visitation.

Father O'Malley drove Kathleen and Glenna to the church, where they met Mrs. Oglesby, who sat with Father O'Malley, Glenna between them in the second row facing the coffin and the family arranged in a line just past the coffin. Kathleen was first in the line, and Papa stood next to her, with Mrs. McAllen next to him, followed by Charlie's siblings and their spouses. Kathleen spoke to her mother-in-law, but Mrs. McAllen did not respond. As the visitors passed down the line, Kathleen could hear those from the mill and those from the Catholic church introduce themselves and explain their connection to Charlie and Kathleen to Mr. and Mrs. McAllen. None of these people knew that Mrs. McAllen had nothing to do with Kathleen and Glenna, because Kathleen would never hurt Charlie by talking about his mother. When Kathleen heard her fellow church members tell Charlie's mother how much they thought of her, Kathleen said a little prayer that Mrs. McAllen would not say anything to embarrass her family.

When the visitation was over, Father O'Malley drove Mrs. Oglesby home first and saw her inside, then Kathleen and Glenna. A neighbor had remained at the house during the visitation and offered to stay up all night, but Kathleen thanked her and said it was not necessary. She and Glenna had spent nearly two years in the house without Charlie. Now they had to get used to the fact that there was no hope that he would ever return.

Kathleen helped Glenna undress and put on her pajamas, and she lay down with her until she was asleep. Then she sat in the front room by the light of the lamp they had bought so many years ago. She picked up the framed photograph Mr. Wallace had taken of Charlie and her a few weeks after she had first arrived. She stared at the picture and remembered how happy they had been in spite of his mother's casting them out of her life. Their love was stronger than her hate.

She thought about her mother in Ireland and how she would love to be with her now, how comforting to be welcomed into her mother's arms, especially now. But the Irish were suffering through the Depression like the rest of the world, actually more so, according to the letters she received from her mother and sister.

Here she and Glenna had a comfortable house to live in, and she had a job where they ate well. She had the veterans' check. Would that still come if she moved to Ireland? Then she thought of Glenna leaving everything she knew after losing her father. It would be terrible for her. No, she wouldn't think of going back to Ireland now. Maybe later when the Depression was over.

Charlie's funeral was held on Thursday afternoon at two o'clock. Father O'Malley drove Kathleen and Glenna to the church. They remained in the car until Charlie's family arrived. Then Father O'Malley accompanied Kathleen and Glenna to the church door, the McAllens following. The coffin was now closed, and a beautiful spray of flowers lay on the front part of the coffin. Kathleen had given Father O'Malley the money to arrange for this.

Kathleen, holding Glenna's hand, led the procession to their seats at the front. It was a solemn service that honored Charlie's life as a Christian, a good and decent man, son, husband, father, and soldier. His favorite hymns were sung and his place in heaven assured. At the end, his brothers and cousins left their seats and carried his coffin down the aisle as the organ played "It Is Well with My Soul." They gently laid the coffin on the covered board over the grave. Kathleen and Glenna and the McAllen family followed the coffin to the cemetery where, once everyone had gathered, the Methodist minister read the Twenty-Third Psalm and then prayed, thanking the Lord for the life of Charlie McAllen, the privilege of knowing him, and finally for the promise of seeing him in heaven, where "there will be eternal life."

Afterward, the flag was presented to Kathleen. Then Pastor Markley announced that Kathleen and the McAllens would receive friends at their respective homes.

Renney's had supplied refreshments of coffee, lemonade, and teacakes, as well as the cups and napkins, at Kathleen's house. A neighbor served everyone. No one asked about the unusual arrangement of this event, but some speculated, and eventually word got out that Charlie's mother had never accepted his marriage to a Catholic. Kathleen never discussed it.

When everyone left, Father O'Malley drove Kathleen and Glenna to the cemetery. Charlie's grave was now covered in flowers, mostly picked from fields or flower gardens, the stems lovingly tied with white ribbons. Neither Kathleen nor Glenna would ever pass the cemetery without looking toward Charlie's grave and sending him a silent message that he was loved and missed.

Chapter 13

Nell

IN 1934 MARTIN King celebrated his forty-sixth birthday. Actually, he did not celebrate it at all. In fact, he had not given it a thought until his mother reminded him of it. When she did, he was distracted by something else, but later, as he sat in his comfortable chair with a book in his hand, the thought of being forty-six years old and well into middle age returned to him, and he began looking back.

He had been successful in achieving his dream of owning property and a house by the Wide River, and now that he had electricity, with lights at the flip of a switch, and indoor plumbing, and an oil-burning furnace to heat the house, it was perfect. He no longer was compelled to chop down trees for firewood for his house or the restaurant, though he did keep a fire in his fireplace just for the joy it brought him on a cold day.

Ethel Ann had settled down, especially after she completed the sixth grade and absolutely refused to go any further. He had always known she was "slow" and would struggle in school, and she had, and he had had to make her work at it every day. It was a relief when she announced that she was finished with school. His mother and Renney gave her a job cleaning and washing dishes at the restaurant, and Gloria, Renney's oldest daughter, had been put in charge to see that she did her job with no shortcuts.

The biggest problem they had with Ethel Ann was her love for doughnuts. Ethel Ann was not allowed any, so she would swipe them when no one was looking. If caught, Gloria took it out of her pay. Her pay she spent at the general store on other sweets, and now, with electricity to power refrigeration and a freezer, this meant Coca-Colas and ice cream. Ethel Ann was Mr. Wallace's best customer.

There was another problem, Martin had to admit, with Ethel Ann. Whether it was caused by her mother's death, her lack of intellect, the teasing over her weight, or a combination of these, his once sweet little girl had become a difficult person to be around. She lacked empathy, was defensive and selfish. She was not allowed to wait on customers, not only because she was likely to mix up orders, but because she just wasn't a nice person. She could behave well, and did so at the restaurant to keep her job, and mostly she behaved well enough at home because Martin required it, but over the years there had been many instances of her hurting someone's feelings. It was as if there was some anger deep inside her that had to be expressed. Martin had tried to figure this out, had tried to help her identify the cause, but the truth was she just was not smart enough to do that. So he had decided to accept that this was who she was, she was his child, and he would love her and take care of her the best he could.

The Depression had hit this area particularly hard because so many were employed, including Martin, at the St. Claire textile mill, and textiles all over had been hit hard. Most of the workers had been laid off, and the men were working on government projects like the building of the Blue Ridge Parkway. He was fortunate to keep his job, though at a lower wage and with fewer hours. But he had another source of income. He had kept Bess's house because, at the time, he thought it important for Ethel Ann's sake. He had planned to rent it or sell it eventually. Then one of the managers at the mill asked him about renting it for a weekend to a group of his college friends who wanted to get together and do some fishing. Martin agreed. There were only the two double beds in the house, so he bought two cots to accommodate this group of six men, as well as sheets, blankets, towels, and soap. He spent several days cleaning the house and making certain that everything worked.

What he charged these men covered his expenses. He learned that they had been very pleased with the accommodations and decided to make this an annual reunion. What was more, they went back to their respective homes and spread the word among their acquaintances about the excellent accommodations and reasonable rent. Martin had left his telephone number at the house in case there were any problems, and the men had copied it and given it to others who called Martin at night and on weekends to reserve the house, mostly for weekends but occasionally for a week, and once for several winter months to a woman who was writing a book and needed peace and quiet.

Cleaning the house and washing the linens after each rental was the downside of his new business venture, and eventually he hired a woman laid off from the mill to do these chores. The upside was that Martin had more money than he had had in his life, and in the summer of 1929, when it was certain that electricity was coming to the mountain, he bought pumps and installed them in both the wells of his two houses. He also installed sinks and a bathtub in the rental house, and all the pipes to carry the water inside.

He also bought himself a 1929 Ford coupe and enlarged the building that housed his truck to accommodate the coupe. He had nearly cleaned out his bank account for these purchases, but five months later, he said a rare prayer and thanked God for this lucky break, because if he had not spent the money, he certainly would have lost most of it in the crash.

The rentals slowed down with the Depression but did not stop, because there were still people with money, and he was thankful.

So, by 1934, Martin was getting by financially, Ethel Ann was fourteen years old and working, and he was continuing to attend the Thursday-night lectures at the college. During his marriage to Bess, he had given these up, but after her death, and after Ethel Ann seemed ready, Rebecca told him she and Mitch would look after the child so he could resume one of his favorite activities. Ethel Ann would spend the night in his old room, and he would see her the next morning. He was grateful to his parents for this "night off."

At the first lecture of the new series in September 1934, there were a number of new faces, some of them new students at the college but one who obviously was not a student. She was a very attractive young woman with short curly blond hair and blue eyes. She was wearing a navy blue pullover sweater and a gray skirt fitted over the hips with stitched pleats that fell loosely over her knees. She wore black lace-up oxfords. Martin had looked her over from head to toe, then remembered he was forty-six and much too old for this lovely woman. But throughout the lecture, his attention and his eyes kept returning to the back of her head, because she was sitting one row over in the front seat.

The next week he took special care to bathe, wash his hair, and shave, and to iron his clothes before class.

Because of all these preparations, he was running late to class, so when he entered the room and stood looking for a seat, their eyes met, and he smiled without meaning to, and she smiled back. He was certain he might have blushed, so he quickly took his seat. When the lecture was over, he stopped to chat briefly with a fellow from lower management at the mill, then headed to his car. When he got to the bottom of the hill, he saw the young woman walking. He stopped and rolled down his window. "Miss, my name is Martin King. I know you don't know me, and I have always told my daughter never to get into a car of someone she doesn't know, but it's starting to rain, and I would be happy to give you a ride home."

She said, "My name is Nell Riley, and my father always told me the same thing, but I'll be drenched if I walk home in this rain, so I will accept your kind offer." That said, she ran around the car and got in. She told him she lived in Mrs. Archer's boardinghouse. He said he knew where that was, and he drove her there. On the way, he learned that she taught first grade at the St. Claire elementary school. He told her he was the fixer at the St. Claire mill. She asked how old his daughter was, and he told her Ethel Ann was fourteen. "So she must be in high school."

"No, she is slow. She went through sixth grade and refused to go any further. It was a terrible struggle for her and for me, so I accepted it, and I'm happy she at least learned to read some. Now she works at my parents' restaurant in The Falls."

"That must be Renney's. I have heard it's a good place to eat. Is Renney your mother?"

"No, she is my sister." He explained why the restaurant was called Renney's. By this time, they had reached the boardinghouse. "This is a long way for you to walk, especially at night. I'll be glad to give you a ride to the lecture and back home every week."

"Won't your wife mind if you do that?"

"My wife died eight years ago."

"Oh, I am sorry. I hate to put you to the trouble, Mr. King, but it would be very nice to have a ride."

"It's no trouble. I'll pick you up at a quarter till seven next Thursday night." Martin drove home looking forward to next Thursday night.

Over the following weeks and months, Martin and Nell became acquainted. She had always wanted to be a teacher and was in college in her third year when her mother died from an infection, leaving a baby and six other children at home. Her sixteen-year-old brother was about to graduate from high school, but the others needed a mother, and Nell had been like a second mother to them before their mother's death. Their father was an engineer on a train and away much of the time. If Nell didn't leave school and come home, his only choice would be to farm the children out separately to relatives or put them in an orphanage. She could not let him do that. So she left school, went home, and raised her brothers and sisters. When the baby finished high school and took over keeping house for their father, Nell went back to school, completed her degree, and was offered a job over the summer teaching at the school in St. Claire.

Martin was surprised that Nell was thirty-seven years old. She could have easily passed for someone ten years younger. He felt younger just being with her. The third night after he had begun taking her to the lecture, he suggested they have some ice cream before he took her home. This became a routine, and they discussed the lecture as they enjoyed the ice cream.

Nell was the first person since Bess with whom he had had the pleasure of discussing the lectures. The difference was he and Bess had been just friends, but he was in love with Nell. For the first time in his life, he was in love. Bess was right when she said what they had experienced was not being in love. Falling in love was wonderful but also torture. He could hardly wait for Thursday night, but when he took Nell home and watched her disappear behind Mrs. Archer's door, he wanted to run after her. And the sad thing was he was afraid to tell her, afraid of rejection and never taking her for ice cream again. She had done nothing to encourage his feelings. She probably thought of him as just a friend.

On the last night of this series of lectures, Nell was quieter than usual. They had stopped for hot chocolate, but he sensed something was not quite right. When he took her home, before he got out of the car to open the door, he said, "What is wrong, Nell? Is something bothering you?"

She turned to him and said, "You have talked about the next lecture beginning in January. I think I'll not be going to any more of the lectures."

"Why, Nell? I thought you enjoyed them."

"Oh, I do enjoy them, but…"

"But what, Nell? Is it me? Have I done something to offend you?"

"No, Martin, you've done nothing wrong. You are a fine man. I enjoy being with you. In fact, I enjoy being with you too much. I'm afraid I am falling in love with you, and I don't want to be hurt."

Martin reached out and took her in his arms and kissed her. "Nell, I love you with all my heart. I was afraid to say it. I am so much older than you." Then he kissed her again and held her until she said, "Martin, if I don't go in now, Mrs. Archer will throw me out."

"If she does, we will have to get married in a hurry, and I'll take you home with me."

In the weeks that followed, they spent every possible minute together, settling issues such as that they wanted no more children. He had one, and she had raised five already. She would continue to teach school. He didn't go to work so early now, so he would drive her to school each morning and pick her up in the afternoon, or she could drive his car and he could drive his truck.

He told her that Ethel Ann was a difficult person but was not at home very much. "She is unlikely to leave home and live on her own or marry, so you will need to get acquainted with her and decide whether you can live with her, because I cannot abandon her."

* * *

The next day Martin told Ethel Ann that he had met a very nice woman named Nell Riley, and he wanted her to meet Nell. "I've invited her to have lunch with us Sunday."

"Are you going to marry her and bring her here to live with us?" she asked without emotion.

"Maybe. I do love her, Ethel Ann. But nothing is certain."

Nell had begun attending church in St. Claire, so after the service Martin was waiting for her. "Ethel Ann and I have prepared lunch. We usually go to my parents' for lunch, but I thought it best for you to meet her at our house and spend some time together, just the three of us." Martin had urged his daughter to take a bath and dress nicely, and she had done this. She had set the table properly and helped him a bit in the kitchen. Though it was a very cold day, she came out onto the porch when they drove up.

Ethel Ann watched as Martin got out of the car and went around to open the door for a very blond and very slim woman who stepped out of the coupe. Jealousy filled her heart, but she had learned that Martin would not put up with bad behavior, so she fought down her real feelings and assumed the act that enabled her to keep her job in the restaurant. She smiled when Nell came up the steps and greeted her. Martin introduced them to each other. Ethel Ann said hello and followed Nell into the house as Martin opened the door for them.

Lunch was ready, so they sat in the dining room and ate and chatted. Martin had taught Ethel Ann that it was nice to ask a guest about herself because it showed interest, so Ethel Ann asked Nell where she was from and about her family. When Nell talked about her mother's death, Ethel Ann became genuinely interested, and she told Nell that her mother had died. She went on to tell her what had happened, and how she was not able to waken her mother or get the pies out of the oven. Tears formed in Ethel Ann's eyes.

Nell said, "That had to have been so frightening for you, Ethel Ann."

It was the first time anyone had expressed to her just what she had felt that awful day, and now she felt a flood of relief and warm feelings for Nell. "Yes, I was so scared, and I didn't know what to do."

Nell said, "Of course you didn't. You were five years old."

Martin sat in stunned silence. He had been living under the assumption that Ethel Ann had forgotten all about that day and her mother. He could not remember the last time Ethel Ann had mentioned Bess.

Later Ethel Ann showed Nell the house as Martin did the dishes, and then they sat in the front room around the fire and talked. Nell spoke about teaching school, and Ethel Ann admitted that school had been hard for her, but now she had a job cleaning the dining room and washing dishes. Nell said those were some of the most important jobs in the restaurant, because if a customer came into a restaurant and the windows were grimy and there was trash on the floor and crumbs on the seats, the customer would figure the kitchen was probably just as dirty, and he or she would walk back out the door and never taste the food, no matter how good it was.

Ethel Ann was pleased to hear how important her job was, and she was further endeared to Nell. Martin was very pleased with Nell's visit and Ethel Ann's reaction to her. He did wonder, though, if this goodwill toward Nell would last. He shouldn't have worried. Once Ethel Ann made up her mind about someone, those feelings were stuck. She really did not think through her feelings. She just felt them and acted on them.

Martin and Nell were married during the Christmas holidays in a small service at the church in St. Claire. Only their family members were present. Mrs. Archer hosted a small reception after the wedding. The newlyweds left on the train to Virginia Beach for their three-day honeymoon, which, of course, included visiting the historical sites of Yorktown and Williamsburg.

Chapter 14

AS GLENNA WAS mourning the loss of her father, twelve-year-old Eduardo Morelli, in Barre, Vermont, was mourning the loss of a job he had hoped to get because he needed to earn money and save for a very special reason. But the job had gone to another boy, and Eduardo was very sad and angry.

At home, Antonio and Rosa noticed the change in Edo, and they asked him what was wrong. He told them that when he had passed Mr. Dickens's store the day before, there was a sign in the window, "Delivery Boy Needed." He had gone inside and grabbed the sign just in time to see Mr. Dickens giving the job to another boy. "He knew I wanted that job. All he had to do was catch me walking home from school. He didn't have to put up a sign. That boy who got the job is a blond-headed boy. Mr. Dickens didn't want an Italian boy. It's not fair!"

"Edo, don't you realize how many other fellows have asked Mr. Dickens for a job? He put up that sign and hired the first one to show up. If you had been first, he would have hired you. Now buck up. These are hard times. We can't get discouraged. We can't let this old Depression defeat us."

Edo knew his father was right, but he was still disappointed. Then he learned that the boy who got the job had desperately needed it. His father, who had been a stonecutter for over twenty years, had recently died of a lung disease, leaving his family without an income. Besides the boy's pay, they would be able to get the free wilted vegetables Mr. Dickens would have sold for hog feed. Now Edo was glad that he had not been the first to see the sign.

When Eduardo was born, his three-year-old brother, Marco, could not say Eduardo, so he called his baby brother Edo, and the name stuck.

Their father, Antonio, was a stonecutter. He had learned his trade in northern Italy as an apprentice in the marble industry. When he completed his training, he had returned home to a small port city in southern Italy, married his sweetheart, Rosa, and immigrated to America and to Barre, where he had been assured of a job cutting granite.

The young couple rented a house in the Italian section of town where Antonio's cousin, who had lured him there, also lived. Everyone there was Catholic and spoke Italian, learning only enough English to get by.

Rosa was different. She knew her children would have to learn English when they started school, and as they struggled with the language, they would fall behind and never catch up.

Besides this, she had grown up in a family who owned a restaurant. She had even, as a child, spent much of her time in the restaurant and had, over time, picked up bits of the foreign tongues of their customers and later, as a waitress, observed that when she spoke a bit of the customer's language, his face would light up with a smile. So she had learned to say, "Good morning/afternoon/evening. What may I bring you to eat?" in a number of the languages of people of the Mediterranean world. These men were pleased to hear the words of their own tongue, and they returned to this restaurant when they docked here again.

Still another explanation for Rosa's attitude about language was her father's story. Eduardo spoke Spanish and also Arabic due to his having spent so much time in Arabic-speaking countries, but he'd spoken almost no Italian when he landed here. In fact, to communicate with her mother that day long ago, speaking to her in Spanish, he had frowned, rubbed his stomach, and pulled out his empty pockets to tell her he was hungry and had no money. Then he had grabbed a broom and started sweeping to tell her he would work for his dinner. Her mother had laughed at his antics, but she understood what he wanted. Of course, he learned the Italian language but often broke out into Spanish when he was excited or vexed over something. Rosa learned to speak Spanish, as did her half siblings.

When Rosa and Antonio became engaged, she knew the plan was to immigrate to America. With her affinity for language, she decided early on that she must learn to speak English. She visited a former teacher and explained her situation. This teacher knew someone who had a friend who lived in Trento, where there was a university.

Several weeks passed, and one day a package addressed to Rosa arrived at the restaurant. It was a very much used book for the Italian student learning English. A note explained that this book had been owned by an elderly person who had passed away, and it was among other books that his daughter had donated to the university. There was no return address, so Rosa wrote a note of appreciation and took it to her former teacher to pass along to the person who had sent the book.

Armed with this book, Rosa spent every spare minute learning English one page at a time. Soon, when she wrote her weekly letter to Antonio, she would write a line in Italian and underneath translate the line into English as best she could. Once in America, in Barre, their priest helped her further improve her English, particularly her enunciation.

When her children came along, she would speak to them in Italian, then repeat what she had said in English. (This was the way her father had taught her to learn Spanish. It had helped both of them.) So the Morelli children were bilingual from the beginning. Later, much to the teacher's delight, Rosa would help other children and their mothers in their community to speak English and would help them understand when something came in the mail or from the school. If it was a note from the teacher, though, it would be taken to the priest for translation, because the mothers did not want their neighbor to know if their children had misbehaved or were not doing their homework or were having trouble learning.

Edo was never behind in school. He was very bright and sweet natured and enjoyed learning. When his teacher read a story to the class, he sat spellbound. This was especially so in fourth grade when Miss Evans described the Indians she had seen sitting on a bench in a railway station in New Mexico and had gone on to describe the Pueblo Indian village, with homes and buildings carved out of the rock high above the plains. This had led to a discussion about what materials people used to build their houses. The conclusion was that they used what was available, and in the case of the Indians in ancient New Mexico, it was rock. There were no trees, no wood, as there was in Vermont.

Edo wanted to see these houses carved out of rock, and he wanted to see the desert in bloom after a rain, and the great Mississippi River, and Niagara Falls. At home he would tell his mother about the places Miss Evans had described, and in time he made up his mind that he would visit these places himself one day. Thus the map Rosa had given him for Christmas.

Miss Evans had planted a seed, and Rosa had fertilized and watered the seed, and the seed had grown into an ambition for Edo. He was going to travel all over America. When a later teacher told him he had definite writing ability, he added to his ambition to not just visit but to write a book about his travels.

At one point, he began to think about how he would travel to these far-flung places. He knew that automobiles were expensive (his father could not afford one), and so were railway tickets. Besides that, trains did not always go very close to the places he wanted to see. He needed affordable transportation. One day, walking home from school with Marco and Sophia, a fellow drove past on a motorcycle. Marco commented that the fellow must be traveling, because he had a large bundle secured to the panel over the back wheel. Edo had not thought about traveling long distances on a motorcycle before. He had thought of them just as something to ride around for fun locally. But now he knew it would be possible to see America on a motorcycle. At the time, he didn't know that some motorcycles cost more than some automobiles, but for now he could keep his dream alive. So he decided that day in November 1929 that he would begin earning and saving money to buy a motorcycle. Surely, he thought, by the time he graduated from high school, he would have the money to buy his motorcycle. He also thought as he traveled, he could pick up jobs along the way to support himself.

Occasionally when he went to the market with his mother, she would give him a penny for a piece of candy. He decided he would forgo the candy and save the penny. Also, the family who lived next door had a set of twin boys three years old and a new baby. Over the summer their mother had given Edo a penny to read stories to the twins while she nursed the baby. He would ask her if she needed any more help when he got home.

Edo was vaguely aware of something called the Depression because he heard the adults talking about it, but nothing in his world had changed, so he had not worried about it. But the next week when he stopped at the market and asked Mr. Dickens for a job putting up stock, sweeping, making deliveries—Edo was willing to do most anything—Mr. Dickens said he couldn't take on any more help at the present time. "Come back when things are looking better. Maybe I'll have something then." When he went to the other shops on the street, he was given the same answer.

When he told his father, Antonio explained as best he could that a lot of wealthy people had lost a lot of money, and this affected many other people. "Things like this happen sometimes, but we will be all right," he assured Edo.

Antonio kept working for a while, but with fewer hours, and as orders slowed down, he was eventually laid off. He and Rosa were frugal people. They had, from the beginning, put away a portion of Antonio's pay. They had taught their children to take care of their clothes and shoes so they could be passed down to a younger child once they were outgrown. The youngest son, Emilio, wore clothes that Marco, Edo, and Niccolo had once worn, and Diana inherited clothes from Sophia. Both girls, like their mother, had learned to sew at an early age. They made the shirts Marco wore and kept all their clothes in good repair.

When Franklin Roosevelt became president, government relief programs were initiated and provided jobs in Barre to improve streets and sidewalks, build a playground, and improve sewer and water distribution systems. Antonio was able to work on these projects.

Though Vermont had a short growing season, Rosa had successfully grown tomatoes, celery, greens, beans, and herbs. A neighbor taught her how to can the tomato sauce she made each September.

The Morellis then were able to keep a roof over their heads and had enough to eat most of the time, and they were thankful. The few pennies that came Edo's way he turned over to his mother to buy eggs and milk, and cheese when she could find it.

President Roosevelt was doing his best to relieve the suffering, but the Depression kept hanging around like a dark cloud. Nineteen thirty-four found Edo fifteen and in his second year in high school. He had always been a good student, but a sadness and a resignation that things were not ever going to get better began to overtake him, and he began letting his schoolwork go.

Then one day an unexpected ray of sunshine broke through the dark cloud.

Chapter 15

WHEN MARCO MORELLI graduated from high school in May 1934, Antonio signed for him to join the army, as he was not yet eighteen. He was sent to Fort Bragg in North Carolina for basic training, and then to Fort McClellan in Alabama for advanced infantry training.

Rosa was terrified that Marco had been sent for infantry training. Antonio said, "Rosa, there is no war going on. Marco will be fine, and he will be sending home money so we can pay the rent and have enough to eat."

Edo wasn't terrified, he was just sad. He missed Marco terribly. Marco had been his protector on more than one occasion, and it was Marco who told him all he needed to know about girls. But Marco had no solutions for Edo's increasingly impossible dream of owning a motorcycle. His only suggestion was to finish school, join the army for two years, and save his money. Then he could buy his bike. He said two years would fly by.

But Edo did not want to join the army or put off his plans. He entered the tenth grade with little enthusiasm, but he was a conscientious student, so he tried hard to do good work and make good grades. For two months, he forced himself to study and turn in all his assignments. But as time passed and he continued to be unable to find work, he grew more discouraged and sad and began to struggle to complete his schoolwork. Any time he tried to read or study, his mind went back to the motorcycle he would not be able to buy, the ride across America he would not be able to take, and the book he would not be able to write.

One day at the end of November, Mr. Duncan, his English teacher, asked him to come by after school. Mr. Duncan was an elderly man, and Edo hoped that he might need someone to chop firewood or do some other chore for which he would pay Edo. But Mr. Duncan had no job for Edo. He was concerned that Edo was not doing the work he knew the boy was capable of doing.

"Something is wrong, Eduardo. Tell me what is bothering you."

So Edo told him about the plan he had had for years to work after school and in the summer, save his money, and buy a motorcycle. Then after graduation, he'd work his way all over America, and then write a book about it. "I will write my mother letters describing everything. She will save the letters so I'll have a record of everything when I write the book."

"What a splendid idea, Eduardo! I wish I had thought of it when I was your age."

"Thank you, sir, but…"

"But you haven't been able to get a job because of the Depression."

"Yes, sir. There is no work for someone my age, and not enough for grown men."

"Well, I have one suggestion: build your motorcycle."

"Build a motorcycle? I wouldn't know where to begin, Mr. Duncan."

"You begin by finding someone who owns a motorcycle. I think that men who own them tend to know others who own them. They probably get together and talk about their machines and their experiences riding them. Find one, and tell him what you want to do. I'll bet he can tell you who can help you."

"I will do that. Thank you, sir."

Edo left Mr. Duncan in high spirits. He knew of a man who owned a motorcycle, and he went to his house, introduced himself, and told the man he wanted to build a motorcycle. This fellow worked in the tool factory, and he also farmed and raised much of the food his large family consumed. As much as he would have liked to help Edo, he just did not have the time to spare, but he knew of a fellow, a welder, who just might be interested, and as it turned out, he was.

Jack Willis, from a young age, had been fascinated by taking things apart and putting them back together. He wanted to know how things worked, and he made it his business to find out. His father had died before he was born, and his mother died soon after. His grandparents had reared him. Mr. Willis was a mail carrier and owned a small farm on which he kept a few sheep, a pig, a milk cow, a plow horse, and chickens. There were five acres of pasture, apple trees, sugar maples, and spruce pines where Mr. Willis could always find a nice Christmas tree.

Fortunately, Jack's grandfather, like Jack, possessed an aptitude for all things mechanical. And out of necessity he would take something apart, repair it, and put it back together. He did enjoy the process, and he encouraged Jack and often sought his help and advice.

One day the plow broke in half, and Mr. Willis took Jack with him to have it welded back together. At a safe distance, Jack watched as Alister Brodie welded the broken pieces back into one piece and as good as new. He decided he would like to learn how to do this, and several years later he approached Mr. Brodie about teaching him his trade. Mr. Brodie agreed, and Jack became his apprentice. He was so pleased with Jack that he eventually gave him a job.

Jack, now grown, continued to live with his grandparents, and when he was not working, he helped his grandfather on the farm. Since they both had jobs, it required both of them and Mrs. Willis to produce and conserve what they grew and to care for the animals. As Jack had taken on more and more of the physical labor from his aging grandparents, they insisted he keep all his earnings for himself. Most of his earnings went into a savings account because Jack wanted to buy a motorcycle.

His grandparents did not approve of Jack's plan to buy a motorcycle. They were afraid he would be hurt or worse. But he was grown and past the age they had any say in the matter. One Saturday morning in June 1928, Jack boarded a train to Springfield, Massachusetts. The next day he returned riding an Indian Scout motorcycle. In his old age, he would say that June 3, 1928, was the most exciting day of his life.

Six years later, Jack arrived for work to find a teenage boy waiting for him. The boy introduced himself as Edo Morelli and addressed Jack as Mr. Willis, and Jack fought the impulse to say, "Mr. Willis is my grandfather. I am Jack." Instead, he asked Edo how he could help him.

Edo explained his plan to see the country traveling on a motorcycle but said he had not been able to earn the money to buy the bike. One of his teachers suggested he build one, but he needed help. He wondered if Jack would be interested in helping him do this.

"When are you thinking of taking this trip?"

Edo wanted to say, "The day I graduate from high school," but he didn't want to seem pushy, and because he had no realistic idea how long this would take and didn't want to sound completely ignorant, he said in about three years.

Jack was immediately interested in this idea. It was just the sort of challenge he liked, needed even. But he felt an obligation to warn the kid that most roads in the country were unpaved and rough and really hard on the backside of a motorcyclist. He also reminded Edo that he would be exposed to all kinds of weather. But Edo was determined, and Jack was captivated by the idea and the challenge of the process of locating the necessary parts and finally assembling them into a running machine.

The following Sunday afternoon, Jack and Edo sat at the table in the Willis kitchen. Jack showed Edo the list of all the parts they would need. They discussed each part and its function. To find motorcycle parts, they would put out the word of their need and hope word of mouth would bring results. In the meantime, they would visit the larger cities, share their plan with law enforcement, and visit junkyards and individuals connected to motorcycle accidents.

Over the next two years, Jack and Edo managed to collect enough parts for two motorcycles. Most were free for the taking, but some Jack purchased. They were stored in one of the barns on the Willis farm. Jack kept scrupulous records of his expenses: long-distance telephone calls, gasoline for his grandfather's truck, and purchased parts.

During the summer, Edo worked on the Willis farm in exchange. When he graduated from high school, he moved into the Willis home, took over all Jack's chores, and helped Mr. and Mrs. Willis with theirs. By then, Jack had met a girl, and he wanted free time to court her. Edo's doing his chores allowed him to spend time with this girl he would eventually marry.

By the fall of 1936, they were ready to assemble the parts they had collected. Under kerosene lamps hung overhead, the two young men who had become partners and friends set to work first building a wooden frame to secure the metal bike skeleton. Night after night they sanded, welded, assembled, fit, adjusted, and refit the disparate parts of the motorcycle.

It was hard work, sometimes maddening, but neither Jack nor Edo ever considered giving up. To accommodate an extra set of clothes and a few other essentials, they attached a lightweight metal box behind the seat. Edo would wear the key to the box on a chain around his neck. The box was the last piece, and afterward they stood back and looked at their work. Then they looked at each other and burst into laughter.

They couldn't take it down and start the motor and ride it, because the animals in the barn would be frightened. But the next day, they shoveled enough snow to back the truck up to the barn door, loaded the motorcycle into the back of the truck, drove to one of the few paved roads in the county, and unloaded their precious cargo. Edo offered to let Jack go first, but Jack refused, and Edo hopped on, started it up, and drove down the street. Jack took his turn, then Edo another. Then they returned the bike to its home in the barn, where it rested for the remainder of the fall and winter and early spring.

Chapter 16

ON SUNDAY MAY 2, 1937, Edo attended Mass with his family as usual, but nothing else about this day was usual, because this was the last day he would spend with Rosa, Antonio, and his sisters and brothers for four years. The next day, he would be off on the trip he had dreamed of since he was ten years old. Resigned that he was really going through with his plan, his parents had managed to buy him a helmet, and each, unaware of what the other was doing, had saved a penny here and there, and at dinner with all the family on the eve of Edo's departure, each had taken him aside and given him the money.

The priest presented him with a letter "To Whom It May Concern" to be presented to other priests along the way, vouching for Edo's good character in the hopes they would give him a bed and a meal in exchange for some work he could do for them. His mother had advised Edo to seek out a priest for needed help or advice, just as her father had sought the same from the imams, rabbis, and priests on his travels around the Mediterranean. Their priest agreed and had written the letter.

When Rosa pulled him aside to slip him the two dollars she had saved for him, she said, "You will write to me, Edo?"

"Yes, Mama, I will write to you, and you will save every letter, just as your grandmother saved your father's letters. Only I will come back!"

"Promise?"

"Promise!"

Early the next morning, Mrs. Willis prepared a big breakfast for her menfolk, which included Edo. She packed sausage biscuits for his lunch. "When you get back, come and see us. We will want to hear all about your travels," Mr. Willis said.

Jack went out to the barn with Edo. He said, "I've kept a record of all the time and money I spent on the bike, and all the time you spent doing my work here, and the truth is I owe you money." He handed fifteen fifty toward Edo.

"Jack, you don't owe me any money. I couldn't have built the bike without you. I wouldn't have known where to start."

"Edo, I enjoyed every minute of it. It was the most fun I've had in years. You, on the other hand, put in many an hour of hard work on this farm. I keep records. I owe you money, and here it is. You will need it."

With that, Edo set off to discover America.

Edo spent the first night in Albany, New York. He located a Catholic church and presented the letter to the priest. He was welcomed and given his supper and a cot to sleep on. The priest was young and able and had no work for Edo, but he was delighted to hear Edo's plans. He signed Edo's letter with "Good luck and God bless."

On Tuesday, May 4, Edo drove to New York City. He wanted to see the Statue of Liberty and the Empire State Building, the tallest building in the world. The elderly priest to whom he had been directed agreed to feed and house him, but he did have one job he needed Edo to do. This priest wanted Edo to accompany him on a visit to a parishioner who had fallen recently and broken his right arm. The man had no family to look after him. He needed a bath and some house cleaning and laundry done, as well as a meal.

While the priest prepared a meal for his parishioner, Edo drew a bath and bathed, shaved, and dressed the old gentleman, then dusted and vacuumed the apartment and cleaned the bathroom while the man ate the meal the priest had prepared. Then he took the laundry to the basement of the building and washed the clothes and hung them on a wooden rack in the apartment while the priest washed the dishes and visited with his parishioner.

When all was done, the priest took Edo to a restaurant and bought him a fine supper. That night Edo was treated to a comfortable bed in the priest's guest room, and the next morning they returned to the parishioner's apartment, where Edo ironed the clothes he had washed the day before while the priest prepared breakfast for the three of them. The priest and the parishioner expressed their gratitude to Edo, and the priest wrote a note of gratitude on Edo's letter.

On May 6, Edo arrived in Philadelphia and easily located the priest who had received a telephone call from the priest in New York. He welcomed Edo with open arms. He had no chores for Edo but insisted on accompanying him to the historic sites of the city: Independence Hall, the Liberty Bell, the old city. He was full of information and enjoyed sharing everything he knew.

Late the next day, Edo arrived in Washington, DC. Again he found himself welcomed by the priest to whom he had been directed. The priests were calling ahead on his behalf. After a fine supper and a warm bath, Edo went to bed. The next day the priest told Edo to put his dirty clothes in the washroom. The priest had household help who would be happy to add his clothes to the priest's. Edo was happy to hear this. Later that evening he would find, on his bed, his things freshly washed and ironed. He left the laundress a note of thanks and a small bag of chocolates he had bought for her earlier in the day.

The priest had a busy day and could not accompany him on a tour of the city, but he had mapped out a walking tour: the Capitol, the White House, the Lincoln Memorial, Arlington Cemetery, and Mount Vernon.

When Edo returned that evening to the rectory, he and the priest enjoyed a simple supper and an evening of conversation. The priest was well versed in American history and in particular the city of Washington. He had met the last five presidents.

"Tell me about them, Father. Which did you like the best?"

"Oh, I like the present one, Mr. Roosevelt, best. He is courageous; he is doing all he can to help people. He encourages workers to join unions, and he passed the Relief Act to help the unemployed, and Social Security to help the old." This comment was followed by the priest's store of memories both serious and amusing of Hoover, Coolidge, Harding, and Wilson. Finally he said what a shame it was that the other victors would not follow Wilson's advice to avoid requiring the Germans such harsh reparations for starting the war. "The German people terribly resented this and this fellow Hitler came along and took advantage of their resentment. He went about the country making speeches proclaiming that the Germans were superior to all other people and how he would make Germany great again, and got himself elected chancellor. He is a dangerous demagogue. I think the Germans will someday wish they had run him out of the country."

"Now," he said, I've talked enough. I want to hear how you came to this idea of traveling all over America."

Edo told him about his fourth grade teacher and another teacher who suggested he build a motorcycle. Then he told him about Jack and described how they collected the parts and built the bike.

"Where do you plan to visit next?"

"I am torn between the Williamsburg, Yorktown, Jamestown sites, and Charlottesville."

"I hope you will choose Charlottesville. It will take you about four or five hours to get there and another two or so to visit Jefferson's home. Then ride on to Lynchburg. I will call ahead, and you'll be welcomed at the church. Then ride west to the Appalachian Mountains. There is a lovely town there on the Wide River and a Catholic church where you would least expect to find one in the midst of strong Protestantism and anti-Catholicism.

"The priest there, Father O'Malley, is an old friend of mine. We were in seminary together. We keep in touch and visit occasionally. The place is called St. Claire. It started as a mill town but evolved into a college town. You'll want to stay a few days and fish and relax and enjoy the surroundings."

Edo was torn between going south to visit where George Washington had defeated the British or southeast to visit Thomas Jefferson's home. It was the thought of how kind the father here in Washington had been, and how he seemed to really want Edo to visit his friend in St. Claire, that made up his mind. It might prove to be a very interesting place, so he told the father he would go to Jefferson's home, Appomattox, and St. Claire, and the father called his friend, who was delighted to have a visitor. Then he made a map to help Edo find his way and wrote Father O'Malley's telephone number on the map just in case he had trouble.

Edo attended early Mass on Sunday morning and left just after breakfast. He made good time to Charlottesville, where he paid thirty-five cents for lunch, then drove on to Monticello, where he viewed the house from a distance but did not want to spend the money for the ticket to go inside. As he drove on toward Lynchburg, he stopped several times just to get off the bike and walk a little.

It was nearly six o'clock when he arrived at the church and was welcomed by the priest. After a simple meal was prepared and eaten, Edo told the priest he needed to walk to recover from the ride, so the priest accompanied him around the neighborhood, and they chatted about the town and the short trip he would make the next day to Appomattox.

After a restless sleep, Edo ate breakfast with the priest, attended early Mass, and headed to the tiny village that saw the end of the Civil War. Edo had studied the Civil War in school and read about the carnage at Gettysburg and on other battlefields. Someday he would visit those places. Here at Appomattox, as he walked through what was left, he thought of the Confederate soldiers, starved, bedraggled, and heartsick, who had been caught up in an unworthy cause and had watched friends die and no doubt wondered every day if they were next.

Edo left Appomattox feeling sad and discouraged that humans would ever learn to settle their differences peacefully. But as dark clouds formed overhead and thunder sounded in the distance, his thoughts turned to seeking shelter. When he saw a farmhouse, he stopped and asked the farmer if he could take shelter in his barn. The farmer was reluctant at first but asked him where he was going. Edo explained where he was from and where he was going.

The farmer relented and allowed Edo to wheel his bike into the barn and out of the rain, and to come into the house. The farmer's wife asked if Edo had eaten dinner, and since he had not, she fixed him a plate. Afterward, as the rain poured outside and they sat by the fire, Edo told them that he had earlier visited Appomattox Court House.

The farmer said, "My grandpappy was there that last day. He had been itching to join up since the beginning, but he was too young. Finally at sixteen, he joined the Army of Northern Virginia in 1864. Years later when he was an old man he told me he had felt proud wearing that gray uniform and carrying a gun. He said, 'I was gonna kill me some Yankees. I felt like a man.'

"But then he saw the killing, and he felt sick, and he just wanted to go home, sleep in his own bed, and eat his mama's cooking and feel safe. He said that final day, when Lee surrendered, and Grant had them lay down their guns and printed those parole papers so they could go home, and then saw they were starving and made sure they were fed, well, he was so grateful tears ran down his face and he didn't care. He said he thanked God he was alive and not maimed like some other fellows, and he was free to go home."

When the storm moved away, Edo thanked the couple for their hospitality and headed to the Blue Ridge Mountains. The roads were rough, but thanks to the father's directions, which included the names of the little towns and communities along the way, Edo made as good time as was possible in this terrain. A few miles out of St. Claire, though, he heard unusual sounds coming from the bike's motor. He was alarmed, but the sound stopped. Darkness was setting in as he entered St. Claire. He passed small white houses on both sides of the road and many others on the hill to his right. Between the houses, he caught glimpses of what he was sure the river at some distance, and on the far side of the water, a dark forest rose to the dark blue sky. He passed quickly through the business district and, just as the father had described, came to the church and the rectory on the left.

Chapter 17

WHEN HE PULLED in beside the rectory, Father O'Malley came running out calling his name. "I was beginning to worry about you, Eduardo. A storm came through here earlier. Did you get caught in it?"

Edo shook hands with the priest and explained that he had fortunately found shelter at the home of a farmer and his wife.

"Oh good. That was very kind of them. Come now. You must be very hungry."

As Edo ate a bowl of fish stew the father had kept warm for him, he asked why he had not seen anyone on the road nor any lights in the houses as he came in.

"Everyone is inside in bed or getting ready for bed this time of night. At five o'clock in the morning, a giant bell will be rung to wake everyone to get up and get ready for work. Not all of them are working now, but the mill still rings that bell. So 'early to bed and early to rise' is the motto in St. Claire. The bell was here from the beginning, when few people could afford timepieces. Truthfully, even now a timepiece would be an extravagance for many people here. Wages are lower here in the south than up north. On the other hand, it costs less to live here than up north."

When Edo finished eating, they decided to delay visiting further until morning because Edo was tired, and they both would be wakened early by the bell. Father O'Malley showed Edo to the guest room, and he soon fell into a sound sleep.

The following morning, Father O'Malley prepared four scrambled eggs and biscuits. "I have plenty of eggs, Eduardo. The lady who does my laundry and cleaning lives on a farm. She keeps me supplied with eggs and milk and butter." As they ate, Father O'Malley told Edo what he had planned for them for the day. But he had hardly finished when his telephone rang, and he hurried off to answer it. When he came back, he said, "I am sorry, but I've been called to give last rites to a parishioner. I'll need to remain with the family, Eduardo. You'll be on your own today. If you want to go fishing, everything you'll need is on the back porch."

After he left, Edo washed the dishes, cleaned the table, and swept the kitchen. Then he walked out back to the river. He knew why it was called the Wide. It was wide and shallow. He decided he would fish later, but now he would explore the town. The air was chilly, so he opened the metal box and dug out his sweater, then locked it back with the key he kept on the thin leather necklace he wore under his shirt.

As Edo walked to the right past the Wide River Hotel and another church, he immediately saw that this was a pretty street with trees and benches between the businesses, sidewalks swept clean, and windows sparkling. There were a series of businesses on both sides of the street, including a hair salon, a barber shop, a jewelry shop aptly named the Jewel Box, a general store, a sandwich shop, a lawyer's office, and a restaurant called The Fish House. The most imposing building was the Jane Lawrence Auditorium, and Edo found himself wanting to know who this Jane Lawrence was.

An elderly man was sitting on one of the benches, and Edo asked if he might join him.

"Certainly, young man. Have a seat."

Edo introduced himself as Eduardo Morelli, and the man told Edo his name was Barnard James. "Everyone calls me Barney."

"Everyone calls me Edo."

"Well, there are thousands of Barneys across America, but I would bet you are the only Edo."

"You may be right about that, Mr. James. Speaking of names, I am wondering who this Jane Lawrence was or is."

"You are new to St. Claire?"

"Yes, sir. I am visiting with Father O'Malley."

"He is my priest. Are you related to Father O'Malley?"

"No, sir." Edo then told Mr. James his story, and how his mother had suggested he stay with priests along the way and work for them in exchange for a place to sleep for a night or two.

Then Mr. James told Edo about the founding and building the town of St. Claire and the contributions of Jane Lawrence.

Edo thanked Mr. James for sharing these stories.

Later at the general store, Edo bought three pieces of writing paper and an envelope for four cents, and bread and cheese for lunch. Then he returned to the rectory to write to his mother about his visits to Monticello and Appomattox, the farmer and his wife who had taken him in out of the storm, the farmer's grandpappy, and what he had learned today from Barney James about St. Claire and a woman named Jane Lawrence.

Then he rode his bike to the post office to mail the letter, and on to the filling station to buy gas. On the way, the noise he'd heard yesterday came back. At the station, he told the attendant, but the fellow said he had no idea of the cause, all he did was sell gasoline. He said there was a good mechanic in The Falls who could tell him what was wrong. Edo asked him where The Falls was, and he gave him directions.

Edo decided he would wait until tomorrow to go to The Falls. He wanted to fish and catch something for Father O'Malley's supper. So he filled the tank and rode back to the rectory, where he gathered the fishing pole, waders, a bucket and hoe to dig worms, and a tin can for the worms.

He caught two nice trout right away and was having so much fun he considered staying and trying to get two more, but he wanted to fry these and some potatoes and thought he had better get started.

By the time Father O'Malley returned, supper was almost done. He was surprised and delighted that Edo had prepared the meal. As they ate, Edo told him about his long conversation with Barney James. "Oh, Professor James is a fine fellow," Father O'Malley said.

"He's a professor?"

"Yes, he teaches chemistry and physics at the college."

"He didn't mention that. But I didn't really ask him about himself. I asked him about Jane Lawrence, and he told me that she raised the money for the auditorium and later for the college."

Father O'Malley then told Edo that Jane had loved music of all kinds, and she thought everyone should have the opportunity to learn to play an instrument, so she gave piano lessons without charge to the children of mill workers. She had pianos installed in several of the rooms at the auditorium so they could practice, and she hired a woman to supervise them when she couldn't do it herself.

"John St. Claire built this as a mill town and filled it with people to work in his mill. How did he feel about Jane Lawrence building a college here?" Edo asked.

"I am told he was furious, but there was nothing he could do about it. There has never been a shortage of people to work in the mill. The college is liberal arts with a concentration in music. There are many talented musicians in this area, and though they don't possess college degrees or even high school diplomas, they teach classes at the college to students who want to learn 'fiddling' or how to play the banjo, and they continue to work in the mill.

"Of course, the college has an orchestra and a fine chorus, whose members sing in our church choirs, and they perform at the auditorium from time to time. The college also sponsors a drama club called The Players, who put on plays and often they recruit local talent for some of their productions.

"It is a rare Saturday night when the Jane isn't absolutely packed. Think about it, Eduardo, in this small town you have basically two groups of people: very well educated and basically uneducated. Music and fun bring them together."

Chapter 18

AFTER BREAKFAST THE next morning, Edo attended early Mass and said goodbye to Father O'Malley. His plan was to ride to The Falls, find Roy Capps's garage, have the noise in the motor identified and repaired, and hopefully head south to Charleston, South Carolina, and Fort Sumter, where the Civil War had begun. As he drove the three miles to The Falls, the strange sounds would come and go. He kept an eye out for Renney's Restaurant, and when he saw it, he turned left and drove past it to the garage just down the road on the right. There was no sign but no other garage in sight, so Edo pulled in, parked the bike, and walked inside, where he found Roy Capps under the hood of a truck. "Mr. Capps?" Edo said.

"Be right with ya," came the reply.

"Yes, sir."

About five minutes later, Roy closed the hood of the truck he was working on, wiped his hands on a greasy towel, and asked, "What kin I do fer ya?"

Edo explained about the sound his engine was making.

"Sounds like it's missin'. Les' take a look. Roll 'er in here."

When Edo returned, Roy circled the bike, looking at it from every angle. Then he looked at Edo. "Where'd ya git this?"

"A friend and I built it from parts we collected from wrecked cycles."

"Well I'll be," he said, a big grin filling his whole face. "Start 'er up." Edo started the motor, and Roy listened. "Turn 'er off." Edo turned the kill switch. After removing the distributor cover, Roy said, "It's the points, and they have to be ordered. I don't have 'em here. It'll take 'bout three days to git here."

"Where's the nearest place I could get them?"

"'Bout forty miles. Ya might make it, but if ya don't, you'll be settin' on the side of the road till somebody picks ya up, and when ya git back with the points, this bike will be gone."

"Is there any place to rent a room here? Edo asked.

"Naw, they ain't here. Renney's rooms'er rented out to schoolteachers. "The preacher might let ya stay at the Avery place." He explained that the Averys were an old couple who had lived on the other side of the waterfall. He died some years ago, and she died several months ago and didn't leave a will, just a dog, some chickens, and a cow. The preacher was looking after the place while the state decided what to do with it. The preacher and deacons decided to give the cow and chickens to Renney because she had been so good to feed people who could not pay during the Depression.

"The preacher might let ya stay there. Ya can ask 'im."

"What happened to the dog?" Edo asked.

"Oh, the preacher took the dog home with him. He wouldn't take nothin' fer that dog."

Edo waited while Roy called to order the new points and make sure they would be mailed this afternoon. Then he left the bike and walked to Rev. Markley's house, where he found him mowing the lawn. Edo introduced himself and explained his situation, then repeated what Roy had suggested about his possibly staying at the Avery place. He shared the letter from the priests with their comments. The preacher looked it over and said he would call and check it out with Father O'Malley.

While he was gone, Edo finished mowing the preacher's lawn and cleaned the mower blades. The preacher enjoyed a cold glass of lemonade and watched through the window as Edo mowed his grass. When Edo was about finished, he called Father O'Malley.

When he returned, he handed Edo a glass of lemonade and told him he could stay at the Avery house in exchange for cutting the weeds and mowing the grass at the place. Edo agreed and thanked him, and then the preacher took him in his car back to Roy's for his things, and then on past Renney's and straight across the highway onto a dirt-and-gravel lane, and across a bridge by the waterfall. "That's how The Falls got its name, son," he explained.

They continued on the lane bordered on both sides by catawba rhododendron, some with pink blossoms and some with purple, and then, as they drove on, the woods on the south side disappeared, and Edo beheld the extraordinary view of the lowlands. Edo's eyes were drawn away from this only as the white clapboard house set in a mass of blooming plants and shrubs came into view. The preacher pointed them out by name—Virginia mint, snow-on-the-mountain, mountain hydrangea, black-eyed susans. Edo could not keep up and would later ask the preacher to name them all again so he could record the names in a letter to his mother. Only the weeds and overgrown grass marred the scene.

A path of flat stones led to the steps and the front porch, where a swing and four green rocking chairs sat, two on either side of the front door. The preacher took a key from his pocket and unlocked the door. Inside a small entryway stood an oak hall tree and umbrella stand. Several canes and umbrellas stood in their places. A man's cap and a woman's straw hat hung on either side of the mirror. The preacher said they had belonged to Olan and Lilah Avery. "I just didn't have the heart to remove them."

To the right, a door stood open to the front room. The first thing Edo saw were floor-to-ceiling bookshelves completely filled with books covering one wall. "Look at that!" he said.

"It's a wonderful collection. Both the Averys were readers and lifelong collectors. After weeding and mowing, you can come in here and relax with a book," the preacher said with a grin. Then he turned Edo's attention to the opposite wall, in the middle of which was a fireplace ready to be lit, with kindling sitting in the grate and logs in a stand to the side. Over the mantel was a painting of Rachael Avery. "She was Olan's mother. I'll tell you about her and Olan's father later," he promised with another smile. Edo noted a small desk a few feet to the left of the fireplace.

About two feet in front of the bookcase was a love seat and, on either side, a small table holding a lamp. Overstuffed chairs sat cattycornered beside the tables. An ottoman sat at the foot of each chair. On the front wall, a radio sat between two windows, and an archway in the opposite wall opened into a small dining room. A door to the right of the fireplace led to a hall. A door opposite the door from the front room opened to the bedroom, whose fireplace shared the chimney with the front room. There were two three-quarter beds with a night table and lamp between them facing the fireplace. A chifforobe stood in the corner. As in the front room, two windows looked out to the beautiful view of the lowlands.

The hall led to the kitchen. An electric stove and refrigerator seemed out of place in this kitchen with its otherwise nineteenth-century furnishings, including a metal cabinet with a flour bin, a pull-out shelf for rolling dough or pastries, and enclosed shelves on top and bottom for storage. A pine cupboard held dishes and glassware, and enclosed shelves underneath held pots and pans. Drawers, Edo assumed, held utensils. A small pine table and chairs sat in the middle of the room. A door on the left opened to the spare bedroom. There was another three-quarter bed, a night table with a lamp, a small rocking chair, and a chifforobe. "You should be comfortable here, son."

The back door led to an enclosed back porch with a bathroom and a washroom, where an electric washing machine sat. From the washroom, there was a door to the outside. The preacher led Edo to an outbuilding close to the house. He unlocked the door and pointed out the sling blade, clippers, and lawnmower. He said to be sure to lock these up when he finished with them and handed Edo the keys to the house and to the outbuilding.

Then they went back inside the house, where the preacher opened the refrigerator and took out two Coca-Colas and handed one to Edo. He opened a drawer in the china cupboard and found an opener, opened his, and handed the opener to Edo. They took their drinks out onto the front porch, sat in the rocking chairs, and the preacher told Edo about the Averys.

"Greene Avery was a gambler, and he won this property in a poker game. There was a rough cabin on the property at the time. It had a fireplace and a dirt floor and a great view, because the owner had cut down trees here and out front and down the hill, which he used to make logs to build the cabin. What logs he didn't use to build the cabin, he burned in the fireplace, and all that was left was this outstanding view. Greene loved that view. If he returned after a gambling spree and found something growing to block the view, he'd cut it right down.

"Soon after he won the property, he was over the mountain somewhere and met Rachael. She was a beauty. So he bragged to her about his house and land. Now Greene was a tall, handsome man, and he could be quite charming. Rachael fell in love with him and married him, and they rode together on his horse to The Falls. They stopped first at the tavern—Renney's was originally Renegar's Tavern. They had a nice supper, and then they rode over here to Green's house. When Rachael saw the inside of that cabin, she threw a fit. She hadn't come from wealth, but she had grown up in a decent house with a floor. She took off back to the tavern on the horse, Greene running right behind her. Seeing his dreams of a night of wedded bliss disappearing, he began promising to make improvements to the house. So they spent their honeymoon in a room he rented upstairs over the tavern.

"After a week or two, Greene took off to ply his gambling trade. When he won big, he would come back to Renegar's and visit Rachael at the tavern. On one of those visits she became pregnant, and she had a baby boy she named Olan.

"Albert Renegar, who owned the tavern, was a bachelor, and he had early on taken a shine to Rachael. He offered her a job cooking and cleaning for room and board, and she accepted. She and Olan had a permanent room upstairs where Albert lived and rented out rooms.

"Whenever Greene had a big win at the card table, he would head home with plenty of corn whiskey to celebrate. After a hot bath and a reunion with his wife and son, he would take his whiskey to his cabin, build a big fire in the fireplace, set a chair in the doorway—winter, summer, spring, or fall—and sit and drink and look out over his domain.

"Greene was an affable drunk. He always shared his winnings with Rachael and Olan, and his grand plans for his property—plans that evaporated when the whiskey was gone and he sobered up. Rachael would just shake her head and go back to work. Olan listened, and though he knew his father would never realize his drunken dreams, he did share Greene's feelings for this place. He often slipped away from the tavern and came to Greene's cabin to dream his own dreams, which, unlike his father, he had the self-discipline and confidence to achieve.

"One January, Greene showed up with his winnings and whiskey, stopped by the tavern to see Rachael and Olan, and have a meal, and then headed to his cabin where he built a big fire, set his chair in the doorway, and sat down with his whiskey. During the night, the temperature dropped. When Rachael got up early as she always did, she noticed how much colder it was, and she woke Olan and sent him to go build a fire for his father. Olan found him still sitting in his chair frozen to death.

When the ground thawed enough to dig a grave, they buried Greene right over there." The preacher pointed to a place at some distance from the house, where Edo could see a mass of flowers. "If you walk over there, you'll see a small headstone that Olan placed there years later. It has Greene's name and dates on it. Rachael always kept flowers planted there.

"She put Greene's winnings in the post office at the general store, saving the money to send Olan to school because she knew early on how smart he was. To please her, Albert talked the men in the community into building a schoolhouse and hiring a teacher, and Olan went there through the eighth grade. By then, there was a high school in Norfolk, and Rachael sent Olan there. In the meantime she and Albert got married. When Olan graduated from high school, they sent him to college to study engineering, and after college he joined the Army Corps of Engineers.

"Early on, Rachael deeded this property to Olan. He would come back here often and cut trees, which he had sawed into lumber and stored in the cabin. Eventually he built this house for Rachael. Albert wouldn't leave the tavern, so she stayed with him and only moved in here after he died, but before that, she spent all her free time here planting shrubs and flowers.

"After she died, and later when Olan retired, he and Lilah moved here."

Edo had listened to the preacher's story thinking that he would definitely write about this. He was already realizing that it wasn't just the great physical wonders of America, but the stories of the people of this country that were so interesting. When the preacher stopped speaking, Edo said, "I believe Rachael and Olan must have really loved Greene. This place is a sort of monument to him. It's a beautiful place. I wish my mother could see it. She loves flowers. I wish I had a picture of it."

"Well, a picture would be in black and white, and that would be a poor representation of this place. Now, I must tell you there is no food here. I just keep a few of these drinks here, but we removed all the food. We didn't want to have mice moving in. You can walk back to Renney's. She has good food at good prices, or if you want to cook, you can go to the store and buy what you need. The stove works just fine."

As soon as the preacher left, Edo got busy. The preacher had warned him about snakes and pointed out the knee-high boots sitting on the back porch. They were a bit too big, but with an extra pair of socks, they fit well enough. He decided to clean up Greene's grave site first, so he gathered his tools and went to work using the sling blade to cut down the tall weeds around the grave. When he finished, he raked them up and moved them some distance to where he would later burn them. Then he mowed the area and raked the clippings into the pile. Finally, he weeded the flowers growing on the grave.

After a short break drinking ice water and sitting on the porch, he mowed the front lawn and cleaned the mower blades. Using the rake, he made sure there were no snakes in the weeds around the shrubs, and he pulled weeds and made a new pile, which he took to the growing pile he intended to burn. He had not eaten since breakfast and began to feel weak, so he decided to stop and go to the restaurant and have lunch. He put the tools away, locked the shed door, and went inside to wash up. He was surprised to see by the clock in the kitchen that it was almost three o'clock. "No wonder I'm hungry," he thought as he went out the door.

Chapter 19

AS EDO WAS crossing the highway on his way to Renney's, he noticed a girl holding what appeared to be books and opening the door to the restaurant. She had coppery red hair pulled into a long ponytail. Once inside, he looked for her, but she was nowhere in sight. The only person in the restaurant was a woman behind the counter. "Good afternoon," she said and showed him to a booth on the left side of the restaurant. He sat down, facing the inside because he didn't want to miss the girl if she happened to appear again.

The waitress handed him a menu, and he said, "I really need to wash my hands." She told him where the men's room was, and he got up and crossed the restaurant and walked down by the booths on the right and into the restroom just beyond. He noticed books on the table at the last booth and thought they might belong to the red-haired girl.

A few minutes later, when he came out of the restroom, he saw her with her head down, reading. When she looked up, he found himself staring into the greenest eyes set in the loveliest face he had ever seen. She smiled, acknowledging his presence, then returned to her book.

Edo couldn't remember if he had returned her smile. All he wanted to do was sit and look at her. He was reminded of a day in eighth grade when his class was in the library. He didn't feel like reading, so he had chosen an oversize art book and just sat browsing, looking at the paintings. Then he came to Vermeer, and there on the page was *Girl with a Pearl Earring*. He began to wonder about her—her name, her age, her relationship to Vermeer. He suddenly wanted to read, and he learned that she was a servant girl in Vermeer's household, and the earring belonged to Vermeer's wife.

As he read, he kept looking back at the painting. This was a book students were not allowed to check out, but on subsequent visits to the library, he would always take it off the shelf and find the picture. One day he was struck by the thought that he had fallen in love with a girl who had been dead for four hundred years. He returned the book to the shelf and never looked at it again.

But this girl in the restaurant was very much alive, and he knew that somehow he was going to become acquainted with her. He decided that she must have a close connection to the restaurant. She was using that table as a desk, and no one had brought her any food. He decided that she probably came here every day after school, so he would plan to be here tomorrow at the same time.

Edo knew he would be hungry again before bedtime, and he would need eggs for breakfast, so when he left Renney's, he walked to the general store. When he walked inside the store, the first thing he saw was a wooden plaque that read in large letters, "Gossiping Is a Sin." He decided there had to be an interesting story behind this, and he needed to learn what it was. He bought eggs, milk, bread, and coffee, and when he got back to the house, he stored the eggs and milk in the refrigerator, took off his clean shirt, hung it up in the chifforobe, put his dirty shirt back on, and went back to work again wearing the boots. He had found a pair of work gloves, and he put these on also.

He got out the tools and resumed his weeding around the shrubs and then the flower beds, being careful to watch for snakes. As he worked, the red-haired girl kept returning to his thoughts. He knew he should not think about her, because he needed to concentrate on what he was doing. He fought this battle for two hours until dusk set in, and then he called it a day. He returned the tools to the outbuilding, locked the door, and went inside.

He drew a bath, then realized he hadn't thought to buy a bar of soap, so he looked into the medicine cabinet and found a new bar of Ivory. A clean towel and washcloth were hanging on the towel rack. He didn't remember these being there when he had earlier taken a tour of the house. He got in the tub and took a bath, and thought about the red-haired girl, but when the water started cooling down, he got out, dried off, and put on clean underwear and pants. Then he put his dirty clothes into the tub and washed them, let the water out, and rinsed them. He had noticed a wooden clothes rack in the washroom, so he hung his laundry on this. It was getting chilly, so he put on his shirt and made sure all the doors were locked, feeling silly that he hadn't done this before he took a bath. The girl was getting to him.

A fire would have been nice, but he didn't want to clean up the mess or burn the house down. So he put on his sweater and padded in stocking feet to the front room, turned on both lamps, and began looking through the books. He found the autobiography of Ulysses S. Grant, took it down, and sat in one of the overstuffed chairs with his feet on the ottoman and began to read.

He read the first chapter, which dealt with Grant's growing up and his years at West Point. Then, feeling hungry, he went to the kitchen and boiled two eggs. When they were done and peeled, he ate them with a glass of milk, washed his glass, found a dishcloth, and turned the glass upside down on it to drain. He put the eggshells in a bowl and into the refrigerator. He would empty these outside tomorrow. He returned to the book and read another chapter about the lead-up to the war with Mexico. Getting sleepy, he put the book on the table and got ready for bed.

Edo went to sleep thinking about the red-haired girl. He woke up before daylight and made his breakfast of fried eggs, coffee, and bread he toasted in the oven. He put on his sweater and took his second cup of coffee out on the porch. As the sun came up, he watched and listened as the world woke up. The air was still and cool; the only sound he heard was a dove calling its mate. He wanted to write about this place so he could remember it always. Then he thought about the desk in the front room. He got up, went to the desk, and opened it. There were envelopes but no paper. Then he thought about the red-haired girl. Maybe he could buy a few sheets of notebook paper from her. He really needed the paper, and it might be a way to get acquainted with her.

Edo worked all day, stopping only to drink a glass of water every hour or so. By two o'clock he was so hungry, he decided he couldn't wait any longer. He took a bath, put on clean clothes, and walked to Renney's, where he ordered fried chicken, biscuits and gravy, mashed potatoes, and green beans. He was still eating when the red-haired girl walked in with her books and notebook.

"Miss," he called out.

Turning toward him, she answered, "Yes?"

Edo rose from his seat and asked, "Do you have a few blank sheets of paper in your notebook that I could buy from you?"

"No, I won't sell you any paper," she said as she laid her things on a table, opened the notebook, and took out three sheets, "but I'll give you three sheets." She handed him the paper and asked if he needed a pencil.

"No, I have a pencil. Thank you for the paper."

"You're welcome," she said as she closed her notebook, picked up her books, and made her way to the last booth on the right side.

When Edo finished his meal and went to the cash register to pay his bill, he very quietly asked the waitress what was the red-haired girl's favorite treat, and she whispered, "A chocolate milkshake." He had her add this to his bill and asked her to make one for the girl after he left. She agreed to do it but decided the milkshake would ruin her supper if she made it now, so she waited until Glenna had eaten and was ready to go home, then presented the milkshake and told her it was from the boy to whom she had given the paper.

"Really? He bought this for me?" She took the milkshake home and put it in the freezer. Later, she took it out and drank it. She had hardly stopped thinking about him since she saw him the day before. She had tried not to think about him. He was probably just passing through, and she would never see him again, yet there was something very special about him. She was thrilled that he was in the restaurant again today. She hoped he hadn't noticed that her hands were shaking as she removed the paper from her notebook and handed them to him. For the second night, Glenna went to sleep thinking about the handsome boy with the black hair and eyes.

Meanwhile, Edo sat on the front porch and wrote a letter to his mother describing the motorcycle problem that had brought him to a tiny village called The Falls. He told her about the beautiful place he was staying and the story of Greene Avery. He did not mention the red-haired girl who gave him the paper. She was a secret he would keep just for himself.

On Friday morning, Edo took his coffee and sat on the porch to enjoy the view and quiet. Then he washed his clothes and hung them on the line out back. After that, he walked to the general store, which also served as the post office. He bought a stamp and put the letter in the mail, then walked over to the garage to see if the points Roy had ordered had come in. They had not.

Edo then walked to Renney's to treat himself to a good breakfast. Before ordering, he went to the restroom to wash his hands. He had noticed on his previous visit that the water continued a slow drip drip drip after being turned off, then increased to a small stream. Edo knew this could easily be repaired, so he told the waitress about the problem and offered to fix it. She soon returned with Renney, who told him she was aware of the problem, but her husband was too busy getting his crops planted to stop and come fix it. She had forgotten to mention it to her brother, and her dad was visiting his brother in Asheville. She said she had tools in the kitchen storeroom. So Edo removed the old washer from the faucet, took it to the general store, bought a new one the same size, returned to Renney's, and installed the new washer.

Renney had planned to pay him for his work, but he refused, so she served him a big breakfast on the house. He had completed the weeding at the Avery house, so he asked Renney if there was anything else he could do for her in exchange for meals. She told him there was something she needed to be done.

For some years, a schoolteacher, Miss Kennely, had rented a room upstairs, and she had eventually rented a second room so she could have a sitting room for the furniture she inherited when her mother died. When electricity came to the mountain in 1930, Martin had taken another room upstairs and made two bathrooms, one adjoining Miss Kennely's bedroom, the other for guests who rented the other two remaining rooms. Miss Kennely's two rooms had not been painted in over twenty years, and there were cracks in the plaster that needed repairing also. Edo's father had, over the years, done these things in their house because their landlord was slow about making such repairs. Antonio taught Marco and Edo how to do these jobs, so Edo told Renney that yes, he would repair the plaster and paint Miss Kennely's apartment in exchange for three meals a day.

When Miss Kennely came home from school, she was delighted to learn that her apartment would be painted and the plaster repaired. She had a friend in St. Claire with whom she could spend the weekend and not have to smell the paint, so she called and confirmed that she would be welcome. Earlier, Edo and Renney had gone to the general store, where Renney bought supplies. After Miss Kennely's friend picked her up, Edo set to work taking down paintings and moving and covering furniture with a collection of old threadbare sheets Renney had supplied. Knowing that the red-haired girl was probably downstairs, he worked quickly, and when finished, he went down determined to meet her.

As he expected, she was sitting at the booth with her books. When she looked up and saw him, she smiled. He introduced himself as Edo Morelli and asked if he could join her. "Please do," she said. "I'm Glenna McAllen. Thank you for the milkshake. It was such a nice surprise."

"You're welcome. Your name is Glenna? That's a beautiful name. Is it Irish?"

"Yes, I was named for my grandfather, Glenn. He was Irish."

"I was named for my grandfather Eduardo. He is Spanish."

"You're Spanish, then, and your name is Eduardo?"

"I am mostly Italian, but my name is Eduardo. Marco, my older brother, couldn't say Eduardo, so he called me Edo, and it stuck." He then told her about his grandfather's travels and how he ended up in Italy and married his Italian grandmother. Then he asked her if her grandfather had come to America, and Glenna told him that it was her mother who came to America after marrying her father, an American soldier she had cared for during the Great War. She told him how her father had died.

"I am so sorry, Glenna. You must miss him."

"Yes, it was terrible, but my mother and I are close, and we talk about him and how after he lost his sight, he learned how to do all sorts of things so he could keep taking care of us. We'll never stop missing him, but you have to go on living. Are your parents still living, Edo?"

"Yes, they are. In fact, the reason I needed the paper was to write a long letter to my mother about St. Claire and the beautiful Avery place where I'm staying." He started to tell her how he came to be in The Falls, but as he spoke, a large group of lumberjacks came into the restaurant and filled the booths on the right behind Glenna and Edo. They were so happy to have work and pay on this Friday evening they were in high spirits, laughing and joking with one another, so as Edo explained where he was from and where he had been, Glenna caught only part of what he said. She would remember the names of places she had heard of—New York, Philadelphia, Washington, Monticello, and Appomattox—but the rest became a blur of words.

When he finished, Glenna went to the kitchen and brought out their supper. She had learned earlier about his job upstairs. After they had eaten, she asked if she could help him, and he said he would welcome her help. So they went upstairs, and she sanded some rough places in the plaster on the walls while he stood on a ladder and filled the crack in the plaster that ran across the ceiling. When Kathleen called up the stairs that she was going home, Edo went to the stairs and asked if it was all right if he walked Glenna home. She said not to be late. When they finished, Glenna gathered her books she had left in the kitchen. Edo insisted on carrying them for her, so she gave him two, and she carried one and her notebook. On the way to her house, she learned that he had graduated the year before last, and this past year he had worked on Jack's grandparents' farm to repay Jack for all he had done on the motorcycle.

Edo asked her if she ever went to the concerts at the Jane Auditorium on Saturday nights. "We used to go often when Daddy was alive, but not since he died," she said.

"Would you go with me tomorrow night? We would have to walk. I don't have a car, but it's not too cold."

"I'd love to go, but we don't have to walk. We have a car. It's a 1924 Model T, but it runs."

"You do? You have a Model T?"

She assured him it was true.

"Would your mother let us borrow it?"

"I think so. I will ask her and let you know tomorrow."

When they got to her house, she told him to wait outside while she went inside for a minute. When she returned, she handed him a flashlight so he wouldn't have to walk home in the dark. "Oh, if the minister's dog is out when you walk back, his name is Buddy. He's really sweet, but he does bark if he sees someone walking by."

After Edo left, Glenna went back inside, and in the darkened front room, she stood by the window and watched him walk back down the hill, past the school, past the cemetery, and past the church. She could see the light of the flashlight and hear the minister's dog barking. Edo stopped to pet the dog, who stopped his barking, and then Edo walked to Renney's and disappeared as he rounded the front of the restaurant.

"Glenna? Is that you?" Kathleen called out from the kitchen.

"Yes, Mum, I was just watching to make sure Edo got past Buddy without getting bit."

She joined her mother in the kitchen and told her Edo had asked her to go to the concert at the Jane the following night. "He doesn't have a car, and we'll have to walk, unless you will let us use the Model T."

"Well, I certainly don't want you to be out walking three miles in the dark. Of course you may use the car, but he'll have to buy a gallon of gas."

"Thank you, Mum. I am so excited to have a real date. I need to see what I have to wear."

Kathleen smiled. She didn't want to throw cold water on Glenna's happiness, but she was concerned that Glenna could end up getting hurt. She followed Glenna as she headed to her room to look through her few clothes.

She pulled out a skirt and laid it on the bed where Kathleen was sitting. Kathleen took the skirt and examined it closely. "You did a fine job on this skirt. You do so many things well. I'm awfully proud of you, Glenna. One more year of high school, then off to college."

"If I get a scholarship, you mean."

"You will, but even if you don't, we will find a way. This old Depression can't last forever. Things will get better." She wanted to remind Glenna of her plans.

"Edo seems like a fine young man, and it's only natural for you to feel attracted to him," her mother went on. "But keep in mind, Glenna, he'll be leaving as soon as his motorcycle is repaired. He'll be off to who knows where, living his dreams. I just want you to remember that you have dreams and plans too."

"I know he's leaving soon, Mum. But it's really nice to have a boyfriend, if only for a few days. Please don't spoil it for me."

Kathleen grinned. "I'm afraid it's my duty to spoil it a bit, Glenna. I'm thinking about your future. I want you to be happy—not just happy now, but happy in the future."

"Don't worry, Mum. I'll be fine."

Chapter 20

THE NEXT MORNING Edo rose early and went straight to Renney's, where he ate breakfast, then headed upstairs to Miss Kennely's apartment. He sanded the spackling he had applied the previous evening to a smooth finish, then gathered the sheets that had caught the sanded particles and took them outside to shake them out. Back upstairs, he replaced the sheets so that all the furniture and the floor were completely covered. Then he opened the windows and set to work painting the ceiling.

When he finished the ceiling, he went downstairs and asked for a glass of water. Kathleen told him that he could use the car to take Glenna to the Jane, but he would need to buy a gallon of gasoline. He said he would do that, and thanked her for allowing him to drive her car. Then he walked to the garage to see if the points had arrived. They had not; Roy assured him they would probably be delivered before the day was out. If not, he would call to make certain they had been put in the mail.

His arms rested, Edo returned to Renney's and painted the walls of Miss Kennely's sitting room. When he finished, he went downstairs for lunch. Glenna was there, and they ate together and discussed their plans for the evening but didn't linger, because they both had things to do. He went upstairs and painted Miss Kennely's bedroom ceiling, then the walls. He then cleaned the paintbrush, put the paint away in the storeroom, and went home to take a long warm soak in the tub. He had ironed his clean shirt and pants the night before. He dressed in these, pulled on his sweater, and headed for Roy's garage. The points had come in, so Edo took the bike for a spin, ending up at Glenna's. Glenna was ready, dressed in an off-white pullover sweater her mother had knitted and the brown pleated midi skirt she had made. Brown was not her favorite color, but it went well with her only pair of shoes, the brown oxfords, which she had polished and shined. When she heard the bike, she walked out of the house. "I take it the points came in today."

"They did. I thought I would leave the bike in your garage while we are gone, if that's all right."

"Of course. It should be safe in there. I'll unlock the garage door." She handed Edo the key to the car. The garage door was secured with a padlock, which Glenna unlocked. Edo opened the door and went inside. Only a person familiar with the Model T would be able to start the engine, and when Edo had been in the garage about two minutes, Glenna began to worry that he might not know how to start it, but then she heard the engine come to life, and the Model T backed out of the garage and into the driveway. Edo stopped, got out, and mounted the bike and drove it into the garage, then closed the door and secured the padlock. Glenna breathed a sigh of relief. Edo opened the passenger door, and Glenna took her seat. He closed the door and walked around to the driver's side, got in, and drove back to Roy's, where Glenna had to get out so Roy could lift the seat to fill the gas tank. Edo paid Roy for the points and the gas, and they drove to Renney's for supper.."

During supper Edo asked Glenna if she had family here.

"As long as my papa was alive, yes, I had family here. He was a wonderful grandfather. Then she told him about her grandmother's shunning Kathleen because she refused to leave the Catholic church. "I have seen her but never met her. She has never acknowledged me as her granddaughter. Daddy's sisters and brothers don't agree with her, but they don't want to cross her so they do visit sometimes but not as often as when Daddy was alive, and it's usually at night. We aren't close.

"Having nothing to do with your own granddaughter is terrible, Glenna. I'm so sorry. It's her loss," Edo said.

"Thank you, Edo. I appreciate you saying that, but I do have a sort of adopted family. I've spent so much time here at Renney's that they are like family."

"Well, one of your family apparently does not like me."

"What do you mean?"

"You know how you can feel that someone is staring at you? Without fail, I'll be eating my lunch or passing through the kitchen and get that feeling, and I'll look up to see this girl staring at me with a dirty look. If I smile at her, she looks angry and walks away. She's never waited on me or spoken to me."

"That's Ethel Ann, Renney's niece."

After a long pause, Edo asked, "Is that all you're going to say? Is something wrong with her?"

Glenna told him what happened when Ethel Ann was five years old, and what a hard time she had in school.

He asked what she does at the restaurant.

"She cleans the dining room and washes dishes, takes out the trash. Edo, don't think twice about those ugly faces she makes at you. It's nothing you've done. I think Ethel Ann is unhappy, and you are always happy and smiling and friendly. She's probably jealous of you because people like you."

"I plead guilty to being happy, but I didn't lose my mother or have trouble in school. I've been lucky in so many ways."

Down the street from the auditorium, they found a parking place. Edo came around the car, opened the door, and held out his hand to help Glenna step out. He walked on the street side of the sidewalk and gently rested his right hand on her back as they made their way to the Jane. Glenna felt protected and proud to be with this handsome and well-mannered young man. She was not surprised by his protectiveness or his gentlemanly behavior. She couldn't shake the feeling she'd had the first time she saw him, the feeling that she knew him. She wasn't surprised that he felt bad for Ethel Ann, because somehow she knew he had a big heart.

They were a bit early, but the auditorium was filling up. They found seats in the middle section closer to the back than to the front. Settled in their seats, Glenna looked around as other people came in and found seats. She judged by their dress that many were mill workers, some mill management, some college professors, and many were college students. They were of all ages, and they had gathered here together to enjoy the music. It made her heart swell to be a part of this. She looked at Edo and felt so grateful to him for making this possible. He was smiling, and he said, "What is it, Glenna?"

"I am just so happy to be here. Thank you."

"I'm happy to be here too." He squeezed her hand and thought, "How on earth am I going to be able to leave her?" Antonio had said more than once that the first time he saw Rosa, he knew he loved her and would marry her someday. Now Edo knew just how his father had felt.

He had barely finished that thought when the program host stepped onto the stage, welcomed everyone, and introduced a college student who sang "America the Beautiful," accompanied by the college orchestra. She sang several verses and encouraged the audience to join in on the chorus. The crowd roared their approval.

The host returned and introduced a local group of musicians called the Mountain River Boys, who played "Cluck Old Hen" on the fiddle, mandolin, bass, and banjo. The crowd clapped along with the music, and when the audience thought they were finished, a group of youngsters clogged onto the stage and performed as the group played "Cluck Old Hen" one more time.

After this, the orchestra reappeared, and a young man sang, "Are You Lonesome Tonight?" Next the Ramey sisters sang in perfect harmony "The Little Church in the Wildwood," which was followed by the Mountain River Boys, who performed "The Wabash Cannon Ball" and several other selections that displayed their outstanding talents.

The show ended with a sweet and soulful rendition of "My Wild Irish Rose" sung by the young man who had performed earlier and who was accompanied by the college orchestra. Throughout this sweet melody, Edo found himself stealing glances at Glenna. He desperately wanted to take her into his arms and hold her close.

On the way home, they talked about the various singers and musicians and cloggers. "I would love to learn how to do that," Edo exclaimed.

"Well, if you stick around, I'm sure you could find someone to teach you."

"Oh, Glenna, I wish I could, but I would soon run out of money. There are no jobs here."

"I know."

"What are you going to do when you finish high school next year, Glenna?"

"I love math. I want to be a bookkeeper. I have one more bookkeeping course to take, and when I graduate, I hope to get a scholarship to college and earn an associate degree in bookkeeping, and maybe study some accounting."

"I am so glad there are people like you who love math, because we need people who can operate banks and all kinds of businesses. If people like me tried to do those things, the whole country would go bankrupt. Do you think you will get a scholarship?"

"I think I have a good chance. My grades are really good. What about you, Edo? After you have done all the traveling and seen all the sights you want to see, what are you going to do?"

"Now I'm not bragging, but I'm a pretty good writer, and everywhere I go, I write my mother a letter describing the place and the interesting people I meet. Everybody has a story, and every story is different and interesting. This is something I had not really thought about until I actually got on the road and started meeting people. Before, it was only the places I really thought about. Anyway, my mother is keeping all my letters, and when I go home, I hope to use them to write a book."

"Oh, Edo, that's a wonderful idea. That's so exciting."

"It is, isn't it? You know what else I've been thinking? How nice it would be to bring all those letters back here to the Avery place and do my writing there. It's such a peaceful, beautiful place. But of course, that would take money, and I'm not sure I will have any money when I'm finished traveling but it's a nice thought. Glenna, only my family know about this—writing a book, that is. This is just between us, all right?"

"Of course. My lips are sealed." She hesitated, then asked, "You said you write to your mother about the people you meet. Did you tell your mother about me?"

"Oh no, Glenna." He took her hand as he said, "You and me, that's personal and private."

Chapter 21

KATHLEEN AND GLENNA at their house, and Edo at the Avery house, were all up early preparing and having breakfast and getting ready for early Mass in St. Claire. When Edo arrived on his motorcycle, the Model T was sitting in the driveway, and the door to the garage was standing open for Edo to park his bike inside. He closed the door and set the padlock as Glenna and her mother stepped outside. Kathleen said she wanted to be chauffeured to church, so Edo helped her into the back seat, Glenna in the front. On the way he told them that though his father did not own a car, the grandfather of his friend Jack did own a Model T and had taught him how to start and drive his during the time he'd lived with them over the past year. He told Glenna she should learn to drive, and her mother agreed but said Glenna couldn't get her nose out of a book long enough to do that. Glenna said she would make that one of her goals for the summer.

When Mass was over, Father O'Malley expressed how glad he was to see that Edo had become acquainted with Kathleen and Glenna and that Roy Capps had been able to take care of Edo's motorcycle. Edo thanked him again for his hospitality.

When they returned home, Glenna put the roast and potatoes and carrots she had cooked the day before into the oven to warm, then made biscuits and set them on the table under a cover. Then she and Edo walked to the restaurant with Kathleen's key to the back door. She let Rebecca and Mitch, who had returned from Asheville, know they had come to put Miss Kennely's apartment back in order. Mitch said he would be glad to help, but he had gotten too old to be moving furniture.

They were quiet as they moved the furniture back into its proper place and hung the curtains back over the windows. Edo had left the nails in the walls, so it was easy to rehang the paintings. As he was doing this, he asked Glenna if she and her mother would always live here in The Falls.

"Goodness, no! My mother will return to Ireland the first chance she gets. She misses her family. As for me, I don't know where I'll end up, but it won't be in The Falls. All my classmates have best friends. All except me, that is, and it's because of being a Catholic. Mum says the Methodists are afraid for their children to get too close to me for fear I'll turn them into Catholics."

Edo had stopped what he was doing and stood listening to Glenna. He said, "Oh, Glenna that is terrible. Who do you talk to?"

"My mother, but there are things you don't want to talk to your mother about, so you just keep those things to yourself."

"If you had a best friend right now, what would you tell her?"

"I would tell her that I met a handsome boy who is kind and considerate and sweet, and he's going away and taking my heart with him."

Edo closed the gap between them, put his hands on her shoulders, and said, "You tell your friend that's okay, because that boy is leaving his heart here with you." He took her in his arms and kissed her, and then he said, "I love you, Glenna. With all my heart, I love you."

"I love you, Edo, and I'm going to take good care of your heart." They held each other close until they heard Mitch coming up the stairs.

When they finished putting things back in place in both rooms, Mitch called Rebecca to come and see how nice everything looked. She was pleased and certain Miss Kennely would be also. They walked back to the house and heard the Methodists singing a familiar hymn, familiar to Glenna but not to Edo. "It's called 'He Leadeth Me,'" she told him.

"How do you know that?"

"Mum and I have always attended early Mass, and then Daddy and I went to his church for the eleven o'clock service."

"Wasn't that confusing to you?"

"Not a bit. They're both Christian churches. They just have different rituals. Mum said she once was invited to the home of a schoolmate to help her with an assignment. While she was there, they ate supper in their dining room, and the food was very good, but there was no conversation during the meal other than 'Please pass the potatoes.' At home they ate every meal in the kitchen: there was no dining room, and there was lively conversation and laughing always. In both places, the object was to eat, which is necessary for life, but the rituals were different."

"Well, that's one way to look at it. Do you still go to the Methodist church?"

"No, it would be too sad to be there without Daddy."

Back at home, Glenna opened a can of green beans, added a small piece of fatback, and set them on the stove to cook. Edo wanted to go fishing, so he dug some worms he put in a can, then joined Kathleen on the front porch, where she was knitting a sweater. She told him her father had been a fisherman in the Irish Sea. "We ate a lot of cod and were happy to have it."

Soon Glenna called them for dinner. After Kathleen said grace, they ate the meal Glenna had prepared. Edo learned that Glenna had been in charge of Sunday dinner for several years. "Mum cooks six days a week all day, so Sunday is her day off," she explained. Knowing that Edo would be eating with them, Glenna had bought a larger roast than she did when cooking for her mother and herself. It was a good thing, because eighteen-year-old boys were ravenous eaters. When the meal was over, there was nothing left. Edo said everything was absolutely delizioso! And he thanked them for inviting him to eat with them.

Then he insisted on washing the dishes. "You should dry and put them away because you know where everything goes," he said to Glenna. She agreed, and in no time the task was completed. Glenna had changed clothes earlier before doing any cooking, so all she had to do was put on her rubber boots before they gathered Charlie's fishing gear. His boots were too large for Edo, but Glenna gave him a pair of socks to stuff in the toes of the boots. They left promising Kathleen trout for supper.

They took the shortcut through the woods, being very quiet and watchful for rattlesnakes. When they reached the road, Edo asked if he could talk now. Glenna laughed and said yes.

"I'm sorry, I do love to talk," he said, "and when you come from a large family who all also love to talk, you have to take advantage of every opportunity."

"I am listening. Tell me about your large family."

"All right. Marco is the oldest. He's in the army. I'm next. Then there are Sophia and Dianna, Niccolo, and Emilio."

"I can't imagine what it's like to have brothers and sisters. Where do you all sleep?"

"There are two bedrooms upstairs, one for the girls and one for the boys. In our room, there are four cots, and in the girls' room two cots. There's a dresser in each room, each with four drawers. The smallest kid has the bottom drawer and the tallest the top drawer. Before Niccolo and Emilio were born, Marco and I were hoping for girls because we were used to having a lot of room, but it turned out to be fun mostly having the little fellows with us. Now those two have the room to themselves. Niccolo and Emilio cried when I left. We all cried when Marco left."

Glenna recalled wanting a baby sister and asking for one for Christmas. Her mother told her it didn't work that way, that it was up to God to decide such things. She had accepted this explanation then but now wondered if her parents had decided it was best not to have any more children. Certainly if they had had a boy, there would have been a problem in time of where to put him.

They came to the path to the river, and she said, "Here's the path we need to take."

They were quiet again as they made their way through the woods to the river. Edo had expected to bait Glenna's hook, but she did it herself. He waded out into the river, protected by Charlie's waders, while Glenna, in her shorter boots, remained just barely in the river. "We want only trout, Glenna, and a good size," he called out to remind her. She gave him a thumbs-up.

Edo caught several small fish and threw them back in, returning each time for more bait. Glenna was too close to shore in shallow water, but she didn't care. She was enjoying the sight of this boy she loved as he fished for their supper. She studied his expressions of disappointment at the little fish and the happiness of success when he caught a big one. She would store away these memories and return to them many times.

When Edo had finally caught three good-sized trout, he said he thought this would be enough. He carried the fish in the bucket of water, and Glenna carried the poles and the empty bait can as they made their way back home. Before they reached the road, they heard someone calling their names. Edo, who was walking in front to avoid the fishing poles Glenna carried over her shoulder, called out, "We're coming." Glenna was alarmed and worried that something was wrong. She sped up so that she was right behind Edo by the time they reached the road.

It was the minister, Mr. Markley, who was waiting for them. He told them that Miss Louise, an elderly member of his church, had been watering her flowers and had fallen. Apparently she had broken her hip and was asking for Kathleen to ride with her in the ambulance on the way to Richmond. Kathleen had seen this lady through a number of illnesses in the past, as she had no family.

They got in the minister's car, fishing poles sticking out the open window and Edo holding on to the bucket of fish and water as the minister drove carefully back to the house, where the ambulance sat waiting with Miss Louise inside, Kathleen giving her sips of brandy to alleviate the pain. Kathleen stepped out of the ambulance to tell Glenna they were going to take Miss Louise to Richmond and that the minister would follow them and bring her back when they got Miss Louise settled.

"You eat the fish," Kathleen said. "Don't try to save any for me. We'll get something to eat. If I'm not back, let Renney know where I am." Kathleen wanted to tell Edo to go home after supper because she didn't entirely trust him, but she did trust Glenna, so she just hugged her and was gone.

Chapter 22

AFTER KATHLEEN LEFT, Edo told Glenna he wanted her to see the Avery house. She had never been there, though Kathleen had visited Mrs. Avery once or twice when she was sick. Glenna had been in school on those occasions. Glenna knew her mother would not approve of her going to the Avery house with Edo, but she wanted to see the house and the flowers, and she wanted to be with Edo. So after they put away the fishing gear, they cooked supper together. Glenna washed, peeled, and sliced the potatoes into thin pieces, seasoned them, and put them in a baking dish with a little water and into the oven while Edo prepared the fish. When the potatoes had baked, he turned up the heat in the oven, then put the trout in to bake. Glenna told Edo if they went to the Avery house together, someone would see them, and it would get back to her mother. So they decided that Edo would leave on his motorcycle first, then Glenna would go through the woods on the path, walk down the road to the waterfall, and meet Edo there. After they ate, they quickly cleaned up, and Edo took off on the motorcycle. Glenna locked the doors and headed for the path. It was getting close to dusk, so she wore her rubber boots and walked as carefully and as quickly as she could. When she came to the road, she breathed a sigh of relief. Then she walked faster in the hopes of avoiding any traffic.

Edo was waiting for her at the waterfall. His face lit up in a big smile when he saw her. He took her hand, and they walked down the lane heavily wooded on both sides and bordered by the rhododendrons, the only sounds birds chirping and the occasional rustle of a small animal in the underbrush. Then about a quarter mile from the waterfall, the world seemed to open up to the setting sun, which cast a pink glow on the flowers everywhere. Glenna slipped her hand from Edo's and walked from one flower-laden shrub to another. She held her arms out and exclaimed, "This is the most beautiful place I've ever seen. I can't believe this has been here all my life and I never knew it."

"Look this way," he said and pointed out the view of the lowlands.

"It's breathtaking. I understand why you would like to live here while you write your book. This is a little piece of heaven."

Edo took her to see Greene Avery's grave, where he had weeded the flowers and around the headstone. Then they sat on the porch, and as dusk turned to darkness, he told her Greene and Rachael's story.

When he came to the end of the story, describing how Olan had found his father sitting in his chair at the door, frozen, Glenna said, "That's a sad story. The things Greene loved the most—whiskey and that view—killed him."

"That's true. But in the end, Olan built this house for his mother, and she planted all these beautiful flowers and shrubs, and after she died, and after Olan retired, he and his wife lived here for the rest of their lives, all thanks to Greene."

"I hope Greene knows that."

"I hope so too. Want to go inside now?"

"Yes."

"Wait until I turn on the lights." He went inside and turned on the lamps, then invited her in. She stared at the books.

"This is like a library in a house. I've never seen anything like this. Mum didn't tell me about this. Edo, do you have something like this in your house?"

"No, of course not. Books are expensive. We check out books from the school library or the library in town. I was as shocked as you are when I saw this. The preacher said the Averys had both collected books all their lives."

"They must have had a lot of money. Look, there's a set of encyclopedias!"

"And here, biographies of all the presidents at least through Wilson."

"And novels by Jane Austen, Charles Dickens, and Mark Twain. This is a gold mine. I don't know how I can go on living here knowing all these books are here and I can't get to them. You must not leave. You must stay here at least until I have read every one of these."

"And what will I do for money?"

"We'll figure out something."

"Don't you want to see the rest of the house?"

Glenna turned around, facing the opposite wall. "Is that Rachael?" she asked, pointing to the portrait over the fireplace. Edo said it was.

"She was beautiful. I wish there were one of Greene too."

Edo showed her the rest of the house, and as they moved from room to room, they accidentally touched as they brushed past each other. Back in the front room, Edo turned on the radio, and music filled the room. He took Glenna in his arms, and they began dancing. When the music stopped, he kissed her and held her close again. She drew away and looked at him. She said, "Edo, before you came here, I was satisfied with my life. It wasn't perfect, but it was comfortable and safe. I was living on dreams and working on making my dreams come true. Over the past week, I found more than comfort and safety. I found happiness." He saw that her eyes were glistening with tears. "When you are gone, how do I go back to the way it was?"

"Glenna, I love you. I want to come back here and marry you and spend the rest of my life with you. Will you wait for me? Will you add me to your dreams? I've already added you to mine."

"Edo, I love you with all my heart. I will wait for you."

"I want to make love to you, Glenna." She nestled her head on his chest, then he took her hand and led her to his bed.

Chapter 23

WHEN GLENNA WOKE up, she didn't know where she was until she realized Edo was sleeping beside her. She woke him up, and they hurriedly dressed. A check of the clock told them they were probably safe, that Kathleen had not had time to make it back home. With the flashlight, they made it to the waterfall, then turned the light off at the road. At the minister's house, they saw his car was not there, which was a relief, but his dog was outside and began barking. They ran as fast as they could to Glenna's back door and rushed inside as soon as she unlocked it. Once inside, they burst into laughter. Edo said, "We made it." Then he held her close to him and asked, "Are you all right?"

"I guess so," she said without conviction.

"Sweetheart, it's all right. What we did is all right. We pledged our love for each other. We're engaged. I am going to find a job, and the first thing I'm going to buy is an engagement ring, and I'll send it to you. Let's don't spoil what we have feeling guilty. We are so lucky to have found each other. Let's celebrate that."

"You're right. I do love you, Edo."

"And I love you, Glenna. Now I'd better get out of here before the preacher and your mother come driving up. I'll see you after school tomorrow."

"Wait." She located the bread basket and handed him a biscuit. "Throw this to Buddy when he starts barking."

"Thanks."

When Kathleen had still not returned by six o'clock, Glenna ate breakfast and hurried to Renney's. Renney told her Kathleen had called her at home last night to say they had decided to wait until they saw the doctor this morning and got some idea of what to expect. They should be home this afternoon.

Glenna went back home and made coffee, and while it brewed, she washed her breakfast dishes and made her bed. She turned on the radio and listened to the news as she drank her coffee, but thoughts of Edo crowded out the morning news, and she turned it off and sat thinking about Edo. She knew she loved him with all her heart, and she was certain he loved her. But she knew what they had done, no matter what Edo said, would be considered a sin by her mother and the church.

God would expect her to confess to the priest what she had done. On the other hand, God would know that she and Edo had pledged their love for each other, that they were sincere. Surely He would approve. In her heart, she now pledged to God to be true to Edo. Out loud, sitting in her chair early in the morning, Glenna pledged to God that she would always love and be faithful to Eduardo Morelli. No confession was necessary.

Buddy was still out when Edo passed the minister's house, but the biscuit proved to be enough to stop his barking. Once back at the house, he went back to bed and thought about Glenna. His heart ached at the thought of leaving her, but he knew he couldn't stay. There were no jobs here except lumberjacking, and those were sporadic. There were no guarantees of staying in this house long term, and where would he go if not here? But more important, he had to get back on the road and see the country, and meet people and write about it. He lay awake thinking for hours before he finally fell asleep and didn't wake up until almost eight o'clock.

He boiled several eggs, made coffee, and toasted bread in the oven. After he had eaten, he took a second cup of coffee to the porch to think things through. Even if he could find work and remain here to be with Glenna, what would that mean? She was only sixteen years old. Her mother would never allow her to marry at such a young age. They would be forced to sneak around to be together. If they did marry, sooner or later she would become pregnant and have to drop out of school. (He wasn't worried about her getting pregnant now. Everybody knew that didn't happen the first time.) But Glenna had plans to go to college, and he had plans to travel and write a book about it.

No, he could not stay. That would ruin all their plans for the future. He would tell her today when they met for supper. Someday they would find their way back to each other. For now, they would write letters. It was the only answer.

He went back inside, took the sheets and pillowcase off the bed, and put them, along with his laundry, into the washing machine. He reminded himself to thank the minister and his wife for the detergent they had left so he could do his laundry. While they were washing, he washed his dishes, rinsed and dried them, and put them away. Then he swept the kitchen and dusted the furniture in the front room. When the laundry was done, he hung everything on the line out back.

Edo knew he would be leaving early in the morning, and he wanted to leave a letter of thanks to the minister, along with the keys in the minister's mailbox, and of course a letter to Glenna. At the general store, he had seen some small notebooks that were narrow enough to fit into the metal box on his bike. So he rode there and purchased a notebook and a package of envelopes. Now he would not be having to borrow paper and envelopes.

He then rode his bike to Renney's to see if she was pleased with his work in the apartment. She said she was, and so was Miss Kennely, who had returned early this morning. She thanked Edo for taking care of this and asked him what he would like for lunch. He told her he would save his last meal for supper. She said, "You can have both. Sit down." So he ate a hamburger for lunch, then left on his bike for St. Claire.

It had been a week since he had ridden on the open road, and it was exhilarating. He found himself smiling and felt the old longing to begin his travels again. But he had something important to do first.

On the day he had spent a little time in St. Claire, he had noticed that beside the general store was a smaller store called the Jewel Box. Now he parked his bike outside this store and walked inside, a bell over the door alerting the owner of his arrival. From the window on the back wall, a middle-aged man looked up, smiling, and quickly left his seat and came through the open door to the right of the window.

"Good afternoon," he called out. "How may I help you?" He was wearing a perfectly pressed shirt and tie. He had a kind face, and Edo felt welcome though he was aware he was standing in an upscale store.

"I want to buy a ring—a special ring for a beautiful girl. I'm going to marry her someday, but I want her to know how much she means to me."

"I understand, and I'm sure I can help you. Do you know her ring size?"

"No, I don't but she is a slender girl, not overweight and not thin. Does that help?"

"Yes, it does. I take it she doesn't have large hands, nor does she have tiny hands. There is nothing unusual about them. Correct?"

"Yes, that's right."

"Very good. Then we'll go with a size six. If it's a bit too large, she can come in, and we have a way to make it fit better. I assume she is young like you, and that means in time she'll probably grow a bit, and it will fit better. Now is there anything in particular you have in mind?"

"Well, she has beautiful green eyes. Do you have a green stone? Affordable, of course."

"Yes, I do. I'll be right back."

When he returned, he held up a ring with a small green stone set in a gold-plated ring. "This is an emerald. As you can see, it is small but beautiful."

"Yes, it's perfect, but I'm afraid to ask the price."

"It is seven dollars."

"I can do that."

"Very good, sir. I'll get a box."

When Edo returned to The Falls, it was only two o'clock, so he went back to the Avery house, set up the ironing board, took in the laundry from the clothesline, and set to pressing the linens. At ten minutes before three, he wasn't finished, but he unplugged the iron and drove to Renney's. He parked the bike behind the restaurant and walked toward the school. The minister's car was parked by the house, so Edo knew they were back. He walked on and met Glenna as she and the other students poured out the school door. Her face lit up when she saw him.

"How was school today?"

"I had a hard time concentrating, and it's your fault, Edo."

"Will you forgive me?"

"Yes, probably. Do you know if Mum has gotten back yet?"

"The preacher's car is back now. It wasn't back at lunchtime, so they haven't been back long."

"I need to go home and check on Mum. She's probably exhausted. I'll meet you at Renney's in a little bit."

"Okay."

Glenna ran home and found Kathleen had just finished a long soak in the tub. She had had little sleep and planned to go right to bed. "Have you eaten anything?" Glenna asked.

"Yes, we stopped at a café. Mr. Markley bought my lunch."

"That was nice of him. How is Miss Louise?"

"She has a broken hip. She's not like likely to recover from this. They gave her pain medication, so she is resting."

"I'm sorry. She's a sweet old thing. How much brandy did she drink on the way to the hospital?"

"A lot."

"Good. Well, I'm going to Renney's to have supper with Edo. I'll be quiet as a mouse when I get back."

"All right. Don't be too late. Tell Renney I'll be there good and early in the morning," she said as she crawled into bed.

Edo was waiting in the booth when Glenna got there. She told him her mother had gone to bed. "She'll be up in the middle of the night. If you like, we can sit on the porch later if we're quiet."

He agreed and thought that would be a good place to give Glenna the ring. He didn't want to do that here in the restaurant, and there would be no more taking her to the Avery place.

They both knew he was leaving soon, but neither wanted to talk about it, so they talked about Miss Louise and what was likely to happen to her, and about school and what courses Glenna would be taking her final year. Finally, she asked what his plans were, and he told her he was leaving in the morning. He told her his heart wanted to stay, but his head knew it was the wrong decision for both of them. They would both be giving up their dreams. "We just have to put off being together for a time until we're both ready."

"I know you are right, Edo, but I don't have to be happy about it."

He reached across the table and took her hand in his. "No, we don't have to be happy about it. We just have to be brave."

They ate supper, then went into the kitchen. Glenna gave Renney the message from her mother, and Edo thanked her for all the fine meals she had given him. She thanked him again for his work on Miss Kennely's apartment. It was a really busy time in the kitchen, so Edo didn't tell her he was leaving and prolong the visit.

He left his bike at the back of the restaurant, and they walked slowly hand in hand toward Glenna's house. Buddy was in the preacher's yard, and he came to them wagging his tail. Edo said, "He hopes I have another biscuit for him. Sorry, old boy, I'm fresh out," he said as he reached down to pet him.

"Supper, Buddy," Mrs. Markley called, and he ran to the back of the house.

Across from the school, they stopped briefly to watch a group of young boys and girls playing softball. There were no adults present, but the children were managing the game just fine.

They walked on to the house and sat in the swing. Edo said, "Glenna, last night I told you I want to marry you someday, and I mean that, but I don't want to wait to send you a ring. I want you to have a ring now to remind you every day that I love you and that someday, I'm going to be your husband and you're going to be my wife. So I bought you a ring today." He slipped the box out of his jacket pocket and opened it to reveal the green gemstone mounted on the gold ring.

In a whispering voice, she said, "It's beautiful."

He removed the ring from the box and placed it on the ring finger of her left hand. "I want you to know that this means I love you, and I will be true to you always, Glenna."

"I love you, Edo, and I will be true to you always." He gathered her in his arms and kissed her.

When he finally let go, he said, "It's going to be hard for us to be apart, but there is no other choice. Both of us have things we need to do. I'll write to you, and I'll temporarily settle down in one place sometimes to work, and I'll save money, and those times, you can write to me. I want you to save my letters. That will help with the book. You finish school here and go to college. We will both be so busy, and before you know it, I'll be back, and we can get married. There is something I want you to do if you can. Have your picture taken, and send it to me when I send you an address."

"I have a picture you can have now." She went into the house and came back with the photograph. "Renney has a camera. She loves to take pictures of her children. She made this one of me last Christmas. Mum got the negative and had copies made and sent one to her mother. She kept one and gave me this one."

"This is really good. I'll treasure this. Thank you. I really want this, but I hate to take the only one you have."

"I want you to have it. You can bring it back to me someday."

"No. You can have me, but I'm keeping the picture."

Before she could answer, a clap of thunder came from the west.

"A storm is coming. You need to get inside," he said as he stood up. He took her hand as she stood up and pulled her close. Then he opened the door and saw her safely inside. Holding the screen door open with his back, he kissed her one last time and was gone. To try to beat the storm, Edo headed for the cow pasture. Glenna watched smiling as he braced himself with one hand on the split-rail fence, then jumped over it and ran toward Renney's, repeating his fence jumping at the other end. By the time she heard the motorcycle roar to life, tears were running down her cheeks. She stood there watching him ride round the restaurant and disappear from view, but she didn't move until the sound of the bike faded away.

Edo just made it back to the Avery house before the rain came. He parked the bike in the small barn, removed the notebook and envelopes, put them inside his jacket, and ran inside. Not knowing when he might have access to a tub and hot water again, he took a bath and dressed. Then he gathered the towels and his underwear and washed them in the machine, finished ironing the sheets, made up the bed, dusted the furniture in the bedroom, and vacuumed the rooms he had used. When the towels had finished washing, he hung them and his underwear on the rack. Then he took the notebook and envelopes to the desk in the front room and wrote a letter to the minister:

May 18, 1937

Dear Pastor Markley,

I am leaving The Falls early tomorrow morning and want to tell you how much I appreciate the use of this house for the past week. I have been very comfortable here. I cleaned and vacuumed and washed and ironed the bed linen. (Tonight I will just sleep on the quilt so you don't have to do any laundry.) I also washed the towels. If they are not dry in the morning, I'll leave them on the rack.

Again, thank you for your kindness and generosity,

Sincerely,
Edo Morelli

He folded the letter and put it in an envelope and wrote the pastor's name on it. Then he took the second page and began to write.

May 18, 1937

Dearest Glenna,

You are probably surprised to receive a letter from me so soon, but I forgot to tell you that I am going to Charleston, SC, first, where, as I'm sure you know, the Civil War started at Ft. Sumter. Also, it is, I am told, a beautiful city. If I find work there, I will stay awhile and send you my address. If not, I will move on. I love you and miss you already.

Love,
Edo

P.S. I'm leaving this letter in Renney's box because I forgot to get your box number and I don't want to ride up to your house so early and wake everyone up.

After rereading the letter, he wrote her name on the envelope, placed the folded letter inside, and sealed the envelope. He gathered and folded his few clothes and packed them in the pouch his mother had made for him. He would add the underwear, his shaving gear, toothpaste and brush, and his comb tomorrow. Then he made certain all the doors were locked, turned off the lamps in the front room, and went to his bedroom, where he took two quilts from the chifforobe. He removed the freshly washed and ironed pillowcase off the pillow and draped it on the chair. He spread one quilt on the pillow and the other on the bed, took off his shoes, and lay down on the bed, turned off the lamp, and pulled the quilt around him, and listened to the rain hitting the tin roof. He went to sleep thinking about Glenna and the good life they would have someday.

Chapter 24

WHEN EDO WOKE up, the rain had stopped, and the faint light told him it was early. He got up, folded the quilts and put them back in the chifforobe, then straightened the quilt on the bed and put the fresh pillowcase on the pillow and back on the bed. In the kitchen, he made coffee, toast and four scrambled eggs, ate his breakfast, and took a second cup of coffee to the porch to enjoy one last time the scene he had come to love. The rain had not been hard enough to disturb the blossoms, and he was glad because he wanted to remember this place as it had been the first time he saw it. As he gazed around him, he was overcome with the desire to ditch his plans and go to Glenna and tell her he would stay, and somehow they would make it work. Almost as quickly as the thought had come, though, it evaporated into the cool morning air. He had to go, and he had to go now.

Returning to the kitchen, he washed, dried, and put away the dishes, emptied the coffee grounds outside and rinsed the pot, and cleaned the table and stove top. He left the remaining eggs, bread, and coffee in the refrigerator with the pastor's Coca-Colas. Then he shaved, brushed his teeth, and finished packing his things. The towels were not quite dry, so he left those on the rack. He looked around to see if he had forgotten anything, locked the front door, and put the letters in his jacket. He picked up his pouch and went out the back door, locked it, and was soon on his way down the lane and to Renney's, where he parked the bike and walked to the minister's house. He placed the letter and the keys in the minister's mailbox, then walked back to Renney's. He considered going inside and leaving the letter to Glenna with Renney or with Kathleen if she was there but decided against it. He had spent a lot of time here with Glenna, and to go back inside would make him even sadder than he already felt. So he drove his bike up to Renney's mailbox and placed the letter to Glenna inside it. He didn't know that someone in the restaurant was watching him.

Later that morning, Ethel Ann spent a lot of time cleaning the dining room. She was waiting for an opportunity to see what Edo had put in the mailbox. When the last customer had left and Jackie, the waitress, took a bathroom break, Ethel Ann ran outside to the mailbox. She saw it was a letter to Glenna. She slipped it into her pocket. When she walked back into the restaurant, Jackie asked her where she had been.

"Oh, to check the mailbox, but there was no mail."

"It's too early yet. You know the mail doesn't get here this early."

"Well, I've been so busy, I thought it was later than it is."

When the mail was delivered, Ethel Ann was out the door to get it. This was something she had never done before. Ethel Ann was lazy and found more ways to get out of work than ways to be of help. Today, though, she took the mail to the office and handed it to Renney. Renney was aware of all the cleaning her niece had done that morning, and now she was bringing the mail. She smiled at the thought that Ethel Ann was turning over a new leaf. "About time!" she thought, but smiled and said, "Thank you, Ethel Ann. It was thoughtful of you to get the mail."

Kathleen woke up very early that morning and couldn't go back to sleep, so she got up, made coffee, and sat at the kitchen table thinking. At the hospital, when she and Rev. Markley had discussed whether to return home that night or remain to speak with the doctor, he asked her if she wasn't worried about leaving Glenna with "that boy" here. She told him she had done her best to teach Glenna right from wrong, and sometimes you just had to trust your child to do the right thing. She had said that, but she knew that young people were not very wise and were vulnerable to temptation. She just hoped that nothing had happened and that Edo would soon be on his way. Later at Renney's, she heard the motorcycle pull up out back. She thought Edo would come in, but he didn't, and a few minutes later, he started the bike again and drove around the restaurant and was gone.

A little past three, Glenna came to Renney's as usual but didn't stay. She took a plate home with her. Kathleen figured she didn't want to sit at the booth where she had sat for years, because now it would be a reminder that Edo was gone.

When Kathleen got home, Glenna was sitting on the sofa with a book. "Long day, Mum? You look tired."

Kathleen agreed as she sat down in the chair next to the table and lamp. "It feels good to sit down. How was your day?"

"Lonely. Edo left, and I miss him so much. I know I've known him for only a week, but I love him, and he loves me. He gave me this ring last night." She held out her hand for Kathleen to see.

"It's lovely, Glenna. It looks like an emerald."

"It is an emerald. We're engaged." Before Kathleen could speak, she said, "Don't worry, Mum. It's going to be a long engagement. I'm going to finish high school and go to college just like we planned. And Edo is going to travel all over the country. He writes his mother about the places he goes, and now he's going to write to me, and when he's finished traveling, he'll use the letters to write a book. Don't repeat that, please. I wasn't supposed to tell anyone, but I want you to know."

Kathleen was relieved that he was gone, but her heart hurt for Glenna. Still, she was glad to see the last of that boy for a long while. The ring, if it was really an emerald and not a pretty piece of green glass, told her that Edo and Glenna were very serious about their feelings for each other, but a lot could happen between now and Glenna's finishing high school and college, and heaven knew what Edo would get into or how many girls he would meet over the next few years. Young people fell in love easily and often passionately. Sometimes it worked out, but often it didn't. Kathleen had been a witness to her older siblings' growing pains as they loved this one and then that one. But she would voice none of this to Glenna. What Glenna needed now was her understanding.

"It's not hard to understand why you love him so. He's quite handsome, and he's really nice. He certainly has a good deal of confidence in himself. He's like you in that respect. These are hard times, and most people don't have many choices. They just do what they can to keep food on the table and a roof over their heads. But even in good times, most people don't have the confidence or imagination enough to set out all by themselves to chase a big dream. Most people make safe choices, stick close to home, don't take chances, and work for other people instead of going out on their own."

"You were one of those confident people, weren't you, Mum? I'm sorry it didn't work out."

"Well, there are often unforeseen circumstances, darling. But my life isn't over yet."

Chapter 25

GLENNA DIDN'T EXPECT a letter for the first three or four days, but when a week went by, she was very disappointed not to hear from Edo. When May became June, and still no letter, she feared something had happened to him. She became so upset that she walked to the college, and in the library went through the North Carolina and South Carolina newspapers for the past month to see if there were any reports of accidents that could have involved him. He had not told her where he was going, but so far he had been traveling south. She found nothing, which was a relief but did not relieve her worries.

One morning in late June, Glenna woke up feeling sick. Kathleen was at work and unaware, and Glenna recovered during the day and did not mention this when her mother came home. Glenna was, by then, suffering from anxiety. She knew in her heart that Edo loved her, and she was terrified that something had happened to him. She decided the nausea was connected to her sadness. Her mother had told her she was going to make herself sick if she did not try to take her mind off Edo. She had tried to do that. She did her chores, though her lack of energy made it difficult. She had checked out books from the school library at the end of school but was unable to concentrate.

Occasionally, doubt about Edo's feelings for her crept into her mind, but reliving their time together quickly erased the doubt. Then she was back to worrying that something bad had happened. Not knowing was maddening.

On the day following the first attack of nausea, Glenna woke up sick again. The thoughts of food sent her outside to throw up. But again she recovered and did not mention this to her mother.

The next day was Sunday, her day to cook for her mother. She told Kathleen she felt sick. Kathleen took her temperature. It was normal. "You've probably caught something," she said.

"Well, maybe, but it's strange because this is the third morning in a row that I woke up sick. Yesterday I threw up. But it goes away after a bit."

Kathleen stood staring at her daughter as she listened to words that made her want to scream. But she didn't scream.

"Did you have sexual relations with that boy?"

"What? Why are you asking that? What does that have to do with being sick?"

"Morning sickness is one of the first signs of pregnancy."

"Pregnancy? That's impossible!" She began to cry.

Hoping against hope, Kathleen asked, "Why is it impossible, Glenna? Tell me why it's impossible."

"Because it only happened once."

"Sometimes once is enough, Glenna."

The smell of the coffee sent Glenna outside, once again, to throw up.

When the coffee was perked, Kathleen poured a cup and sat at the kitchen table to think. Her thoughts about sex education had always been that when a child asked a question on such matters, a parent should answer truthfully in language the child could understand, but no more. Too much information would lead to questions the child wasn't ready to have answered. Eventually, as the parent answered one question after another, all would be covered.

Kathleen had followed this plan with Glenna. As the role of the male had come up, she had explained, and added that the sexual union between male and female should take place only within the sanctity of marriage. Outside marriage, it would be a sin. Kathleen thought she had covered all the bases, and Glenna had shown all through her young life to know right from wrong and had always demonstrated her desire to please God and her parents.

But now, Kathleen decided she had failed. She had trusted Glenna, and she had underestimated the girl's feelings for Edo. And Edo! She thought, "I am going to find that boy if it's the last thing I do!"

She found Glenna lying in her bed crying. She said, "Glenna, when you are feeling better, we have to talk. Just stay in bed until it passes." Then she went back to the kitchen, poured more coffee, and did more thinking. Later, with her thoughts in order, she checked on Glenna and found her asleep. She returned to the kitchen and made batter for pancakes, heated the griddle, and perked fresh coffee. Glenna came into the kitchen and watched her mother. "Let's eat, and then we'll talk," Kathleen said.

After the meal, when the dishes were washed and put away and the table wiped clean, Kathleen sat down opposite Glenna.

Before Kathleen could begin, Glenna spoke in a tearful voice. "Mum, I am so sorry."

"I know you are."

"I have shamed you."

"Glenna, you made a bad decision; we're all guilty of making bad decisions. Some are easily remedied, and some are not. But it's important to look at any situation with a clear head so you can decide how to go forward."

"What do you mean?

"Well, first, does anyone know about this besides the two of us?"

"No, of course not."

"That's good, Glenna, because sometimes pregnancy ends in a miscarriage. You may have heard about someone losing a baby. It happens, and usually early in the pregnancy, in the first few months. If that happens this summer, then you will be able to return to school in the fall, and no one will be the wiser. If it doesn't happen, you will not be able to return to school."

"I've ruined everything."

"You've changed everything. Maybe in time, you can get books and study bookkeeping on your own. We'll see. But in the meantime, we've got to find that boy. Now we're assuming he went south; we just don't know where. But he came from somewhere, and you say he planned to write to his mother. She'll know where he is, and how to get in touch with him. Where did you say he was from?"

"He told me where he was from and all the places he'd been, but it was the night all those lumberjacks came in. You remember they were laughing and talking so loud it was hard to hear what Edo was saying. And he named so many places he had been through. All I can remember are the big cities he visited. I don't know where he's from."

"Well, Father O'Malley might know. Edo spent the night at his house, remember? I'll go see him and ask if he knows."

"Oh, I hate for him to know about this."

"Glenna, he's going to know sooner or later, and there's another reason I need to tell him. The church has places—convents that take in unwed mothers before the baby comes, and they find couples who can't have children, and they adopt the babies of these girls."

"No, I will not do that! This is Edo's baby, mine and his, and I won't give it away."

"Glenna, don't reject the idea without thinking it through. You are sixteen years old, will be seventeen when the baby comes, and you won't have a high school diploma. If we can't find Edo, and if something happens to me, how will you live? Think about that. As long as I'm alive and able to work, I'll do my best by you and the baby, but there are no guarantees. You have to consider this."

"Is that what you want me to do, Mum? Go away to a convent, and give away the baby?"

"No, Glenna, I don't want any of this. There aren't any great choices here, and you're the one who has to decide."

The next Sunday, Kathleen drove alone to St. Claire to early Mass. Between morning sickness and the dread of facing Father O'Malley, Glenna refused to go. After Mass, Kathleen stayed back so she would be the last to speak with the priest.

"Kathleen, so good to see you. But where is our Glenna this morning?"

"Father, I need to speak with you privately."

"Of course. Let's go to my office." He led the way back through the nave. They passed before the statue of the Virgin, bowed and crossed themselves, passed the sacristy, and went into the hall and finally to the office, where Father O'Malley held the door open for Kathleen to enter. It was a beautiful room. The walls and woodwork as well as the floor-to-ceiling bookcase behind the father's desk were solid cherry, shined and gleaming. On the adjacent wall was a double window that framed the flower garden, carefully tended by the priest. The river lay beyond. To the right were two leather chairs separated by a small round table. Most of the floor was covered by a large Oriental rug with a floral motif in red, white, and navy blue with green accents throughout.

"This is the most beautiful room I've seen since coming to America," Kathleen said.

"John St. Claire spared no expense when he built this church, including the office. I feel fortunate to spend time here. Please have a seat, Kathleen," he said as he motioned toward the chair closer to the window.

They sat and turned toward each other. It was then that Kathleen noticed the wooden cross on the wall midway between the door and the bookcase. It was made of rough wood. She wondered if the priest had made it himself. It reminded her of the rough wooden cross on which Jesus had died. She imagined that a cushion for kneeling lay below it, and later, before she left, she saw she was right.

"Father, you of course remember the boy, Edo, who came through here in May. Work was needed on his motorcycle, and Roy Capps had to order the parts. It took most of the week to get them, so he made a deal with Rev. Markley to stay in a vacant house in exchange for cutting the weeds and mowing the grass. I think he also mowed the minister's grass. He also painted the apartment over the restaurant in exchange for his meals.

"As you know, I cook for Renney, and mine and Glenna's meals are part of my pay, so Glenna comes to the restaurant after school every day. She and Edo became acquainted, and she says they fell in love. I didn't worry too much about it. He seemed like a responsible young man, and I knew he would be leaving as soon as his motorcycle was repaired. But on the Sunday he, Glenna, and I came to church—you remember? Well, that afternoon an elderly woman I'd cared for from time to time fell and broke her hip. Rev. Markley came to the house and said she was begging for me to go with her in the ambulance to Richmond. So I went with her and gave her brandy to ease the pain. I was gone until the next afternoon. In the meantime, Edo and Glenna were alone. Now Edo is gone, and Glenna is pregnant. He promised to write, but she hasn't heard a word."

"Oh, Kathleen, I am so sorry. How can I help?"

"We have to find him, Father. Glenna is certain he's sincere. He bought her an engagement ring, said one day they would get married. She is afraid something happened to him. She searched through the North and South Carolina newspapers at the college for the time since he left but didn't find anything. She is pretty sure he was going south, but she doesn't know exactly where.

"He told her he writes letters to his mother and tells her all about the places he visits, and she is keeping the letters because he plans to use them to write a book someday." She explained how Glenna forgot where he said he was from. "Do you know where he was going and where his parents live?"

"I am sorry, Kathleen, I don't know where he is from or where he is going." He explained how late it was when Edo had arrived, and how the death of Mrs. Ellison had taken him away most of the next day. "We spent little time together, but I did get the impression that he is very interested in places with historical significance. He visited Washington and Appomattox. If I had to guess, Charleston, South Carolina, would be the place he'd have gone from here. Of course, he would likely have moved on by now, but maybe if he is continuing to stay at rectories, we may be able to track him down. Also, I'll call the priest in Washington. He's a friend of mine. Maybe he will know where Edo's parents live. As soon as I know something, I will pay you and Glenna a visit."

"You know, Father, we were taught that it was rude to ask a person a lot of questions, that a person would tell you what he wanted you to know. I wish I had violated that rule with Edo."

"Yes, I've heard a number of people express that 'rule,' as you say, and the truth is that most people enjoy talking about themselves and like it when someone is interested enough to ask questions. A member of the church had a conversation with Edo. I'll ask him if Edo mentioned where he is from, and you might do the same in The Falls—without giving away the reason you need to know, of course."

Kathleen said she would do that, thanked the priest, and made her way home. She told Glenna what he intended to do and said he would visit and let them know what he had learned. Glenna was not happy about his plan to visit, but Kathleen told her that she couldn't hide for the rest of her life. "Father O'Malley won't be coming to preach to you. He isn't like that."

Over the next week, Kathleen and Glenna casually asked every person they knew who had had any contact with Edo if they remembered where he was from. No one knew where Edo was from.

Father O'Malley wasted no time trying to learn Edo's whereabouts. He called the most likely rectory in Charleston and spoke with the priest, who told him Edo had shown up there, but he'd had a house full of relatives from out of town and had to turn him away. He said he would call around, though, to see if Edo had gone to another church and would call Father O'Malley back when he learned something.

Next, he called the priest in Lynchburg, but the priest there said Edo had been very tired from his long ride and needed to walk a bit to improve his circulation, then went to bed and left early the next morning. He didn't know where Edo was from. Father O'Malley then called his friend in Washington, who told him that Edo was interested in hearing about the presidents he knew.

"You know I enjoy talking about that," he laughed. He said Edo was from somewhere up north, but he could not remember where. "I will call the priest in Philadelphia and see what he knows, and I will call you back."

The next afternoon, the priest in Washington called back. He said the Philadelphia priest did not remember where Edo was from, and the priest in New York had died since Edo's visit, but this priest had called him after Edo's visit and told him that he had taken Edo to the apartment of an elderly man who had a broken arm and needed assistance. He repeated what all Edo had done for this man. The priest and his parishioner were very pleased and grateful for Edo's care. He said he did not remember where Edo was before New York. No one, including Father O'Malley, remembered this either.

The following day, the priest in Charleston called to say he had remembered that there was a boardinghouse in the neighborhood and had called there. Edo had spent two days there as he visited places around the city. The landlady asked the other boarders who had been there at the time of his visit, but no one remembered where he was from except up north somewhere, or where he was going next. (Later, at supper one night, they would talk about Edo, and one of the fellows said Edo had told him his father was a stonecutter. It did not occur to anyone to pass on this information.)

After this conversation, Father O'Malley called Renney's to tell Kathleen he would like to visit after she got off work. He told her not to get her hopes up. He still did not know where Edo was, but he wanted to visit Glenna. She told him what time she would be home.

Glenna had dreaded the father's visit. She had thought if it were not for the pregnancy, she could have kept her secret to herself and enjoyed reliving those intimate moments with Edo unbeknown to anyone else. But soon everyone else would know what she had done and would say Edo had used her, that she had been foolish. They would gossip about her, make fun of her. Those thoughts made her wish, even pray for the miscarriage her mother had mentioned. Then she would look at the ring and be reminded that Edo loved her. He didn't have much money, yet he had spent some of what he had to buy this ring for her. The ring was a symbol of their love and commitment to each other. No matter what other people would think and say, she knew the truth, and come what may, she would get through this.

As Father O'Malley made his way to Kathleen and Glenna's house, he was reminded that the last time he had been here was when Charlie died. It occurred to him, not for the first time, that most of his home visits were in times of trouble and sorrow. This made him sad because he truly cared about his small flock. He said a prayer that this situation would end well.

Kathleen answered his knock on the door and invited him into the living room, where Glenna sat on the sofa. He went to her, bent down and held out his hand to her, took hers, and said, "Glenna, I haven't come here to admonish you but to assure you that God loves you. He knows all us humans make mistakes, but He just keeps loving us and rooting for us. He hopes we learn from our mistakes and that our own problems increase our compassion for our fellow human beings. I want you to know that I will help you in any way I can."

"Thank you, Father," she said, barely above a whisper.

Kathleen invited him to sit down and offered him a cup of decaffeinated coffee, which he accepted. She had prepared the coffee ahead of time so was back quickly with a cup for him and one for herself. Glenna had declined a cup.

"I am sorry I do not have news of where Edo is nor where he is from, but I will tell you what little I have learned." He shared that Edo had gone to Charleston and, unable to stay at the rectory, had spent two nights at a boardinghouse. The owner said she didn't know where he was going, that he'd spent little time there, was out most of the time seeing the sights of the city, and she did not know what state or city he was from, but said he was "very nice for a Yankee."

He then told how helpful Edo had been to the elderly man in New York City. The priest there was an elderly man, and he had asked Edo to help an elderly parishioner who had a broken arm and needed assistance. The priest called the priest in Philadelphia to tell him how much Edo had done for this man. Unfortunately, the priest himself had died since Edo's visit, so the trail had gone cold on both ends.

"This was almost two months ago. He could be anywhere by now." As he said this, he noticed that tears were coursing down Glenna's cheeks, and his heart hurt for her. "Glenna, maybe some mix-up somewhere we can't know about is keeping him from writing or, if he is writing, keeping the letters from getting to you. I have no idea what it could be. But you must consider the possibility that he changed his mind when he left. That doesn't seem like the person he appeared to be, but some people are fickle. You didn't know him for very long. If he had stayed around for a long time, you might have seen this. I am not judging him, but you have a big responsibility facing you. You have another human being to think about, and you must take care of yourself so that little one will be healthy."

"I know," Glenna said, again barely above a whisper.

"You are going to bring a new life into the world, and I know you have the heart and the ability to be a good mother. Pray that God will give you the courage to let go of grief and prepare yourself for this responsibility. I will be praying for the same."

Chapter 26

GLENNA UNDERSTOOD THAT Father O'Malley and her mother doubted that she would ever see Edo or hear from him again. But she would cling to the possibility that something she couldn't explain was keeping him from writing or keeping his letters from her. She couldn't believe she had been wrong about him. He had given her the ring to remind her how much he loved her, and she had pledged to God to be true to him. She would keep that pledge. But the father was right. She was going to become a mother, and she had a responsibility to take care of herself, to stay healthy so the baby would be healthy. She would do what he said. She would pray that God would help her to stop grieving for Edo. She would do this every time she thought of him, and she would also pray for his safety and pray that God would assure him that she loved him.

Glenna spent the summer working at Renney's at every opportunity. At home, she did the housework and read the books she had borrowed, though she would often read a page, realize she had no idea what she had read, and have to read it again. She saved the money she made for the baby. The morning sickness passed and was replaced with the need for naps and early bedtime.

Glenna had worked hard to distract herself from thinking about Edo, but one day in mid-July, nothing worked. As she thought about him, she realized not only had he sent no letters, he had not sent the promised photograph of himself. The fear that she would forget his face overtook all other considerations. She walked to the store and bought a small package of stationery.

Back at home, she began sketching his face with her pencil. Glenna was not a particularly talented artist, and there were many erasures, but after an hour she was satisfied that she had captured on paper the face she loved. She held the portrait out at arm's length and imagined him sitting across from her in the booth. "I love you, Edo," she said, and brought him close and kissed him. Then she placed the picture in the drawer of her nightstand.

While Glenna was busy sketching Edo, Ethel Ann was sitting at Renney's desk taking one of her breaks. It was nearly four in the afternoon, and Renney and Kathleen were busy cooking. The telephone rang, and in her nicest voice, Ethel Ann answered, "Renney's Restaurant. May I help you?"

"This is Edo Morelli. Could I speak with Glenna, please?"

Ethel Ann turned toward the wall of the office and lowered her voice. "She's not here. She and her mother don't live here anymore," she lied. Ethel Ann had overheard Kathleen telling Renney that she would love to take Glenna and move back to Ireland. "They moved back to Ireland."

"When did they go?"

"Right after school let out."

"Is this Gloria?"

"Yes."

"Do you have their address?"

"No. They said they would send it when they got settled, but we haven't heard a word."

"Gloria, would you write down my parents' address and send them a letter with Glenna's address when you get it?"

"Of course." Ethel Ann wrote down the address as Edo told her. He thanked her and started to ask why they had moved, but the operator interrupted and asked Edo for another quarter, so the call ended. Ethel Ann put the paper with Edo's home address in her pocket. Later, when no one was watching, she dropped it into the stove.

When Ethel Ann came out of the office, Renney asked her who had called. Ethel Ann said, "It was for me," and grinned.

When she waddled out of the kitchen, Renney asked Kathleen, "Could Ethel Ann have a fella?"

"I've heard it said there's someone for everyone," Kathleen said as she rolled out dough for biscuits.

Before school started, Kathleen visited the principal to tell her about the pregnancy. The principal was saddened and shocked that one of her most outstanding students would not be graduating. Kathleen asked if Glenna could do her schoolwork at home, but the principal said no.

Kathleen also told Renney, who was shocked and angry that this young man she had trusted would "take advantage of Glenna and take off without a word." She agreed to allow Glenna to keep working as long as possible. By the end of October, Glenna's pregnancy was beginning to show, and she stopped working at Renney's.

Now at home full time, Glenna made herself several shifts. Kathleen had saved all Glenna's baby clothes packed in a box and stored under the bed. Glenna now took them out and began washing them in Ivory Snow. Kathleen gave her knitting lessons, and she knitted an afghan for the baby, and later several hats and booties and finally a sweater.

Months passed and still no word from Edo. Glenna did not speak about it anymore, but in her heart, she never wavered from her belief that he loved her and that he would be there if he knew about the baby. She did realize that if he had written to her and received no answers, he would stop writing, thinking she had changed her mind, which made her heart hurt for him.

Any time she heard the sound of a motorcycle, she would stop what she was doing and go out on the porch. She would stand there listening, watching, hoping. Sometimes she could tell the rider had stopped at Renney's, other times at Roy's garage or the general store. But Edo never appeared. By December she had stopped going out on the porch but couldn't help herself from staring out the window.

For Christmas that year, Kathleen and Glenna agreed they would spend no money on gifts for each other but would celebrate only with a special Christmas dinner and enjoy the music and programs on the radio. On Thursday, the twenty-third, Glenna shopped at the general store, where she bought a fat hen, sweet potatoes, canned green beans, and canned pumpkin. Mr. Wallace loaded her purchases in the wagon, and she pulled them home thinking of the days her father had done this after he lost his sight. She hated to think how he would feel now if he knew what she had done.

Christmas Eve, she went into the woods and cut small bunches of pine and holly and made an arrangement for the kitchen table and another that she placed on top of the radio cabinet in the front room. She made a third arrangement that she took to the cemetery and placed on her father's grave.

Back at the house, as carols played on the radio, Glenna made the pumpkin pie. Kathleen brought home vegetable beef soup for supper. Renney had kept the restaurant open all day, serving only soup and sandwiches. With Christmas on Friday, she had decided to remain closed until Monday morning. This reminded Kathleen of the long four-day holiday she had had the Christmas before Charlie's accident. Glenna was just a little girl then, but she also remembered. She knew Kathleen wanted to attend the midnight Mass tonight, but Glenna hadn't wanted to go, so Kathleen wouldn't go either. Now she said, "Mum, let's go to Mass tonight."

"You want to go?"

"Yes, it will do us good."

The next day, Kathleen and Glenna cooked together and ate listening to the carols. After cleaning up, they sat in the front room and talked and listened to the music. They remembered past Christmases when Charlie was alive, and how Papa always brought them a fresh ham. They were both gone now, and their absence was deeply felt.

Kathleen reminded Glenna that she still had a large family in Ireland. She described the fun, laughter, the love they'd shared. "They would welcome us and the baby with open arms," she said.

"I know you miss them all, Mum, but I can't leave here."

Kathleen did not say that Edo wasn't coming back. She would not ruin what little happiness they had on Christmas Day. "Well, it's just a thought."

So they passed the afternoon listening to music and chatting about the goings-on at Renney's. "How is Ethel Ann doing now?"

"You remember how last summer we all thought she had turned over a new leaf. She was cleaning everything in sight out front and doing a really good job. Renney really thought she was growing up. I told you about that telephone call she got. We thought she had a fella. But if she did, it didn't work out. Not long after that, she headed back to her old ways. Now all she wants to do is eat. I know she had a terrible experience when she was little, and I hate that, but something is badly wrong with that girl."

Chapter 27

BY FEBRUARY, GLENNA was ready to have pregnancy over. She was uncomfortable and anxious. On Sunday, February sixth, she began to have contractions. Her due date was the eighth. Kathleen knew that the due date for most pregnancies was an educated guess, but in Glenna's case it was probably very nearly accurate. She was as prepared as she could be, already having had Roy check the car and fill it with gas. She and Glenna had packed a bag with a little dress, the sweater, cap, booties, and afghan Glenna had knitted, as well as rubber pants and cloth diapers. Glenna had made blankets of three pieces of flannel on which she had sewn a pretty edging. They had packed two of those also.

At four o'clock in the afternoon, Kathleen and Glenna drove to Renney's house to let her know that Glenna was in labor and Kathleen might not be at work in the morning. She also used Renney's telephone to call the doctor Glenna had been seeing for her prenatal care to let him know they were on their way to the hospital down the mountain.

By five thirty, they had arrived at the hospital to begin the long night. Kathleen waited out the night in the room reserved for fathers. She had brought with her a sweater she was knitting for Glenna. She wanted Glenna to have something new to wear when this was over. She knitted through the night, stopping only to drink coffee and eat the sandwich she had packed, and several times to visit the restroom.

At 5:33 the next morning, she had finished the sweater and was putting the needles in her bag when a nurse came to tell her she had a beautiful seven-pound-two-ounce granddaughter. She said that Glenna was fine. When Kathleen went to the viewing window in the nursery, a nurse brought Anna Kathleen McAllen close for her grandmother to see her. Looking back at her was a baby with black hair, olive skin, and bluish brown eyes that within months would be almost black. Katie, as she would be called, was beautiful. Kathleen could not hold back the tears.

At Renney's, they had set on the counter a quart jar with a pink ribbon tied in a bow just below the rim to let everyone know about Katie's arrival and give everybody in The Falls the chance to contribute a few pennies to help with Kathleen's expenses. Nearly everyone who could contribute did, including Charlie's brothers, who felt bad because they had not taken their brother's place and been substitute fathers to Glenna. Both brothers put a dollar in the jar. Before the week was out, the jar was full of mostly pennies, nickels, dimes, and quarters, and when counted on Friday night, the total came to fourteen dollars and eighty-seven cents. Renney added thirteen cents to make it an even fifteen dollars.

Several women in the community had quietly asked for used baby and toddler clothes, which they had washed and pressed. One of them had covered a box with a pretty pink-and-blue feed sack fabric. She had cut and glued another cardboard box to make the top for the box, covered the top with the same fabric, and filled the box with the used clothes. Charlie's oldest sister had loaned Glenna a crib and assured her she would loan her a baby bed when it was needed.

Renney had asked Kathleen for a key to her house so that when Kathleen and Glenna arrived home on Saturday with Katie, the jar of money and the box of clothes, as well as a fine meal from Renney's, were waiting for them. During the afternoon, neighbors came by to see the baby, and each brought something small but useful: a thermometer, a teething ring, a small teddy bear, a bib. After closing hours, Mr. and Mrs. Wallace came with a package of diapers, two pairs of rubber pants, and two bars of Ivory soap.

On the following Monday, Glenna, needing some essentials, wrapped Katie from head to toe and took her to the general store. Mr. Wallace was delighted to see her, and he got out his camera right away and took a picture of Katie and one of Glenna holding Katie. "Bring her back every month, and I'll take a new picture. You can make an album and see how she changes over time." He didn't want payment. "This is my hobby, Miss Glenna. It makes me happy to do this."

If Glenna had worried that she and the baby would be shunned, the outpouring of love and support by the community relieved her of that fear. She had fallen in love with Katie on first sight of her. Her fierce sense of protectiveness surprised her a bit. She really didn't want visitors to hold her baby for fear they might pass on a budding cold or some other malady. She wanted to learn everything she could about childcare and quizzed Kathleen as soon as her mother walked in the door. Sometimes she had even written down questions.

Kathleen was certain the nurses at the hospital had spent a lot of time with their young patient and had given her good advice. She was proud that Glenna was receptive, that she loved Katie and was eager to be a good mother. Glenna was conscientious about keeping Katie clean and dry and about washing out diapers immediately. Kathleen bought a bucket especially to use as a diaper pail. "Just rinse them out and put them in the pail," she told Glenna. "Then wash them in the machine when you have enough. You'll ruin your hands if you keep scrubbing them by hand each time." She bought Mr. Wallace's best hand cream for Glenna.

* * *

For the next two years, Glenna's life was consumed with caring for Katie and keeping house for her mother. She would talk to Katie, sing to her, tell her stories, read her stories, and, in good weather, walk her around the neighborhood in the stroller borrowed from Renney. On Sundays when there was enough fuel in the car, Kathleen would take them to church. Glenna had worried that Katie might not be accepted there, but Father O'Malley assured her she would be welcomed "with open arms." "Glenna, Jesus said, 'Bring the little children unto me.' He made no exceptions. He meant all the children."

Glenna checked the mailbox every day, but she no longer expected a letter from Edo. She did hope though that when he had completed his travels, he would come back this way to see her again, and perhaps explain what had happened. She continued to wear the ring he gave her, and at some point she had taken the picture she had drawn of him out of the drawer and told Katie, "This is your daddy, Katie." Now when Katie saw the picture, she said, "Daddy," and she kissed it as she had seen her mother do.

In December 1939, Kathleen received a letter from her sister informing her that their mother was ill and asking for Kathleen. She asked that Kathleen come home and care for her. She said her hands were full caring for her own large family. Their brothers and their wives were in London, too far away to help, and two sisters had jobs they could not afford to give up, as their families would starve without their income. She said their brothers were willing to pay Kathleen's passage over.

Kathleen desperately wanted to return to Ireland. She regretted she had not done so when Charlie died, but word from her sister then had been discouraging. There were no jobs. Poverty was rampant. Here at least she had a job and a place to live, and that part of Charlie's savings account not wiped out with the bank failure in '29. She had withdrawn what was left, but once the government insured savings accounts, she had redeposited it, and it was earning a little interest. The veterans' check had been reduced when Glenna turned eighteen, but Kathleen continued to receive the widow's pension. The jar of money collected at the restaurant had covered the hospital bill, and the used clothes and diapers had been a blessing. Soon, though, Glenna would need to start making things for Katie to wear. Kathleen could use the money in the savings account to pay Glenna's and Katie's passage to Ireland, but Glenna was now eighteen years old, and she refused to leave The Falls.

Kathleen told her if Edo came back, Renney could tell him about Katie and where they were. But Glenna could not be persuaded. So Kathleen reluctantly decided she must leave Glenna and Katie behind and go to her mother. She said she would return as soon as she could.

In the meantime, Renney would have Gloria take Kathleen's place in the kitchen, and Glenna could take Gloria's place as a waitress. A place was made in the kitchen for a playpen for Katie. This was a huge change for her, but Glenna was in and out of the kitchen all day, and Katie took naps in the morning and afternoon and played with her few toys when she was awake. During down times, Glenna took her out of the playpen, and outside in good weather. Soon, though, Glenna realized that this arrangement was not good. When Katie needed to be fed or go to the bathroom, as she was now two and being potty trained, Glenna had to stop working and see to this. One day after work, Glenna and Katie visited Mrs. Oglesby, and Glenna asked her if she would be willing to care for Katie while she worked.

"Why, Glenna, I thought you would never ask! Of course I'll keep Katie." They agreed on three dollars a week. Mrs. Oglesby became a new grandmother for little Katie and a reason to get up in the morning for Mrs. Oglesby. They talked and sang songs and read stories, and in the spring they planted tomatoes and flowers. Katie thrived, and so did Mrs. Oglesby, as at night now she had no trouble falling asleep.

Letters from Kathleen indicated that her mother was gradually recovering under her care, but not to the extent that she could leave her. France and Great Britain were at war with Germany, and though Ireland was not involved, it soon became clear that Kathleen was stuck where she was, even if her mother recovered completely, as travel would be dangerous.

The economy was somewhat better due to FDR's policies, but tips were still not good, and the rent was twenty-five dollars a month. Had Glenna been staying home, she would have made Katie's clothes, but her days were long, and Sundays were a day for cleaning and laundry and spending time with Katie. She shopped then at the general store for Katie's clothes and shoes. Kathleen had added Glenna's name to the savings account, and she sometimes had to withdraw money to make ends meet. When the United States entered the war in December 1941, the textile mill soon rehired many laid-off workers as the mill began to manufacture cloth for uniforms for the army. Unfortunately the workers had gotten used to giving small tips and were slow to increase these. By June 1943, the bank account was empty, and the rent was overdue.

Chapter 28

ON FRIDAY, JUNE 4, 1943, Serena packed the last few items into the car George had bought in 1937, before the war, before the Germans and Japanese began taking over their neighbors. She remembered how reluctant George had been to sell the Model T Ford coupe he had bought in 1925. He had taken excellent care of it, had built a shelter for it behind the house where he had added on to the driveway carved out of the lawn. He had thought about keeping it but decided that would mean enlarging the shelter, and he didn't want to take up more of the lawn or go to the expense. So he finally sold the Model T. She knew it had hurt him to let it go, but now she was glad that he had. It would have been one more painful reminder of him, and she did not need any more of those.

She had finished the school year and packed up the items she had collected over the years, things she would need for the teaching job she had accepted in St. Claire. She had said her goodbyes to her fellow teachers and to Patsy and her family. They would stay in touch. Now she called Jimmie, and he came right away and settled onto his quilt, which she had placed in the front passenger seat. She took one last look at the house, then got into the car and drove to her new/old life in St. Claire. She had plans for the summer: gardening and cleaning out the house. She tried to think about that as she left the town where she had first tasted the freedom of being on her own, working at the profession she loved, falling in love and marrying.

These thoughts crept in, and the tears began. She pulled the car into a store parking lot and cried until Jimmie began to whine. "Jimmie, I can't help it," she said. He sat up in the seat and, as if to answer, barked three times. What she heard was, "Yes, you can." She caressed his head and petted him. "You are right, I can help it. I'll always love George, but he's gone, Jimmie, and all the tears on earth won't bring him back. I've got to go on living, Jimmie, and I'm going to."

With a determination she had willed for herself, she pulled back into the road and headed for St. Claire. Long before she got there, she decided to stop at Renney's and have lunch. She hoped Glenna would be there so she could thank her again for the kind letter she had sent after George's death.

When they arrived, she attached a rope to Jimmie's collar, led him to the wooded area on the left side of the restaurant, and tied the rope to a tree. Then she returned to the car for his bowl and a jug of water and filled the bowl. He wasn't happy about this arrangement, but she assured him she wouldn't be long.

It was early for lunch, and there were no other customers. Glenna saw her and came outside to greet her and meet Jimmie. Serena explained how Jimmie had come to her as they walked to the door and went inside.

"Glenna, thank you again for the letter you sent. It meant a great deal to me."

"I just wanted you to know that I care."

"It helps to know that. How are you doing? How is your mother?"

"She went back to Ireland to take care of her mother, who seemed to be dying. That was three years ago, and she's still living. I doubt Mum will ever come back here, but certainly not as long as the war is going on." She showed Serena to her seat and handed her a menu.

"You must miss her. Who takes care of your daughter?"

"An elderly lady in the village. She's really good with her, loves her, and Katie's happy there. Would you like tea?"

"Yes, please."

While Glenna fetched the tea, Serena saw the fried chicken and gravy on the menu, and she ordered this and vegetables when Glenna returned.

Later, as Serena was finishing her meal, she noticed a man come into the restaurant and speak to Glenna, who said something to him. He left, and Glenna disappeared into the kitchen. Serena was watching them, and when she placed her fork on the plate, a bit of gravy fell into her lap. She got up immediately and went to the restroom to wash the stain from her dress. As she was dabbing the stain with soap and water, she heard voices outside, as the window had been left opened a bit.

"Mr. Norris, I don't have the money. Tips have been terrible lately. Please give me another week."

"Glenna, Glenna, it's the same every month lately. We're gonna have to work something out."

"Well, I've thought about that. I could do your wife's ironing without charge."

"Oh, she'd like that, but how's that gonna help me? No, that won't solve this problem. But I have an idea. What time does that young'un of yours go to sleep at night?"

"Why do you want to know that?"

"Glenna, don't play dumb with me. I've got something you want, and you've got something I want. I could come by once a week or so on Sunday night, and we can have some fun. I'll see you about nine o'clock Sunday night."

Serena was shocked at what she heard. She forgot about the stain on her dress and left the restroom. She hurried back to the table, fished a five-dollar bill out of her purse, and laid it on the table. Gloria was behind the counter, Glenna nowhere in sight. Serena paid Gloria for her meal and left. Outside she quickly opened the car door and settled Jimmie inside, gathering his bowl and the water jug, and was soon back on the road.

As she drove, it occurred to her that she didn't know how much Glenna owed this Mr. Norris. The five dollars might help, but what if she owed him more than that? Would he force Glenna to move out or to make a terrible decision? "I'll pray for her," she thought, and immediately heard the minister's words: "The hands that help are holier than the lips that pray."

"But how can I help?" she asked out loud. But she knew the answer. "I don't want to do that. Glenna and I hardly know each other." Yet she knew enough about Glenna, a teenager with aspirations to become a bookkeeper. She had been an excellent student who had fallen in love, gotten pregnant, and been abandoned. She had kept her child and worked long hours for little pay to support the two of them, and she had been thoughtful and caring enough to write Serena a letter of condolence.

Serena came to the bridge over the river, turned to the side, stopped, and turned off the engine. She needed to think this through. Glenna was in a desperate situation, and Serena had the resources to help her out of this situation, possibly even help her realize her long-ago dreams.

On the other hand, Serena wanted to live a quiet life with Jimmie as her only companion. She wanted to clean out the house, have some painting done, and tend the garden she had paid Bob Gilley to plant for her. She had planned to teach, read, and ease herself back into church and eventually a social life as she felt up to it. Her plans didn't include living day in and day out with two other human beings. And yet, could she turn back on someone she had the means to help? No, she couldn't.

Serena started the engine and headed for the St. Claire high school. Fifteen minutes later she was sitting in Louise Carter's office, Jimmie on a leash sitting beside her. She told Mrs. Carter Glenna's story including her father's disability caused by his service in the war and his death, "We both know that girls who grow up without a father are vulnerable to young men. She fell in love, became pregnant, and was abandoned. She had to drop out of school and work to support herself and her daughter. She had to give up her dreams of completing high school and college. We can help her get back on tract." Mrs. Carter agreed to help.

When Serena arrived back at Renney's there were only two cars parked out front. Serena again tied Jimmy's leash to a tree and went inside. Glenna was at the cash register ringing up a customer's bill. When he left she walked around the counter and toward Serena and held out the five dollar bill. "I guess you left this by mistake."

"Oh no, that was no mistake. I left that for you."

"Really? But—"

Serena interrupted, "Glenna, we need to talk. Can you get off for an hour? It's really important."

"Well, I suppose I can. Let me ask Renney if Gloria can cover for me. I'll be right back."

"I'll be outside with Jimmie."

When Glenna returned and said Renney had agreed, Serena asked if there were somewhere they could speak in private, and Glenna suggested they go to her house. Serena made a place for Jimmie and his quilt in the back seat, and they drove up the hill to the house.

Glenna invited Jimmie inside, where he sat in the kitchen at Serena's feet as the two women sat at the table. Serena said, "I debated whether to tell you this, but I decided you should know. Earlier, I spilled a bit of gravy on my dress and went to the restroom to wash it off. The window was open a bit, and I overheard the conversation you had with Mr. Norris."

Glenna sighed and said, "This is embarrassing. It explains why you left the five dollars."

"Yes, that's true. But as I drove up the road, I realized that five dollars might not be enough, and even if it was for this month, this is going to keep happening. I also realized that I can do something about it. You see, I am not visiting Amelia, I am moving to St. Claire. My grandfather left me the house. It's a big comfortable house."

"He left the house to you and not Amelia?"

"That's right, but don't worry about Amelia. He left her all his money. She and her friend, Carole, retired from the college, and they moved to Key West. They bought a house, and they intend to rent rooms to travelers. They are as happy as clams."

"You must miss her."

"Yes, I do. She is the only family I have left, and she might as well be living on the moon. It's over a thousand miles to Key West, and there's no train that goes there. But back to business. Glenna, I'm offering you a job and an opportunity. The job would be as a housekeeper and cook in exchange for room and board for you and Katie and ten dollars a month. There are two bedrooms and a bath upstairs as well as an open space. That would all be yours and Katie's. I'll use the downstairs bedroom and bath. The rest of the house would be for all of us."

Glenna sat quietly and listened.

"Now the opportunity I mentioned is your finishing high school and later attending college."

"That would be wonderful, but they won't let me attend school at my age."

"When I left here earlier I went to see the principal at St. Claire High School. She has agreed to help you."

"Really? I don't what to say. I'm stunned."

"I know I am springing all this on you, Glenna, but Sunday night is only two days away."

"What would I do with all this furniture?"

"All this is yours? The house wasn't furnished?"

"Only the stove and refrigerator were furnished. The rest is mine."

"That's great. Amelia took every stick of furniture from the upstairs. There's nothing left but the dust on the floors. Those rooms are large. I'm sure everything you have will find a place. This table, for example, could be your desk."

"What if I quit my job here and give up this house, and then it doesn't work out?"

"Why wouldn't it work out? We are two mature women. If a problem comes up, we'll work it out. If it doesn't work out, I promise you I would never throw you out. I'd find you another place to live and another job. Glenna, we can make this work."

"Mum wanted us to go with her to Ireland, but I just couldn't do it. I couldn't leave here."

"What is holding you here, Glenna?"

"You'll think I'm crazy, but I keep hoping Katie's father will come back, and if I'm gone, I'll miss him."

Serena thought how sad it was to hope for something that wasn't going to happen, but she didn't say that. She said, "Renney will tell him where you are. You could even leave a letter for him."

"Yes, I suppose I could do that. This is awfully generous of you. But it seems wrong to run off and leave Renney short a waitress."

"Tell her the truth, Glenna. She'll understand."

They discussed the logistics of moving. Serena knew a man with a truck. He could make multiple trips, and Serena would pay him. They discussed the taxes that would soon be due on her father's land. Serena said she might have to let it go or sell it whether or not she moved.

"I'll call Renney's tonight at seven o'clock, and you can tell me what you decide to do." Glenna agreed.

Later at the restaurant, Glenna told Renney about her conversation with Mr. Norris, and how Serena had overheard it and had offered her a job and the possibility of completing her education. Renney was not shocked about Mr. Norris. She had heard rumors about him. She urged Glenna to accept the job. "This is a wonderful opportunity for you, Glenna. You're not likely to have another." She also assured her that two women had been asking her for work. "I'll call one of them to come in tomorrow. You need to start packing." She also promised to tell Edo where Glenna was should he turn up.

On the way home, Serena talked to Jimmie. "I've done it now, Jimmie. I've invited Glenna and Katie to live with us. This isn't the way I planned our future, but I just couldn't not do it." She rubbed his head and said, "I hope you understand. Maybe you and Katie will become friends. Won't that be nice? We have to look at the positive side of this, Jimmie. I always wanted a sister, and I've always liked Glenna. It's a big house. There is plenty of room for privacy. It will be good for us, Jimmie. We'll make this work."

Chapter 29

AT SEVEN O'CLOCK, Serena called. Glenna was waiting by the telephone and answered on the first ring: "Serena?"

"Yes, Glenna. Are you going to accept my offer?"

"Yes. Yes, I accept your offer. It is more than generous. It's a life saver."

Serena told her that she had also spoken with Bob Gilley, a mill worker she had known all her life. "He will be at your house tomorrow at two o'clock to load your furniture. He will also bring some boxes to pack things, but if you can get some more, that would be good." Serena gave Glenna her telephone number in case she needed to call her. Glenna wrote it down for herself and for Renney. Then, carrying the boxes Renney gave her, she walked to Mrs. Oglesby's house to pick up Katie and tell Mrs. Oglesby the good news. Mrs. Oglesby had come to love Katie as an "adopted" grandchild, and although thanks to President Roosevelt she now received a small pension from the government, she enjoyed the three dollars a week Glenna paid her for keeping Katie.

Glenna left the boxes on the porch and went inside, where she was greeted with smiles and hugs from Katie, who was always eager to tell her what she and Mrs. Oglesby had done that day. Glenna sat down and listened to all the details as Mrs. Oglesby looked on, grinning. When Katie finished, Glenna said, "It sounds like you had a very good day. Now I need to tell you about my very good day.

"A nice lady I've known since I wasn't much older than you, Katie, came to the restaurant today and offered me a job. I'll be her housekeeper and cook, and we are going to live with her in her big house in St. Claire."

Mrs. Oglesby said, "Oh, Glenna, that's very nice for you. You won't have to be away from Katie all day."

"Are you coming with us, Mrs. Oglesby?" Katie asked.

"No, dear, but I'll come to visit you, and you can tell me all the things you've been doing, and you can show me the big house you're living in. Will you do that?"

"Yes, ma'am."

"Good. Now, run along and get your things, please. When will you be moving, Glenna?"

"Tomorrow. I know this is a shock, and I'm sorry. I wish you could go with us. I need to tell you what happened, but not in front of Katie. Could you come to the house in the morning?"

"You don't need to explain, dear. To tell you the truth, I'm sad about this but also relieved. I'm too old to keep looking after Katie. I can't keep up with her. I'll miss her, but this is for the best."

Glenna gave her the three dollars, hugged her, and said, "I don't know what I would have done without you."

As soon as they got home, Glenna turned on the radio to entertain Katie while she began clearing out the cupboards in the kitchen and packing the contents into the boxes. She would have no need for the cooking utensils at Serena's, but she would keep them for future use. She used the extra bed linens to wrap the dishes, cups, and glasses. She worked for an hour, stopping only to help Katie wash and dress for bed.

She wanted to get back to it, but Katie had questions about the place they were going and why. Glenna told her she could not make enough money to pay the rent, and that was why they were moving. She reminded her that St. Claire was not very far away, and they would come back and visit. She told her about Jimmie and what a good dog he was, and how nice Serena was, and how now she would be staying home with her in the big house. "We will have our own inside bathroom with hot water coming right out of the spigot. We are taking all our things with us. You don't have to worry. I'll be with you all the time." Katie seemed reassured and soon drifted off to sleep, and Glenna resumed packing up the kitchen and finally fell into bed at midnight.

She woke up at her usual time at five in the morning and made coffee for the last time in this house she had known all her life. She felt sad as she drank her coffee and the memories ran through her mind of Charlie and her mother and Edo. There had been so many happy times here, and many sad ones too. But, she thought, that was life. The past years since her mother left had been a struggle, especially since the savings account had been depleted. She wondered what on earth she would have done if Serena hadn't spilled gravy on her dress and overheard Mr. Norris's crude suggestion. Maybe she and Katie could have moved in with Mrs. Oglesby, but even so, she would have still been stuck at Renney's with no future to look forward to. Now the future held real possibilities. She could finish school and get a job she would enjoy, and maybe the war would end, and maybe Edo would come back.

Glenna washed, got dressed, and woke Katie. They walked down to Renney's, where they were seated at Glenna's booth and served a breakfast of bacon, eggs, and pancakes. Before they left, there were hugs and kisses and tears. Glenna reminded them that she was not going far, and they could visit. Ethel Ann had not worked in nearly a year because she had gained so much weight she had trouble getting around. She had been told that this was Glenna's last day but said, "Good riddance." Of course, no one repeated this to Glenna, and Glenna had not expected her to be there.

After breakfast, Glenna and Katie walked to Roy Capps's garage, where she explained their plans to move. He agreed to store Charlie's truck until she could find a buyer. He walked home with them and drove the truck back to the garage.

Glenna spent the morning packing clothes and storing them in boxes in the car. She removed the bedclothes and all the curtains her mother had made, folded them neatly, and laid them on the sofa, waiting for the boxes Mr. Gilley would bring. Neighbors Dan and Jean Campbell, who had eaten breakfast at Renney's and learned about her move, came over to help. He broke down the beds, and Glenna saved the screws in jars she labeled "Katie's bed" and "Glenna's bed." Jean took Katie home with her to play with their children.

Glenna knew the Campbells had no washing machine. Before Dan left, she told him to take the washing machine her mother had bought when electricity came to the mountain. He said he didn't have the money to pay her for it. "I have no place to put it where we're going, and I don't want to leave it here. Please take it," she said. He left and came back with a borrowed wheelbarrow, disconnected the washing machine, thanked Glenna, and took it home.

Mrs. Oglesby came when Glenna was cleaning out the refrigerator. Glenna took the opportunity to tell her about Mr. Norris's suggestion as to how Glenna could pay her rent. "He's a disgusting character. I'm so glad you don't have to put up with him anymore," Mrs. Oglesby said.

Glenna filled a basket with odds and ends from the refrigerator for Mrs. Oglesby, and she left with it to find Katie to say goodbye.

At lunchtime, Suzanne, Renney's youngest daughter, brought sandwiches, tea, and doughnuts for Glenna and Katie, and they had a picnic on the porch. After lunch, Glenna put Charlie's tools in the car's trunk. Bob Gilley and his grandson arrived shortly thereafter. Glenna took the boxes he'd brought and packed the bed linens and curtains. The Gilleys moved the sofa onto the truck and secured the chairs on top of the sofa with ropes. They were gone for over an hour. When they returned, they lay the chifforobe down on a quilt on the bed of the truck, then wrapped it with another quilt. Beside it, they added the radio, the end tables, and Katie's nightstand, which no longer held Edo's picture, as Glenna had removed it and packed it in the bottom of a box with her clothes on top.

The Gilleys were back more quickly this time because Mr. Gilley had summoned two of his sons to help unload and carry the furniture into the house and upstairs. It would take them five trips to move all of Glenna's furniture and boxes.

While the Gilleys were emptying rooms and moving the furnishings, Glenna was cleaning. This little house had been her home, and she would leave it for the next tenants as she would want someone to leave it for her. When she finished cleaning, she sat down at the table with paper and pencil to figure how much rent she owed Mr. Norris for the five days, counting today, that she had occupied the house. Then she wrote a note.

Mr. Norris,

As of the end of Saturday, June 5, 1943, my daughter and I will have vacated your property. Enclosed is the $4.28 I owe you for these five days we have lived in your house. I have cleaned out the refrigerator and turned it off. I am leaving it open to air out.

Glenna McAllen

First thing Monday morning, she would call the power company and have the power disconnected immediately.

The Gilleys took the table and chairs, and the rocking chairs and swing on the front porch, and drove off one last time to St. Claire. After one final look around in the house and the garage, Glenna and Katie said goodbye to their neighbors and drove to their new home.

Chapter 30

SERENA HAD GIVEN Glenna directions to her house, but as she quickly caught up with Bob Gilley and followed him to the house, no directions were necessary. On the way, she thought about the money she had saved by moving. The five dollars Serena gave her, added to the nineteen dollars she had after paying Mrs. Oglesby, wasn't quite enough to pay the twenty-five she would have owed to Mr. Norris. In her head, she figured she had nineteen dollars and seventy-two cents left after leaving the four dollars and twenty-eight cents for the five days' rent. She had not had time to do the math on paper, but she would later. She realized Serena would owe Mr. Gilley and his sons and grandson quite a sum for their work and gasoline. She would give Serena all she had to help pay them. No doubt Mr. Gilley had used all his gasoline rations for the month also, but she couldn't do anything about that.

When Glenna and Katie arrived at the house, they pulled onto the side of the street by the gate to the fenced-in yard rather than behind Mr. Gilley, because she didn't want to block his truck when he was ready to leave. Katie looked up at the house and asked, wide eyed, "Mummy, are we going to live here?"

"Yes, darling, we are going to live here."

They got out of the car, opened the gate, and were walking up the stone walkway when Serena, followed by Jimmie, came out of the house. Katie squealed when she saw the dog. Serena held him back with her left hand, and when they came up onto the porch, she took Katie's hand in her right as Glenna introduced Katie to "Mrs. Lowell." Serena said, "I am delighted to meet you, Katie, and this is Jimmie. If you let him sniff your hand, you can make friends with him."

Katie did as she was told, then asked if she could pet him. Serena said she could. "He licked me," she said.

"He's telling you he likes you," Serena said. Before the evening was over, Katie and Jimmie were best friends.

"You must be exhausted, Glenna. I have lemonade for everybody. Let's go inside and have some, and then you can go upstairs, and the fellas will arrange the furniture where you want it."

Glenna drank the lemonade quickly because she didn't want to keep the Gilleys any longer than necessary. They had to be tired after all they had done today. Upstairs she found the sofa, chairs, and end table, as well as the kitchen table and chairs and the radio, and her mother's sewing machine in the large open area at the head of the stairs. She told Mr. Gilley that where they had placed everything was fine. Then she went through the rest of the rooms. Just beyond the open space was the first bedroom. Down the hall, it turned to the right, and on the immediate left was the door to the bathroom. Straight ahead about six feet was the door to the other bedroom. She decided this would be Katie's room, because if Katie got up and wandered around, she would have to pass Glenna's room before going downstairs, and Glenna would want to know that. So Glenna directed the men what to take to Katie's room.

One of the men said they would put the beds back together, which reminded Glenna that the jars of screws were in the car. "I'll be right back," she said as she ran down the stairs and out to the car. On her way back inside with the screws, she met Serena, Katie, and Jimmie coming down the hall. Serena said they had been cooking supper, and it was almost ready.

"I have to take these upstairs so they can put the beds back together, and I'll be right back." Glenna delivered the screws, quickly directed where the bed and chiffo-robe were to go, then did the same in Katie's room. She thanked the men for their hard work and went down-stairs, following the sounds of Serena's and Katie's voices to find her way to the breakfast room, where the table had been set, and into the kitchen. "This smells good. What can I do to help?"

"Not a thing except eat my cooking," Serena said. She had prepared fried pork chops and gravy, creamed potatoes, green beans, stewed carrots sweetened with honey, and a pan of biscuits.

After they sat down, Serena said a brief blessing, and they passed the food. Glenna spooned small servings of each dish onto Katie's plate. She cut a pork chop in two and placed half on Katie's plate, then cut it into small pieces. Katie waited patiently until her mother finished before she began to eat.

Serena and Glenna chatted about the day they had had throughout the meal. Katie did not interrupt but sat quietly and ate and drank her milk. When Serena asked if she would care for seconds, Katie said, "No, thank you."

Serena had taught school for a dozen years, and she knew some children would be difficult to live with. Katie was clearly not one of those. She was a sweet, unspoiled, well-mannered child. Serena felt a sense of relief.

When the meal was over, Glenna said, "This meal was a treat, Serena. Thank you."

"This is a special occasion, Glenna, your and Katie's first night here. Besides, I knew you would be tired and hungry after all the work you've done today."

"Speaking of work, Bob Gilley and his sons and grandson have really done some work today. I don't know how much you intend to pay them, but I want to help you with that. I left the rent for the five days we lived at the house this month, but I have the rest."

"You keep that, Glenna. I'll pay the Gilleys. I can afford it. You'll need your money. I imagine you'll have a power bill to pay."

"Yes, but it won't be very much. I'm going to call the power company Monday and have it disconnected immediately."

"That's a good idea. If you don't do that, that Norris man would use your power all month, and you would get the bill. I would love to see his face when he realizes you had the power turned off."

"So would I, but Serena, I really don't feel right about your paying all my moving expenses."

"Glenna, I have considerable resources, most of which I did not earn. I inherited them. I want to share some of those with you. It makes me feel good, and I need that."

"All right. Thank you, Serena."

"You are welcome, Glenna."

When the men had been paid and left, Glenna moved her car behind Serena's car and brought up boxes of her and Katie's clothes. When she got to the bottom of the box of her clothes, she took out the picture of Edo. She put it in the drawer of her nightstand. She decided since she had some money, she would buy a frame for the picture and keep it on her nightstand.

She made her bed, then went to Katie's room and unpacked and put away her clothes and made her bed. She unpacked the towels and washcloths and put them in the cabinet in the bathroom. Then she went downstairs to find Katie, who was sitting in the living room with Serena and Jimmie, listening to the radio. It was past Katie's bedtime, and she was getting sleepy. Glenna had planned to give her a bath but decided against it. They told Serena and Jimmie good night and went upstairs, brushed their teeth, washed, put on their pajamas, said their prayers, kissed Edo, and went to sleep.

Glenna woke up at five o'clock. Katie was still asleep. She got up quietly and found her clean underclothes and bathrobe, went to the bathroom, and drew a bath. This was the first time in her life she had bathed in a real bathtub, and she enjoyed everything about it: sitting in the warm water, turning on the spigot for more hot water, the feel of the smooth surface of the tub on her skin. She hoped she would never again have to heat water on the stove and sit in a cold tin tub to take a bath.

When she returned to the bedroom, soft morning light had begun to replace the dark. Katie was still asleep, her teddy bear on one side and Mamie, her doll, on the other. Glenna sat down at the foot of the bed and watched her sleep, her heart so full of love she thought it might burst. Katie opened her eyes and looked around, then smiled. "I didn't know where I was, Mummy."

"Do you know now?"

"Yes, I'm in Jimmie's house. Where is he?"

"I expect he's downstairs or maybe outside doing his business."

Katie laughed, and Glenna said maybe she had better get up and do her business, and take a bath. "It's Sunday. We need to tell Father O'Malley that we have moved and we'll be coming to Mass every Sunday now."

Later, when they went downstairs, they found Serena in the kitchen. She had made coffee and pancake batter, and the griddle was hot. She asked if they slept well, and they assured her they had, and she had also. Katie asked about Jimmie. "He's outside getting some exercise and probably chasing squirrels. Let's hope he never catches one. He'd get a nasty bite if he did." Serena had already eaten, so Glenna made the pancakes for Katie and herself. As she was doing this, Serena told her when she had time to just begin looking through the cupboards and drawers to see where everything was.

"There are enough leftovers for lunch, and I'll make more biscuits so we don't have to do much cooking today. I bought tomato soup, so we can have that for supper if that suits you. We are going to need to talk about what you like to eat. Of course, with the rationing we will have to eat what we can get. We stock maple syrup at the general store, so I do keep that most of the time for pancakes."

Glenna said, "We have never tasted real maple syrup."

"You'll love it," Serena said as she handed the bottle to Glenna.

Later Glenna and Katie walked to early Mass and afterward told Father O'Malley about the change in their circumstances. He had never met Serena but knew a bit about her because he was acquainted with Amelia. He recognized that this was a great improvement in Glenna's and Katie's lives and was delighted for them.

When they returned to the house, Serena was still there getting ready for church. Glenna told her she would make the biscuits for lunch and heat the leftovers. They changed clothes, and Katie went outside to play with Jimmie. "Do not go outside the fence, Katie," Glenna told her. While they were playing, she found the ingredients, rolling pin, dough board, and a bowl and made the biscuits and set them aside ready to bake.

Then she went through the large kitchen to see where everything else was. Satisfied that she could find what she needed to cook an entire meal, she heated the oven and put the vegetables into small pots ready to heat them. Over the course of the hour, she checked on Katie and Jimmie. On the back porch, Katie had found a ball with his teeth marks, so she had spent some time throwing the ball, which he brought back to her. Then they had wandered around the yard, which had been recently cut.

Glenna decided that Bob Gilley had probably been the one to do this. She had had to mow the grass at her house in The Falls. She would do that by taking off after the lunch rush, running home and cutting the grass, washing up, and running back to Renney's. Her only other choice would have been to mow on Sunday, but that was something she just couldn't do. She did do laundry on Sunday, but the clothesline was hidden from her neighbors' view by the large evergreen trees in the backyard. If she'd had the money, she could have paid someone to help her. She knew she had put herself in that situation. She couldn't blame anyone else, not even Edo, because she could have said no. Well, she would never make that mistake again. She would get her diploma, go to college, get a job, and have money enough to support herself and Katie. She hoped with all her heart that Edo would come back. If he didn't, she had already learned to live with an aching heart, but she would not live without money.

When Serena returned from church, the table was set and lunch was ready. As they ate, Katie told them about throwing the ball to Jimmie and how he found it every time and brought it back to her. Serena said her former neighbor had taught him to do that. Glenna told her she had taken stock of the kitchen and knew where everything was. They talked about the things they liked to eat. Serena mentioned the garden and the vegetables they would can. Glenna had never done any canning and was surprised to learn that Serena knew all about it. Her grandmother Ann Lawrence had taught her, and she had spent many a summer day picking and stringing green beans, shelling peas, cutting corn off the cob, and canning them all. There were apple trees, a pear tree, and a peach tree on the property, and these fruits would need to be dried or canned also.

After lunch, Katie went down for a nap upstairs, and Glenna washed the dishes and put them away. Serena suggested that she show Glenna the house. There had not been time the day before. They started at the front door, where Serena opened the door to the left to reveal a library. "This was my grandfather's study, but everyone was welcome here except when the door was closed. That was the sign that he was doing serious work."

As Serena spoke, Glenna was only half listening, as all these books reminded her of the Avery house where she and Edo had made love. She had to force herself to stop thinking about that night and concentrate on what Serena was saying.

"My great-grandparents William and Jane Lawrence actually started this collection, and then my grandfather Thomas added to it. There are encyclopedias, biographies, autobiographies, nonfiction, history, religion, science, and of course many novels. When you begin your studies, you'll find the books on these shelves helpful. I want you to feel free to use this room and its contents as much as you like."

"This is so unexpected, Serena. It's wonderful. I love to read, but I don't own a single book. Every book I've ever read came from the school library."

"That's true for most people. The only book you'll find in most homes is the Bible. We are lucky to live in a country that supports free public education, and most towns of any size have a public library. The college library here is open to the public."

They walked across the hall to the living room. Glenna had already been in this room briefly. Now Serena showed Glenna the radio, which stood against the wall to the right of the doorway. "You may want to play it while you're down here." Then she pointed out the piano. "This was one of the first baby grands. Great-Grandmother Jane," she said as she pointed to Jane's portrait on the wall behind the piano, "was a talented musician. She owned a grand piano, but it was too large for this space, so she donated it to the college later, and this one replaced it.

"Glenna, I'm sure you understand this is not a toy. I would love to give Katie lessons when she is older, but please tell her now it is off-limits."

"Of course, I'll talk with her about it."

From the living room, they walked through an archway into the dining room, which Serena said they wouldn't use except when they had guests or on special occasions. They continued into the kitchen. "If we find something broken or worn out, we'll replace it. I don't think either of my grandmothers ever threw anything away. If there is something you really need, let me know."

They walked out onto the enclosed back porch, where there were wicker chairs with faded floral cushions. "This was always a comfortable place in warm weather to shell peas or string beans or read or just rest." Then Serena opened the screen door, and they stepped outside. "Let's have a look at our victory garden," she said, and she led Glenna to a fenced-in area beyond but attached to the fenced yard. Serena opened the gate, and they stood outside and gazed at the green shoots breaking through the earth.

Back in the kitchen, as they entered from the porch, Serena opened a door perpendicular to the porch door and led Glenna into the laundry room. There was a large sink for soaking items that were particularly soiled, a washing machine, a sewing machine, and floor-to-ceiling shelves that held laundry and sewing supplies, flower vases, canning jars, and Christmas decorations in boxes labeled "Christmas." An iron and ironing board stood ready to be used. Overhead were metal lines for drying clothes. "This room speaks for itself," Serena said.

As they left the laundry room, Serena pointed out the third door directly across from the porch door. "That goes to the basement. The furnace is down there and by the way your porch swing and rocking chairs also." Then she walked through the kitchen, the breakfast room, and into the hall, where she opened a door to the right. "This is the powder room. When you are working down here and need to go to the bathroom, you won't have to go all the way upstairs to your bathroom."

"Nice," Glenna said.

Down the hall on the right, they walked into Serena's bedroom. "This was my grandparents' room. Now it's mine." It was furnished with a four-poster bed of cherry, night tables on either side, a dressing table, a chaise longue with a table beside it, and a tall floor lamp behind it. Stacks of books lay against the wall. "These are my books. Most belonged to George. I'll find a place for them in the library or have shelves built in here." Then she showed Glenna her huge closet. "When this house was built, ladies' dresses took up a lot of room." As you entered the closet, on the wall to the right hung a seven-foot mirror that reflected everything from your shoes to the tip of the hat you might be wearing. From there, there was a clear path to the bathroom door on the right and, straight ahead, a door to the laundry room.

The remaining wall space featured hanging rods, and above these were shelves where several decorative hatboxes sat. On either end there were built-in boxes, some large and some small. These were for boots and shoes, Serena explained.

"Did you and George have a house like this, Serena?"

"No, our house was about the size of your house in The Falls. No schoolteacher could afford a house like this."

The tour over, Serena said she was going to do some reading and maybe take a nap. Glenna went upstairs to check on Katie, who was still asleep. Then she found the pack of stationery and envelopes she had packed the day before. She went out to the table, took a seat, and wrote her mother a letter to let her know that she and Katie had moved into Serena Lowell's house in St. Claire, that she would be keeping house for Serena, and that the house was beautiful and had three bathrooms (well, only two with a tub, she corrected). She said that Serena had had all their furniture moved into the second floor of the house as her aunt Amelia had moved to Key West and taken all the furniture up there with her. She told Kathleen that she would be working on her high school diploma and might even have a chance to go to college. She told her that Katie was just fine and they hoped that she was too, and they missed her and sent her their love. "Our new address is on the envelope," she added.

Two months later Glenna received a letter from Kathleen:

August 30,1943

Dear Glenna,

Your letter of June 6, was the answer to my prayers. I am so happy that you have the opportunity to finish high school and go to college as you always planned to do, and I am relieved that you will not have to struggle to pay the rent. All those times Serena visited Renney's I was in the kitchen and never met her. Please tell her how much I appreciate what she has done for you and Katie. I will sleep easier now knowing you are in a better place in your life.

Mum is doing well for an eighty-three old woman. In good weather we take a short walk every morning; if the weather is bad we walk around in the house. Some of our neighbors do not have radios so they come to listen to the news and other programs in the evenings. We are thankful that my brothers bought one for Mum before the war. We enjoy the programs and the company.

My sisters visit frequently and often bring their grandchildren with them. I am always happy to see them, but they remind me how much I miss you and and Katie so far away in America.Please write again soon and let me know how things are working out.

Love,
Mum

Chapter 31

FIRST THING MONDAY morning, Glenna called the power company and had the power disconnected immediately. She gave the clerk her new address so they could send her the last bill. Then she called Mr. Wallace at The Falls General Store to tell him she had moved in case she got any mail so he could forward it to her new address, which she gave him. He told her to bring Katie by near her birthday, and he would take another picture. She said she would do that and thanked him. "You have been so kind to us, and so generous, Mr. Wallace. We will miss seeing you."

"And we will all miss you, Miss Glenna," he said.

She and Serena had sat on the porch on Sunday evening and watched Katie and Jimmie play as they made out a grocery list. Now this morning they rode in Serena's car to her general store. Mrs. Carter, the high school principal, had issued a new ration book to Serena to cover her, Glenna, and Katie on Friday. They bought as much as they were allowed of the rationed items, such as Kraft macaroni and cheese, dried beans, stew beef, and sausage, and stocked up on the items not rationed.

On the way home, Glenna told Serena how her father, after he lost his sight, would pull her wagon to the store, put the groceries in the wagon, and pull it home. She would go with him and be his eyes. She had loaned the wagon to her neighbor for her children. Serena said she had a wagon stored in the apartment above the store. She would get that later for Katie.

They had been home only a few minutes when the telephone rang. Mrs. Carter wanted to meet Glenna that afternoon to discuss the plan to allow her to work toward her diploma. An appointment was made for two thirty. They decided to have an easy lunch of macaroni and cheese, black-eyed peas, and corn bread. Glenna quickly made the corn bread batter and put it in the oven, heated a can of the peas, and prepared the macaroni and cheese. Serena suggested that stewed tomatoes would be good with this also, so she opened a can of those and poured the tomatoes into a bowl. They ate lunch, and Serena did the dishes so that Glenna could put Katie to bed for her nap and freshen up for the appointment.

Mrs. Carter was on time. Serena introduced her to Glenna and left them alone in the living room to talk. Glenna said it was very nice to meet her and offered her a seat. Mrs. Carter wasted no time. She asked Glenna why she was so interested in getting her diploma.

Glenna told her that she had always loved school, loved learning, loved to read, but arithmetic had been her favorite subject from the beginning. She enjoyed solving problems and working with numbers. "When my daddy lost his sight, my mother went to work at Renney's, and I spent a lot of time there," Glenna explained. "Sometimes I'd be in the office when Renney was working on her books. I'd beg her to let me do it, but of course she wouldn't. But I knew that's what I wanted to do—become a bookkeeper. To do that, I know I need to learn everything I can about it.

"Besides that, I want an education. I hope to go to college if possible. I want a good job doing what I enjoy and making enough money to support myself and my daughter."

Mrs. Carter told her that several of her teachers would be required to do extra work in order to make this happen, and she needed to know that Glenna was serious about this endeavor. She said that unlike when Glenna was in school, there were now four years of high school beyond eighth grade.

Glenna assured her that she was serious and that she was aware of the fourth year.

They discussed the courses she would need to take. Mrs. Carter said that Glenna would need to call the school in The Falls and request that her transcript be mailed to Mrs. Carter. Glenna said she would do that. She thanked Mrs. Carter.

As soon as Mrs. Carter left, Glenna called the principal in The Falls and requested her transcript be sent to Mrs. Carter.

Two weeks later, Mrs. Carter asked Glenna to come to the school that day. When she arrived, she was surprised that a curriculum had been planned for the two-year courses: English III and IV, General Science (since chemistry and physics would require lab work), World History, Civics, Spanish I, and Bookkeeping II and III. These courses, combined with those she had already taken, would give her the eighteen units required for graduation. She was pleased, but even more pleased to receive all the first-year assignments. "When you have completed a week's worth of assignments, you will turn them in to me, and I will give them to the teachers. You'll receive those back on Monday morning graded.

"At the end of each unit, a test will be required. Serena will need to verify that no help was given. The teachers have all agreed to begin now because they understand that you are probably anxious to get started."

Glenna thanked Mrs. Carter and said, "I appreciate this so much."

When Glenna returned home and told Serena that she was to begin now with her studies, Serena said not to worry, that they would work out ways for her to have time to do the schoolwork. "You could prepare a large meal for lunch, and we can have leftovers for supper. That will free you to study in the afternoons. You do the laundry for yourself and Katie, and I'll do mine. Any time you're in a pinch, I'll look after Katie. It won't be until the vegetables are harvested that it will get rough, but we'll manage. I'll do the shopping." She put a pencil and a sheet of paper on the kitchen counter. "Write down anything we need or will need soon. I'll see to Katie in the afternoon when she finishes her nap, and we will fix supper."

"But Serena, I'm supposed to be working for you."

"Well, I am not going to sit around all day while you do all the housework and cooking and have no time for schoolwork. I want you to succeed. It will be a pleasure to help you do that. Besides, I sleep better when I put in a busy day. It's good for me, so let's don't argue about this."

The truth was that though she liked Glenna and always had, and Katie was a sweet little girl, cooperative and well-mannered, Serena would have preferred to be living alone with Jimmie as her only companion. She could talk to him and express the deep sorrow she continued to feel that George would never come back. Now she had to hold that in.

She also would have preferred to expend all the energy she could muster on the house. Amelia had emptied the upstairs, and Serena could have cleaned, repainted, and planned how to restore and decorate those rooms. But Glenna had now refilled it. Her grandfather's desk needed going through, as well as her grandmother's desk in the living room and the drawers in her bedroom. Cleaning out the kitchen would take a massive effort. And the whole place needed cleaning and painting inside and out.

She had planned to work on all these projects, gardening, and getting her classroom organized before school started. And if she were alone, she could cry anytime she felt the need.

But as much as she would have liked to be alone, she would never go back on her word. Her conscience would never allow that.

Serena went out every morning to weed the vegetable garden and all around the house in the shrubs and the perennial flower beds. She enjoyed the solitude. It gave her time to think uninterrupted. One morning she was in the garden when Katie opened the gate and came into the garden, Jimmie close on her heels. "Katie, Jimmie isn't allowed in here," Serena said as she rushed forward to shoo him out and close the gate.

"Why can't he come in?"

"Because he's liable to step on the plants, and then they won't grow. You know not to do that, but Jimmie would get excited and run all over the place and tear up jack. We would have to replant everything."

"Who is Jack?"

"Oh, nobody. It's just an expression."

Katie was quiet about three seconds, then said, "I thought you weeded yesterday."

"I did. I check for weeds every morning unless it's raining."

"How come?"

"If I check every day, there won't be many, and what few I find will be easy to pull up. If I waited for a week, there would be lots of weeds with big roots, and they would be hard to pull up. I would have a really hard job then."

Katie frowned. "What's wrong with weeds?"

Serena stood up as the teacher in her took over. She recognized that Katie wanted to learn, which thrilled the heart of any good teacher.

"There are three things you need to know about weeds. Number one, the soil these plants are growing in has what are called nutrients. Plants won't grow without nutrients. Nutrients are food for the plants. If weeds grow beside the plants, they steal some of the nutrients from the good plants, and the good plants won't be healthy, and won't produce good vegetables for us to eat.

"Number two. What animal do you think loves to hide in weeds?"

"Snakes."

"That's right, and we surely don't want snakes to set up housekeeping in our garden, do we?

"No, ma'am."

"So I pull the weeds so the snakes know they are not invited.

"Number three. When I come out in the afternoon to look at my garden or walk around the yard to look at the flowers and shrubs and trees, all that beauty lifts my spirits. If the place is covered in weeds, it would make me feel bad."

"Can I pull weeds?"

Serena started to correct her grammar, but then she thought that in this case "can" was correct. "You can if you learn the difference between a weed and a good plant. I'll teach you how to do that." And so began a lesson and a relationship between a sweet little girl and a broken-hearted woman who just really wanted to be left alone.

Soon after this, as Serena walked around in the yard, she looked up at the huge oak tree that had once held a swing. Memories came flooding back of her grandmother and sometimes Amelia pushing her gently in that swing, and later, as she was older, propelling herself, swinging higher and higher. "Katie would love a swing," she thought to herself. "I'll speak to Glenna, and if she is okay with it, I'll call Bob Gilley." A week later the oak tree boasted a new swing.

Chapter 32

THE SUMMER OF '43 was passing quickly. The two women fell into a pattern of sharing the work and Serena looking after Katie more and more, giving Glenna time to read, answer questions, study, and take tests. Thinking ahead, Serena realized that besides Jimmie, Katie had only a teddy bear, a doll, one book, and now the swing to occupy her time and imagination, and soon the garden would demand both Glenna's and her attention.

She remembered her intention to bring the wagon home from the store, and there were other things stored in her childhood bedroom there that Katie would enjoy. One afternoon while Katie napped, Serena walked to the store, and an hour later walked home pulling the wagon, on which were her tea set packed safely in a box and her little table and chairs secured with ropes.

Back home, she moved the breakfast room table and chairs to make room for the little table and chairs, which she cleaned with a damp cloth. Then she unpacked, washed the tea set, and set the table for three. When Katie woke up from her nap and came downstairs with Mamie in her arms as usual, Serena met her at the bottom of the stairs. "I hope you had a nice nap, because you and Mamie and I are going to have a pretend tea party."

"What is that, Miss Serena?"

"Come, I'll show you," she said, and she led Katie to the breakfast room. When Katie saw the little table and chairs, the little cups and saucers and teapot, a smile lit up her face.

"Please take your seats, 'Miss Katie and Miss Mamie,'" Serena said.

Katie carefully placed Mamie in her seat, then took her seat to the right. Serena sat opposite Mamie, and the party began. Serena poured pretend tea from the teapot into each of their cups, hers last of course. Then they pretended to drink tea as Serena told Katie that she had been given this tea set many Christmases ago when she was about Katie's age. "I thought you and Mamie and Teddy might enjoy using it."

"How about Jimmie?"

Serena assumed a haughty accent and, waving her hands as she spoke, said, "No, my deah, Jimmie is entirely too rambunctious to attend a tea party. He would likely upset the table, break all the dishes, and have tea spilled all over the floor." Katie laughed so hard she nearly fell out of the chair. Glenna, coming out of the library, heard the laughter, and came to see what was going on. Serena assumed the accent again and said, "So sorry, my deah, you just had to be heah."

When the party was over, Serena told Katie, "These are real dishes, and they will break, so we must not let Mamie or Teddy drop them." They found a place in a low cabinet to store the tea set. "Any time you want to have a tea party, you may get the things out and set the table."

Serena had explained to Katie that growing up, she had lived in an apartment over the general store, and the tea set had been stored there. Now she said she had brought something else, and she and Katie went out back where the wagon sat. "You can take Mamie and Teddy for a ride. Katie laid the doll in the wagon and began pulling her around the yard. Jimmie ran alongside barking.

"I think Jimmie wants to ride too," Katie said.

But Jimmie would not get in the wagon.

Finally Serena picked him up and put him in the wagon, but when Katie began pulling her passengers, he jumped out.

"Jimmie, don't you want to ride?" Katie asked him. He barked.

"I think he said no, Katie. You get in, and I'll take you for a ride. Let's see what Jimmie does." He ran alongside and barked.

As the garden began to produce, Glenna put her books aside, and she and Serena washed jars, shelled peas, strung green beans, stewed tomatoes, cut corn off the cob, and canned it all. They also dried squash and canned peaches.

Katie entertained herself swinging under the oak tree and giving rides to Mamie and Teddy as Jimmie ran alongside the wagon. She had many tea parties for Mamie and Teddy and could be heard telling them to be careful not to drop their cups. On rainy days, she would "read" to Jimmie her only book, *The Poky Little Puppy*, which she had memorized. She would always show him the pictures.

Glenna would return to her books after supper each night until time to give Katie a bath and put her to bed. Then she would take her schoolwork into her "living room" and sit at the table and work until the need for sleep forced her to stop and go to bed. Not once, even with all the canning she did during the day, did she fail to turn in her assignments on time.

When the summer harvest was finished, Glenna's thoughts turned to Katie's entering kindergarten. She both looked forward to and dreaded this. She knew Katie would enjoy learning and being with other children, and Glenna could use the time at home alone to work on her assignments. But she dreaded the inevitable questions about Katie's father. She could do nothing about that, but she could make certain that Katie was dressed as well as any children in her class.

Toward the end of July one Monday morning, she and Katie walked uptown to the general store, where she bought patterns, material, and notions. She also bought yarn to knit Katie two sweaters, one red and the other navy blue. When she was here earlier in the summer with Serena, she had noticed that the store carried picture frames, and she chose one for Edo's picture.

As soon as they got home, she washed the material because any shrinking it was going to do she wanted done before she did any sewing with it. She hung it up to dry and went upstairs with the package containing the picture frame inside. Glenna had little to no control over the situation with Edo. She didn't know where he was or how to reach him, but she loved him and had kept her promise to be true to him. She had not had the money to properly frame his picture, but now she did and she would enjoy the process before her. She took out the glass and, in the bathroom, washed it and dried it with a lint-free cloth. She took Edo's picture out of the drawer, laid it on the table in her living room, and centered the glass on top of it, and then, with a pencil, drew an outline all around the glass. She removed the glass, cut the lines she had drawn, inserted the glass into the frame, laid Edo's picture against the glass, placed the cardboard filler on the back of his picture, and inserted the back piece into the frame. She lifted out the support piece and carried the picture to her bedside table and set it on top. She stood back and looked at Edo's smiling face, no longer hidden in a drawer but in its proper place where she and Katie could see him throughout the day. She was pleased.

When July became August, Glenna noticed a change in Serena. She was quieter and spent more time in her bedroom. Glenna knew the reason. The first anniversary of George's death was coming up. She knew he had died in August but didn't remember the day. She hated to bring it up, but to ignore it felt wrong.

One night after Katie went to bed, she went downstairs to do a bit of sewing on the jumper she was making for Katie. Serena was sitting in the living room with an open book on her lap, but she was staring straight ahead.

"What are you reading?"

"I was trying to read this...but it's no use. I can't concentrate."

"You're thinking about George."

Serena looked at Glenna. "Yes. It will soon be a year ago, you know."

"What was the date when he died?"

"August the ninth. It was a Sunday. I went to church that day, and in God's house, as hymns were sung and the minister was speaking, as the organ was played, I prayed that God would protect my husband. I felt that He would listen better there in His house. But even as I was praying, the Japanese were bombing that ship and killing my husband. And he ended up in the bottom of that big ocean.

"It would be some comfort if I could have buried him, put up a stone marker with his name and dates, could take flowers to say I remember you, I loved you. Now it's like he never lived. I want people to know that George lived, that he was a good and brave man."

"I don't know any reason you couldn't put a marker somewhere, even on an empty grave."

The next day Serena went to see the superintendent of city properties. She knew that her grandfather had purchased burial lots for his family but did not remember how many. She was told there were a total of eight, and four had been used. She discussed her desire to have a monument of some kind for George. This man knew what had happened to George. He showed her pictures of ledgers that some people had placed over graves of especially prominent people. She did not feel that this was what she wanted or what George would have wanted, but she did want to remind people of his service to the country. The superintendent suggested a smaller ledger. "Go home and write out what you want to say, then come back and see me. I'll help you make the arrangements."

Serena thought first she should write to Amelia and tell her what she wanted to do and make sure her aunt had no objections. Amelia wrote back and said to save plot number five for her, and suggested Serena use number six for George, seven for herself, and eight for her second husband, "because you're too young to never marry again."

Serena followed Amelia's suggestion, though she had no intention of marrying again. The last plot would remain vacant, she was certain. On a cold November day, with the wind blowing snow, the ledger was laid. Underneath the carved United States Navy seal were the words:

IN MEMORY

Of

GEORGE JOSEPH LOWELL

OCTOBER 2, 1902 – AUGUST 9, 1942

BELOVED HUSBAND and TEACHER

DIED IN SERVICE TO HIS COUNTRY

and

LOST at SEA

She had stopped at the florist and bought a spray of pine with cones and a red bow, which she laid at the top of the ledger, then stood at the foot and read the words. She told George how much she loved him and missed him. She would come often, bring flowers, and talk to him. She would tell him about moving to St. Claire, about Jimmie and Glenna and Katie, about school, and always how much she missed him.

* * *

When Glenna finished making Katie's clothes for school, she took her back to the store for a pair of shoes, socks, and new underclothes. She had kept the yellow rain slicker and boots she had when she started school, and those, though a bit large for Katie now, would do fine for a year or two. Katie was beside herself with excitement over her new clothes and going to school. In good weather, she would walk with Serena to school. On rainy or very cold days, Serena would drive them. Katie would stay in Serena's classroom until school began each day and return to Serena's classroom after school until they returned home.

The issue with Katie's father did not come up. Perhaps it was because of Katie's close connection with Serena, who came from a prominent St. Claire family and was the owner of the general store. Serena was respected, and she accepted Glenna and Katie. If there was talk, it was discreet and did not filter down to the children.

Serena did not just accept Glenna and Katie. As time went by, she grew genuinely fond of them. She had returned to teaching seventh grade, always with its challenges, but ones she met with stern kindness. When she and Katie returned home each day, they were met with the pleasant aroma of supper. Even with the rationing of butter, oil, and most cheese, Glenna prepared hearty meals. Sometimes it was chicken and dumplings with a little chicken and a lot of dumplings, or meatballs with more bread than meat. Often it was Kraft macaroni and cheese. Always there were the vegetables they had canned the previous summer, and sometimes a dessert sweetened with honey, corn syrup, or maple syrup. Whatever it was, Serena was grateful to come home to a warm meal and pleasant company.

Now that Glenna had more time during the day for her studies, she would join Serena and Katie and Jimmie in the front room after supper to listen to the news and other programs on the radio. They would laugh together at *Amos n' Andy*, listen spellbound to *The Adventures of the Thin Man*, or enjoy the concerts presented by The Bell Telephone Hour. During these programs, Katie often colored in the coloring book Glenna bought her.

Katie was always bathed and in bed by eight o'clock. Glenna would read to her from Serena's book of Mother Goose or *The Poky Little Puppy*. She continued to sleep with her mother, but as time passed, she spent more time in her room and began taking naps in there most of the time. Glenna wisely did what she could to make the room attractive. Pink was Katie's favorite color, so with Serena's permission, she had painted the room pink. Katie loved it. Only the blackout curtains pulled at night spoiled this very feminine décor.

One day as Katie looked out the window, she saw a man walk up to the house next door. Katie knew no one lived there. She ran downstairs and into the breakfast room, where Serena and Glenna were sitting, and told them what she had seen and her hope that the man was moving in and might have a daughter her age.

Serena said, "Katie, I'm sorry to disappoint you. You saw Mr. Barnes. He looks after the house for the owner. He checks it over every few weeks just to see that everything is all right."

Then followed a barrage of questions: "Who is the owner? Why doesn't he live there? Does he have a daughter?"

Serena explained that the owner was Ben Hadley, who had inherited the house when his parents died. "He doesn't live here because he's in the air force. All he ever wanted to do was fly. And now that's what he does. When he retires, he'll probably come back here to live, but he doesn't have any children." A dejected Katie returned to her room.

But Glenna asked Serena if she had known Ben.

"Oh yes. He was five years older than me. I was born in this house so that Amelia and my grandmother could look after mother and me for several weeks. When Mrs. Hadley brought Ben over to see the baby—me—I was told he took one look and said, 'She's a squirt,' and after that he always called me 'Squirt.'

"As I got older, I spent most afternoons here, and I would see him outside, and I'd go over and try to insinuate myself into whatever Ben and his friends were playing. They didn't seem to mind much. They would let me have a turn at bat, and whoever was pitching would throw a ball easy for me to hit, and if I actually hit it, they would pretend they couldn't catch it or, if one did, would drop it, and I would make it to first base, then second, then third, then home. I'd be so proud, but eventually I caught on to what they were doing.

"I told my daddy what they were doing, so he took a bat and ball out of the store, and after the store closed, he'd take me out back and give me lessons on how to keep my eye on the ball, how to hold the bat, and when to swing. Bless his heart, he was sixty years old and had worked all day in the store. He must have been so tired. But I learned, and one day when I went over to play with Ben and his friends, and the pitcher pitched an easy ball to me, I smacked the ball over their heads and into the woods, and I made a real home run. That was the proudest day of my nine-year-old life."

"Did you keep playing with them?"

"For a while, but they started throwing hardballs to me after that, and I did pretty well, but I lost interest in playing ball. By the time I was eleven, I had developed a huge crush on Ben, who was sixteen then. When I learned he had a girlfriend, I was crushed. He eventually married that girl."

"So he's married but has no children."

"No. They divorced. He joined the air force right after high school, and they married a year after that. But she didn't like the military life, moving around the country or coming back here when he was stationed somewhere she couldn't go. So they divorced, and he never married again, unless he has since I saw him last when he came home for his mother's funeral. That was before Pearl Harbor. That was two years ago. A lot can happen in two years," she said almost to herself.

Fall was always a busy time. There was school, of course, and the three residents at the big house on the hill overlooking St. Claire and the river were busy with school. Then there was Halloween, which was celebrated as a fall festival at the school. Children dressed in costumes their mothers made gathered to bob for apples, go through the haunted house constructed by high school students, buy and eat the penny treats their mothers made, and finally enter the Best Costume contests for each grade. The prizes for the winners were cupcakes made by home economics high school students.

Katie liked the nursery rhyme "Little Miss Muffet" and wanted to go as Miss Muffet. But Serena said if it were her, she would go as the spider. Katie laughed and ran around imitating the scary spider. She decided she would be the spider.

So Glenna rummaged through the old clothes Serena had found in her grandparents' closet and found several black dresses. From those, she made a costume consisting of a padded head with holes for Katie's eyes, nose and mouth, and a fitted bodysuit, to which she attached six legs filled with cotton saved from a raggedy old quilt. To hide Katie's hands, she made black gloves.

Serena found a pair of her grandfather's black socks. She cut off the toes and sewed a new seam to fit Katie's feet. Katie would wear her brown shoes, so she would be black from head to toe. Serena took her picture before they left for the festival.

Needless to say, Katie won Best Costume for the kindergarten class. She offered to share her cupcake with Glenna and Serena, but they declined. Later, Katie commented that the cupcake was good, but not as good as Renney's.

Chapter 33

HALLOWEEN WAS BARELY over when plans were laid for Thanksgiving. Glenna asked Serena if it would be possible to invite Mrs. Oglesby, who had kept her for a while when she was a child and had also kept Katie until they moved here. Serena thought it a good idea and offered to give up her bed so Mrs. Oglesby wouldn't have to climb the stairs. Serena suggested they invite Father O'Malley if he did not have other plans. They had become acquainted while shopping at the general store, and Serena found him to be a pleasant and interesting person. He had told her how pleased he was that she had given Glenna an opportunity to complete her education. He said he didn't worry so much about Glenna and Katie anymore. Both he and Mrs. Oglesby accepted the invitation.

Serena had her store manager, Jacob Brooks, save a turkey for them. (Jacob was a local fellow and would be having Thanksgiving with his family.)

School let out at eleven on Wednesday, the day before Thanksgiving, and Glenna and Katie drove to The Falls to pick up Mrs. Oglesby. She was ready and waiting with her little bag packed. Katie ran to the door and hugged Mrs. Oglesby. It was a sweet reunion. Glenna had decided she would visit Renney and Gloria Friday when she returned Mrs. Oglesby home, but this day they had to get back home. All the way to St. Claire, Katie chatted to Mrs. Oglesby about Jimmie, her tea parties, her spider costume, and kindergarten. Once inside the house, Katie asked her what she had been doing in the months they had not seen each other.

Mrs. Oglesby listed reading, knitting, listening to the radio, and taking naps.

"When do you take naps, Mrs. Oglesby?"

"Whenever I feel like it, Katie," she said, and they both laughed.

Mrs. Oglesby thanked Serena for inviting her to share the holiday with them.

Serena said, "We are so happy you could join us. Thank you for coming."

For lunch, Glenna had made a pot of vegetable soup with a bit of beef left over and frozen from a roast they had eaten some weeks before. As they ate, Mrs. Oglesby told them that at Thanksgiving she was always reminded about growing up on a cotton farm in South Carolina. She said she would never forget picking cotton and how it pricked her fingers, and she always remembered to be thankful that she didn't have to pick cotton anymore.

After Katie went down for her nap, Mrs. Oglesby told Glenna that on the Monday after she moved, Mr. Norris came to her house. "He was as mad as an old wet hen. He said you left with no notice whatsoever, that you owed him the entire month's rent, and he wanted to know where you'd moved.

"I told him I couldn't tell him that, and he said, 'Do you expect me to believe that?' and he insisted I tell him where you were, but I didn't. He said he would find out one way or another. I said, 'Mr. Norris, Glenna went to work for a very prominent person. If I were you, I'd let sleeping dogs lie.'"

"Thank you, Mrs. Oglesby."

"You don't have to thank me. I enjoyed it. Now tell me, how have you been?"

Glenna told her that she was studying at home and working on finishing high school. So far she had made straight As and hoped to complete the junior year by Christmas. "Then I'll start on the final year's work and hopefully be finished by June. After that, I plan to take some college courses in bookkeeping."

"Glenna, I am so proud of you. I know your mama must be too. Do you hear from her often?"

"We write back and forth, but the mail is slow because of the war. But yes, she is very pleased about what I'm doing. It's what she always wanted for me."

While Mrs. Oglesby took a nap, Serena and Glenna made pumpkin pies. After supper they all gathered around the radio to listen to the news and the programs that followed.

The next morning, Serena prepared stewed apples from those they had dried in September. Then she fried fatback and made gravy while Glenna made a large pan of biscuits and a pot of coffee. Katie entertained Mrs. Oglesby, showing her all the pictures she had colored in her coloring book.

After breakfast, Glenna put the turkey in the oven while Serena did the breakfast dishes. They worked together preparing the candied sweet potatoes, green beans, stuffing, and more biscuits. They put the padding on the dining room table and covered it with the tablecloth Serena had ironed the day before. Then they set the table with Serena's grandmother's china and silver, which she had washed the day before. Serena placed washed, dried, and shined apples in a pretty crystal bowl in the center of the table. She would send the apples home with Father O'Malley and Mrs. Oglesby, keeping one each for Glenna, Katie, and herself.

Father O'Malley arrived promptly at one o'clock with a jar of cranberry relish he had ordered from a store in Richmond. "Oh, Father, thank you. This is perfect," Serena said. She introduced him to Mrs. Oglesby, but they remembered they had met years ago when Glenna's dad died. As they got reacquainted, Serena went to find a small crystal bowl for the relish.

Soon they were all seated at the table. Father O'Malley asked the blessing, and at Serena's request, he carved the turkey. The food was excellent and conversation pleasant. Mrs. Oglesby shared how she and her husband had come to live in The Falls. Mr. Oglesby worked for a company that sold machinery and parts for textile mills, and the mill in St. Claire was part of his territory. He grew very fond of the little village, its cool weather in summer and the quiet, and the lovely views. He told her he wanted to retire there. She said it was not her first choice, but she went along with it, and they bought a little house, and he soon retired. They joined the church and got acquainted with the villagers, raised a garden and grew flowers, and ate supper at Renney's every Friday night. Sometimes they went to concerts at the Jane. Then Mr. Oglesby got sick and died, and she had been alone for ten years.

"I have a sister in South Carolina. She says we should live together in The Falls in summer and in South Carolina in the winter. Of course the truth is she would never leave her daughter and grandchildren for the summer. They live just down the road from her."

The conversation then turned to Father O'Malley, but as he talked about his growing up, Serena's mind was stuck on Mrs. Oglesby's situation. The feelings of loneliness and sadness that lay just below the surface threatened to overcome her. Only her responsibility as hostess forced her attention back to Father O'Malley.

After the meal, Glenna took Katie upstairs for her nap, then rejoined the others. They had all insisted on helping to clear the table and put the food away. Father O'Malley took Jimmie outside for a walk around the yard, but the cold soon drove them back inside. They and Mrs. Oglesby settled themselves by the fire in the front room while Serena and Glenna washed the dishes. When they finished and joined their guests, they found Mrs. Oglesby and Jimmie fast asleep and Father O'Malley sitting with his eyes closed but insisting he was awake. They chatted quietly until he admitted he needed to go home and take a nap. Mrs. Oglesby woke up as he was leaving with a small bag of apples. She excused herself to finish her nap on Serena's bed.

Glenna made coffee, and she and Serena, now revived, sat and talked. Serena told Glenna how sad she'd felt as Mrs. Oglesby talked about all the years she had been alone after her husband died. Glenna admitted this had made her feel sad also. "Of course, I have Katie, but she will grow up, and I could be all alone. I do plan to have a job, but to work all day and go home to an empty house, well, that's not something I want." She then told Serena how she had promised God to always be true to Edo. "What if he never comes back, and I never know whether he is dead or alive? What if I marry someone else and he turns up? I can't stand to even think of that."

Serena said, "Glenna, you were sixteen years old when you made that promise. I don't think God would hold you to that. We are human, and God is forgiving. And surely there is some way to find out if he's alive."

"If there is, I don't know what it is. Mum tried. Father O'Malley tried. We traced him to Charleston, but the trail went cold."

Serena didn't reply, and they were quiet for a minute or two. Finally Glenna asked, "What about you, Serena? I know it's been only a little over a year, but you're young, with most of your life ahead of you. Do you imagine yourself being alone from now on?"

"Really all I've thought about most of the time is how desperately I miss George. But since June, when you and Katie came into my life, I haven't been able to dwell on that nearly as much. I thank you for that. Now I'll be doing something, schoolwork or tending to Katie or planning a meal, and it will hit me out of the blue that George is gone and he's not coming back, and it feels almost as shocking as the moment I received that terrible telegram. I really hadn't thought much about the future until today, when Mrs. Oglesby told us about being alone all these years. I was genuinely relieved to hear she has a sister. But it made me realize that I don't just dread living without George. I don't want to live alone for the rest of my life."

A few minutes later, they heard Mrs. Oglesby coming down the hall. Serena got up and said, "We're still in here having coffee. May I fix you a cup?"

"Only half a cup, with a little cream or milk, please." She came in and sat down in the chair near where Glenna was adding a few pieces of wood to the fire.

"Were you able to get back to sleep?"

"Oh yes, but I've slept enough for now. I don't want to miss the opportunity to enjoy good company. Is Katie still asleep?"

"Yes, it was later than usual for her nap. I expect she'll sleep another hour or so."

"You've done a wonderful job with her, Glenna. She's so sweet. I've really missed her."

Serena handed her the coffee. "Thank you, dear."

Serena freshened Glenna's coffee and her own and returned the pot to the kitchen. When she returned. she said, "Mrs. Oglesby, I'd like to ask you a question. You said earlier The Falls was not your first choice for a place to retire. What was your first choice?"

"Oh, I didn't want to move at all. We lived in a bustling little city down the mountain. There were textile mills, a furniture factory, lots of businesses, places to shop, many churches, a good library, and a community theater. I belonged to the garden club. We had a number of friends. We didn't have children—I wanted to adopt one or two, but Arthur wouldn't consider it. But I kept busy, taught Sunday school to the little folks. We were Presbyterians. I'd have liked to stay right there, do some traveling but not move.

"Arthur brought me up here to The Falls a few months before he retired. It is a pretty place, a nice little village, but I was appalled that he wanted to live there. There's nothing there, one Methodist church. The Methodists are as bad as the Baptists. They find sin in everything. There's one store and of course Renney's. We came up here to St. Claire, and while he visited the mill, I walked all over the place. When he finished at the mill and we got back in the car, I said, 'Why don't we move here, Arthur? There's the river. You can fish, and the college. A college town always has interesting people and concerts and speakers.' But he said he wanted to get away from the hustle and bustle. So we went back to The Falls and looked at a house that was for sale. Then we went to Renney's to discuss what we could do to improve it. I was heartsick, but I felt I had no choice but to go along with what he wanted.

"So we moved, and we began going to church, and we met the Averys and became friends with them. They were a bit older than we were, but it didn't matter. We had a lot in common, especially gardening. I tried to start a gardening club, but Lilah Avery and I would have been the only members. Then Katie began staying with me. I miss her terribly. She was such a joy, but I couldn't keep up with her. If I could sell my house, I'd kiss The Falls goodbye. But who would want it?"

"Have you tried to sell it?" Serena asked.

"No, I wouldn't know how to go about it."

"The first thing to do is have it appraised so you know what it is worth and what price to ask for it. Then you can advertise it in the paper. Of course there is a real estate broker here in St. Claire. You could turn it over to him. When he sells it, he gets a small percentage of the selling price, and you keep the rest unless there is some money owed on the property. That would be paid first, and you get what's left."

"There's nothing owed on it. Arthur had a good job, and we had a nice home, but he was tight with money. He put half of every paycheck in a savings account, and we managed on the remainder. When he bought the house in The Falls, he withdrew every penny from that savings account. He paid cash for the house and kept the rest of the money in a metal box so it would be handy to pay for the improvements. This was 1928. It was '29 when our house sold, and he put most of the money from that sale in the bank here. When the crash came a few months later and the banks failed, we lost most of that money. I had always wanted to go to the coast. I've never seen the ocean. We had some money in the metal box, but we had to live on that because Arthur was no longer working. We felt sorry for ourselves at first. We regretted we didn't put all that money in the box. But we looked around and saw what other people were going through, and we decided to be grateful for what we had.

"Arthur built a henhouse and fenced it in, and he raised chickens, so we always had eggs and occasionally fried chicken. The preacher's wife is feeding my chickens and gathering the eggs while I'm here. And we raised a big garden, and we bought milk and butter from the Averys. They kept a cow.

"After Arthur died and Mr. Roosevelt insured savings accounts, I put the money that was left in the box into a savings account where it makes a little interest. I have to take out a little to pay property taxes, but other than that, I leave that money where it is. I get a Social Security check every month, and it covers what I have to buy at the store and the electricity bill. I can't complain. I could be much worse off. But I do believe I'd like to see that real estate man you mentioned tomorrow."

The next morning after breakfast, Serena called Mr. Todd at Todd Properties and explained the situation. He agreed to accompany Glenna as she took Mrs. Oglesby back home. He would look over the property, take measurements, and work up a market analysis. She told him she would pay him for his work but not to mention this to Mrs. Oglesby. He agreed.

Later at Mrs. Oglesby's, he went from room to room measuring and making notes. Mrs. Oglesby showed him a copy of the plat, which indicated the property was 3.4 acres. He looked over the land, the spring, and the chicken house, noting the fence.

While Mr. Todd was busy at Mrs. Oglesby's, Glenna and Katie went to Renney's and visited with Renney and Gloria, who shared that she was dating the new science teacher at The Falls High School. He was deferred from the military due to asthma.

The next day, Mr. Todd called Serena to say he had completed his analysis. He told her all the things he had considered and said if he were to list the house, he would price it at $4,200. Serena visited his office later and paid him for his work. She also mailed a letter to Mrs. Oglesby with the results of Mr. Todd's analysis.

A week later, Serena received a letter from Mrs. Oglesby, who said she wanted to talk with her sister over the Christmas holidays before she made the final decision. She thanked Serena for all her help and for having her for Thanksgiving, saying, "I enjoyed it so much."

Chapter 34

CHRISTMAS 1943 WOULD be the second Christmas Serena had spent without George. Last year she had spent the holiday here with Amelia and Carole, and they had done their best to help her get through it. But it had felt like someone had stabbed her heart with a sharp knife. This terrible pain threatened to return as memories came flooding back. But this was the first Christmas Serena would spend with a child, and it didn't matter the child was not her own. She had come to feel something like an aunt to Katie, and she sincerely wanted to make the holiday special for her, and also for Glenna.

Over the past six months, Serena had come to admire Glenna. She was a good mother to Katie. Glenna was busy with housework, cooking, and her schoolwork, but she managed to keep Katie on a schedule: mealtimes, nap times, bedtime, and story time. Serena knew this helped a child feel secure. Also, Glenna was a tenacious worker, well organized and dependable, and she was good company, with a pleasing personality and a sense of humor.

Serena could find no fault with Glenna except for her foolish belief that Katie's father would someday appear. Serena remembered the first time she had taken Katie upstairs for her nap because Glenna was working on an especially difficult assignment. There on the nightstand was a framed sketch of a young man. "That's my daddy," Katie had said.

"He's very handsome," Serena had replied.

It was really none of her business, but she hoped Glenna wasn't leading Katie to believe that her daddy would show up someday. Heavens, he could be dead, or married to someone else, and have other children. Serena feared that heartbreak lay ahead for Glenna and Katie. And heartbreak was something Serena knew all too well.

Serena steeled herself to put aside her sorrow and concentrate on making Christmas a joyful season for her little family. Though she could afford to buy lots of presents for Glenna and Katie, she knew this would be embarrassing for Glenna, so she had a chat with Jacob Brooks and asked him to be especially attentive when Glenna shopped for groceries each week. If she really admired something in particular, he should write it down and let her know so she could get it for her for Christmas. Serena had noticed that Glenna's shoes were badly worn, so she was not surprised when Jacob told her that Glenna had tried on a pair and asked if he ever put them on sale at a reduced price. He told her no, but when she left, he took the shoes and set them aside. Serena bought them, of course, and placed them in the trunk of her car. She also bought two Golden Books, *The Three Little Kittens* and *The Little Red Hen*, which she also stored in the trunk. She let Glenna know so she wouldn't also buy these for Katie.

Glenna bought a set of colorful blocks, each with a letter of the alphabet, because at kindergarten the children were learning the alphabet, and Katie was thrilled that she had already memorized it perfectly. With the blocks, she could learn to spell words as well as build things. Glenna had also laid away a toy stove for Katie. Years ago, she had made a stocking for her, and she would fill it with peppermints, chocolate drops, peanut butter bars, an orange, and an apple.

Serena had placed an order with Jacob for a fresh ham and would buy cranberries for a cranberry and apple salad. They would use the vegetables they had canned and make pumpkin pies for dessert. For Jimmie, they would save a soup bone.

During the weeks before, they took advantage of every opportunity to celebrate the season. There were concerts performed by both the high school and the college choruses, Dickens's *A Christmas Carol* by the college players and local children, and a performance of *The Messiah* by the combined choirs of the Catholic and nondenominational churches. Both churches held Christmas Eve services also.

Before *A Christmas Carol* was presented, Serena remembered her mother had told her all about the play before she saw it for the first time, and understanding the plot had made watching the play much more enjoyable for her. When she suggested they do the same for Katie, Glenna agreed, and on the afternoon before the play, they gathered by the fire, and Serena told Katie, "Charles Dickens wrote the book *A Christmas Carol* exactly one hundred years ago in December 1843 in England." Katie already knew about England, where her grandmother had once worked.

Serena told Katie that the story was set on Christmas Eve and Christmas Day, that it was very cold and snowy, and that people then had no central heat, only fireplaces to warm their houses and offices. She named and described the main characters and explained the plot: Scrooge's dead partner, Marley, comes back as a spirit to warn Scrooge he must change his miserly ways and would be visited by three spirits to help him do that.

Katie wanted to know if the story was true. Serena explained that it was not true, that it was fiction, or made up, but she said, "There is always some truth in good fiction."

Katie wanted to know about the spirits and if they were real. Serena and Glenna assured her spirits and ghosts were not real. Katie wanted to know if Scrooge changed his ways, but they said, "You'll have to see the play to find out what happens."

During the play, when the ghost of Christmas future revealed that Tiny Tim had died, Katie cried, and Glenna held her and whispered, "This happens only if he doesn't get the treatment he needs. Let's see what happens." At the end, when Scrooge and Tiny Tim were shown happily walking together, Katie was greatly relieved.

When Glenna turned in her final exams, she received the good news that she had made all As and completed eleventh grade. Serena took them out to eat at the College Café, where they all ordered hot dogs and milkshakes.

Christmas fell on a Saturday, so there was no school the week before Christmas and none the week after Christmas. As the weather had grown colder that fall, Serena had taken several walks in the woods behind the house and found a pretty cedar she thought would be a perfect Christmas tree. She later returned with a brush and a small can of red paint and painted small red marks on the trees along the path to the cedar.

By December 20, several snows had fallen and, as usual on the mountain, had stuck around. On this cold day, the three decided to brave the elements and find a Christmas tree. Wrapped from head to toe, they set out into the woods, Jimmie leading the way but veering off whenever a squirrel caught his attention. Katie ran ahead and found several trees she liked, and Serena would say, "Yes, that's a nice one. We'll keep that one in mind," until they came to the cedar.

Katie ran to it, exclaiming, "This is the best one!"

Serena and Glenna, who had caught on to the red marks, agreed. Glenna said, "Katie, you found the best tree." She and Serena took turns sawing it down and together, one in front and one in back, carried it through the woods and to the house, where a bucket of water waited on the back porch. Glenna made hot chocolate sweetened with honey, and they sat at the table to enjoy this and discuss their adventure.

Later, after lunch while Katie took her nap, Serena and Glenna set the tree up in the stand to the left of the arch between the front room and the dining room. They checked the lights Serena had brought down from the attic and found them all working, so they strung them on the tree, stood back to take a look, and decided they had done a good job. Serena laid the white cloth around the bottom to hide the stand and simulate snow where later the presents would sit.

They decided to wait until Katie woke up to decorate the tree. Glenna had stored her ornaments in the attic and wanted to suggest using them, but this was Serena's house, and no doubt she had expensive store-bought ornaments she would want to use. Except for the glass red balls, all Glenna's ornaments were homemade. But as Serena sat on the sofa and looked through her ornaments, she said, "I'm not sure about some of these." Glenna looked up from the book she was reading. "These glass ones might not survive if Jimmie gets excited and wags his tail near the tree. Also, I wonder if the small limbs will hold them." Then she held up a red ball. "These haven't aged well." She looked over at Glenna. "Did you bring any ornaments with you?"

"Yes, but they're mostly all homemade."

"There's nothing wrong with homemade. Why don't you bring them down?"

"All right." She put down *Little Women* and went upstairs. When she returned, she set down the box and began showing Serena the white stars her mother had knitted and the angels with knitted wings. There were also Santas, snowmen, and Christmas trees.

"These are wonderful, Glenna. I knew your mother knitted, but I would never have thought about knitting ornaments. They're really lovely."

Glenna beamed with pride. "I'm glad you like them."

Serena packed away her ornaments except for a few red balls that were in the best shape.

When Katie woke up and came down, she was eager to help decorate the tree. When they finished, Glenna turned on the lights, and they all agreed it was beautiful. They sat by the fire and listened to the radio, and Serena thought about George, and Glenna thought about Edo, and Katie thought about the baby Jesus and Santa Claus.

The following day, they went back to the woods and cut spruce from several trees, then returned to the house, where Serena and Glenna made six sprays, each with a red bow. Then Serena drove them to the city cemetery, where they cleaned the snow off the markers and George's ledger and placed a spray on each one. Then they drove to The Falls and laid the last spray on Charlie's grave.

On Christmas Eve, Serena went to her church for the eleven o'clock service, then hurried home so that Glenna could attend the midnight Mass.

The next morning, Serena was the first one up. She let Jimmie out, then fed him and made coffee and pancake batter. Soon she heard squeals coming from the front room. She carried her coffee to the tree, where she found Katie examining her stove. "Look, Aunt Serena, look what Santa brought me—a stove!"

Glenna was sitting on the rug grinning and enjoying her daughter's delight. Serena sat down and felt something she hadn't felt in a long time: happiness. Katie soon discovered the wooden blocks painted in bright letters. Serena asked Katie to find the K and set it aside, then the A, then the T, I, and E. "Do you know what that spells?"

Katie studied it for just a moment and said, "Katie!"

Glenna handed Serena a box. "This is from Katie and me."

Serena had not expected anything but was delighted to find in the box a blue hat with a black ribbon and a short blue veil. "Oh, this is just lovely. Thank you. I must try it on." She went into the hall, where a mirror sat above a chest. "It fits just right. I love it, girls," she said as she returned to the front room. "I'm going to wear it tomorrow to church."

Then Serena presented Glenna her present: the shoes she had tried on in the store. "I really wanted these. I really needed these. Thank you, Serena."

"You're welcome. I believe I see another present under the tree. It's for you, Katie, from me."

"For me?"

"Yes, for you."

Katie carefully unwrapped the paper and opened the box to find the two Golden Books. She was beside herself and asked Serena to read them to her.

"How about we have pancakes first. I am starving."

"Okay."

The day that followed was one of eating, cooking, reading, eating some more, cleaning up, napping, listening to the radio, and playing with Jimmie.

When Katie was finally tucked in bed for the night, Glenna joined Serena by the fire. "I know this hasn't been easy for you, but I want you know how much I appreciate all you've done to make this a wonderful Christmas for us."

"Glenna, if it weren't for you and Katie, I'd have been alone today. I wouldn't have even celebrated Christmas. It would have just been another day without George to try to get through. So thank you for taking a chance, uprooting all you'd ever known, and moving here with someone you barely knew. Having you and Katie here has been good for me. I hope it's been good for you."

"Serena, of course it's been good for us. If you hadn't suggested this, Mrs. Oglesby might have taken us in, but I'd have lost all my furniture, and it would have been temporary at best. I would have been still stuck at Renney's with no future. You've given us a wonderful place to live and a future with promise. I am so grateful."

"Then I think we can agree this arrangement of ours has been good for both of us."

Chapter 35

IN JANUARY, MRS. Oglesby wrote to say that she and her sister had agreed that she should sell her house, move in with her sister, and share expenses. On a Saturday, Serena and Katie drove to The Falls to see Mrs. Oglesby. Glenna was busy with her new school assignments so did not go with them. Serena suggested that she take the market analysis that had all the important information about the property home with her and make advertisement sheets to be posted at Renney's and the general stores in both The Falls and in St. Claire. Serena took photographs of the house and property. Mrs. Oglesby said she would ask the Methodist minister to be with her anytime someone wanted to see the house.

Back in St. Claire, Serena took the roll of film, which held photos she had taken at Christmas as well as of Mrs. Oglesby's house, to the drugstore to be sent off and developed. Then she went home and began work on the advertisement sheet. Mrs. Oglesby said that most of the furniture would stay, and they had gone from room to room to estimate the worth of each piece. All were of high quality and in excellent condition. They added $800 to the recommended price of the house and land.

On Monday, with the principal's permission, Serena copied the advertisement sheets and paid for the paper. A week later, the photos came back, and Serena took them and the sheets to Mrs. Oglesby. She was pleased and told Serena to go ahead and post one with photos at her store in St. Claire. Mrs. Oglesby would ask Renney and Mr. Wallace to post the others.

In February, Katie turned six years old. Glenna made a cake, and even Jimmie was allowed a piece. They all laughed as he held his paw in his dish while he licked up every crumb.

In March, they donated all the aluminum cans they had saved to the community can drive to provide ammunition for the troops and, in April, all the paper they had saved for the paper drive.

In May, Bob Gilley came with his mule and plow and plowed the garden. Serena planted the seeds she had saved from last year. Glenna was busy completing her work and studying for her final exams. She had done nine months' work in five months. At the end of the month, Mrs. Carter personally delivered her high school diploma. Glenna sat down at the desk in the library and wrote thank-you notes to Mrs. Carter and each teacher who had generously gone out of their way to make this happen. Then she wrote a letter to her mother with the good news.

On June first, Serena took Glenna, Katie, and Mrs. Oglesby to Renney's for supper and to share the news of her graduation with Renney and Gloria. As it turned out, Gloria had news herself. She and the science teacher were engaged, and he had been approved for a loan to buy Mrs. Oglesby's house.

On the sixth of June, the Allied Forces landed at Normandy and began the push east toward Germany as the Soviets pushed west. Serena and Glenna, like all Americans, were encouraged that this terrible war, at least in Europe, was coming to an end. Glenna felt that Edo was probably fighting the Germans. She said many prayers for all the Allied troops but especially for Edo, in case he was in the midst of these battles.

In July, Serena, Glenna, and Katie visited with Mrs. Oglesby for the last time. She was busy packing the things she was taking with her. Her sister's son would be coming to get her the following week. She and her sister had made an agreement that if her sister died before she did, she would have lifetime rights to live in the house. If Mrs. Oglesby died first, her money would go to her sister. They had both added codicils to their wills to these effects. But then she announced with a big grin, "As soon as this war is over, Sister and I are going to rent a place on the coast. We are going to see the ocean!" She promised to send a postcard. She also gave Glenna her new address, and they promised to write. Katie cried when she said goodbye to Mrs. Oglesby. Mrs. Oglesby hugged her and told her to be a good girl, work hard in school, and write to her. She said she would write back. Katie promised she would.

Glenna learned that if she took a full-time job at the college, she could take one class free of charge each semester. She would be responsible for purchasing her textbooks. She applied and was given a job in the cafeteria beginning in September.

Also in July, the garden began producing, and Serena and Glenna set to work canning and drying the vegetables and fruit. The only respite was a Sunday in the middle of the month to attend Gloria and the science teacher's wedding. They were married at the Methodist church. A reception followed at Renney's. Glenna and Katie attended, and Glenna was surprised that Martin and Nell were there without Ethel Ann. Nell said Ethel Ann was not well enough to attend.

In August, the canning continued, and it was time to make new school clothes for Katie and shop for new shoes and underclothes. Glenna bought new patterns and material and set to work. The war kept going, but Glenna was so busy, time flew by. Each night she and Serena listened to the news, hoping the Germans would give up, but night after night they were disappointed.

In September, Serena returned to school, Katie entered first grade, and Glenna went to work and began her first college-level bookkeeping course. Glenna had to report to work by six o'clock in the morning. She would work Monday through Friday. Other students worked the weekend shifts. Serena agreed to make Katie's breakfast and help her get dressed for school in the clothes Glenna had laid out the night before. Glenna usually made it home by two in the afternoon. She would pet Jimmie, who did not understand why everyone had left him all of a sudden, do her schoolwork, and prepare supper. When Serena and Katie arrived, Katie would show her mother the work she had done that day and tell her anything of interest that had happened. After supper, Katie would play with Jimmie outside unless it was raining.

They would all gather in the front room and listen to the news at six o'clock, then Glenna would return to her studies until time to help Katie with her bath. She no longer took naps, so she went to bed earlier. Tucked in bed, she and Glenna would talk, or Glenna would read her a story. When she drifted off to sleep, Glenna would lay out their clothes for the next day, take a quick bath, then rejoin Serena, and they would talk about their day or listen to the radio. By nine o'clock, Glenna was in bed and soon asleep.

By ten Serena was in bed and asleep. Sometime over the past months, she had stopped having trouble falling asleep. Her life was not as she would have chosen it to be, but it was full. She had come to love Glenna and Katie. She had always wanted a sister, and Glenna had filled that void. She wanted Glenna to succeed, and she was more than willing to help her. She looked forward every day to Katie showing up in her classroom after school and listening as Katie told her what she had learned as she showed her the papers she had filled with letters of the alphabet. Serena would let Katie practice her letters, writing with chalk on the blackboard as she graded papers or did some planning or straightened her room. Then they would walk home together and talk.

Katie loved school, and by October, she was teaching Mamie and Teddy how to read. For Halloween, she wanted to go as Little Red Riding Hood. This was a much easier costume for Glenna to make. Katie did not win Best Costume this year, but she was a good sport and had fun at the festival.

Thanksgiving was a holiday Glenna welcomed even though it did require extra cooking for the day itself, because there were leftovers for several days thereafter. They invited Father O'Malley, but he had already accepted an invitation from another family. Serena and Glenna prepared the conventional roast turkey dinner, but they decided to eat in the breakfast room and save themselves the extra work of a white tablecloth and china. After they ate and did the dishes, Katie said that Mamie and Teddy were sleepy, so she took them upstairs and put them and herself to bed for a nap. Serena made a pot of coffee, and she and Glenna settled in the front room by the fire to chat and listen to the radio. Both women were thankful for the time off. They talked about Christmas and decided to forego giving each other presents and concentrate on Katie.

In December, they again attended the concerts and the play *A Christmas Carol.* All these were presented at the Jane Auditorium, and every time Glenna went there, she was reminded of one of the sweetest evenings of her life, when she and Edo had sat shoulder to shoulder at that long-ago concert. It occurred to her during one of the concerts that if Edo was alive, he was probably in the army, and maybe if she contacted someone in the government, he could be found and told he had a daughter. That thought gave her a feeling of encouragement. She decided after Christmas she would look into this.

A month or so before Christmas, Katie said that Mamie wanted a new dress for Christmas because her old one was faded from being washed so often. "What color dress would she like?" Glenna asked.

"She loves pink," Katie said. Glenna smiled at this coincidence that pink was the favorite color of both Katie and Mamie.

When she told this to Serena, they both laughed. Then Serena asked if she planned to make a new dress for Mamie, and Glenna said, "Of course."

Once again, they found a Christmas tree, but this time they went to Charlie's land and found a pretty white pine, which they secured with a rope wound over the tree on top of the car and through the windows, which they rolled up as tightly as possible. It was a chilly ride back, but Katie and Jimmie snuggled up in the back seat under a blanket. They had also cut greenery for the sprays they would make and deliver the next day to the cemeteries.

This year, Katie wanted to attend the midnight Mass with her mother, so Glenna agreed. Katie managed to remain awake, but she slept late on Christmas morning. Glenna and Serena were up and dressed, had eaten breakfast, and were enjoying coffee when Katie came down the steps holding Mamie.

Santa had brought her a doctor/nurse kit with a stethoscope, a thermometer, and bandages. He had also brought her a xylophone with a songbook, which included numbered notes that corresponded to the numbered bars on the instrument. This allowed Katie to play the correct tunes as she sang the songs. She was delighted with both gifts, and with the two additional Golden Books and the goodies in her stocking. Finally, Katie noticed one last package under the tree. The tag said "Mamie." Katie took the package to Mamie and carefully opened it and cried out, "Oh, Mummy, it's beautiful!" Then she undressed Mamie and put on her new dress. She had a little trouble with the buttons but kept at it until she succeeded.

They ate their Christmas dinner of ham and all the trimmings and spent the day being examined and treated by Dr. Katie, then listening to a xylophone concert. Jimmie did not mind the examination by the doctor, but he raised his head and bayed loudly when the concert began. Serena suggested that she might play the xylophone in her room because some sounds hurt a dog's ears. So Katie read her new books, and later the xylophone was taken to Katie's room. She would spend a great deal of her time now in her room playing the instrument for her audience, Mamie and Teddy.

On January 2, 1945, everyone returned to school, and Jimmie was once again left to wonder why he was alone. Serena drove herself and Katie to school now because it was bitter cold. Glenna bundled up every morning and walked to the college. She had done very well on the first semester exam and would begin the next course today. She was thankful that, once again, the course was taught at midmorning between the breakfast and lunch rushes. She was quite certain she had chosen the right profession for herself.

She had talked to Father O'Malley about her idea of contacting the government to see if someone could locate Edo. He said he would try to find out how to go about this. So one night in late February, as she and Serena sat by the fire after supper and Katie had gone to her room to play the xylophone, they heard a car pull into the driveway. Glenna's first thought was that it was Father O'Malley with news.

Serena peeked out and said, "I think that's Gloria." Glenna looked out and confirmed this.

Glenna opened the door as Gloria made her way up the steps. "Gloria, is everything all right?"

She came in and said, "Glenna, I need to talk to you."

Serena said hello to Gloria and invited her to sit down by the fire. "I'll get more coffee," she said and left the room.

Glenna and Gloria sat down by the fire. Gloria said, "Ethel Ann died this morning."

"Oh no, what happened?"

"I guess her heart just gave out. Over the past several years, she had gained so much weight. For the last six months, she couldn't get out of the bed. Uncle Martin had to hire a woman to take care of her. All she wanted to eat was sweets. If she didn't get what she wanted, she made life miserable for Nell and him. I went over there this morning when I got the call that she had died. Nell and I were looking through her clothes to see if we could find something to bury her in. I was looking in a drawer in her room and noticed part of an envelope sticking out underneath some clothes, so I pushed back the clothes, and I found these." She pulled six envelopes out of her purse and handed them to Glenna.

Glenna took the envelopes. They were addressed to her at Renney's Restaurant, and the return address on each one was the name Edo Morelli.

Glenna grasped the envelopes and held them to her chest and cried out, tears rolling down her cheeks.

"I didn't read the letters, Glenna, but you can tell how handled the envelopes are. She must have read them over and over. I'm so sorry, Glenna. We had no idea she was taking your letters." Now Gloria was crying.

"How can anyone be so mean, so cruel? Why would she do this, Gloria, why?"

"I guess she was eaten up with jealousy. You're so pretty and so smart and so nice. You are everything she wasn't, and your mother was alive and hers was dead. But there's no excuse. I told Nell what I found, and she was horrified that Ethel Ann would do something like this. She said to tell you she is so sorry. She also said she has no right to ask you this, but could you please not tell anyone, because it would kill Uncle Martin if he knew she had done this."

"Tell Nell not to worry. I won't tell this. It's not Martin's fault. But how did she get away with this?"

"She liked to get the mail. Apparently she slipped Edo's letters into her pocket under her apron and brought the rest of the mail inside and put it on Mama's desk. Well, I know you want to read these letters, so I'll go now." She got up to leave but turned back. "Glenna, if there is anything in those letters that helps you find him, and if there's anything Mama or I can do to help, let us know."

"Thank you, Gloria, and please tell Renney I don't blame her for this."

"I'll tell her. Goodbye, Glenna."

Serena had taken her time in the kitchen, as she sensed that Gloria needed to speak privately with Glenna. After Gloria left, she returned to the front room and found Glenna staring at the fire. She didn't seem aware of Serena's presence. "Are you all right, Glenna?"

Glenna turned toward Serena. "Gloria brought me these," she said, holding the envelopes out toward Serena. "These are the letters Edo wrote to me after he left."

"Gloria had them all this time?"

"No. Renney's niece, Ethel Ann, had them. She must have watched for Mr. Wallace to bring the mail each morning, and apparently she slipped letters from Edo into her pocket, then took the rest of the mail inside."

"Why would she do that?"

"I asked Gloria the same thing. She said Ethel Ann was jealous of me. I suppose she wanted to hurt me. Boy, oh boy, did she ever succeed."

"Are you going to confront her about this?"

"Oh, no. Ethel Ann died this morning. Gloria found these letters when she was going through her things looking for something to bury her in."

"What happened to her?"

"She literally ate herself to death. Her job at Renney's was washing dishes and cleaning, but she got so heavy she couldn't work. Renney had to let her go, but Renney told her if she would lose some weight she could come back, but she just went home.

"I knew she didn't like me, but I didn't know she hated me."

"Glenna, I am so sorry. But maybe there is something in those letters that will help you find him."

Chapter 36

GLENNA TOOK EDO'S letters upstairs and sat on the sofa in her little sitting room. She put them in order according to their postmarks and opened the one with no postmark first. In it he said he was going to Charleston first, then explained that he'd put this in the box at Renney's because he didn't want to drive to her house and wake everybody up. He also said he forgot to get her mailbox number. This explained why he kept sending letters to Renney's.

Glenna knew Edo had left a letter to the minister in his box that morning so many years ago. She had wondered why he hadn't left one for her also. Now she knew he had. When she finished reading the letter, she thought it was funny and tragic that Edo didn't realize that in this small place, if he had just written her name and The Falls, et cetera, on the envelope, it would have been delivered to her house. But she was reassured that he had wanted her to know where he was going first and that he "loved her and missed her already."

She picked up the second envelope and removed the letter.

May 21, 1937

Dearest Glenna,

When I left The Falls I drove down the mountain and stopped at a store in a small town in North Carolina where I asked the owner what would be the best way to drive to Charleston. He studied for about a minute, and then he said he didn't know, but he did have maps for sale. I bought two and studied them, but came to the conclusion if I were to drive to the large cities from where I was, I would have to drive many miles out of the way. So I laid the maps on the counter and borrowed a yard stick from the man, lined up the maps and drew a straight line from where I was to Charleston. I stayed as close to the line as I could, avoiding large bodies of water and sticking to roads. The land in both states along this route is flat and filled with farms and small communities that thankfully have gas stations. (I kept the tank filled.)

I camped at a small community a few miles into South Carolina. A farmer let me sleep (my bike by my side) in his barn. His wife fed me supper and breakfast the next morning. They wanted to know where I was from and where I was going and why I was going there. They had never heard of my last name, and when I told them it was an Italian name they insisted I speak something in Italian. I taught them to say a few phrases in Italian. It was obvious they viewed me as entertainment. Before I left, the farmer advised me to avoid the Sandhills Wildlife Refuge as my noisy bike would not be welcome. I drove around it.

Many of the roads here are more like paths, but I made it to Charleston a bit after five o'clock. I went to a Catholic church, but the priest was unable to offer me a bed as he had a house full of relatives visiting. When I left, I spied a boardinghouse not far from the church, so I went there and rented a room. They had already had supper, but the landlady was kind enough to offer me a meal. I slept like the dead last night and woke up early this morning and had a big breakfast including grits for the first time. Then, with directions from another boarder, I drove across the bridge to Mt. Pleasant where I found a fisherman who agreed to take me to Fort Sumter for a dollar. He told me about the fort. He said it was built on a sandbar and thousands of tons of granite from up north (maybe from my hometown?). I did not get off the boat, just viewed the fort from the water.

The rest of the day was spent walking around Charleston. Someday I want to come back here with you. I'll close for now. Tomorrow I am heading to St. Augustine, Florida, America's oldest city.

All my love,
Edo

As Glenna read the words "granite maybe from my hometown," she held the letter to her heart. She got up and ran down the stairs to find Serena, who was sitting by the fire reading. "You were right, Serena! He describes Fort Sumter as being built on tons of granite maybe from his hometown."

"Oh, that is a very good clue. Did you know that many Italian stonecutters emigrated here to places with granite quarries? Maybe Edo's father is a stonecutter. You're certain he came from up north, right?"

"Yes, definitely."

"Well, New Hampshire is the granite state. Does New Hampshire stir any memories?"

"No, but it's a good place to start."

"Have you read all the letters?"

"No, only two."

"Well maybe there's more information to come."

"Right."

On the third letter she saw the address was St. Augustine. She took the letter from the envelope and read it.

Monday, May 24, 1937

Dearest Glenna,

Greetings from St. Augustine. It has a rich history which I am learning and sending to my mother. Mainly today I am sending you my address which you will find on the envelope.

Also, I want to tell you my very good luck. I have a temporary job of two months so we can write back and forth many times. Also, I will be sending you a picture as promised when it is developed.

When I went to the Roman Catholic Cathedral and spoke with the priest, he noticed my last name and asked if I speak Italian. I said I do, and he told me one of his parishioners recently sponsored a couple from Italy. The parishioner's cousin in Italy asked him to do this and find jobs for this couple who desperately needed to leave the country and come to America.

I have no idea how they got here, and I do not plan to ask, but they speak no English, and he has hired me as a live-in tutor to teach them English. The pay is good and will finance my travels for some time. Also, I will have some time off to explore the city and surrounding area, though the couple may go with me for English lessons.

My plan is to accompany the couple around the house and grounds as they do the chores assigned to them, and point out objects in Italian and then in English. I'll also translate into English what they are doing. I'll try to make it fun.

Oh, Glenna, how I wish you were here with me. I take out your picture dozens of times a day and kiss you. You may have to send another picture because I may wear this one out.

I will love you forever,
Edo

Tears came to her eyes as she read how he took her picture out dozens of times a day and kissed it. If she had gotten this letter, she would have sat down immediately and written to him and told him how she missed him and loved him. Then she read the fourth letter.

Friday, May 28, 1937

My Dearest Glenna,

At last the developed pictures came today so I am getting one in the mail to you. I have not received a letter from you, but I know it takes time. You have probably just received my last letter. I will be patient, but please write soon and often.

It is very hot here and muggy. I don't think I could live here in summer. But it's probably nice here in winter. After my job ends here, I may head north for the remainder of the summer and then in the fall ride back south. We'll see. I imagine the weather in The Falls is nice in the summer being at a higher altitude.

To cope with the heat I bought a bathing suit, and every chance I get, ride the twenty miles or so to the ocean and go swimming. Riding back wet is a little chilly but nice. Some of the people here have swimming pools, but unfortunately my boss does not, and I dare not swim in the river or ponds because there are alligators. My break is over, so I will say goodbye for now.

I love you,
Edo

Glenna felt sad that he hadn't gotten a letter from her and wouldn't because she had not received a single letter from him, but he didn't know that. There was no picture in the envelope, and she thought about asking Nell to go through everything and see if she could find it. With a sense of dread, she took the fifth letter from the envelope.

Saturday, June 5, 1937

Dear Glenna,

I go to the mailbox every day in hopes of a letter from you, but I've had none so far. Maybe the mail is slower than I thought. That must be it.

My students are coming along very well. They are smart and eager to learn English. I have written down many common phrases in Italian and English for them to study, and also I've labeled everything in the house with the English word. (No, I didn't write on the furniture. I wrote the names on little pieces of paper and taped the papers on the items.) Then I remove the papers after a few days and "test" them. They are very happy when they pass the tests.

Well, I must get back to work. Oh, by the way, I showed Marcelo your picture and he said in perfect English "Beautiful!"

I love you,
Edo
Please write to me!

This letter was heartbreaking. He was trying to find a reason why she was not writing to him. He'd had no idea why she hadn't, and she'd had no idea why he hadn't written to her. She remembered how painful it was and knew he felt exactly the same way. She had to force herself to take the last letter out of the envelope. Tears rolled down her cheeks as she read it.

Saturday, June 27, 1937

Dearest Glenna,

I made up my mind that I would not write again until I heard from you. I spoke with the postmaster and he said it might take a week to get a letter from me to you, but no more. So I must conclude that you do not want to write to me. I would ask that if your feelings for me have changed, please at least tell me.

I will be here for about two more weeks, but no longer. The heat is terrible. I need the money, but I can't stand it any longer. Besides, Marcelo and Maria are doing well with their English. They will pick up more and more as they live here longer.

I hope and pray that you are all right. I love you and miss you, but I cannot go on like this. Please let me hear from you. If I don't, I won't write again.

Love,
Edo

Glenna sat and cried silently so as not to alarm Katie—Edo's daughter, she thought. Finally, she dried her face and went back downstairs. Serena was still sitting by the fire. She looked up and could tell that Glenna had been crying. She waited for Glenna to speak, but when she didn't, Serena asked if there were any more clues as to where Edo was from.

"No, nothing more. Serena, I've known Ethel Ann since first grade. I always felt that something was wrong with her, something was off. But at Renney's she could behave like a half-normal person. But to do what she did, she had to have been a coldhearted person."

"You're right. She couldn't have had much conscience. Either that or she was so obsessively jealous of you that she felt justified in hurting you. Didn't you spend a lot of time with Edo at the restaurant?"

"Yes."

"Did you notice anything about Ethel Ann during that time?"

"I didn't, but he did. I had forgotten this, but he told me that when he was in the restaurant, he would feel someone staring at him, and he would look up and it was Ethel Ann. He said he would smile at her, and she would give him a dirty look and walk away. He wanted to know what that was all about. I told him about her mother's having a stroke and dying as Ethel Ann lay next to her. She was five years old, and she kept trying to wake Bess but couldn't, of course. Edo felt sorry for her."

"Well that's a terrible thing to happen to a child. But I suspect there's more to it. We're likely to never know the whole story."

"You're right, and I need to think about other things now, like how to figure out which town up north with a granite quarry is also Edo's hometown. It's going to take some money. I'm going to have the timber cut on Daddy's land. It's been almost seventeen years since it was cut. That's a lot of growth."

"Let's think about how best to go about finding Edo's family before you make a decision on the timber."

For an hour, until Katie joined them, they discussed the possible ways of discovering what they wanted to know, including hiring a detective. Finally, they decided that the fastest and most simple way was to determine the names of the companies in each state where granite was mined, call each one, and ask if any employed a man named Morelli. Serena said she would pay for the calls, and Glenna, who was working now, could pay her back.

Later, they brought the encyclopedia of every state in the northeast out of the library and into the front room. All were eliminated except New Hampshire, Massachusetts, and Vermont.

The following day, Glenna called information to get the numbers for state offices in each state capital. She figured that most of these would be closed on the weekend. She wrote the numbers down and waited until Monday.

Shortly after two o'clock Monday, she was home and on the phone. In New Hampshire, she was given another number to call to get the list of companies who mined granite. She wrote down the name and number for each company and made the calls. Glenna had decided that to win the cooperation of whoever answered the phone, she would have to choose her words carefully without being dishonest and, at the same time, not reveal the exact reason for needing to find Edo. So when she spoke with each of the clerks who answered the phone, she gave them her name and said she was calling from St. Claire, Virginia. "About seven years ago, a young man came here and spent a week or so. He has been left an inheritance, and after all this time, no one knows where he is or exactly where he came from. All we know is that his father was a stonecutter for a granite company, and his last name is Morelli. Do you employ, or did you in the past employ, anyone by that name?"

Glenna found that in every case, the person answering the phone was eager to help when they heard the word inheritance. Unfortunately, in all of New Hampshire's granite companies, no one by the name of Morelli was or had been employed there.

Something told her to try Vermont next, so she called the company in Barre, and after reciting her speech, the clerk said, "Oh, that must be Edo you are talking about. He has an inheritance? This is exciting. Of course he's overseas in the army now, so he won't be able to claim it for a while."

Unable to help herself, Glenna said, "Perhaps he has a wife I could call."

"No, he's not married. But I'll give you his parents' phone number."

"Thank you, I appreciate that."

Glenna was so relieved that Edo was alive and not married, and so excited that she had found his family, that after copying the number, she had to put the telephone down and walk through the house. She wanted to scream for joy, but that would frighten Jimmie. So she drank a glass of water and thought about what she would say to his parents.

When she had calmed down, she returned to the library, sat down at the desk, and called the number the clerk had given her. When a woman answered, Glenna said, "Mrs. Morelli?"

"Yes."

"My name is Glenna McAllen. I live in St. Claire, Virginia. Your son Edo came through here about seven years ago. I believe he wrote to you about St. Claire and about The Falls, where he stayed for a week while his motorcycle was being repaired."

"Yes, I remember."

"I was in high school at the time. We met, and we fell in love. Before he left, he gave me an engagement ring, and we promised to write to each other while he was traveling. He did write to me, but he sent the letters to the restaurant where we met, and where my mother worked. He had forgotten to get my home box number. I never received his letters because a girl who worked at the restaurant stole his letters out of the mailbox. She died recently, and her cousin discovered the letters and brought them to me. Of course, I couldn't write him back because I had no address.

"Edo told me where he was from, but there was a lot of noise in the restaurant that night, and I couldn't hear all of what he was saying. And he mentioned so many places he had driven through, I couldn't remember all he had said. If I had, I would have contacted you sooner. You see, a month after he left, I discovered I was pregnant."

"Oh no, you must be mistaken."

"I am not mistaken, Mrs. Morelli. I had never been with a boy before, nor have I been after. Edo is the father of my daughter. She was seven years old this month. I will send you a picture. My mother and our priest, Father O'Malley, tried to find Edo. They traced him to Charleston, but then the trail went cold.

"When the letters were brought to me, Edo described his visit to Fort Sumter and said it was built on tons of granite from up north, maybe from his hometown. This was the clue that allowed me to find you. I would like to write to Edo and explain what happened and tell him that he has a daughter. Her name is Katie. Would you share his address with me?"

"I don't know. He never mentioned you. I will talk to my husband when he gets home."

"Then I will call you back tonight. I'm sorry to have upset you, but he really has a right to know about Katie, and she has a right to know him."

When Glenna called that night, Mr. Morelli answered the telephone. He told Glenna, "We don't know you. Everything you say may be true, but we don't know you. We are not comfortable giving you Edo's address. But we will send him your address, and it will be up to him to contact you." He did give her their address, and she said she would soon send them two pictures of Katie, one for them and one for Edo. She also gave him her telephone number. Now all she could do was wait.

Chapter 37

A MONTH WENT by with no letter, but Glenna had heard others with loved ones overseas speak about receiving letters written three or four weeks earlier. She knew of one woman who received a letter from her brother after the family had received the news of his death. After six weeks with no word, her feelings ranged from anger that Edo knew about Katie and didn't care to fear that he'd been wounded and couldn't respond, or worse, he had been killed.

Spring break was coming up. Serena and Katie would be off for Good Friday on March 30 and Easter Monday on April 2. Glenna would be off the whole week after Easter as the college closed for the break. She decided she would take the opportunity to call the Morellis to see if they had heard from Edo. She had spent over seven years in limbo, waiting for him to come back, waiting for an end, whatever that would be. She would call tonight when Mr. Morelli would be home.

In the meantime, she had decided to treat herself to a new dress. On Tuesday morning, she saw Serena and Katie off to school, cleaned up the kitchen, then freshened up and got ready to walk uptown to buy a pattern and material. It was still cold in April on top of the mountain, so she dressed warmly in her green pullover sweater and gray wool skirt. As she headed to the door, she heard Jimmie barking at the front gate. When she opened the door, she saw a soldier leaning over the gate, petting Jimmie and talking to him.

Glenna stood still, her heart racing. The soldier looked up. In a shaking voice, she called, "Jimmie. Come, Jimmie." Jimmie left the soldier and ran to her. Never taking her eyes off the soldier, she stood aside as Jimmie ran into the house, and she closed the door. She was afraid if she looked away, the soldier would be gone when she looked back.

Now he was unlatching the gate and stepping inside. Tears rolled down her face, and she wiped them away with her hand. As he came closer, she saw that he had changed. The boyish young face was gone. A man's face had replaced it, a beautiful man's face. There were tears in his eyes.

"Glenna, I'm so sorry. I'm so sorry I got you in trouble. I was so stupid."

She took his beautiful face in her hands. "We were kids, Edo. All kids are a little stupid, but I can't regret a single thing. We have the sweetest little girl God ever made. But I have longed for this day for seven years. I've missed you so."

He wrapped his arms around her and held her. When they finally let go, she asked, "How did you get here?"

"Train from Washington."

"Have you eaten?"

"Not since yesterday, and I'm starving."

"I'll make you breakfast. Let's go inside."

Once inside, as he took in the spacious rooms and beautiful furnishings, he asked, "Do you live here?"

"Yes, Katie and I live here. I'll tell you all about it while you eat."

"Katie. I like that name."

"Your parents didn't tell you her name?"

"No, they just said that you said we have a little girl."

"Did they send you her picture?"

"No. They said you were sending them a picture, but they wrote before it came. It will probably show up someday."

"Well, it doesn't matter now. You get to meet her this afternoon. If you want to call them and let them know you're here, you can do that." He said he did, and she took him into the library.

"Wow," he said. "This reminds me of the Avery house." He looked at Glenna and grinned.

"I know what you're thinking. I had the same thoughts the first time I came in here. Now it's just a good place to study."

"Study?"

"I'll tell you about that later." With that, she left him to call his mother, and she went to the kitchen to make his breakfast.

By the time he found the kitchen, the coffee was made, the eggs were ready to scramble, and the pancake griddle was hot. He leaned against a cabinet and watched her make his breakfast. She made a stack of pancakes she kept warm in the oven while she scrambled the eggs. When all was ready, he sat at the table where she earlier had placed oleo margarine and maple syrup, a napkin, and utensils. "This looks wonderful, Glenna." She poured his coffee and said she did not remember if he took cream. He said he did, and she went back to the refrigerator to get it.

He told her what a treat it was to have such a breakfast and how much he appreciated her making it for him. She told him it was a treat to make it for him. As he ate, he asked who owned the house, and she told him how she first met Serena at Renney's when she was eight years old, and how they would see each other there over the years. She told him about George and how happy they had been, then George's death, and that as Serena was moving back here, she'd offered Glenna a job as live-in housekeeper and cook. She told him how Serena had arranged with the high school principal for her to complete high school by doing the work at home. "Now I'm working in the cafeteria at the college and taking one bookkeeping course for free."

"Glenna, you couldn't go back to high school because you were pregnant. I'm so sorry. Is that the reason you and your mother went to Ireland right after I left?"

"Edo, my mother went to Ireland in January 1940 to care for her mother. I've never been to Ireland."

"But I called Renney's right before I left Florida. I asked to speak to you. Gloria told me that you and your mother left, sold all your furniture, and went to Ireland."

"That wasn't Gloria. It had to have been Ethel Ann, and while she was talking to you, my mother was in the kitchen a few feet away cooking. If anyone other than Ethel Ann had answered the telephone, they would have told you about the baby and that my mother had tried to find you."

"All this time, Glenna, I thought you were in Ireland. I didn't have the money to go to Ireland, so I just kept traveling until I was drafted, and I've saved nearly everything I made so when the war was over, I could go to Ireland and find you. I remembered you said your grandfather fished in the Irish Sea. I was going to find you."

"Mum begged me to bring Katie and go with her, but I refused to go. I kept hoping you would come back. See, I knew there had to be a good reason you weren't writing to me. Every time I heard a motorcycle, I would go to the window and look out until I knew it wasn't you."

Edo reached across the table and took her hand in his. "This is breaking my heart, Glenna."

"It's breaking mine too, remembering it. Let's talk about something else, like how did you manage to leave the army? I hope you aren't AWOL."

"No, I'm here on leave. I won't be going back. The war in Europe is just about over. When the letter came from my dad, I was off in the fighting away from our base. When I got back to base three days ago, the letter was there. When I read the letter, the first words out of my mouth were, 'Oh, my God!' I was crying. Lt. Willoughby was close by, and he asked if I'd had bad news. I told him the whole story, and he read Dad's letter. He went to the captain with Dad's letter, and the captain came back and told me I had been a good soldier. I'd served for three years and been lucky, but if I went back out, I could get a bullet between the eyes tomorrow. He said, 'That woman has apparently been true to you all these years, and she deserves to have you back alive and well and not in a box.' He said, 'Go home, son. We'll miss you, but we can run those Nazis out of Venice even if you're not here.' He made sure I got on a plane carrying wounded to Walter Reed in Washington."

"I wish I could thank that captain and that lieutenant."

"I already did."

He had noticed the little table and chairs in the corner, and now he said, "Those are Katie's?"

"Actually, they belong to Serena. She had them stored in her old room over the general store. Her parents owned the store, and they had an apartment on the second story of the building. She thought Katie would enjoy having tea parties, and she does with her doll, Mamie, and Teddy, her teddy bear. Don't be surprised if she invites you to join them."

"I look forward to it. Do you have more pictures of Katie?"

"Yes, they're upstairs. I'll be right back." She went to her room to get the pictures she kept in a box in the nightstand. The sketch she had made sat on top. She decided he might not like it, and she slipped it into the drawer.

When she returned to the breakfast room, she saw that Edo had taken his plate, cup, and utensils to the sink and wiped the table. She laid the pictures on the table in order so he could see how Katie had changed. "Look at that hair!" was his first comment, then, "I should have been there. She is so beautiful. Who took all these pictures?"

"Mr. Wallace at the general store. Remember him? Photography is his hobby. He has a dark room and develops them himself."

"He's also the postmaster, isn't he? Why didn't he tell you I was writing to you?"

"He had no way of knowing that I wasn't getting your letters. He hates gossip. No one would have told him."

"Oh yes, I remember he had a sign in the store, 'Gossiping Is a Sin.' I had meant to ask you about that when I was here."

"I couldn't have explained it. Mum thought that probably someone he loved had been hurt by gossip, but that's just a guess. Anyway, he and his wife have been very kind to me."

Upstairs, Glenna gave Edo a tour of her and Katie's living quarters. She explained that all the furniture had come from her house in The Falls, that Serena's aunt had moved to Florida and taken all the furniture upstairs with her. When Edo stuck his head into the bathroom, he said, "A bathtub!"

"Do you want to take a bath?"

"I would love to take a bath."

While Edo went downstairs to retrieve his duffel bag, Glenna selected her best towel and washcloth and laid these out for him, as well as a fresh bar of soap and a bottle of shampoo. When he disappeared into the bathroom, she saw that he had laid out a clean shirt from his bag. It needed ironing, so she took it downstairs, ironed it, and returned upstairs and laid it on the bed where she found it. Then she went back downstairs, cleaned up the kitchen, and planned the special supper of meatloaf, vegetables, and apple pie she would prepare for supper. Finally, she called the school and asked the secretary to tell Mrs. Lowell that she would walk Katie home from school today, and to tell Katie to meet her outside at three o'clock. She wanted to call Renney's and give them her wonderful news but decided that Katie should be the first to know, and Serena should be the second. Then she remembered that she had earlier let Jimmie out, and he would need to get acquainted with Edo, so she let him back in.

Edo called her name, and she went upstairs. He was putting on the shirt. “You ironed my shirt. Thank you.”

“I was happy to do that for you.”

He took her in his arms and kissed her and said, “I love you, Glenna. Will you marry me?”

“Yes, a thousand times, yes, I will marry you.”

“Will you marry me tomorrow, Glenna?”

She laughed and said, “If you can arrange it, I will marry you tomorrow.”

“I can arrange it.” He kissed her again. “Is Father O’Malley still here?”

“He is.”

“Then let’s go call him.”

They went downstairs to the library and called the father. He was so happy to hear that Edo was back, he agreed to perform the ceremony the next day, as soon as they could get the license. He said he would have a person on hand to witness the ceremony, as they planned to have no guests.

By now, it was almost time for Glenna to go to the school for Katie. Edo wanted to go with her, but Glenna said it would be better for her to meet him here without a crowd around. Also, she wanted to tell Katie he was here before she met him.

At quarter to three, Glenna walked to the school and waited outside until Katie appeared. She began immediately telling her mother all the things they had done that day. About halfway home, Glenna said, "Katie, I have something very important to tell you."

"Is it something good, Mummy?"

"Yes, Katie, it's the best thing I can think of. Your daddy is here. He's waiting for us at the house."

"My real daddy?"

"Yes, your real daddy."

Katie was very quiet as they walked along. Then she said, "Jeanie said when she's afraid, she gets in bed with her mummy and daddy. Where is my daddy going to sleep, Mummy?"

"Well, Katie, for now he'll sleep in your room, I think, and you will sleep with me."

"Okay."

When they walked in sight of the house, Edo came off the porch and opened the gate. He squatted down and said, "Hello, Katie."

"Hello, Daddy."

"I'm sorry I've been away so long. As soon as I got the news that you and your mother were here, I got on the first plane and came here to be with you. I would love to hug you. Would that be all right?"

She said, "Yes, Daddy," and she reached out to him. He took her into his arms, and she put her little arms around his neck.

When he released her, she said, "You smell good, Daddy."

"I bought that cologne in Washington so I would smell good for my girls."

Katie laughed.

Glenna laughed and wiped the tears from her cheeks. Then the three of them, Katie in the middle holding their hands, walked up to the house and inside.

Edo built a fire in the fireplace, and he and Katie sat on the sofa, and she showed him the papers she had worked on that day, and then read to him the stories in her Little Golden books. "You are a very good reader, Katie," Glenna heard him say. At one point, Katie, holding her daddy's hand, led him into the breakfast room and showed him the little table and chairs.

"This is where Mamie and Teddy and I have tea parties. We have real china. It's Aunt Serena's, but she said it's mine as long as I live here.

"Now let's go upstairs. I want to show you my room. Mummy said you can sleep in my room."

"Oh she did, did she?" He grinned and looked at Glenna, who was watching from the kitchen. She grinned and shrugged her shoulders.

While Edo and Katie were upstairs, the front door opened and closed, and Serena greeted Jimmie as he ran to her for some petting. Glenna, hearing this, ran to meet Serena.

"Edo is here. He arrived this morning."

"Oh, Glenna! That is wonderful," she said as she hugged Glenna. "Where is he?"

"Katie took him upstairs to show him her room." Glenna described Katie's reaction when she learned he was here. "I told her he could sleep in her room, but if that's not all right with you, he can get a room in the hotel."

"Glenna, I wouldn't think of asking him to leave. Of course he can stay here."

"Thank you, Serena. The truth is I don't want him out of my sight."

"I understand completely. Now what can I do to help you with supper?"

"Actually, it's all ready. I'll go up and get them."

Serena was setting the table when Glenna, Edo, and Katie came down. Glenna introduced Serena and Edo, and they shook hands. She told him she was so happy to meet him. "If there's anything you need, let me know. It's wonderful that you're here."

"Thank you, Serena. It's wonderful to be here."

Glenna had made a meatloaf using most of their ration of ground beef, creamed potatoes, green beans, carrots sweetened with honey, and biscuits. She had also made an apple cobbler using the apples they had dried the previous fall. Before they ate, Serena said the blessing, thanking God for Edo's safe return.

After supper, Edo spoke privately with Serena and told her if she was uncomfortable with his spending the night, he would understand and go to a hotel. "I'm sure you know Glenna and I have a child, but we are not married."

She told him she wouldn't dream of asking him to leave his family. He also told her he had called his mother earlier and would like to call his father later, and he would pay for the charges. She told him he was welcome to call as much as he liked.

Shortly after this conversation, Antonio Morelli called Edo to welcome him back to the States and ask when he planned to come home. Edo told him that he and Glenna were getting married the next day and that Katie had two months of school left. "We haven't actually talked about this yet, as I just got here today, but it will probably be June when we get to Barre."

Edo asked about Marco, who was still serving in Europe, and his father said he was all right as far as they knew. When the call was over, Edo told Glenna that he couldn't wait for her to meet his family. "I know they will love you and Katie, and I hope you will love them."

"Katie will fit in just fine. She looks like a little Italian girl with her black hair and eyes and olive skin," Glenna said.

As he took her in his arms, he said, "And you are my beautiful Irish rose, and all my brothers are going to fall in love with you."

"I will try to resist them."

He laughed and hugged her.

They gathered in the front room and listened to the news. The British and Americans moving east and north and the Russians moving west were closing in on Hitler.

There was no longer any doubt that Germany and the Nazis would be defeated. But the Japanese were another story.

After the news, they listened to the Jack Benny show, which Edo heard for the first time. It was a relief to laugh at his antics and forget for a few minutes the horrors of war and the monumental tasks of rebuilding and rehabilitation that lay ahead. Afterward, Glenna and Katie went upstairs for her bath, and Edo soon followed. He wanted to read Katie a story.

Serena locked all the doors and checked to make certain all the blackout curtains were closed. Though it was highly unlikely that any Germans would be attacking St. Claire, the Japanese were still out there with their kamikazes. Who knew what they might be up to? She hated the Japanese. They had killed George. She knew she should forgive them. Her hatred wouldn't bring George back, and it wasn't doing her any good, but she wasn't ready to let it go. Instead, she picked up the book she had been reading for the second time, Charlotte Brontë's *Jane Eyre*. She knew there would be a happy ending, and she needed to believe that all the pain she had suffered would, like Jane's and Glenna's, have a happy ending.

After her bath and a story and another story Edo could not refuse, Katie told her daddy that she and her mother said their prayers after they read a story. He told her to say her prayers, and he listened as she asked Jesus to take care of her grandmother in Ireland, her mummy, Aunt Serena,

Mrs. Oglesby, and Jimmie. Then she thanked Him for taking care of her daddy and bringing him home.

"Now we always kiss your picture," she said as she turned toward the nightstand. "It's gone."

As she scrambled on all fours across the bed, Edo said, "I didn't know you had a picture of me."

Out of the bed, Katie went to the nightstand saying, "Mummy drew it." She opened the drawer. "Here it is." She handed Edo the sketch of his face. He recognized himself and realized what had happened. All those years ago, when the promised photograph didn't come, Glenna was afraid she would lose the memory of his face and had sketched this.

She walked into the room. "You found the picture."

"Katie found it."

"Katie, we don't need the picture anymore. We can kiss Daddy now before we go to sleep."

"I'd really like that, Katie." He picked her up, and she kissed his cheek, and he put her back in the bed and pulled the covers over her. Then he bent over and kissed her forehead and said, "Sweet dreams, my little love."

Edo turned out the light, and they walked out to the sitting room. "Thank you for not giving up on me. I don't know how you did it, how you kept loving me. Anyone else would have felt abandoned, would have hated me, wished me dead."

"Never, never could I hate you, Edo. I knew there was some reason I hadn't heard from you. I was terrified at times that something had happened to you. Not knowing was terrible. The anxiety was making me sick. Then Father O'Malley reminded me that I had to take care of myself so our baby would be healthy. So every time I felt anxious, I thought of the baby. I washed all my old baby clothes. I learned to knit and made an afghan and a little sweater, and booties and a cap. I went to work at Renney's and saved my money for the baby. In a way, Katie saved me. I learned to live with an ache in my heart, but because of her, I couldn't give in to it. It was only this morning, when I opened the front door and saw you bent over the fence petting Jimmie, that the ache went away."

Edo pulled her close. "I am so sorry for all the pain I've caused you. I'll spend the rest of my life trying to make up for that."

"Edo, you were not responsible for that pain. You did what you promised to do. You wrote to me, sent your picture and your address. Ethel Ann stole your letters, and we are likely to never know the reasons why. You don't need to feel guilty. Let's celebrate that we are here now together, you, Katie, and I."

"I should have called you sooner; maybe someone else would have answered."

"We cannot change the past, Edo, only enjoy the present." Then she put her arms around him, drew him close, and kissed him passionately.

"You are right, Glenna, but I may need to be reminded often."

She grinned and said, “I love you, and I'll be happy to remind you every day for the rest of my life.”

“All these years, what did you tell Katie about me?”

“I told her the truth, that when you left, you did not know that she was coming. If you had known, you wouldn't have left. I told her that you were traveling all over the country, and I didn't know where you were, but I believed you would come back someday. I didn't mention that you had not written any letters, because I always thought you probably had but something happened to them. I thought that would confuse her. Every night we would pray that God would take care of you, and we would kiss your picture.”

“Don't hide that picture. It will always remind me that even though you were very young and hurting, you never lost faith in me. There will be hard times ahead; there are for everybody. That picture will remind me how very lucky I am.”

Later, while Edo slept, Glenna washed the shirt he had worn on his way home, and she cleaned and pressed his uniform and shined his shoes. Up at five o'clock, she ironed the shirt, then took a bath.

After breakfast, Edo drove Serena and Katie to school in Serena's car. She was disappointed that she would not be present for Edo and Glenna's wedding, but she understood that they wanted to marry without delay. They had not told Katie their plans.

While they were gone, Glenna dressed in her green wool suit with matching hat. She had saved her money for months and kept her eye out every time she had shopped for groceries for material and a hat to match. It had been a present to herself for her high school graduation and getting the job at the college. She had made the suit in the fall, bought her first pair of black patent leather shoes with low heels, and worn it to church at Christmas. Today she would wear it to her wedding.

When Edo returned and called up to Glenna, she said, "I'm coming," and came down the stairs as he waited below. She had gathered her hair into a French twist crowned with the green hat with a matching veil. Serena had loaned her pearl earrings and a black patent leather clutch bag that matched Glenna's heels.

Edo couldn't take his eyes off his bride as she came down the stairs. And she couldn't take her eyes off him as he stood there so handsome in his uniform.

"You are beautiful, Glenna, just like the day I first saw you."

She smiled and took his arm, and they walked out the door together.

Epilogue

AFTER GETTING THE marriage license, Edo and Glenna went to the Jewel Box, where he bought wedding rings, then to the florist to buy a bridal bouquet. Father O'Malley had arranged for the church organist and a soloist to participate in the ceremony. Adjustments were made as there was no assembly, but it was a lovely service. Afterward, they went to the office of an attorney to file papers for Edo's legal adoption of Katie . She would now have his name. They decided to forego a honeymoon trip because Edo had missed so many years away from Katie. Instead, they would enjoy a honeymoon the rest of the week during the hours Serena and Katie were at school.

After Glenna read Edo's letters and learned he had sent a picture of himself, she called Gloria and asked her to discreetly let Nell know that the picture was not in the letter. Nell looked through everything in Ethel Ann's room but found no picture. Then one day Martin said he wanted to burn the mattress in Ethel Ann's room because it smelled. Nell agreed, but it occurred to her that Ethel Ann might have hidden the picture of Edo under the mattress where she would have easy access to it. Sure enough, that was where she found it. She gave it to Gloria, and Gloria mailed it to Glenna not long after Edo's arrival.

Several weeks after Edo and Glenna's wedding, Serena hosted a reception for them on a Sunday afternoon. Everyone associated with Renney's was invited, as well as Glenna's uncles and aunts and their children, Father O'Malley and all his parish, Mr. and Mrs. Wallace, Mr. and Mrs. Markley, Roy Capps, Glenna's close neighbors in The Falls and of course Mrs. Oglesby and her sister, whose invitation included train tickets and a night's stay at the Wide River Hotel.

To explain Glenna's not having received Edo's letters for so long, they settled on a story that in Florida, the man who'd hired Edo to live in his house and teach an Italian couple to speak English had a six-year-old daughter who was mentally handicapped. As she got older, she became too difficult to handle at home and was placed in an institution. When her mother cleaned out her room, she discovered Edo's letters to Glenna. Apparently she was watching when Edo put a letter in the box, and she would go and get it out and hide it in her room. Her mother sent the letters in a large envelope with a letter of apology. Mr. Wallace sent them on to Glenna. (Mr. Wallace had been given a heads-up, and he agreed to go along with this story.)

When school was out, Edo, Glenna, and Katie boarded a train for Vermont, where they spent two weeks with Edo's parents and his siblings, including Marco, who was home on leave. The rumor of Edo's "inheritance" had gotten around, and then the truth of his marriage to the mother of his seven-year-old daughter had followed. There was some laughter about this among some in the community, but when friends and neighbors met the beautiful Glenna, all laughter was forgotten. Edo was right. His family loved Glenna and Katie, and his brothers fell in love with their new sister-in-law. He took his family to visit the Willises. Mr. and Mrs. Willis were growing feeble but were delighted to see Edo again. Jack and his wife and children continued to live with them and do the work on the farm. He and Edo showed Glenna the barn where they had built the motorcycle.

Edo withdrew the money his parents had saved for him, and when they returned to St. Claire, he repaid Serena for the taxes she had paid on Charlie's land, and he organized the letters he had written to his mother and began writing his book. Throughout the day, he would take breaks and spend time with Katie.

One day as Edo was pushing Katie in the swing, Serena and Glenna sat on the back porch stringing beans. Serena confessed to Glenna that she had never really thought that Edo would come back after all those years. "I was astonished that you kept on believing that he would. How were you so certain?"

Glenna looked at Serena without answering but finally said, "It was because of what happened the first time I saw him. I've never told anyone this before because I suppose I didn't think anyone would believe me. I had just sat down in the booth to do my homework when I heard someone close one of the restroom doors, and I looked up, and Edo was walking toward me. The instant I saw him, this feeling came over me that I knew him and I loved him, but I hadn't seen him in a long time. I was embarrassed by this and looked down immediately. My heart was racing so I had trouble breathing, but I found myself smiling. I was overcome with joy. I knew this boy, whoever he was, was the one. There was no doubt."

"That's remarkable. I've heard of love at first sight, but this seems more than that."

"But how could you explain love at first sight unless you thought you already knew the person somehow? I can't explain it, so I just decided that God had arranged for us to meet, just as He arranged for you to overhear that conversation I had with Mr. Norris. They were gifts, and I am grateful."

In September, Glenna went back to work at the college and signed up for an accounting course. Katie entered second grade, and Serena began another year teaching seventh grade. Edo worked in the library all day on his book without interruption, except to let Jimmie in or out. Mrs. Oglesby sent a postcard from Myrtle Beach, where she and her sister were enjoying their first vacation by the sea, and Ben Hadley retired from the air force and returned to the house his parents left him next door to Serena.

Ben and Edo became friends, bonding as they shared their experiences in the war. Ben became a frequent guest, then a regular at the supper table as he contributed to the larder. He insisted on taking Glenna's place as she and Serena washed the dishes and cleaned up the kitchen. As they worked, they recalled the times of their youth. On one occasion, Serena confessed to him that she had had a big crush on him, and he confessed he had known and was flattered. "I was in love with Valerie at the time," he said, then added, "I should have just waited until you grew up."

By Christmas, it was obvious to all that Ben and Serena were falling in love. Edo, Glenna, and Katie were sailing to Ireland to spend Christmas with Kathleen and meet the relatives she had known only through the stories her mother told her. Kathleen had been hired by her mother's doctor, who was impressed with Kathleen's medical knowledge. He would go on to teach her everything any nurse should know and more. Ben, Serena, and Jimmie were taking the train to Florida and going by boat to Key West to spend Christmas with Amelia and Carole. Before they left, they had an early Christmas dinner and opened the gifts, for whom they had drawn names. They had set a limit of five dollars per gift.

Ben gave Edo a new dictionary, Edo gave Katie a large storybook, Serena gave Glenna a small bottle of her favorite cologne, Glenna made a large batch of pecan shortbread cookies for Ben, and Katie gave Serena a pretty tin of chocolate candy. Everyone was pleased.

In time, Ben and Serena married. Ben enrolled in college and eventually taught science at the St. Claire high school. Edo sold his book and wrote others. He and Glenna bought Ben's house and moved next door. Glenna got a job at the college in the accounting office. She and Edo had two more children, a boy and another girl. Ben and Serena became their aunt and uncle. They adopted another dog so that when they were away during the day, Jimmie had a playmate. Serena and Ben bought a small house on the beach. Anytime they were not using it, the Morellis were welcome to it, but often Edo, Glenna, Katie, Milo, and Olivia spent their summers traveling to Barre and Dublin, and to historical places Edo had longed to share with Glenna. One very special trip was to Italy to meet Edo's grandparents. Edo would write a book about his grandfather's adventures.

Serena sold the house that she and George owned to Patsy's daughter and her husband.

Before the closing she visited Patsy. They had stayed in touch with Christmas cards and an occasional letter, but today Serena needed to thank her again. "I have no doubt that you saved my life with those orange and egg milkshakes, and you looked after Jimmie while I was at school. You took 'Love thy neighbor' seriously. I am so grateful."

"I was happy to help you, Serena, and I am very pleased that my family will now be permanently living next door." After hugs and promises to stay in touch, Serena left and drove to the attorney's office for the closing.

After the closing, Serena went by the church, where she found the minister in his study. He was surprised and delighted to see her. She told him she had sold the house. "I don't expect I'll ever have reason to come back here, so I wanted you to know what a difference your words meant to me," she said.

She told him about Glenna and how she had stopped to see her on her way home, and what happened. "I didn't want to do what I knew I should do, but your words kept running through my mind, so I went back to the restaurant and offered her my home and a job. Living with her and her little girl changed my life. She is now the sister I never had."

She told him the whole story about Edo and Ben. "Ben and I are getting married. I will always love George, but I discovered that you can also love someone else. I am very happy."

"It means a great deal to me that you took the time to come here and share this with me. You've given me encouragement. Thank you, Serena."

When she drove through town on her way home she passed Lindsey Hardware and thought of the letter she had written to Jimmie not long ago. She had enclosed a picture of Jimmie and Katie sitting together contentedly by the fire as she read to him.

Jimmie had joined the army the day after high school graduation. After basic training he had been sent to advanced infantry training where it was discovered that he had an outstanding talent as a sharpshooter. For the duration of the war he was assigned to train new recruits how to become excellent marksmen. He never left the country. Serena was relieved that Jimmie Lindsey survived the war without a scratch.

March 10,1946

Dear Jimmie,

You may think this letter is long overdue and you are right, but when a terrible thing happens and turns your life upside down it takes time to recover and look back with perspective. You gave me a puppy, and he helped me to survive my husband's death especially in those early days when I couldn't have gotten out of the bed were it not for needing to let Jimmie outside or feed him. It isn't always easy to express your deepest feelings to another human being, but I could tell him just how I felt and he really seemed to understand my sadness and didn't mind my tears. He was truly a comfort to me, and I will always be grateful to you for giving me Jimmie. He was just what I needed.

I also want you to know how relieved I am that you survived the war by remaining stateside to teach young soldiers how to shoot accurately. Countless American and British soldiers are alive and at home with their families today because of your efforts. I am so proud of you.

The little girl in the picture is Katie Morelli. She is eight years old and loves to read to Jimmie. She is the daughter of my dearest friend, Glenna.

I will always remember your kindness.

Sincerely,
Serena Lowell

Ingram Content Group UK Ltd.
Milton Keynes UK
UKHW040807120423
420037UK00004B/186